Dolls Behaving Badly

Dolls Behaving Badly

A Novel

CINTHIA RITCHIE

GRAND CENTRAL
PUBLISHING

NEW YORK   BOSTON

Copyright © 2013 by Cinthia Ritchie
Reading group guide Copyright © 2013 by Hachette Book Group, Inc.
All rights reserved. In accordance with the U.S. Copyright Act of 1976, the scanning, uploading, and electronic sharing of any part of this book without the permission of the publisher is unlawful piracy and theft of the author's intellectual property. If you would like to use material from the book (other than for review purposes), prior written permission must be obtained by contacting the publisher at permissions@hbgusa.com. Thank you for your support of the author's rights.

Grand Central Publishing
Hachette Book Group
237 Park Avenue
New York, NY 10017

www.HachetteBookGroup.com

Printed in the United States of America

RRD-C

First Edition: February 2013
10 9 8 7 6 5 4 3 2 1

Grand Central Publishing is a division of Hachette Book Group, Inc.
The Grand Central Publishing name and logo is a trademark of Hachette Book Group, Inc.

The Hachette Speakers Bureau provides a wide range of authors for speaking events. To find out more, go to www.hachettespeakersbureau.com or call (866) 376-6591.

The publisher is not responsible for websites (or their content) that are not owned by the publisher.

Library of Congress Cataloging-in-Publication Data
Ritchie, Cinthia.
  Dolls behaving badly : a novel / Cinthia Ritchie.—1st ed.
      p. cm.
  Summary: A hilarious and heartwarming debut novel about a single mom living in Alaska trying to make a life for herself and her young son.
  ISBN 978-0-446-56813-5 (trade pbk. : alk. paper)—ISBN 978-1-4555-1827-2 (ebook : alk. paper) 1. Single mothers—Alaska—Fiction. 2. Mothers and sons—Fiction. 3. Alaska—Fiction. 4. Domestic fiction. I. Title.
  PS3618.I7655D65 2013
  813'.6—dc22

                                    2012025864

For my sisters, Christine, Cathie, and Candace,
and for Gramma Lucas

Acknowledgments

Thanks to the Rasmuson Foundation and the Alaska State Council on the Arts for the financial boost, and Hedgebrook and Hidden River Arts writing residencies for providing a quiet writing space.

Special thanks to Tony Hall, for not firing my sorry ass when I missed work deadlines; Rich Chiappone, for always answering my frantic and obsessive e-mails; Ronald Spatz, for helping me get started; Sherry Simpson, whom I can never thank enough; Jo-Ann Mapson, for reading a shorter draft of this story and saying, "This sounds like a book"; Nikki Jefford, for her dedication and writing support; Kathleen McCoy, for teaching me to edit my own work; Mike Dunham, for the gift of paper; Jeanne and Mark Haas, for the house-sitting gig; Michael Fierro and Cissy, for food, comfort, and the "dungeon" desk; David and Jonnie Mengel, for the doggie babysitting, the meals, and the fresh produce; my Alaska Newspapers work buds Van Williams, Victoria Barber, Rose Cox, Tammy Judd, Alex DeMarban, and Roy Corral, who kept me sane during insane times; Dawnell Smith, for the runs and great talks; Sarana Schell, for the great hugs; Susan Morgan, for the everlasting friendship; John Edmonds, for loving me even when I was unlovable; Candace Ritchie, for being the best sister in the world; my son, for being who he is; my mom; The Beebs, for being my own personal Killer Bee; and Mike Mitchell, for the runs, the camping, and the delicious hugs.

And lastly, thanks to my agent, Elizabeth Wales, who never lost faith in me, even when I lost faith in myself; my editor, Beth de Guzman, who totally "got" my book; and my old high school English teacher, Clare Blakeslee, whose enthusiastic literary rants gave me the courage to buck convention and write.

Dolls Behaving Badly

LESSON ONE

The Giant on the Oprah Show

Keep a diary, and someday it will keep you.
—*Mae West*

Chapter 1

Thursday, Sept. 15, 2005

THIS IS MY DIARY, my pathetic little conversation with myself. No doubt I will burn it halfway through. I've never been one to finish anything. Mother used to say this was because I was born during a full moon, but like everything she says, it doesn't make a lick of sense.

It isn't even the beginning of the year. Or even the month. It's not even my birthday. I'm starting, typical of me, impulsively, in the middle of September. I'm starting with the facts.

I'm thirty-eight years old. I've slept with nineteen and a half men.

I live in Alaska, not the wild parts but smack in the middle of Anchorage, with the Walmart and Home Depot squatting over streets littered with moose poop.

I'm divorced. Last month my ex-husband paid child support in ptarmigan carcasses, those tiny bones snapping like fingers when I tried to eat them.

I have one son, age eight and already in fourth grade. He is gifted, his teachers gush, remarking how unusual it is for such a child to come out of such unique (meaning underprivileged, meaning single parent, meaning they don't think I'm very smart) circumstances.

I work as a waitress in a Mexican restaurant. This is a step up: two years ago I was at Denny's.

Yesterday, I was so worried about money I stayed home from work and tried to drown myself in the bathtub. I sank my head under the water and held my breath, but my face popped up in less than a minute. I tried a second time, but by then my heart wasn't really in it, so I got out, brushed the dog hair off the sofa, and plopped down to watch Oprah.

What happened next was a miracle, like Gramma used to say. No angels sang, of course, and there was none of that ornery church music. Instead, a very tall woman (who might have been an angel if heaven had high ceilings) waved her arms. There were sweat stains under her sweater, and this impressed me so much that I leaned forward; I knew something important was about to happen.

Most of what she said was New Age mumbo jumbo, but when she mentioned the diary, I pulled myself up and rewrapped the towel around my waist. I knew she was speaking to me, almost as if this was her purpose in life, to make sure these words got directed my way.

She said you didn't need a fancy one; it didn't even need a lock, like those little-girl ones I kept as a teenager. A notebook, she said, would work just fine. Or even a bunch of papers stapled together. The important thing was doing it. Committing yourself to paper every day, regardless of whether anything exciting or thought provoking actually happens.

"Your thoughts are gold," the giant woman said. "Hold them up to the light and they shine."

I was crying by then, sobbing into the dog's neck. It was like a salvation, like those traveling preachers who used to come to town. Mother would never let us go but I snuck out with Julie, who was a Baptist. Those preachers believed, and while we were there in that tent, we did too.

This is what I'm hoping for, that my words will deliver me something. Not the truth, exactly. But solace.

Sunday, Sept. 18

Already I'm slacking. Writing is like working out. If you miss one day, it's easy to convince yourself to miss another.

I'm an artist. I write this rather shamefully, as if admitting to an embarrassing medical problem that I have no right to be embarrassed about since I clearly brought it on myself.

"She's obviously talented," the art teacher informed Mother during my fourth-grade teacher conference, and Mother hung her head, her white-gloved hand tightening around the Ivory soap sculpture I had fashioned into a Campbell's soup can. By the time we walked out to the car, my sculpture had melted under the wrath of Mother's grasp.

Growing up in Dowser, a little southwestern Michigan town whose only distinction was an award-winning badminton team, I took every art class the high school offered. I even managed to win a few "prestigious" awards: the Dorothy Maloney Fellowship for Duck Drawings; the Hardings Grocery Store Cuts of Meat Award; and the Southwestern Michigan Lookalike Contest, where I painted the assemblymen in drag and almost got Mother kicked out of the Women's League.

All this might sound heady and exciting, except that in our stuffy little farming community, the liberal arts were looked upon as a minor sin. Mother squirmed each time I brought home another award, while my older sister, Laurel, sighed and squared her shoulders, knowing it was up to her to do something with her life, since I was so obviously throwing mine away.

I slid through my senior year with Cs and Ds, skipped graduation, and hitchhiked down to the Greyhound station, where I made a one-way reservation to Farmington, New Mexico, the farthest my money would take me. I wore my lucky peasant blouse and carried my new Kmart suitcase, stuffed with art supplies, stray earrings, photocopies of Frida Kahlo's paintings, and a brand-new diaphragm.

Things didn't quite work out as planned. Trying to make it in the art world is like trying to have an orgasm when you're not in the mood:

You strain and struggle and twist yourself into impossible positions until you almost, almost (oh god, oh yes, oh pllllleeeassee) get there. But you never quite manage, and instead of being blissed-out on pleasure, you find yourself attending other people's shows and pretending to be happy for them when all you want to do is give them a swift kick in the ass.

That's what happened to me. I lost my orgasm. My resolve followed shortly afterward, along with my standards. I started settling for a little less here, a lot less there, and before I knew it, I found myself living in Alaska, a state so far removed it's not even included on national weather maps.

Then I met Barry and *really* lost my steam. Years passed in a blur and the minute Jay-Jay popped his head from between my legs, it was sore nipples, sleepless nights, and Barry and me arguing about whose turn it was to buy diapers. Our arguments quickly escalated until he moved into a shabby apartment in Spenard, a down-on-your-luck neighborhood famous for its cheap hookers and even cheaper drugs, and I bought a shabby trailer less than a mile away. This is typical of Barry and me. We've been divorced almost three years yet neither one of us has the gumption to move on. We claim that this is so Jay-Jay can move back and forth between us but really it's because we don't know how to let go. Sometimes, I'm ashamed to admit, we still...

Whew, there's the groan of the school bus grinding its way up the hill by Westchester Lagoon. In a minute Jay-Jay will charge through the door. "Mom," he'll scream, demanding food and attention, love and understanding. And I'll give it to him, messily, badly, my hair falling down, my armpits reeking because I forgot to put on deodorant this morning. Jay-Jay is tall and blond, his legs starting to thin, poor kid. He's caught in that awkward stumble of pulling away from the cute-little-boy stage. He's choosy about food and movies, and so good-natured it's easy to forget how smart he really is. He's just Jay-Jay, a skinny kid with freckles who picks his nose when he thinks no one's looking. He smells of milk and grass. What I like is the smell of his feet.

Embarrassing, but while he sleeps I sometimes sneak into his room, lift his foot to my face, close my eyes, and inhale: subtle and slightly sweet, not yet sour, a bit musky.

Soon he'll wear huge sneakers and clomp around the house. He'll smell of sweat and get pimples and hard-ons. He'll jack off in the bathroom and borrow the car without asking, while I sit home reading trashy magazines, hoping and praying that he doesn't turn out to be as big an asshole as his father.

WHAT'S ON MY KITCHEN TABLE

Alaska Airlines Visa bill: OVERDUE!
JCPenney credit card bill: PAST DUE!
Anchorage Pet Emergency bill: DELINQUENT!
Ken doll, with the head cut off
Sex and the City DVD covered in ketchup

Wednesday, Sept. 21

It's 9:30 a.m. on a sunny autumn day, and I'm sitting at a cleared space on the kitchen table, munching on Chex Mix and watching the dog dig holes in Mr. and Mrs. Nice's yard. It's almost time to pull on my wrinkled blouse and stained apron and head out the door.

My food service career began over fifteen years ago at a truck stop in Camp Verde, Arizona. *Easy money,* I thought, and a perfect way to supplement my art, which I was sure was about to take off.

When it didn't, I hit the road and spent the next three years following the festival circuit in the summer and waitressing during the winters. I spent my days out in the desert sketching naked men I picked up in bars, transforming their tired bodies into paintings of cowboy butts floating in the air like helium balloons and penises shaped like the arms of saguaro cacti. I hadn't snared a gallery show, but I was getting by. I had my own business cards (my name misspelled, but you can't have everything) and a faithful following of women in Birkenstock sandals.

One night, camped out on the Navajo Reservation in northern Arizona, red sandstone smeared across my face and arms, I dreamed that Gramma was standing in front of me, a white egg in each palm. I woke up sweating and irritable. Gramma, my father's mother, was Polish and fat and smelled of onions and garlic. We had always been close. We were the messy ones, the stumbling ones, the ones who goofed up and knocked things over. Mostly, though, our relationship went like this: She cooked and I ate. She talked and I listened. She made messes and I played happily in their wake. Just thinking of Gramma made me so lonely that I broke down and called her from Holbrook the next morning.

"Yah," she answered in her heavy Polish accent. "That you, Pushski?"

I asked her what it meant to dream of an egg. "Raw," I told her. "In a shell. In someone's hand. And white, almost luminous."

"It mean," she said slowly, "that you is *brzemienny.*"

"That's ridiculous," I shouted.

"You sure?" she asked. "You got the blood?"

"Yes," I lied. After I hung up, I sat on the wilted ground outside the phone booth. I knew Gramma was right. I was pregnant and I had no idea who the father might be: That cowboy from Winslow who never wore underwear? That cowboy I picked up outside of Flagstaff who had a belt buckle larger than my head? That older cowboy who walked with a limp and lost three fingers off his left hand to a horse bite?

To make a long story short (and the less I talk about this phase of my life, the better), I had an abortion at the clinic down in Tucson. As soon as I was declared "normal" at my six-week checkup, I walked to the highway, stuck out my thumb, and waited for a ride. I left everything behind, even my car. It was the price I had to pay, was still paying, since as soon as it was gone that child connected to me tighter and firmer than if I had birthed it myself. I learned too late that some things can't be left behind, that they seek you out, show up at your doorstep late at night.

"Sins make you fat," Gramma used to say. I thought she meant it literally, that sins would cause weight to form on your body. But after the abortion I understood what she was really saying: sins bring you down, make you heavy. That they make you fat with your own misgivings.

I eventually reached Alaska, met and married Barry, and worked and quit and worked and was fired from a variety of waitressing jobs. We had Jay-Jay and our own house and a golden retriever named Almond Joy. I stayed home most of the first year, stumbling around in a sleep-deprived haze while Barry stormed off to work every day. As soon as I put Jay-Jay down for his midmorning nap I'd hurriedly pull my art supplies from the closet (I was down to two colors by then, phthalo green and cadmium orange, which sucked since everything came out a grainy, brownish mess). I was halfway finished with an Alaska nude *Last Supper*, but I was having trouble with the toes, which resembled slugs. Jesus' thighs looked especially nice, though, very strong and competent and tinted an almond shade I was particularly proud of (I had mixed in a small bit of Jay-Jay's infant formula to lighten the paint colors). Right when I hit on the brilliant idea of covering the apostles' feet with bunny boots, Barry up and quit his job. I tried to keep painting but it was impossible. I threw my supplies back in the closet (just the phthalo green—the cadmium orange had given out the week before) and joined my husband on the couch for morning marathons of PBS shows: *Mister Rogers*, *Barney*, *Reading Rainbow*. I ate too many bowls of cereal, lulled into a sugary stupor so that I would often look at us all curled up in our pajamas at one o'clock in the afternoon and think, *Isn't this cozy?*

The day I pinned a dish towel around Jay-Jay's squirming butt because we had run out of diapers was the day I shook off my inertia, pulled on the only skirt that still fit, and marched around the restaurant circuit. I hit all the places that frequently hired but rarely advertised: Sea Galley, Sourdough Mining Company, Peanut Farm.

"I'll call you," everyone said. But no one did. It wasn't my spit-

stained shirts or lackluster hair that turned them off as much as my
desperation, which emitted from my skin like a nasty odor.

One night in the Safeway, as I hurriedly wrote out a check I couldn't
cover for milk and crackers, the scrappy manager from the Denny's accidently rammed my shopping cart. He remembered me right away—
I had worked for him a few years before, quitting to hike the Resurrec-
tion Pass Trail, only to be hired back again, only to quit to kayak Prince
William Sound. He eyed my meager purchases and slyly mentioned a
day shift opening. Would I be interested? I swallowed my pride, added
three Mounds bars to my order, and said I would. Then I drove home to
share the good news with my soon-to-be ex-husband.

"I got a job," I yelled. Barry grunted from the couch.

"Cool," he said with disinterest. "Where?"

"Denny's." A long pause, and was it my imagination or did he actually sneer?

"Well, it ain't the Hilton, but you'll do just fine," he said. Then he
turned to Jay-Jay and patted his dish-toweled butt. "Sport, get your
daddy another one of them beers."

This is the truth: I used to lie awake and imagine my husband's
death. I imagined this right down to the clothes I would wear to his
funeral—a simple black dress and a pair of designer shoes. In these fantasies, my expensive feet floated a few inches above the ground like in
those pictures of the saints on holy cards. Like I was suddenly blessed.

For the past two and a half years I've worked at a restaurant called
Mexico in an Igloo. It's as tacky as the name implies, a monstrous igloo-
shaped building that squats over half a city block, with cacti and tequila
bottles jutting around the door and window frames. Tourists love it and
locals tolerate it because the food is homemade, the drinks stiff, the salsa
hot enough to knock sweat inside your winter drawers.

I start off each shift strong but fizzle halfway through. I don't have
the pizzazz it takes to be cheerful seven hours a day. By the time I pick
up Jay-Jay from his after-school Camp Fire program, I'm itchy and ir-

ritable. He usually has the good sense to keep his mouth shut on the ride home. Once we walk in the house, however, he lets loose, his words shooting from his mouth so fast I often jump back as if under attack. Poor kid, it's not his fault his mother hates her job. I try to listen, I really do. But some evenings I stare into his eager face as he goes on and on about some complicated story and want to yell, "Stop! Stop being so happy!"

Instead I smile my fake waitressing smile and make little cooing sounds of approval.

Then I warm up some bread. It's my favorite thing after work, thick, sturdy wedges of brown bread so dense I have to rip pieces with my teeth. Jay-Jay munches the crust while I work my way through the middle sections. It's satisfying to eat this way, no plates or silverware, only our mouths chewing. On Fridays, I spread open the paper to the entertainment section and daydream of myself as Talented Artist, my hips swaying under a long silk skirt as I give an interview to the snotty arts reviewer from the local paper.

"I know what it's like at the bottom," I say as he eyes my breasts (in this fantasy, I have hefty and enviable cleavage). "I lived in a trailer park for years, and the shading from this period was influenced by Kmart blue-light specials."

These little fantasies calm me down enough so that by suppertime, Jay-Jay and I are able to enjoy a nice meal out in the living room, eating on TV trays while we watch Vanna applaud as contestants spin the big wheel.

"She's pretty old, huh, Mom?" Jay-Jay says. "She's been on *forever*."

"Yes, honey, she has," I reply. And I stare at the screen, the wedges on the wheel going round and round, my stomach full and gurgling, the dog lying on my feet, and the TV gives off a tint that makes everything around us, from the mangy carpet to the cracks in the wall, look homey and warm and inviting.

It isn't, of course. But it's a nice illusion.

LETTER #1

Ms. Carla Richards
202 W. Hillcrest Drive #22
Anchorage, AK 99503

Dear Ms. Carla Richards:

We regret to inform you that your application for a Platinum Alaska Bank Visa Card has been declined.

After reviewing your rather entertaining credit history, we feel it is in our best interest to keep you securely focused on your current plan.

As always, thank you for choosing Alaska Bank Visa Card.

Sincerely,
Douglas R. Winnington
Junior Account Supervisor

P.S. Did your August payment get lost in the mail again?

Chapter 2

Friday, Sept. 23

SHHH! I'M CROUCHED IN THE CLOSET, hiding from my sister, Laurel, who this very minute is pouring herself a glass of my generic orange juice. I can see her through the cracks along the door hinges.

"Yoo-hoo, Carla," she yells. "I've got wonderful news."

I hold my breath and pray for her to go away. No such luck. She sits down at the kitchen table and shuffles through a magazine.

"Carla, listen," she shouts toward the closed bathroom door; she must think I'm in there. "I sold the McPherson place, can you believe it? On the market for almost a year and I sell it in two weeks. Isn't that amazing?"

She walks down the hall, her heels *click-clack-click*ing on the linoleum, and knocks on the bathroom door. "I've got to go, Carla. I'm meeting someone for breakfast." A nervous cough, followed by a giggle. "No one special, you know. Just a . . . this client."

She lets herself out and I wait a moment to make sure the coast is clear, then slip out of the closet and hunker down at the table to finish this entry.

I know it sounds a bit mad, hiding from my very own sister. But if you saw Laurel, you'd know what I mean. Two years older, Laurel is perfect, or at least she likes to think she is. Smart, talented, beautiful—that's how Mother used to explain it to me. Laurel was the favorite. The shining star in an otherwise mediocre family. My brother and I (poor Gene, working as a manager for a Chickin' Lickin' back home in Dowser) were pushed to the background, half-hidden, like those relatives they used to keep in attics.

Now Laurel lives up on the Hillside in a perfect house with an immaculate lawn, expensive art dangling from the walls. Her husband, Junior, is a flat, white wall: no surprises, no deep shades or textures. He is a corporate lawyer for British Petroleum, and Laurel is one of the top-selling agents at Southwest Alaska Real Estate. She and Junior are among the Alaska jet set. They play racquetball on the weekends, tennis in the summers, take exotic vacations twice a year, and keep their cars so clean you could put on your makeup in the reflection of the chrome.

Laurel and Junior weren't always Alaskans. They used to live in Chicago, a glorious six-hour plane flight away. Then one afternoon about five years ago, someone knocked at the door as I was untangling Barry's fishing line. Jay-Jay, who was almost three at the time, raced to answer.

"Mom! Auntie Laurel's at the door."

"Laurel?"

"She has funny shoes." Jay-Jay stared at his socks. "Like animal claws."

I hurried out to the kitchen and found my sister leaning against the dishwasher, the toe of her expensive boot jutting across my path.

"Carla," she cried.

"I didn't know you were on vacation," I said.

"Vacation?" She giggled. "We're moving here." Her voice was high and screechy. "We're looking at houses up on the Hillside. It's supposed to be the best neighborhood for people like us." She nodded at my shabby kitchen as if to say, *as opposed to people like you.*

A few months later, they were tucked tidily away in an expensive house by the Chugach foothills, Laurel maneuvering her BMW along potholed roads and bitching about the general lack of basic traffic law obedience. I initially envisioned the two of us drinking tea and sharing pieces of our lives, like sisters in Hallmark Cards commercials, but that never happened. Laurel remained as unapproachable as ever, though she did soften toward Jay-Jay. Oh, the way my sister changes when Jay-Jay is around! Her face lightens, and the lines around her mouth even out. Laurel and Junior don't have children. Laurel says she can't, but I think she has willed her body not to reproduce, frightened as she is of the idea of pregnancy. And labor! Blood and sweat, screams and flailing legs: Laurel would die before she would allow herself to be seen like that.

I could go on, but writing about someone who is so goddamned perfect is like drinking too much. At first you feel brave and superior, but as soon as the alcohol hits your blood, you flatten out and realize that underneath it all, you just want to sit on a barstool and sob.

Monday, Sept. 26

Every Sunday the Oprah Giant posts a blog to give us poor diary-writing slobs hope. This week's was about loss. "You can't see the center of the pond when the water is muddied with regret," she wrote. "Make a list of all the things you lost—socks and pets and that teacup from Aunt Mabel. Draw little hearts beside them. Treasure them! Love them! They're not lost, they're still hiding inside your heart."

I snorted as I read this. List the things I've lost—please! What exactly was her point?

But then I remembered the winter after the divorce, when the snow and darkness settled in and I felt so alone that I called Laurel in the middle of the night. It was all too much, I sobbed. I couldn't take it.

"I'll come over Saturday and take Jay-Jay," she offered.

"Thanks," I sniffed. But it wasn't a babysitter I needed as much as hope. I wanted someone to offer me a slice of hope, the way Gramma used to offer me a slice of lemon meringue pie, the middle shiny with promise.

"I'll never love anyone again," I cried dramatically.

There was a long pause. "Love isn't what you expect," Laurel finally said. "It doesn't necessarily make you happy."

I ignored the implication that my sister's marriage wasn't working. I was too selfish, too mired in my own pain to acknowledge anyone else's.

"I'll never meet anyone like Barry," I continued. Now that he was gone, I forgave him his faults and remembered only the good. What had I done? Why had I left such a prince of a man?

"He chewed with his mouth open," Laurel reminded me. "He hung dead animal heads on the walls. And remember your wedding? He wore hiking boots with his tux."

"Those are no reasons to leave a good man," I cried.

Laurel snorted in disgust. "What exactly about him do you miss?"

"He loved to eat," I said. "He was a great hiking partner. He had a nice furry chest."

"So get a dog," Laurel snapped.

Enter Killer Bee. Like everything else around here, she isn't much to look at. Part beagle and part Labrador retriever, her eyes are slightly crossed, her tail bent, her coat speckled with outlandish white spots, the largest one in the perfect shape of Florida, right down to the panhandle. Killer is afraid of loud noises, cats, small dogs, kites, the garbage truck, and plastic bags blowing in the wind. She also has a nervous stomach and throws up if anyone yells too long, too loud, or too often.

But Killer is loyal to a fault, patrolling the hallway at night, her toe-nails clicking on the floor like a demented sentry.

We rescued Killer Bee from the back of a pickup truck at the supermarket. Jay-Jay took one look at the squirming puppies and refused to budge.

"Can we get one, huh, Mom, huh?" He asked for so little, how could I possibly refuse? I gave the man a twenty and we drove home with that puppy licking Jay-Jay's face. He named her the next day, after watching an advertisement for a movie about killer bees swarming a Texas town.

I have to admit that through all the housebreaking, the chewed-up shoes and coats, and the torn upholstery, it helped having another body in the house. Nights after Jay-Jay is asleep and I pace the dark living room, it's reassuring to know that anytime I want, I can reach my hand out and she'll trot over and greet me. She'll always be happy to see me.

Jay-Jay wasn't happy to see me when I picked him up from his after-school program this afternoon.

"You smell," he hissed, glaring at my grease-splattered uniform. "The *other* mothers don't wear stupid aprons."

Well, what could I say? The other mothers had neat hair and I'm-a-respected-member-of-the-community clothes and wedding rings that flashed when they waved their hands. Jay-Jay attends the gifted program in a school located in an upper-middle-class neighborhood, and while he's too young to understand the significance of class structure, he's smart enough to decipher the nuances. He knows it's not good to have a mother who works as a waitress and has rightly decided that this must be my fault. Once we got in the car, though, he was more civil, and by the time we hit the first traffic light, he was explaining a science class fiasco.

"Julia was supposed to only count the green colors," he said. "But she didn't, Mom. She counted everything *but* green." Jay-Jay shook his head. "We came in *last*. It took us forever. We had to recount every single green."

I had no idea what he was talking about but I nodded my head. I was looking forward to a long bath and a bowl of tomato soup with little oyster crackers floating around the top, like Gramma used to make. She called the crackers "little darling dumplings," and thought they were the cleverest thing.

"Crackers that float," she marveled, and none of us had the heart to tell her that all crackers float, to one degree or another. I was remembering Gramma's tomato soup recipe when I pulled in the driveway and met up with the sight of my bearded ex-husband sprawled over the porch, his face hidden behind a hunting magazine. A bear growled out from the cover.

"Jay-Jay Jiggers," he yelled, standing up and brushing off his pants. "Wanna head over for dinner? Got a nice piece of salmon and I'll fry them little brown potatoes you like so much."

"Can I, Mom, huh?

I hadn't planned anything for supper but even so I bit my lip and acted like it was a big deal. Barry and I officially have joint custody; unofficially, I have custody and he has visitation whenever *he* feels like it. Usually this means every other weekend and a good chunk of the summer, plus fishing trips when the kings and silvers are running. I can handle impromptu visits, and Jay-Jay doesn't appear to have a problem with them, either. What I have a hard time handling is the way Barry tries to weasel out of child support payments.

Right now Barry owes me over $1,600 in back support. When I mention this, his mouth tightens and his eyes narrow and he flashes that "don't tell *me* what to do" look men have been giving women since we all started stumbling around upright. Don't get me wrong, he loves Jay-Jay. He would die for him in an instant. It's just that, like me, money isn't his strong point. He doesn't know how to save; he insists that it's not in his genetic makeup, but really it's because he blows all his money on fancy outdoor equipment.

"I *said*, can I?" Jay-Jay yelled, interrupting my thought process.

"I suppose so." I sounded just like my own mother. "Don't forget your homework, and take a sweatshirt in case you get cold and—"

"Mom!"

A few minutes later they roared down the driveway in Barry's ridiculous camouflaged Jeep. Barry is a chef. I have to mention this because it explains so much. The man loves food. That's how we met. We were both stuffing grapes in our mouths at the Carrs produce section, those large black Concord grapes we used to pick back home. I was new to Alaska and couldn't get used to the summertime light or the way the mountains looked when I walked out of my apartment each morning: stern and reproachful, like a father waiting for me to make a mistake. I was terribly unhappy. I had ditched a short-term fling in Homer and hitchhiked up to Anchorage with an old man whose dog chewed the zipper off my pack. I was homesick and couldn't sleep, so when I noticed the grapes I felt redeemed. I looked up, saw Barry throw a handful in his own mouth, and grinned at him with purple teeth.

That's how it started. It wasn't at all romantic, but then again, nothing ever is.

LETTER #2

Killer Bee Richards
c/o Ms. Carla Richards
202 W. Hillcrest Drive #22
Anchorage, AK 99503

Dear Killer Bee Richards:

Your owner is in trouble. He/she hasn't paid his/her monthly bill. Please give a bark/meow in his/her direction to start the bone/catnip rolling.

If payment isn't made by Oct. 15, your owner will be smacked with a newspaper and sent to a collection agency.

Woof woof, meow meow,

Dr. Francis Sterling and Dr. Emily Goodman,
Anchorage Emergency Clinic

Wednesday, Sept. 28

I. Am. So. Depressed.

After work today I trudged over to an appointment at the Consumer

Credit Counseling agency. Laurel set this up for me after I mentioned that I was trying to get my life together.

A fattish woman who smelled of Jergens hand lotion, the credit counselor patiently explained the counseling motto: a penny saved is a penny saved.

"Clever," I muttered as I pulled my dirty waitressing skirt over my knees. For some reason it was important that I make a good impression with this homely woman who knew how to save her pennies.

I answered questions and turned over copies of my pay stubs and income tax returns while she printed out a spreadsheet with my take-home pay on one side and my basic expenses on the other. No matter how she prodded and subtracted and crossed out items, she couldn't get the columns to balance.

"You don't *need* to buy name-brand food," she said. "You don't *need* Playtex tampons; generics work just as well."

After half an hour of hard-grit figuring, she wiped her hands on a tattered Kleenex and looked up. Sweat dotted her forehead.

"Any additional income?"

I lied and shook my head no.

"Child support?"

"Four hundred a month, but I never see it."

"Never?" she challenged.

"Not for four, maybe five months. But wait! I got a couple of twenties a few weeks ago, but that's only because he wanted me to watch his bird for the weekend and—"

"I think I've heard about enough." The counselor glared me into silence. "The best solution," she continued in a stern, no-nonsense voice, "is to find a better-paying job." She scanned my application. "It says here that you're a what, a waitress? And you're almost forty?"

"Thirty-eight," I said meekly. "I'm thirty-eight."

She ignored this and pulled out a new form. "Let's talk retirement. Any stocks? Money market accounts? CDs? IRAs?"

I opened my mouth, about to mention my closet filled with art supplies and half-finished paintings. I had invested thousands of dollars in my art. Surely dreams, however far-fetched, however misconstrued, must be worth something. But I knew that this sensible woman with her freshly ironed blouse wouldn't see it this way, so I wisely shook my head no.

"Savings?"

"Five hundred and seven dollars," I whispered.

"Health insurance?"

I shook my head again.

"Emergency funds?"

"N-n-no."

"Mrs. Richards, may I be frank?"

I nodded.

"Your financial life is a mess," she said. "At the rate you're going, you'll be bankrupt in two years."

A whimper of shame escaped my mouth.

"The best you can hope for at this point is to maintain your current level of debt and make every effort—and I mean every—to not dig yourself in any deeper."

"Yes," I whispered again.

"And cut up your credit cards, or at the very least put them in the freezer." She leaned forward and glared straight in my face. "You can't afford to spend another—and I mean another—aimless dollar."

She handed me an appointment card for next month, shook my rather limp hand, and escorted me to the door. I was so depressed I stopped at JCPenney on the way home and bought a cookie jar that plays five different songs when you pop the lid. It was rather pricey, but the tag said it was dishwasher safe, so I knew it was a good deal. Besides, it was round and fat and reminded me of Gramma, who used to march down to the gas company every month and demand a handful of the free lollipops they handed out to the kids.

"I gotta pay, you gotta pay," she'd say, her three chins wiggling with the indignation of having to hand over her hard-earned money to a company that heated her bathwater. If Gramma were still alive, she'd tell me to not worry, that a little debt never hurt anyone. Then she'd make chocolate chip cookies, which she called little brown chippies, and we'd sit at the table and eat them while they were still warm. Gramma used to say that as long as my belly was full, nothing bad could happen. It was a fib, of course, but it brought me such comfort that I've passed it along to my own son. Some nights that's all I can manage for supper, a batch of chocolate chip cookies with tall glasses of milk, along with a side of cucumbers or tomatoes so we don't get scurvy. I make Jay-Jay promise to never breathe a word that his mother feeds him cookies for supper.

"Big deal," he says. "Malcolm's mom forgot him at the state fair last year. He had to sleep with the *cows*, so you don't have to worry. Cookies are nothing."

GRAMMA'S LITTLE BROWN CHIPPIES

- 2½ cups flour
- ½ cup margarine
- ½ cup Crisco
- 1 cup sugar
- ½ cup brown sugar
- 2 eggs
- 2 cups oatmeal
- 2 cups chocolate chips
- 1 teaspoon baking soda
- 1 teaspoon vanilla
- ½ teaspoon salt

Preheat oven to 350°. Mix everything together. Roll in small balls, stick on cookie sheet, cook at 350° for 12 to 15 minutes. Remove from oven. Eat while still warm. Serves four, or one premenstrual woman.

Friday, Sept. 30

It's late at night, Jay-Jay asleep, the house quiet. Outside the wind blows, a cool autumn breeze filled with the smell of damp leaves and silt from the inlet. I'm sitting at the kitchen table, my art supplies huddled around a Barbie doll arm, three Bratz doll legs, a Ken torso, and two vintage heads with the hair scalped off. As soon as I finish drinking my tea and writing this entry, I'll start my second job. No one knows I do this, not Laurel or my best friend, Sandee, or the snotty credit counseling woman. It's best to keep quiet about it, at least for the time being.

I've already spread newspapers across the table and assembled my X-Acto knives. I love the way they feel in my hand: cool and smooth and promising. Each time I pick one up I experience a tremendous urge to cut something, and once, after an especially brutal fight with Barry, I sliced holes in all of his socks, clever little rips that wouldn't become apparent until halfway through the day, when his toes would suddenly pop through the seam and give off that itchy feeling that can drive you crazy. X-Acto knives make you think of things like that. They make you slyer and smarter than you really are.

Across the table I've lined up my paints and glue, sandpaper and drill, dental floss and various tricks of my trade along with the red storage containers I keep at the back of the closet filled with my "work" dolls, most of them bought for a steal on eBay because of cracks or missing eyes. Such flaws mean nothing to me. Like that *Six Million Dollar Man* show I used to watch growing up, I have the technology to make my dolls better and faster. Much, much faster. Because I make them anatomically correct. I drill tiny little vaginas and labia lips between those poor sexless thighs, and then I cover these private parts with seductive underpants, cheerleader outfits, or nursing uniforms with push-up bras stretched across newly expanded boobs so big it would be impossible for these dolls to see their feet if they had the misfortune of coming alive. I make dirty dolls. X-rated, but mildly so.

I don't do anything radical like butt plugs or fisting or foursomes, and I always make sure Ken carries a condom.

I sell these on an adult website and they're more popular than you might expect. My agent is Jimmie "10-inch" Dean (no relation to the sausage), a former porn star who found Jesus during a stint in rehab and became so excited pondering the age-old question of whether Joseph and Mary had ever *done it* that as soon as he got out he started Thinking Butts and Boobs, an artsy adult website that speaks frankly and honestly about sex and desire and why we want what we want. It's *the* adult site; it's even been written up in such stuffy publications as *The New Yorker* and the *Wall Street Journal*.

I happened upon this site by accident one night as I was surfing the web looking for ways to make extra money. One minute I was reading about My Points accounts and the next I found myself at Jimmie's website, which I like to think was fate since he was hosting his My Body and Why? art contest. First prize was $500, so I grabbed a Barbie, made her boobs bigger and her butt rounder, and then I went all the way and drilled a tiny vagina, complete with real-life labia (which was harder than you might expect, with so many folds and all). I only came in third, but Jimmie was so smitten that he called me the very next day to see if he could market the idea. I was sure he was joking: did the world really need dolls with cunts and pubic hair?

It turns out it did. The first five sold out in less than a day, and even though Jimmie has twelve other artists working on his Really Real, Really Feel Me doll line, mine are the most popular. I make four to eight a month and average $50 apiece. I could make more money if I branched out on my own, but I don't want the hassles. Jimmie has an ongoing legal battle with the Mattel toy company and besides, I like the anonymity. I don't have to suffer the embarrassment of walking into Jay-Jay's school conference knowing his teacher knows I'm the creator of Purple Pussy Patty or Suck Me Harder Sammy.

My dolls actually sell more among women than men. This is a fact. It's also a fact that women think of sex a lot more than men give them credit for. It's just that we think of sex as a whole outfit, while men only think of ripping off the clothes and getting the deed done. Women dress up their fantasies, right down to the weave of the silk undies and the peek of lace around a push-up bra. We imagine not only hairstyles but the shapes of barrettes and the shades of toenail polish. Once we're satisfied that our fantasy looks exactly as we want, only then do we bring in the men. And here's the secret, the thing we all know but rarely admit: in our fantasies, the men don't matter that much. Oh, we need their parts and their presence, but they are shadowy and often faceless because it's mostly about us, our bodies, and the way we look and move. Sex for men is all about the orgasm. For women, it's all about getting to the orgasm. I understand this, which is why my dolls are so popular. I take care with every detail, from the handbags to the toe rings to the fake designer camisoles, one strap slipping coquettishly down a shoulder.

I love sitting at my kitchen table late at night and chopping my dolls to bits. I feel so inexplicably happy that I often get up and dance around the kitchen. It's not just about the money, which I so desperately need. It's the knowledge that I'm creating something, and so what if it's slutty dolls? I'm choosing colors and shading textures, I'm figuring lines and confronting angles. Lately I've begun dabbing small canvases on the side, sketching an identity for each doll. These paintings are embarrassingly sloppy and amateurish; it seems I've gotten out of touch these years I've been away. Yet I can feel a difference in my brush the nights I work on these, a thumping like a heartbeat, a tingle much like someone's breath against my hand. Often I get so carried away I fall asleep right at the table, my head pressed on small tubes of acrylic paint so that when I wake in the morning, streaks blaze across my face like tribal markings. I don't wash these off, I wear them as long as I can: to the post office, the grocery store, the bank, the color marking me as someone with a purpose, someone trying to find meaning, decipher nuances. Someone who matters.

LESSON TWO

Remember to Praise Thy Mailman

When we praise the good things, the universe rewards us by subtracting from the bad. Think of it as a math problem with a smaller solution!

—*The Oprah Giant*

Chapter 3

Tuesday, Oct. 4

"It's not that I *DIDN'T* want to sleep with him," Sandee said the moment I walked in to work this morning. "I just didn't want to listen to him make a big deal out of it later." She pulled a large tray out of the pantry cooler and began sorting salsa: green, hot, mild, and chunky. "It's so pathetic when men try to thank you for sex."

Sandee is my best friend. She's a small-town girl from the Florida bayou who hates the heat and doesn't know how to swim. She has platinum blonde hair and dimples and wears high-heel shoes even while waiting tables, her shapely calves flexing with each step. We work side-by-side stations during the lunch rush, and over and over, she saves my life. Unlike me, she actually likes to wait tables.

"The money's not bad and I don't have to wear career-girl bullshit outfits," she says, tugging her apron over her hips. Sandee is fifteen pounds overweight, but on her it's perfect. She looks ripe, like fruit waiting to be picked. She also has a way of making people feel right at home that nets her more tips than the rest of us.

"Honey, I'll be right back," she says, patting shoulders and soothing tempers so that even the older women, the hard, over-fifty women with sagging chests and bad haircuts, feel a need to protect her. No matter what she does, drops her tray or mixes up drink orders, the customers forgive her.

"Oh, darling, it's just not my day," she gasps, her hand held up to her mouth like a parody of old movies.

Sandee lives out in Eagle River, an upper-middle-class area about thirty minutes outside Anchorage, in a house with large windows overlooking the mountains. She was married once. On their third anniversary, her husband, Randall, surprised her with a Las Vegas vacation. He settled her in an expensive hotel, told her he was going out for breakfast, and never came back. He left her with a hefty hotel tab, a $1,600 monthly mortgage, and four maxed-out credit cards. Every three months, she receives a postcard from a peculiar location: Tupelo, Chattanooga, or Hell, Michigan, the backs holding strange and badly poetic messages scrawled in Randall's stilted handwriting. "In the morning, the sky is the color of pumpkin pie," the last one said. Sandee fumes for days after receiving one of these. It's her theory that Randall is hiding out in Vegas and making a killing as a blackjack dealer. The postcards, she believes, are mailed by tourists after they return home from vacation.

"That would be like Randall, making someone else do his dirty work for him," she says.

She isn't sure if she's still married ("He could be dead for all I know," she says in more optimistic moments), and when men ask her out, which is often, she usually agrees. These dates rarely end well and the next morning she shares the unhappy details with me. Today it was a guy she met at the car wash over on Minnesota Drive.

"I knew he was left-brained—come on, he's an accountant—but even that can be sexy. Remember that guy from British Petroleum who wore my underwear?" She tossed lettuce for the Caesar salad special. Croutons and cherry tomatoes flew. "Then he goes on and on about this digital recorder he got to capture rutting moose. I should have left right then but no, I hang around for the inevitable sex. Which was—surprise!—

accompanied by the roaring and thumping of horny moose." Sandee licked her fingers and stuck them back in the salad. "Why do I bother?"

I shrugged and headed to the empty dining room to set up my tables. The air was hazy with the smell of spilled tequila and old grease, and as I wiped chairs and tightened salt and pepper lids, I hummed along with the Mexican elevator music piped over the speakers. Since I'm the only all-day server—the others work split shifts and return for dinner as I'm finishing up the last of the afternoon tables—I get the prime corner station, five cozy booths plus two tables. Most days they're covered through two p.m., which is a good thing: more tables equal more money.

Today was busy, and after everyone was cut from the floor I got caught with a busload of retired dentists from Wisconsin, all of them straggling in with that peculiar pallor of the overly stimulated tourist. They had been to Portage Glacier and Denali, cruised Kenai Fjords, walked along the Alaskan Pipeline, and were just now returning from a day jaunt along Turnagain Arm, where they had encountered two heaps of bear scat. A fat man shoved his camera's viewfinder in my face.

"See?" He pointed to a blurry speck on the ground. "Scat so fresh it was steaming. Five minutes earlier, we'd have been ripped to shreds."

I didn't have the heart to tell them that they had photographed dog poop, not bear. They were having such a good time—what right did I have to ruin it for them? They ordered premium margaritas and steak fajitas, left me a fat tip, and promised to send autographed pictures of The Scat as soon as they got back home. By the time I tallied up my bank, the dinner shift was in full swing and I was late picking up Jay-Jay. I found him slumped in front of the locked multipurpose room, a big-bosomed lady with a clipboard glaring down at me. Did I know, she barked, that I would be charged an extra dollar for every minute late? I shook my head and signed the form; I had barely broken even. The re-tired dentists had left $55 in tips, yet their staying late had cost me $35 in extra child-care fees.

"I had to wait with Mrs. McCallister," Jay-Jay complained as we walked across the darkening parking lot. The air was cold and crisp—

Halloween weather, I always call it, these midautumn evenings when the wind blows with damp promise and everything feels suspended and mysterious.

"She talked about when she was a *girl*." Jay-Jay shuddered and pulled his coat tighter. "It was awful."

"I was a girl once," I said.

He gave me a disgusted look and climbed in the backseat. Once home I couldn't muster the energy to cook, so we had TV dinners. Jay-Jay and I secretly love TV dinners; we love the brightly colored cardboard wrappers and the way the food is stacked so neatly in clever little aluminum trays and then covered like holiday presents. We eat these compact meals in the living room while watching movies. Tonight it was *Dr. Dolittle*, and we laughed along with Eddie Murphy, we slurped and chewed and wiped our mouths on the bottoms of our shirts. After we finished, we put on our coats and sat on the porch and ate Fudgsicles until our tongues turned brown. I was stuffing the second one into my mouth when Jay-Jay suddenly asked, "Mom, ever wish you had a penis?"

"Not particularly," I said.

"Maybe then you wouldn't be so grouchy."

I lowered my Fudgsicle and stared at the slope of his forehead, so much like Barry's that I had the sudden urge to smack him. "How so?"

"Because," he explained in a patient, adult voice, "you could pee standing up."

"I'm on my feet all day at work. I like sitting down."

"Whatever." Jay-Jay shrugged. I could tell he didn't believe a word I said. I wondered if he was right, if I would be happier if I had a flap of skin swinging between my legs. I couldn't imagine it, though; couldn't imagine having to tuck it in and constantly rearrange it and worry about whether it would get hard when it wasn't supposed to or, worse yet, not get hard when it was supposed to. No wonder men treated their cocks as if they were the greatest things in the world. It was like stroking a talisman or praying to an unpredictable god: if I worship you and grant you privileges you'll always be there for me when I need you.

But they weren't, that was the thing. Every man I've ever dated for an extended time sooner or later couldn't get it up or got it up but came moments later, or got it up but not quite up enough, lying there and stroking it with a fearful, desperate look in his eyes. As I lay there beside them with my beautiful cunt that was always ready and only needed to be oiled from time to time and could come five and six and seven times in a row and never "petered" out or stopped working.

"Vaginas are really cool things," I wanted to tell Jay-Jay, because I wanted him to understand how it is to always be open, how walking around with that hole between your legs can sometimes feel like a void—if not filled, you could find yourself leaking away. How a man's penis might be more prominent but a woman's desire is just as strong, if not stronger, because she carries it deep inside of her.

Of course I couldn't say this to my son; it would be almost incestuous. Plus it wasn't really Jay-Jay I was thinking about but myself and the way I've lived my life, flitting from one desire to the next, never stopping to question if I was moving in the right direction, or even any direction at all. If men follow the lead of their penises, then women follow the path of their wombs. We follow our nurturing instincts. We call this passion or sex or love, but really it's deeper and more binding. It's our true voice, pure and pink and strong. It's the thing we seek yet fear and doubt because, think of it: how many of us really want to know the truth about ourselves? Most of us, I believe, are happier with lies.

LETTER #3

Ms. Carlita Richards
202 W. Hillcrest Drive #22
Anchorage, AK 99503

Dear Ms. Carlita Richards:
Congratulations! As head librarian of Anchorage Community Libraries, I would like to commend you for having the highest outstanding

library fine so far this year: $120.60, accumulated in daily fees for How to Save Your Own Life, *by Erica Jong.*

Please arrange payment as soon as possible. Until balance is paid in full, your library card will no longer be honored at local branches.

Shame, shame, shame on you, Ms. Richards!

Sincerely yours,
Margaret M. Miller,
Head Librarian
Anchorage Community Libraries

Thursday, Oct. 6

I lie. I can't help it, they just slip out. Gramma never made a big deal out of my lies, at least not the small ones, which she called fibskis. She believed fibskis were the only thing holding the world together.

"Think anyone wanna see themselves like they really is?" she'd snort. Then she'd roll dough out over the kitchen table and cut noodles while she told the story of her name, which was supposed to be Rachel but ended up Bethany; the midwife refused to write Rachel in the registry, since it was the name of the woman who stole her husband, so she wrote the name of her dead sister instead. By the time anyone realized this, it was too late and Gramma became Bethany, a combination of two names and similar to a small town in northern Alaska. Perhaps it was fate, for not only did I end up living in Alaska, but my name is also a fibski. It's not really Carla, it's Carlita. I don't admit this often because it's obvious to anyone looking at me that I don't have an ounce of Spanish blood in my veins. Laurel could get away with it, since she is darker, but I have that pasty skin of someone who should have been blonde but turned brunette. I wasn't purposely given a Spanish name. Mother, drugged out on painkillers and flying from champagne, goofed. I was supposed to be a boy and Mother had the name Charles all picked out, after her great-uncle, who started his very own tire company and made a fortune, only to lose it on a mad gambling binge when he was eighty-four, but that's beside the point. He was the only rich one in a family of middle-class people trying to toe the line and pull themselves up. I was supposed to be a lawyer or a doctor. "Or maybe even a movie producer," Mother used to sigh when telling the story. Then she'd take two aspirin and lie on the couch with a washcloth over her eyes. Talking about our muddled family history gave her a fierce headache, and we all knew to keep it down at such times.

When the doctor handed me to Mother, all wrapped in a pink blanket with a frilly cap on my head, Mother tittered and tried to hand me back.

"I seem to have the wrong baby," she fretted, still groggy from the drugs. "I ordered a boy and this seems to be, why, it's a girl." Her face was all scrunched up and puzzled, and at that exact moment Daddy took a picture, which is still plastered in the photo album, Mother holding me away from her body and looking at me with distaste, while I stuck out my tongue and crossed my eyes.

Later, when the drugs wore off and it finally hit Mother that she was stuck with another girl, she worried about what to name me. "Charles is such a good, solid name," she insisted. "It seems a shame to waste it. Maybe we should name her Charles anyway? If we gave it a cute little spelling..."

Daddy refused. Even then he was secretly plotting to try again. So when the Mexican aide came in to change the sheets and pointed at me and asked Mother, "What you name," Mother explained her dilemma. I don't know how much the woman understood, but at one point she excitedly pushed back her massive braid and screamed out, "Carlita!"

"Carlita? That sounds so, well, ethnic," Mother replied, but when Daddy looked it up in the baby book and found out that it was the female equivalent to Charles, he couldn't be swayed. So I ended up a Polish-looking child with a Spanish-sounding name in a family with a mother who put on airs and a father who bought me baseball gloves and took me to football games and couldn't seem to remember that I was really a girl. You'd think that when Gene finally came along, three years later, he would have given up, but he dragged Gene and me to every sporting event possible, and instead of making us athletic, all it did was give us a lifelong aversion to any type of game that required a ball.

Saturday, Oct. 8

"Think you'll ever get married again?" Laurel was splendidly attired in a navy blue Halston blazer and skirt so slim she was forced to mince her way across the kitchen. "I'm not getting personal. I just showed a new-lywed couple a condo over in Independence Park." She plopped down on a kitchen chair without bothering to brush off the dog hair.

"So?" I took a savage bite of the peanut butter toast left over from Jay-Jay's breakfast. I had been up late the night before, supposedly finishing a transvestite G.I. Joe doll order but actually working on my *Woman Running with a Box* painting. The box, now tied with red and yellow ribbon, was cradled against the woman's chest as lovingly as if it were a child. I had no idea what was inside but believed that if I kept painting it would soon be revealed to me.

"... out of my mind," Laurel was saying.

"Huh?"

"The newlyweds. I can't stop thinking of them. 'Are you sure these are the counters you want?' he kept asking. They were so endearing, so careful of each other's feelings."

"Give them a few years and they'll be fighting over those very counters," I snorted.

"Maybe not. If you find the right man it doesn't have to happen that way." Laurel's voice was dreamy, as if she were talking from far away. I got up and stuck another piece of bread in the toaster.

"The question is whether this is a sign or merely a coincidence," she said.

I didn't know how to answer. Laurel has been acting strange, calling and asking off-the-wall questions: If I were a bug, would I rather be a beetle or a grasshopper? Were socks invented before shoes? And why do we care what color our car is when we can't see it while we're driving? These questions make me cringe. They're like seeing Laurel without her bra, her pale, sad breasts forlorn and defenseless without their normal wedge of armor.

"Some days I put on a yellow sweater yet all day I feel as if I'm wearing black," she was saying. "Oops, there's my phone." The theme from *Jeopardy!* blared as Laurel pulled out her cell and hurriedly tapped out a text message reply. When she looked up, her face was flushed.

"Where was I? Oh yes: if you had five hundred dollars, would you spend it on a swimsuit that makes you look perfect or a new radiator for the car?" She leaned back in her chair and flashed me a hopeful smile; lipstick gleamed against her teeth.

If I had five hundred dollars, I'd pay off some of my credit cards and buy a new pair of work shoes, but I knew that wasn't what she meant. "I guess it depends on how often I used the car."

Laurel's face fell for a moment. "Okay, it's your *second* car, the one you don't use much. The one you keep for summer."

"Summer?" I repeated stupidly. I knew she was trying to tell me something but it was too early in the morning to make the kind of mental leaps I needed to understand my sister. I nodded and chose the swimsuit.

"Yes!" She tapped the tabletop with her hand. "That's *exactly* what I thought. So you agree, then? That I'd look good as a redhead?" She pulled a strand of her hair and stared at it with fascination.

"We're talking about hair?"

"What did you *think* we were talking about?"

I paused. "I thought Junior hated redheads."

"Oh, *him*," Laurel said with disinterest. "I need something new, you know? Something bold. Something that shouts, 'Here's a woman who's not afraid to take chances.'"

Laurel *was* afraid to take chances, but I knew better than to point that out. "Red is bold," I agreed. "But I've heard that it's hard to cover back up."

"I know!" Laurel cradled her head in her arms. "It's such a dilemma, Carly. I can barely sleep thinking about it. I want to look as if I'm in charge, but sexy in charge, you know?"

I was at loss for words. Except for the few days before her period, Laurel doesn't allow her emotions to get the best of her. She's logical and precise and careful. Yet there she was, sitting in front of me and revealing more moods then she'd had in years.

"The time!" Laurel stood up and pranced her way to the door without bothering to rinse out her dirty coffee cup. "I'll call you," she yelled over her shoulder. "About the hair, okay?"

The slam of the door, followed by the purr of her car's expensive motor as she glided down my driveway. I watched out the window and wondered what was going on in my sister's mind. Women always try to change their hair when they really want to change their lives. I did this myself, back before the divorce, before Barry and I dared utter the word, when we were still rolling it around on our tongues with an almost frenzied joy, each of us sure all our failures were the other's fault. Instead of bringing up the subject of divorce, I began cutting my hair. It had been long when I married Barry, down past my waist, and I often wore it in a fat braid that hit comfortably against my spine. I loved my hair. It was a shiny, dark blonde that picked up yellow highlights in the summer. Sometimes I wove ribbons through it or curled it in a mad array around my face.

"Getting loose," Barry yelled when I let my hair down. "My baby's a'gettin' loose."

I sacrificed my hair to free myself from my marriage. I hacked away, inch by agonizing inch, with Jay-Jay's toenail scissors, ripping and tearing until my hair lay in uneven strips across my back, slowly creeping up toward my shoulders. Barry never uttered a word, not even when my hair littered the bathroom floor and stuck to the sides of his socks.

To retaliate, or maybe to keep up, he started killing things: a few spruce hens here, a rabbit or porcupine there. King salmon so fat and heavy the middle of the kitchen table sagged, and then a coyote, a lynx, and—god help us—a sheep and finally a caribou. The day I walked in the bathroom and found a moose head floating in a cold bath was the day I knew we had gone far enough. Next time, it could only be a person.

That night I waited up for Barry, who was working an insurance salesman banquet. I waited until he walked in the door, his ridiculous chef's pants dragging on the floor, and then I coughed, cleared my throat.

"Divorce," I said, and we both froze, the silence between us thick and dangerous. I said it again. It was as if I had no control over my mouth.

"Divorce, divorce, divorce," until the very word became strange and blurry, like something you might read about in the newspaper.

"Shut up!" he screamed, which made me scream even louder: "Divorce, divorce, divorce."

He finally had to hit me to shut me up, a gentle tap that didn't even leave a mark, but still my eyes watered and I stared at him, momentarily betrayed. How dare he!

I kicked him, sly and quick, but he didn't bother to fight back, just stood there, his shoulders slumped, his chef's hat sagging against his neck. I hated him then, hated him with a passion so extreme that if someone had handed me a knife, I wouldn't have hesitated to stick it in.

"You win," he said in a horrible, gravelly whisper. "Happy now, god damn it, are you fuckin' happy now?"

But I didn't win. We both ended up losing more than we ever imagined, more than we even knew we had. Divorce sounds so simple, a two-syllable word about two people breaking apart. It's not simple, though, and the break is never clean. And just when you think it can't possibly hurt any more, it hurts more than is bearable, more than you can take. But you do take it, and that's the worst part of it all.

Chapter 4

To: crichards69@gmail.com
From: Jimmie10inch@yahoo.com
Subject: What the fuck?
C:
Your order is late again. Get your fucking ass in gear. Now!
On a cheerier note, the last batch looked good, especially the
Hanging Low, Hanging Hard for Big Daddy military doll. The
camo dick rocked, as did the rocket-flared cock ring.
Keep it up,
Jimmie Dean
President, Thinking Butts and Boobs
www.thinkingbuttsandboobs.com

Tuesday, Oct. 11

I can't seem to finish my dirty doll orders. For the past two nights I've
sat at the table, X-Acto knife in hand, and accomplished nothing. Oh,

I did manage to slice open Ken's buttocks and insert a small wedge of latex to give him a plumper, sexier behind, but my heart wasn't in it and poor Ken ended up with lopsided cheeks and an ugly scar, which I didn't bother to cover with dabs of flesh-coated tint. Instead, I stapled Ken's mouth shut. Then his eyes, and his ears and hands, all the while wondering: what is it I don't want to see or hear or touch or say?

My dolls are a camouflage, a distraction. They keep me from seeing my real self. But what if I were braver? What if I dusted off my brushes and concentrated, really concentrated, on the *Woman Running with a Box* painting? Finishing it would make it permanent, and permanence scares the hell out of me. Which is ironic, because one of the reasons I yearn to be an artist is to leave something behind, a record of my life, a yell in the dark: I was here.

Gramma was the one who first put a crayon in my hand when I was two, and forget the fact that I ate the first couple she handed me (primrose, followed by burned sienna and then midnight sky), I soon began coloring everything in sight, from Mother's good white slip to the bathroom walls.

"*Ach*, you got the gift," Gramma said, *ooh*ing and *aah*ing at every smeary new creation. "You are a gifter."

Gramma always believed I'd make it as an artist. She was the only one in the family who believed I would amount to something; she said she knew it the first time she plopped a piece of honey-glazed cabbage into my mouth. I sucked it slowly, intently, as if trying to draw out every single flavor.

"Greedy for life," Gramma called it. She insisted it was a sign of a strong personality, someone with the gumption to go out and get what she wants. Poor Gramma, with her messy hair and unshaven legs and ugly flowered dresses clinging to her massive hips. Poor onion-smelling, mole-spotted Gramma. She was never good at predicting anything, not even the weather. If she said it was going to be sunny, we all made sure we carried our raincoats that day.

Friday, Oct. 14

"Midway through your diary writing you will be surprised by offerings of mysterious gifts," the Oprah Giant wrote. "It could be money, free car repairs, or a letter from the sister you haven't spoken with in years."

When this happened, she continued, it was our obligation, our duty, to offer up praise.

So praise be the mailman with his balding head, his shuffling gait, his knobby knees (in the summer) and big red ears (in the winter). Praise be his little truck that creeps and coughs up our road each morning before I leave for work. Praise be his gloves with the chewed fingers and his cheery "Good morning, Miz Richards" and his breath that smells of butterscotch candies.

Praise be to you!

Because today you brought me two Alaska Permanent Fund dividend checks, each made out for the whopping amount of $845.76 and tucked inside a small envelope with stars from the Alaska flag running up the side.

In Alaska, October is a holy month. It's when every man, woman, and child, plus a few dogs and hamsters squeezed illegally into the system, gets a portion of the oil profits from the North Slope. Forget the fact that those same oil companies pollute our waters and kill our wildlife. Most of us are happy to receive this money we didn't do a damn thing to deserve. We feel vindicated, as if it is our right, our pat on the back for having suffered through winter after dark winter, along with crappy springs and too-short summers. These checks usually average around a thousand dollars, though they've been known to soar past the fifteen-hundred-dollar range.

For a short space each October, the financial burden lifts from my shoulders and I am left feeling light and airy, as if I can accomplish anything. It's an illusion, of course. Still, it's a welcome reprieve. I buy balloons and decorate the kitchen.

"We're rich," I sing, dancing around the kitchen with Jay-Jay and

Killer. I order take-out pizza—a luxury—and we sit on the worn linoleum and look through catalogs, deciding what to do with this windfall,
this gift from god and the state and our pigeon-toed mailman. Jay-Jay
usually buys video games and I always buy art supplies.

So thank you, Mr. Mailman. For the filbert brush and the bone-
handled fettling knife, the Schmincke soft pastel set and the Totally
Hair Ken doll, and especially for the 1966 blonde ponytailed Barbie I
won on eBay, which is splendid and glorious and should arrive in your
humble little truck sometime next week.

Monday, Oct. 17

Phone call at 8:03 a.m.

"Carla Richards?"

"Mmmmmm."

"This is Darlene, over at Alaska Consumer Credit Counseling. I see
by my records that your dividend checks were scheduled to arrive this
week."

"Oh. Right. Yes."

"Wonderful! Do you still have a copy of our payment budget?"

"I-I guess so."

"Don't worry, I'll e-mail you another."

"Uh, okay."

"You need to send out your payment checks the minute you cash your
dividend, and I mean the minute. This way you can get your foot in the
door, payment-wise."

"Sure!" I lied heartily.

"Now, have you..." I heard papers rustling in the background.
"Have you looked into further education to procure better job opportunities?"

"That's next on my list," I lied again.

"I must say, Miss Richards, you are doing exceptionally well. If you only knew some of my other clients, why, they're practically helpless. But for someone who works in the service industry, you seem to have things well under control."

"Yes." I could almost feel my nose growing longer.

"I'll call in January, to see how you've survived the holidays." She gave a little laugh and hung up.

My hands were slick with sweat by the time I put the phone down. Gramma would have sympathized. Her spending habits were as sloppy and unpredictable as mine. Every Thursday she "borrowed" a handful of bills from the cash register of the deli where she worked and bought as much hamburger as it would cover. Then she cooked up huge vats of goulash and soup, which she took down to the park and left for her poor neighbors. She left dishes as well, bowls and spoons and even cloth napkins. She never worried that people might take things.

"Just 'cause they ain't got money don't mean they ain't got hearts," she'd say, chopping onions and celery, her fat hands moving so fast they appeared to blur.

No one ever stole anything from Gramma, even though she lived in a rough neighborhood and never locked her door. She was esteemed, like Mother Teresa or Gandhi. Even the street punks nodded when she waddled past. They called her Grannie P, for Gramma Polack.

"Hey, Grannie P, what's shaking?" they yelled, giving her high fives.

Gramma pinched their cheeks and asked about their mothers. She knew everyone's names, even though she lived in a predominantly Hispanic neighborhood and few people spoke English. How they understood my grandmother's butchered speech is beyond me. Maybe food speaks louder than words, for at the beginning of the month when the men lucky enough to have jobs got paid and the others received their welfare checks, the women left offerings on Gramma's doorstep: a bowl of fried rice, a jar of homemade salsa, a plate of green chili tamales. Gramma and I ate these in front of the TV while watching *The Price Is Right*. Gramma had a crush on Bob Barker.

"That one spunk of a man," she sighed.

"Hunk," I corrected her, but neither of us cared much about semantics. I sat beside my grandmother eating foods so hot my mouth burned, and I almost wept from the pleasure of it all: the food, my grandmother, the dusty TV set spilling out words in Bob Barker's smooth, silky voice. Food. House. Grandmother.

Good.

Wednesday, Oct. 19

I. Am. So. Ashamed.

"Wake up," I hissed earlier this morning to the lump snoring beside me.

A grunt from beneath the covers.

"I *said*, wake up!"

"Wh-what?" The covers flew back and Barry scrambled out of bed, his naked penis swinging back and forth, as if unsure of which direction it wanted to go.

"Jay-Jay's in the kitchen."

We stared at each other, eyes wide.

"Mom?" Jay-Jay called, his footsteps pounding up the hall.

"Don't come in!" I shouted. "I'm getting dressed."

"You got the wrong kind of cereal," Jay-Jay yelled back. "I said corn-flakes, not bran flakes. *I'm* not the one who—"

"It was on sale!" I rattled dresser drawers so Jay-Jay wouldn't hear the sound of his father sneaking out of his mother's bedroom window after a night of wild and desperate sex. Imagine the confusion! Imagine him thinking we might still love each other!

We don't, of course. At least not in that way. But we still fuck. When either of us is lucky enough to be in a relationship, these sad couplings are supposed to stop. But they rarely do. It has little to do with love or pleasure or even sex and everything to do with the fact that Barry and I can't let go. If we did, we'd have to face the terror of loving someone else again. So we see other people, we sleep with other people, we have relationships, but we never dip below the surface. As long as we're secretly sleeping with each other, everything else is a lie. And this lie keeps us safe; it shields us from taking chances and risking love and finding out that maybe, just maybe, the divorce wasn't the other one's fault. Maybe it was a lot more about our own stuff than either one of us cares to admit.

Sandee can usually tell when I've been with Barry. She says I walk differently, heavier, as if I'm carrying a burden. "A very pleasant burden," she says, "but a burden nevertheless."

She didn't notice today; she was too busy bitching about the guy who wooed and then insulted her at Simon & Seafort's. Right after their appetizer plate arrived, he leaned suggestively forward and whispered that she'd be stunning if only she had bigger boobs.

"Can you fucking believe that?" It was just after eleven thirty and we stood in the alley behind Mexico in an Igloo, furiously smoking unlit Camel Lights while enjoying our first cig dig of the day. Neither of us smokes, but since the only way they'll allow us out of the building is if we're on a cigarette break, we keep packs of Camel Lights in our apron pockets. We're experts at making these fake breaks last as long as possible, sliding our unlit cigarettes to our mouths and pretending to inhale. Whenever the dining room becomes unbearable, one of us mouths, *Cig dig?* and the other holds up her fingers, indicating how many minutes until our escape.

"I should have left right then and there, but I wanted to make it through to the clam chowder. Ever have it? There's this taste that's real distinct but kind of strange."

"It's Barry's recipe," I told her.

"Wow, no way!" Sandee paused for a moment, as if out of respect. "Then he tells me he knows this doctor who could fix my boobs for under five grand, he says this like he's offering me a prize, so I look him in the eye and say, 'Baby, I'm sure he could.' When he goes to the bathroom I call over the waiter and order a bottle of two-hundred-dollar wine and five seafood and steak platters. Then I put on my coat and walk out."

"Good for you." I picked tobacco flecks out of my teeth.

"No," Sandee sighed. "I shouldn't have gone out with him in the first place."

"Barry stopped over last night," I said, as if to console her.

"You fuck?"

My mouth turned up in a guilty little grin.

"If Randall were around I'd fuck him." She dropped her unlit cigarette in her pocket and wiped her mouth over her sleeve. "Then I'd kill him. Or maybe not. He had such tiny ears. I used to worry that if he ever needed glasses he wouldn't have anything to hold them up. You can't kill someone with ears like that."

Sandee sighed and shook her head. "We can't let go, don't you see? We're clinging to the ghosts of our dead husbands. Metaphorically speaking," she added.

I stared at her.

She leaned toward me. "We're both so busy fighting the corpses of our dead marriages that we're half-dead ourselves. There's no room for anything else—how can there be?" She stamped her heeled foot for emphasis. "You can't love the dead and the living at the same time."

I knew what she said was true. I had said the same thing to myself a hundred times. But hearing it out loud was startling. It was like hearing a nun swear.

"I can't keep on like this," Sandee said, more to herself than to me. "I'm so goddamned sick of sex. Some nights I want to cut off my vaggy, leave it in the room with the guy, and say, 'Here, you wanted it so much, you take care of it.' It's just getting too *hard*."

Amen, I thought, remembering the way Barry and I had clawed and pulled and bit, almost as if we were trying to destroy each other or, most probably, some part of ourselves. I stuck my gnawed cigarette in my apron pocket and followed Sandee back inside, weaving slightly as my eyes adjusted to the dim light. Right before we passed the bathrooms, she turned and laid her hand on my arm.

"Think I'll ever love anyone again?" she asked, not a question but more of a challenge.

I stared into her face, her clear and pale complexion, her perfect cheekbones, her wide and too generous mouth, leaned forward, and pressed my lips against her forehead, a mother's kiss.

"Sure you will," I said in my most comforting voice, "I'm positive you will."

It wasn't until later that I realized it was myself I was really talking to.

When I got back home, I grabbed Killer's leash and took her for a quick walk down by the inlet. It was just beginning to get dark, the sky an orangeish tint, the wind cold and sharp. I love late fall, love how thick and large the air feels, love the trees with their bare branches, love the way the frozen ground feels so much more solid beneath my feet. As soon as we reached the beach, I snapped Killer off the leash and let her run over the sand. During low tide, the distant water is silver blue, the mud flat gleaming and damp. Much of the coast around Anchorage is surrounded by a strange, thick clay that smells of salt and old water and sucks at your feet and sometimes, though rarely, acts like quicksand.

There's a story locals love to scare newcomers with about a man who got stuck in the mudflat out by Cook Inlet and, when rescuers tried to rescue him by helicopter, was pulled in half. I don't know if that story is true, but I do know that a handful of people have died in the mudflats and that there have been times when it's sucked me down to my knees and held me fast for a few seconds before letting me up with a loud, gurgling burp.

I always tell Jay-Jay to stay off the mudflats; I tell him it's like quicksand; I tell him if I ever catch him with even one toe in the mud, he'll be grounded until he leaves for college. But who knows what goes through his head, what small tidbits of advice and remarks and petty angers will stay with him, what he'll remember and what he'll discard. Having a child is the bravest thing I've ever done, braver than staring down a bear or encountering a horny moose during rutting season or trying to keep my head during an earthquake. No matter how much I love Jay-Jay, there's no guarantee that it's enough, that I'll be able to keep him safe. There are so many risks! So many things that could go wrong! I could look away for a minute and in that instant, he could be gone.

Of course, love is always like that. Or at least any kind of love worth having.

Tuesday, Oct. 25

"He's here." Sandee tapped me on the shoulder right as the lunch shift was heating up. Her face was flushed, her bangs frizzed across her forehead. "The Swedish god. He requested your station."

"God?" I had just seated a table of argumentative lawyers and couldn't remember if the bald guy with the pink tie had ordered Diet Coke or regular.

"The gorgeous guy with the big feet, you know, always wears high-topped sneakers? Shit, Carly, you have a pimple on your chin." She reached out and rubbed at my skin, as if to erase it. The "god" looked vaguely familiar but I couldn't place him.

"Carla," he said heartily as I approached his table. "I was hoping you'd be here."

"Can I start you off with something to drink?"

"Water's fine. Can't drink on the job. Too much dirt to sift through."

"Construction?" I asked hurriedly. From the corner of my eye the lawyer with the big teeth was frantically waving me down.

"Anthropology." The god stuck out his hand. "I'm Francisco."

"Fr-Francisco?" Sandee was right, he did look like a god. His hair was lighter than mine, but he was tall enough that when he stood up to shake my hand I had to throw my head back to get a good look at his eyebrows, which weren't all run together like some men's. "But aren't you Swedish?"

"Norwegian," he laughed, and his teeth were so white. "I get that all the time. It's an old family name, from the 1800s. My great-grandfather chased a woman down to Mexico..." He stopped for a moment and pulled a pair of smudged glasses out of his pocket. "Sure you want to hear this?"

I nodded and ignored the lawyers, who were whistling and stomping their feet. I stared at the god's hands, which were weathered and capable.

"...and lived there the rest of his life, returning long enough to knock up my great-grandmother with my grandfather and burden him with a ridiculous Mexican name and... What's wrong? Did I say something wrong?"

"Ask me my name, okay?"

"It's Carla, right?"

"My whole name."

"What's your whole name?"

"Carlita."

"No shit." He whistled. "Wow, listen, I'll bet we're the only non-Spanish people with Spanish names in all of Alaska."

"Yeah." I looked at him with interest now that we had something in common. "Yeah, we probably are."

He ordered a bean burrito with green salsa and then excused himself to take a call on his cell phone. I took care of the lawyers, who had decided to order a round of margaritas ("But don't tell the boss, okay, hon?" the fat one said, his hand creeping up my thigh), and by the time I returned to Francisco's table, he had been joined by two more men. He nodded but didn't say anything the rest of his meal. He didn't even leave a noticeable tip, so I was surprised when the hostess handed me a folded piece of paper.

"From that good-lookin' blond guy," she said, peering over my shoulder as I opened it. *Carlita, my pseudo Spanish pal, give me a call sometime. We'll eat hot food and drink Mexican wine. Francisco 555-4289.*

"Nice handwriting," she said. "You gonna call him?"

"No." I crumbled the note and stuck it in my apron pocket.

"Of course you're going to call him," Sandee said during our last cig dig of the day. I was covered with salsa and reeked of tequila—the lawyers had gotten boisterous. "He's smart, funny. For Christ's sake, he's a Swiss god."

"Norwegian," I corrected.

"Did you see his feet? They're enormous. That means he has a big dick."

"As if I care."

"You do. Or at least you should." Sandee fake-smoked in tense silence. Her own love life was a mess, but she felt it was her duty as best friend to boss me toward something better. "You're parked on a cul-de-sac when you've got a whole highway in front of you," she finally said.

"Francisco's a highway?"

"You know what I mean." She stabbed her unsmoked cigarette out on the side wall of the lounge. "He's a possibility. How can you turn away from that?"

I couldn't explain the fear that clutched my stomach when I thought of doing it all again: the anxious first date, followed by the worry that there wouldn't be a second date, followed by the anticipation and worry of the first night of lovemaking, and then the rushed two or three months after that, when all I would think about would be him.

Then the inevitable moment I looked over at him and noticed that his ears were crooked or that he used coasters (coasters!) when he set a glass on the coffee table and something inside of me would come crashing down and I would realize with a start, with a deep sense of betrayal, that he wasn't quite perfect after all. Then, like dominos falling over, his faults and weaknesses, his bad habits and insecurities, would slam down over my head. Worse still would be the realization that he would be looking at me in the same way, seeing all of my own worst traits and failings.

And then would come the talks, the long, agonizing nights spent talking instead of making love, when we would pour out our doubts and decide if we should call it quits or bravely navigate past this rough patch. If we made it through all of that, we would settle down to a life of steady comfort, interlaced with occasional bouts of mad passion, along with a couple of hefty fights where we would throw things and blame the other for all of our faults.

I didn't have the energy to do it all again. I wanted to bypass the beginning and settle down in the middle. I wanted to know the ending to all of a man's stories and sit beside him eating sandwiches and know that he'll always say, "Are you sure this is mayonnaise and not Miracle Whip?" and be certain that we will always have sex on Saturdays and Tuesdays. It angered Sandee when I talked this way because she felt similar. Maybe a lot of women do, once they reach their midthirties and have played all the games and worn the sexy lingerie and had multiple orgasms and multiple partners and multiple heartbreaks. After a while an orgasm is an orgasm is an orgasm, and if truth be known, it's easier to invest in a good vibrator and let your fingers do the walking. Love is too complicated. It takes too much effort. It's something we all want, but we want it our way.

WHAT'S ON MY KITCHEN TABLE

Gas bill: DUE!
Phone bill: PAST DUE!
Visa bill: WAAAAYY OVERDUE!!
Chatty Cathy torso
Francisco's phone number, crumbled into a tight ball

Chapter 5

Thursday, Oct. 27

JAY-JAY WAS IN A QUIET MOOD when I picked him up from school this afternoon, his face pale, a smudge of green marker trailing across his cheek.

"Science sucked," he said. "Mr. Short wouldn't let us look at a book of medical mysteries 'cause one of the women didn't have a shirt on. Duh! We've all seen cable. Like we don't know about boobs."

I cleared my throat, worried I would have to throw out my Let's Talk about Sex spiel, but that was all he said. The minute we walked in the door, Killer Bee charged us from the hallway and Jay-Jay yelled something about corn.

"I don't think I have any." I kicked off my shoes and sank down on the couch. "Are peas okay?"

"No, an *ear* of corn. For Halloween."

I had completely forgotten about Halloween. "You want to be corn? Isn't that kind of, I don't know, different?"

"Exactly," Jay-Jay screamed. "No one will get it. They'll think I'm a superhero when really I'm a farm product."

After dinner we loaded ourselves into the car and headed over to the fabric store, where I asked the middle-aged saleswomen in my most polite waitressing voice where I might find a pattern for a stalk of corn.

"This isn't the supermarket, dear," she said.

"An ear of corn," I repeated. "For Halloween."

"We don't do fruits and vegetables." She peered over her glasses. "It upsets people."

I decided I would make my own pattern. After all, I was an artist—how hard could it be? I bought yards of bright green fabric plus swatches of yellow for kernels and curtain cords for the tassels. As soon as we got home, I spread the material over the not-so-clean carpet, dog hairs sticking across the sides.

"Better sew fast," Jay-Jay said. "We're supposed to come in costume tomorrow."

"Halloween's days away." I pinned a long skinny piece with a short fat one.

"Mr. Short wants to spread out our sugar influx. He says candy at school and candy after school will make our brain cells sag with despair."

"Mr. Short sounds like a smart man," I said.

"He flunked out of Harvard," Jay-Jay said. "He said it's better to flunk out of a top-notch school than graduate from an inferior place."

"Don't," I warned, pointing the scissors in his direction. For a moment, he had sounded exactly like Laurel.

"What? All's I said was Mr. Short says it's better—"

"Put your arms up," I ordered, measuring the badly sewn pieces against his back; they fell short by at least three inches. "Think you could hunch over for the whole day?"

Jay-Jay snorted with disgust and stomped off to take a bath. An hour later, after sewing a malformed corn kernel to my pant leg, I called Sandee, who was home from work faking a cold.

"Hello?" she said in a nasal tone. Then she coughed twice.

"Cut it out, it's me."

"Carla?"

"Jay-Jay wants to be an ear of corn for Halloween and I can't do it."

My voice was dangerously close to tears. "I forgot about Halloween and he needs it by tomorrow, did you hear me? Tomorrow!"

"Calm down," she said. "I'll head over as soon as I finish the dishes." Sandee never leaves the house without washing the dishes. This isn't because she's exceptionally neat but because she grew up in a shack with no running water and four to a bed and pork rinds every Saturday night while her father staggered around blitzed on the home-brewed moonshine that was their only source of income. Her poverty-drenched past waits at the edge of her University of Michigan education and $350,000 house, and Sandee is terrified that one day it will pounce. I doubt that this could ever happen. Sandee is a survivor, not because she's tough but because she isn't afraid to be soft.

"I'm here," she sang out an hour later, her arms stuffed with a jumbo box of Safeway croutons and a half-liter of Diet Coke. "Caffeine speeds up the metabolism," she said, kicking off her shoes and clearing a space off on the coffee table. Then she sat down cross-legged on the floor and arranged the croutons into neat piles.

"Want some?" She motioned to Jay-Jay, who clutched a Harry Potter book to his pajamaed chest. When he refused, she popped a crouton cheerfully into her mouth. "Seven of these have only twenty-four calories," she said, pointing to the piles. "And just an itty-bitty amount of fat."

I reached for the croutons, which were garlicky sharp and delicious. I finished off one pile and began on another.

"Mom's trying to sew," Jay-Jay said, "but she's making a mess. A real fiasco."

"Teeth." I pointed toward the bathroom. "And don't forget to floss."

"Yeah, yeah." Jay-Jay stomped off down the hall.

"It doesn't look that bad." Sandee wiped her hands over her jeans and rummaged through the shoddily sewn material. "Here's a stalk. A leaf. No, wait, a kernel. But look here, they're all the same size. You want to stagger them so they look more real and then..."

I settled back and happily crunched croutons. Sandee was a quilter and sewed fast and neat, her stitches marching like tiny soldiers across

the fabric. I wondered if she'd be up to sewing sexy underwear for my
porno dolls. Right now I paid a grandmother from Texas to do it, but
shipping was a problem. Last month a box of black thongs and furry
handcuffs had gotten lost in the mail. I opened my mouth to ask, but
guzzled a mouthful of soda instead. I didn't want to ruin the mood.
Having another adult around made the house feel warm and safe. I
wasn't alone. There was someone to talk to and argue with. Not that I
wanted an argument. Still, I knew if I needed one, Sandee would give it
her best shot. She handed me one of the sewn kernels and I began stuffing it with quilt batting as I hummed the theme from *Happy Days*.

"Carla?" Sandee asked.

"Hmmmm?"

"Nothing," she said. "It's just, well…"

Sandee crouched over a billowy green leaf, her mouth scrunched tight.

"I need to tell you something." Her voice was eerily low. "Something
I've never told anyone."

"Sure," I said.

"Do you have to go to the bathroom first?"

I shook my head no.

"I used to pray for Randall to die," she said. "I'd say, 'Please, please
get him out of my life.'"

"So?" I munched down on a handful of croutons. "I lit candles at
church while Barry and I were married and he *still* didn't die."

"No one tells you." Sandee's voice rose. "They dress you in a frilly
dress and push you toward the aisle and everyone fusses over your shoes
and worries about your hair but no one says, 'Oh, by the way, in a couple
of years you'll be wishing he's dead.'

"Then I started to think that maybe I had it wrong, maybe *I* was the
one who was supposed to die. I knew one of us had to go. We couldn't
keep on much longer. When Randall came home with tickets for Vegas,
I thought: maybe the plane will crash. It didn't, though, and the heat
slammed us the minute we got off the plane. 'Whoever thought of going to Vegas in the summer?' I screamed.

"I wore a sleazy little dress and strappy sandals because Randall told me to dress like I had class, and I knew Vegas class was the same as Florida small-town trash. I fit right in and won three hundred bucks at blackjack. Randall was furious. Blackjack was his thing. He had taken an online course before we left; I guess he thought he'd make a killing. He ended up losing over a thousand, and of course that was my fault, too.

"Finally I headed back up to the room without him. The elevator had glass walls, and after everyone got off, there was just my reflection staring at me from every direction. I had on too much makeup, I looked cheap and eager, and it scared me. I knew that beneath my healthy skin and good grammar, another woman waited, a back-home bayou woman who ate fried catfish and didn't have all her teeth and let her man beat her every Friday because she knew he would fuck her brains out come Saturday. That's when I suddenly understood that Randall liked this woman better than me, he needed to know that there was something dirty and tainted inside of me so he could feel better about himself.

"When I got to the room I took all of his clothes and threw them in the filled-up bathtub. Then I went to bed. He woke me early the next morning, screaming. I screamed back, and before you know it, it all came out. It was such a relief, Carla, like throwing up when you're really sick and how clean you feel afterward. I got it all out: that he was selfish and self-centered and a coward and woman hater and lazy in bed.

"He yelled I was poor white trash who ate out of garbage cans and my family was so inbred my brother was practically retarded.

"I did the worst thing. I laughed. I couldn't help it. In college I worried so much about people finding out where I came from that finally hearing someone put it into words was a relief. Randall's neck turned red and his fists balled up and for one glorious moment I thought he would hit me. Instead he slumped down on the bed, took off all his clothes, and added them to the heap in the bathtub. Then he sat across from me in just his socks. I waited a moment and did the same. I took off all my clothes and sat across from him naked and silent. The light coming in the window was harsh and too bright. We looked awful, both of our bellies flabby, our arms and legs sunburned, the rest of us white and splotchy. We looked like the ugliest of things.

"Then we were making love like we used to, soft and slow. We made love all that day and night, and when I woke, he was gone and there was a note on his pillow.

"'Out to get breakfast, bee back soon.' He spelled *be* with two *e*'s, I noticed that right away. Like *bzzzzzzz*. I thought he was being cute.

"But he never came back. I waited and waited, and finally I called the police. The older officer wouldn't meet my eyes.

"'Lady,' he said. 'Happens all da time. Da guy gets restless. Wanders off. It's Vegas. All kinda pleasures out there.'

"After they left, I noticed Randall's suitcase was gone. I didn't cry, though. I stayed in that hotel until my credit card maxed out, but he never even called."

Sandee wiped the last ear of corn over her face. Her hands shook slightly.

"I still don't know why he left, and that's the worst part. Was it something I said? Was there someone else? Not knowing is hell. You invent all sorts of reasons in your mind.

"But here's the thing I never told anyone. The second night, when I realized he wasn't coming back, I ordered steak and shrimp for two from room service. I sat down on the bed and ate until I threw up. Then I ate more. I forced down every single bite, even the garnish and cherry tomatoes. Then I thought, 'Whew, that's done. I'll never have to eat *that* again.'

"I was relieved, get it? I didn't love him anymore. So why the fuck am I so angry, Carla? Why do I want to kill him over and over again?"

Sandee flounced the costume and held it up: a perfect stalk with two ears of corn tucked coyly around each side, and a hole for Jay-Jay's face that tightened with a drawstring. Her eyes were red and puffy; her hands left damp smears over the fabric.

"I make dirty dolls," I offered.

She stared at me blankly.

"I know it's not the same as your husband running off," I said. "But you're the first person I've told." I rummaged around the closet until I found Little Bo Peek-At-Me, complete with a sheepherding stick that doubled as a vibrator. Sandee turned it over and peered inside the crotchless panties.

"Holy shit," she said. "You did this yourself?"

"Yeah." I felt strangely proud.

"Wow, well, this is really crazy, Carla." She held it up, squinted and then turned it over again. "I can't believe how real it looks." She ran her finger over the glued-on labia. "How did you get it to look so real?"

"*Playboy* and *Penthouse* spreads," I said. "Plus that squishy stuff from kids' footballs to make it soft."

"Well, shit, honey." Sandee reached over and grabbed my hand. Our fingers wrapped around each other and it was nice, holding another woman's hand, the palm soft, no calluses or scratches—I could feel the shiny tint of her fingernail polish against my fingertip.

"We're two misfits, aren't we?" Sandee said. "I lost Randall, and you, Carla, well, you've kind of lost your mind. But in a good way," she said quickly. "I mean that as a compliment."

"I know," I said.

Monday, Oct. 31

I'm writing this entry by jack-o'-lantern, Jay-Jay's pumpkin grinning moronically between crooked teeth. The candle gives off the scent of spiced apples, while scattered around me packets of Smarties and Now and Laters and thick squares of purple taffy call out my name. "Eat me," like in *Alice in Wonderland.*

Earlier tonight Jay-Jay left for a mad bout of trick-or-treating with a bunch of kids from school, a neatly dressed PTA mother knocking at the door and peering curiously in at our dilapidated trailer that reeked of the casserole I had burned for supper. Two hours later, he staggered back home clutching a bag of treats so heavy he could barely lift it up on the table. His face was smeared with chocolate, his costume ripped down one side.

"We had a blast," he shouted. "Bailey threw up right in front of the stop sign on Gerald's street and Mrs. Jenkins made us stop until she was finished, get it? Stop at the stop sign?"

I poured him a glass of milk, for protein, and got him settled at the table, where he slid his candy into complex patterns and then recorded numbers in the small notebook he carries in his back pocket. When I asked what he was doing, he rolled his eyes.

"I'm *categorizing*," he said. "Color, shape, and favorbility." He slid two packets of Life Savers away from a pile of Hershey Kisses. "Did you know we all lose the same amount of weight when we die? The same amount! Even fat people. Even midgets."

"That's nice." I wondered if perhaps his gifted class was a bit too progressive for my tastes. "Did you learn that in school?"

"Nah, it was from a movie over at Alan's."

After Jay-Jay went to bed and the house was quiet, my belly filled with chocolate, I decided to work on my *Woman Running with a Box* painting. In some demented part of my mind I believed the supernatural promise of Halloween would lend a mysterious aura. I was pulling my supplies from the closet when Killer let out a deep growl and charged for the door. A moment later a distraught vampire flew into the kitchen. A vampire with flaming red hair.

"Laurel?" I squinted at the chalky pancake makeup and bloodred lips. "You colored your hair."

The vampire plopped down in the chair across from me and began devouring a Nestlé Crunch bar. Then a Hershey bar, followed by a Mr. Goodbar, a Kit Kat, and a handful of chocolate coins.

"Holy shit, slow down." I grabbed the candy bowl and hurried it over to the counter. "You're gonna be sick."

Laurel whispered something from behind her chocolate-smeared mouth.

"Huh?"

"I'm seeing someone," she said, staring at the window behind me.

I jumped up and looked out, sure some nasty little goblins were toilet-papering our backyard again.

"I said I'm *seeing* someone." She jammed another Kit Kat in her mouth. "A man," she slurred. "I'm seeing a man. Okay, I've said it. *Are you happy now?*"

"I heard you." I didn't know what to say. Laurel and I don't tell each other private stuff; we stay on the surface as much as possible, where things are as safe and bland as white bread.

"It's not what you think," Laurel sobbed, her vampire makeup smearing down her face. "I love him!" The legs of her chair slammed down as if for emphasis.

"Who?" I finally asked.

"Promise you won't get mad?"

"Why would I care?"

"Promise?"

"Yeah, sure."

"It's Mr. Hankel."

"Who?" The name sounded vaguely familiar, and I ran through a mental list of Jay-Jay's teachers and camp counselors.

"You know. The weatherman."

"On TV? With the broadcaster wife? Holy shit!"

"You promised," Laurel hiccupped. "You promised you wouldn't get mad."

"Well," I stuttered. "I'm not mad, not at all." I forced my voice low and soft, the same tone I used to comfort Jay-Jay. "It's just unexpected, that's all."

"He came to the office about a summer rental on the Kenai earlier this spring," Laurel said. "I was wearing my yellow blouse, you know the one? The creamy silk with the cunning collar?"

"Ummmm." I had no idea what she was talking about.

"We were in the middle of the paperwork and I leaned over, and he smelled so good, Carla, sharp and crisp, like a pair of freshly ironed pants. His neck looked lost and vulnerable above his shirt, so trustworthy that I couldn't help leaning over and kissing him."

I didn't know what to say, so I muttered "Ummmm" again.

"That's when it started."

"It?"

"You know." Laurel gave a proud little laugh. "The sex."

"At work?"

"Carla! Do you think I'm so cheap? Hank took me to a nice hotel."

"Hank Hankel?"

"Yes," Laurel sighed, all dreamy. "Isn't it wonderful?" She wiped her face on one of my dish towels until her skin emerged, pale and beard burned. Then she put her face down on the table and sobbed again. "Oh Carly, I don't know what to do. I love him. I do! But it's impossible. We're both married."

I ate three Milk Duds and waited for more.

"But I love Junior, too. Don't look at me like that, Carla. I've been with him over fifteen years. He can't see without his glasses. He's so *help-less*. He gropes around every morning like a baby bird. Oh, oh. What am I going to do?"

"I'll make you something to eat," I said, handing her a fresh dish towel to mop up her eyes. "How about tuna casserole?"

"Like Gramma used to make?" Laurel asked in a small voice.

"Yeah, just like that," I lied, desperately trying to remember the recipe: cream of mushroom soup, egg noodles, cheese, and something else, something that gave it a strange, spicy taste. Peppers? Cumin? Garlic powder? "Go watch TV." I nodded toward the living room. "There's a bunch of old movies on tonight, a Halloween fest. I'll let you know when it's done."

"Okay." Laurel slumped out of the kitchen. The tuna smelled salty and strong when I opened the can. Gramma used to say that fish was the meat of the gods. Each week she made some type of fish, not on Friday, the typical Catholic fish-eating day, but on Monday, the beginning of the school week. She said the fish would swim up my brain and make me smarter.

"That why you answer all them right on your spelling test," she said.

I didn't have the heart to tell her I cheated off Bobby Wright's paper. He sat catty-corner from me and wrote extra big in exchange for the chance to watch me pee into a jar. Bobby saved the pee to pour over his mother's houseplants and then waited for them to die. When they didn't, he fell in love with me and insisted, in that logical persuasiveness common to eight-year-old boys, that he would never, ever love anyone as much as he loved me. Sometimes I still believe this. Sometimes I'm sure that I will never do anything to impress a man the way I impressed Bobby when I peed in those jars.

GRAMMA'S TUNA CASSEROLE
(WITH MINOR REVISIONS)

- 2 large handfuls egg noodles
- 1 can cream of mushroom soup
- 3 cloves garlic
- 1 can waterpacked tuna
- Pinch of cumin
- Splash of bourbon (for a kick)
- 1¼ cups milk
- ½ cup (or more) cheese

Preheat oven to 350°. Throw everything except the bourbon, cheese, and milk into a large casserole dish, adding enough milk to cover noodles. Splash with bourbon and spread cheese over top. Cook at 350° for 40 minutes. Eat with a large glass of wine. Serves two sad and frustrated sisters plus one greedy dog.

LESSON THREE

Can You See Abundance in This Picture?

At some point during the diary-writing process you will be hit with an insight that forces you to see things as they really are. Once this happens, you'll never be able to go back and see things as you used to. Be forewarned—change isn't a party dress. It doesn't always flatter your life. But like a London Fog raincoat, it will keep you warm and dry.

—*The Oprah Giant*

Chapter 6

Wednesday, Nov. 2

"DID YOU CALL HIM YET?" Sandee asked as we fake-smoked during a cig dig outside of Mexico in an Igloo. A stingy inch of snow covered the ground, and the air was crisp and cold.

"Call?"

"The god, you know, the Swedish guy."

"Norwegian," I corrected. Then I sighed. "I doubt he even remembers. He was just being nice."

"Yeah," Sandee snorted. "Guys are so *nice*. They leave their numbers for the hell of it." She looked at me sharply. "When was the last time you fucked someone, Carla? Can you even remember?"

I opened my mouth to answer, but she waved her finger in my face. "And don't you dare say Barry—he doesn't count."

Well, I couldn't remember, that was the thing. Sex with Barry was fierce and angry and intense, but it certainly wasn't deep. It didn't startle my soul. Afterward I sometimes sat in front of the refrigerator and ate whatever was handy: cheese slices or lettuce dipped in mustard or Jell-O scooped up with my hands. I wasn't hungry but I had to eat. I ached inside. And the few men I've seen since my divorce have been insipid and vague. Sex with them was like watching a rerun, everything dulled and lacking in surprise or wonder. Right after I left Barry, when I still felt adventurous and brave, I had an affair with the Mighty Muffler man. When I dropped the car off I told the young man (and he was young, sweet Jesus, barely legal) that I didn't care what he did, to just fix the goddamned thing. I was crying by then, and Dave (his name stitched across his pocket in blue letters) patted my head as if I were a dog.

"There, there," he murmured, offering me a soiled rag pulled from his pants. "We'll have her ready by five."

What is it about a sad woman that melts a particular kind of man's heart? When I picked up the car, Dave slipped me his phone number. I swore I wouldn't call but two nights later I broke down and did just that. We went at it on the couch, the dishwasher turned on to drown our sounds. Afterward, I cried again, but Dave didn't mind. He had grown up in a family of sisters, so he was used to a woman's tears.

"Baby," he said, kissing my forehead. "Poor sweet baby."

But he was just a kid, barely out of high school. When he invited me over to play video games with a bunch of his buddies, I knew I had to cut the cord. Still, he was such a nice, tender man. Boy. Man-boy. I still have his Midas shirt tucked in my dresser drawer. Sometimes I take it out and trace his name over and over, the curve of the D, the jut of the V, the clever jaunt of the E.

I didn't love him. I was too raw and hurt at the time. But I needed to believe that someone loved me. And he did, I think, his fingers lingering against my skin as if learning the shape of my cells. He was the last one, almost three years ago. He was the last one that filled me up.

LETTER #4

Ms. Carlita Richards
202 W. Hillcrest Drive, #22
Anchorage, AK 99503

Dear Ms. Carlita Richards:

We are returning check number *****756 due to insufficient funds.

But don't worry! We here at Just You Sex Toys understand the complexities faced by today's women. We are therefore holding Order #8594, for one Shady Lady Pleasure Ridged 5-Speed G-Spot Vibrator in playful pink, until Dec. 1.

Thank you for shopping at Just You Sex Toys. We are pleased to help you on your quest toward sexual fulfillment.

Sincerely,
Margaret M. Millerson
Senior Account Manager
Just You Sex Toys

Friday, Nov. 4

Barry stormed over, just as I was starting dinner.

"Hold it!" he yelled from the living room. "Jay-Jay Jiggers, go tell your mama to move away from that stove right this minute."

Jay-Jay charged in from the living room.

"Dad-says-move-from-that-stove-right-this-minute."

I wiped my hands with the dish towel as Barry slumped into the kitchen carrying a large plastic grocery bag.

"Nippy died." He slammed the bag on the counter. "Thought I'd cook up some lasagna. Kind of a tribute."

Barry cooks when he's troubled. He cooks when he's depressed or sad, worried or afraid. Basically, he cooks all the time. Except when he's happy. Then he bakes.

"Who's Nipper?"

"Nippy," Barry said. "With a *y*, not *e-r*."

"As if it matters," I snapped.

He sighed and tore open a box of noodles. "Got any butter? Forgot mine."

"Yeah."

"Butter," he stressed. "Not margarine."

"I said yes."

"Don't gotta yell." He slumped against the counter. "I can't believe he's gone."

"How'd it happen?" I still had no idea who in the hell Nippy was.

"I was driving home from work during that dim-dark time when it ain't light but ain't dark? A couple blocks from the house, right where the road curves, this darkish shape runs right out in the road. 'Whoa,' I thought. 'Some skinny dude with long legs.'"

"That was Nippy?"

"No." Barry was irritated at the interruption. "Not a dude. A moose."

"Ohhhhh."

"Crossing the road with his mama. Right in the crosswalk like they knew what they was doing. Light was even green. Then this lady in an SUV comes barreling around the corner and smacks right into him: Ka-bam!"

He stopped chopping onions and wiped his eyes.

"Nippy didn't have a chance. Been watching him and his mama hanging out in the yard. Left some lettuce one night."

"But I thought—"

"I know, I know." Barry waved his knife. "It's illegal feeding wildlife. But they was so skinny. Darned near broke my heart. Reminded me of the kid who sat behind me in second grade. Hummed under his breath and about drove me crazy, but then one day he moved and darned if I didn't miss all that humming."

He covered the noodles with tomato sauce while I washed the dishes littering the sink.

"Sandee coming over?" he asked hopefully. Barry has a bit of a crush on Sandee. "Got enough for four, maybe five if nobody hogs."

"Working."

"Shit."

After Barry slid the lasagna into the oven, we all sat in the living room and watched a movie about talking ants as the smell of garlic and onions seeped through the air.

"How's the job?" I asked Barry.

"Shhhh," Jay-Jay warned. "This is the good part."

"Banquets are about killing me," Barry said, as he scratched his armpit.

"You're ruining it," Jay-Jay cried. "You guys have to shut up during the good parts."

I didn't bother disciplining him for saying *shut up*. I got up and walked through the kitchen and down the hallway to my bedroom, which is at the back of the trailer. The reassuring thud of Killer's feet followed. I shut the door, stripped down to my underwear, and stared at myself in the mirror. My skin was pasty, my bra straps fraying, my Hanes underpants grayish from too many washings. My stomach, which was rounded but not fat, looked especially lonely. No one had touched it in so long, or at least touched it with gentleness, with adoration. I crawled into the closet and shut the door, the hems of my shirts fluttering my face. A moment later I crawled back out, grabbed the phone, and punched in Francisco's number, counting the rings: three, four, five. On six, the answering machine clicked on, but I didn't wait around to leave a message. I hung up quietly, as if to erase the call from my mind because really, what could a man like that see in a woman like me?

When I finally straggled back to the living room, fully clothed again, the movie was over and Barry and Jay-Jay were setting plates over a blanket spread over the floor. They hadn't even noticed I was gone.

"A picnic," Jay-Jay said excitedly. "Except we don't have any potato salad. Or pickles. Or ham sandwiches. Or..."

I sat down and forked warm noodles into my mouth, a spicy tomato sauce shivering against my tongue. The lasagna was superb: rich and comforting and lingering in my chest like a hug. Jay-Jay told a story about a kid who had thrown up during gym, and Barry told about the mess one of the prep cooks made when he dropped two dozen eggs on the floor.

"Your turn, Mom," Jay-Jay said. They both looked expectantly at me; I didn't know what to say. All of my stories were bleak.

"Sandee thinks Randall is still living in Vegas," I finally said. Barry leaned forward and scratched his foot. "She thinks he was married before and that's why he left, you know. He was living dual lives."

"Parallel lives," Jay-Jay said excitedly. "It's physics, see? Particles exist in more than one place at a time."

"Don't see how that's possible," Barry grunted.

"You can't explain it," Jay-Jay said. "You've just got to trust it, that's what Mr. Short says. If you try and understand this stuff, you'll go crazy."

One of these days Jay-Jay will look around his shabby life and wonder what cruel twist of fate stuck him with two such silly and insignificant parents. Maybe he'll hate us. Or worse yet, pity us. He'll pat our dense heads like beloved but stupid pets.

"Oh, wow, look, Dad," Jay-Jay screamed as he ran toward the window. "It's snowing."

They stood at the window together, Barry's stocky body next to Jay-Jay's slim grace. Jay-Jay takes after Barry; there's no denying the way their bodies resemble each other, how when one shifts, the other instinctively leans forward. Watching them almost broke my heart. I remembered camping at Destruction Bay in the Yukon years ago, the waves wild, the autumn night wicked with wind as Barry and I lay in our sleeping bags staring up at the sky. Just as we were about to close our eyes and drift off to sleep, we were hit with the most magnificent display of northern lights I've ever seen. It began subtly, a vague streak across the sky, followed by a whitish yellow that soon deepened to green. The colors zigzagged here and there, brightening and then retreating, and just when we were sure they were gone for good, they reappeared, swaying and expanding above us, a phosphorus green that picked up pinks and oranges, lilacs and reds. Before long the colors had deepened to a crimson so rich and true it reminded me of our grade school auditorium curtains shimmering and swaying as they opened for school assemblies.

Barry and I lay on the ground and watched. I was newly pregnant with Jay-Jay at the time, my stomach just beginning to puff. I don't know which one of us started, but we were soon shouting at the sky, singing at the top of our voices, "This little northern light of mine, I'm gonna let it shine."

Singing until we were hoarse and even then we couldn't stop. We stood up, kicked off our shoes, and danced barefoot over that cold ground as the colors swayed above us.

"Honey-muffin," Barry cried, lifting me up and twirling me around. He used to call me food names back then: baby buns, sweetie peach, cakey-bakey. We kissed, and the sky was brilliant and Jay-Jay was a fish swimming in my belly.

MESSAGE ON MY ANSWERING MACHINE WHEN I GOT BACK FROM COSTCO

"Hello? Anyone home? This is Francisco, Francisco Freebird, and this number was on my caller ID. I guess you called? I don't know who you are but if you still need to catch me, give me a holler at 555-4289. And hey to you, Jay-Jay. Whoever you are, you sound like a mature young man."

I listened three times before hitting the Delete button. I didn't dare leave the message on the machine; it would be a temptation, like the apple hanging on the tree. Eve couldn't resist, and I doubt I could, either.

All evening, as Jay-Jay chattered on about last year's Halloween costumes and I folded laundry and watched *Who Wants to Be a Millionaire?*, I thought about that apple hanging from a tree, golden yellow with a hint of peach and green, the kind of apple that might be hanging in one of Georgia O'Keeffe's paintings: sensual and erotic and looking more like a breast than a piece of fruit. I saw green happy leaves swaying in the background, I saw myself running in a gauzy summer dress, my feet bare, my hair floating out behind me as I reached out to pluck that perfect apple off that perfect tree. But I didn't call him back.

Sunday, Nov. 6

I spent the evening sanding down the penis on a dirty doll order. It seemed a shame to make it smaller when all over the country men were shelling out thousands of dollars to make theirs larger. But an order is an order and I desperately needed the money so I buckled down, and by the time I finished, G.I. Joe's dick stuck up in a permanent hard-on that looked like nothing more than a crease in his pants. I folded him in bubble wrap, boxed him up, and addressed the label. Tomorrow morning, the FedEx man would stop by and pick him up, and from the looks of the FedEx man's pants, he'll never have to worry about his hard-on not being noticed. His is thick and large and makes such a nice bulge that I want to reach out and pet it—it seems rude to not acknowledge it.

To distract myself from such thoughts I got out my paints and mixed yellow pearl with golden bronze, trying for that unearthly tint of the time right before dusk, when the sun colors the horizon with a yellow-spotted aura. I was struggling with my *Woman Running with a Box, No. 3* painting, which had somehow evolved into a series. Each piece appeared identical to the previous one until I leaned closer; then differences became apparent. The box was smaller and shabbier, and the woman was slowly unraveling. Her hair fell out of its knot, her dress sagged. She was still running but she looked out of breath; her purse had opened, and a trail of belongings spread out behind her: hairpins and tissues, car keys and cell phone, an address book and an opened compact, the broken mirror reflecting the light so that a shadow glared off her lower back.

I had no idea what this meant. Who was this woman and why was she running? More importantly, why was she unraveling? And what was in the box? I began evening out the woman's ear when someone banged on the door. Killer rushed forward, her toenails skidding on the linoleum.

"Open up, it's me!" Laurel cried.

I hurriedly placed my painting on the farthest kitchen chair and opened the door. Laurel leaned against the frame, snow stuck in her hair, which was no longer red but back to its usual glossy brown.

"I'm stuck," she said, tromping across the floor without taking off her damp boots.

"I'll get my shoes," I started, but she held up her hand.

"Not in the snow. I'm stuck in life." She laughed bitterly.

Her lips were chapped, her nail polish chipped. She was slowly coming undone. Was she—oh!—was she the woman from my painting?

"Do you have a white box?" I leaned toward her. "About this big? Tied with ribbon?"

She looked at me as if I were mad. "Hank said he loved me," she said in a weary tone, as she eased herself down into one of the kitchen chairs. "He said I was the one."

"Which one?" I was still trying to imagine her with a white box.

"*The* one, Carla. You know, like in songs and movies." She let out another harsh laugh and fiddled with the T-shirt overflowing from the laundry basket.

"And that's bad?"

"Well, it's not good. He's married. He's a public figure, almost a celebrity."

"I wouldn't quite say that. I mean, it's not like..."

"You're enjoying this, aren't you?" She squared her shoulders and suddenly looked like herself again.

"It's late. I don't want to start."

"Start what?" Laurel challenged, and that was when I realized why she was here. She wanted a fight. She needed to unload her conscience before going home so that she wouldn't say too much, reveal in her tone or mannerism that Junior's supposedly devoted wife of fifteen years was stepping out with the TV weatherman.

"So that's the way it's gonna be, huh?" My tone was tough, the voice I used at work when I had to cut off a customer from the bar.

"I have no idea what you're talking about." She flounced prissily in the chair. "You're just jealous," she murmured.

"Excuse me?"

"Nothing. I just said...Okay, this is for your own good, Carla. I just said you were probably jealous. Not about Hank, because I don't think he's exactly your type, but—"

"No, he's not," I interrupted.

"You just can't stand to see me happy, can you? You want everyone to be as miserable as you." She lifted up her voice. "'Oh, I'm just a single mother who lives in a trailer, please feel sorry for me.' Just because *you* can't get your life together doesn't mean the rest of us have to suffer."

"You're married," I hissed. "You took vows. And now you're running around like, I don't know. Look at you!"

"Like you can talk."

"What's that supposed to mean?"

"Just keep your mouth shut, you hear me? You have no right to talk about Hank and Junior that way, not when...I think I'm going to be sick," she gasped, running for the bathroom and throwing up in the middle of the hallway.

"Sorry," she sobbed, crouching down in front of her mess. "I couldn't make it, I just couldn't make it in time."

"You're drunk," I hissed. "You shouldn't have driven over here."

I helped her to the bathroom and sat her down on the closed toilet seat. Then I wiped her face off with a warm washcloth, gently, gently.

"Three months ago I was happy." Laurel's voice was low and toneless.

"Not happy, but content. Now it's as if my eyes have become magnifying glasses. Everything Junior does is enlarged. Even his footsteps are too loud. He walks on his heels, slams around the house. He practically echoes. How could I have not noticed before?"

"I'll fix the couch up and you can stay over," I said. "Need a shower first?"

Laurel shook her head. "I can't," she whispered. "I don't want to wash off Hank's smell." She buried her face in her arms. "I'm an awful person, Carla. A terrible, terrible person."

"No, you're not." I patted her shoulder awkwardly. "You're just on overload. You've had too much to drink, and—"

"I only had orange juice, not even half a glass." She pulled a towel over her head. "Jay-Jay can't hear us, can he?"

I shook my head. "He's been asleep for hours."

"I couldn't bear for Jay-Jay to think his aunt was a slut."

"You're not a slut." I pushed Laurel toward the living room, making sure neither one of us stepped in her pile of throw-up, and then situated her in the shedding lounger and started making up the couch. "You're just, well, you're confused, that's all. You're looking out for yourself. Men do it all the time and no one thinks twice. But women are supposed to put everyone else before them, and if they don't..." I ran out of steam. "Would you like some water? Milk?"

"An aspirin would be nice."

By the time I returned with four of Jay-Jay's old baby aspirins, Laurel had fallen asleep on the couch, little gasps escaping her throat. I called Junior and left a message that Laurel had had too much to drink and was staying over. My voice was high and shrill, the way it always gets when I lie, but I counted on Junior to not notice. People seldom see what they don't want to until it's too late.

Chapter 7

Tuesday, Nov. 8

I'M NOT SURE WHERE THIS DIARY IS GOING. The Oprah Giant said that writing about our lives would prompt our unconscious needs and desires to surface. Yet skimming over what I've written so far, most of my entries are about lack: Lack of money and lack of artistic merit. Lack of parenting skills and lack of control. Lack of common sense and lack of good sex. There's talk about love, not real love but wishful or regretful love. There's also a lot about Barry, which strikes me as terribly unfair. The man is behind in child support! He borrowed my blender and hasn't returned it! What right does he have to hog so much of my story?

But the truth (and I hate to admit it) is that I will always love Barry George, though I'll thankfully never be in love with him again. He's the first man I ever opened up to. I don't even know if it was him as much as geography. Alaska is so far removed from everything else, tucked away as it is between towering mountains and cold salt water, that you begin to feel free. You slowly shuck off the old layers of who you used to be, throw them down on the ground, and leave them to be trampled on by knobby-kneed moose and nearsighted bears, and you don't even care because you're sure something better waits for you.

I loved Barry more than I loved myself, and then I loved Jay-Jay more than I loved Barry, and one day I looked up and I was no longer there. But sometimes I stand by the window at night and imagine I can see the woman I used to be running down the road, her hair streaming behind her, her thighs strong and muscular. She is so beautiful, my former self. She doesn't trip or hesitate. She runs because she wants to, because she loves to feel the wind against her face.

Thursday, Nov. 10

Mr. Tims, the manager at Mexico in an Igloo, poked his head in the pantry door and informed me that since Velda had unexpectedly quit, he had signed me on for her Saturday night shift.

"I don't have a babysitter." I sliced flan into eight wavering pieces.

"Second-best station in the house, nets a hundred bucks, a hundred and fifty if it's busy." He leaned down and pulled up his socks. Mr. Tims always wears yellow socks—he says they make him less cranky. "Be here by five."

"Six."

"Five thirty."

It was snowing by the time I left work, an obstinate, lingering snow that made driving slow but gave the trailer park a cheery glow. Even the Huberts' blaring red trailer looked festive, the torn window shade flapping merrily in the breeze.

"Oh boy, it's getting deep," Jay-Jay yelled as he charged up the walkway and skidded across the porch. Once he settled down, he poured himself a bowl of Cheerios and cleared a spot on the kitchen table. A dirty shoe sat in front of him, along with two stray socks and a threadbare copy of *Foolish Women, Foolish Choices*.

"If we lived in Finland, it would snow 101 days a year," he said, milk dripping down his shirt. "In Sweden, it'd be 95. That's on average, of course," he added self-importantly. "You can't *accurately* know until it happens."

I peered down into the coffee I had poured, as if willing it to give advice. I could see my reflection; sugar crystals wavered around my nose.

"...desert gets snow but everyone pretends it doesn't," Jay-Jay was saying. "And the mountains? It snows more but melts faster 'cause it's closer..."

"I'm going to start working Saturday nights," I interrupted.

Jay-Jay stared suspiciously at my chin.

"Of course, I'll find you a sitter."

"Drop me at Dad's."

"He's got banquets," I said. "We'll find someone dependable. I wonder if—"

"Can we get high-speed Internet?" Jay-Jay blurted out. "Ours is soooo slow. It's embarrassing, Mom. It's like we're stuck in the Pliocene era."

After he wiped his face with the grimy dish towel and headed to his room to start his homework, I ate the rest of his soggy Cheerios and worried over how I'd find a babysitter on such short notice. The three Sanchez teenagers next door had found more lucrative jobs at Subway, and the girl I used last time, recommended by the neighbor of a neighbor, had gotten high and dabbed Magic Marker circles over the living room walls.

Then I remembered the peculiar note duct-taped to our front door last week. I fished it out of the bathroom wastebasket and smoothed it over the counter:

GOT KIDS? HIGH SCHOOL SENIOR WITH THREE YEARS
EXPERIENCE WILL WATCH, FEED, AND AMUSE YOUR
KIDS WEEKNIGHTS AND WEEKENDS, UNLESS
OCCUPIED WITH A TOTALLY AWESOME DATE.

RATES VARY WITH NUMBER OF KIDS AND HOW THEY
RATE ON THE BRATTINESS SCALE.

CALL FOR APPOINTMENT AND REFERENCES.

STEPHANIE ANNE STEELEY

Below this rather startling announcement was a blurred photograph of a smiling young girl of about seventeen wearing a checkered blouse and one of those pot-shaped hats from the forties, with plastic cherries dangling over her forehead. She looked harmless enough so I called and left a message. She called back in less than ten minutes.

"I can totally be over in an hour." Her voice was loud, with a peculiar lilting tone. "Is your daughter, like, home?"

"Son," I corrected. "His name is——" But she had already hung up.

At exactly seven fifteen, the new babysitter arrived. Her hair was blue and she wore yellow fishnet stockings, a red leather skirt, black boots, and an orange-and-green-striped peasant blouse. She nodded her head at everything I said.

"Oh, Mrs. Richards, I totally agree," followed by an infuriating snap of her gum. I was ready to boot her out the door when Jay-Jay ran in. Immediately, Stephanie reached out her ringed hand. "Stephanie Steeley," she said in a serious voice. "And you are, like?"

"Jay-Jay." He shook her hand, impressed.

"So you must be in, like, fifth grade?"

Jay-Jay giggled. "No, fourth."

"Well, you're totally tall for your age." She turned her attention to me. "Mrs. Richards, I think I should spend time with Jay-Jay to see how we, like, hang together."

An hour later, she walked back into the kitchen and said her boyfriend wouldn't "totally" like her working Saturdays, but she'd be happy to take the job. I hadn't offered it to her yet but that seemed beside the point. We hashed out a price and she asked if she could stick around and catch the end of the movie she and Jay-Jay had been watching.

"If I don't see the end, it will totally *haunt* me. I'll have to, like, *imagine* endings, and that could easily keep me up the whole night."

Wednesday, Nov. 16

Maybe it was the smell of the acrylic paints I had been using, or the way my brush swirled across my latest *Woman Running with a Box, No. 4* painting, my movements fluid and thick, almost sensual. Or maybe it was how the woman ran, her chest stuck forcefully out, her face flushed, her mouth opened in harsh breath, that caused me to finally call Francisco back, my fingers smeared with blue paint as I punched in his number. It was past midnight; I didn't expect him to answer. The phone rang once, twice.

"Hello?" a sleepy voice answered, followed by a yawn. "Anybody there?"

I didn't say anything. I listened to his breath: in, pause, out, pause, pause. He didn't hang up; it was as if he knew it was me, as if he had been waiting for this very call. I clutched the phone to my ear and breathed along with him: in, pause, out, pause, pause.

"Okay," he finally whispered, and then he hung up.

Saturday, Nov. 19

Stephanie showed up promptly at 4:58 p.m. for her babysitting shift, her hair a blaring purple that clashed with her bright pink sweater. Jay-Jay stood expectantly in the doorway.

"Cool," he breathed. "You look like this big grape."

As I tied my apron and spit-cleaned my shoes, Stephanie told Jay-Jay about a friend who had just gotten her tongue pierced.

"She passed right out on the floor and we totally couldn't get her to sit up and Heather tries to call 911 but, like, punches in 844 instead and gets the time and temperature and..."

"I'm leaving now," I yelled, as I rushed through the kitchen looking for my purse. "The number's on the board, Jay-Jay needs a shower and snack before bed, and remember, he can only read for half an hour and no—"

"Chill, Mrs. Richards." Stephanie snapped her gum. "We'll be totally fine. There's this show on PBS? It's about these turtles with wrinkled heads that totally look like my grandfather."

She shooed me out the door. It was already dark but clear and cold, the air crisp on my face as I walked out to the car. It sputtered twice before catching, and I hurriedly drove down the street hoping to make it in time for my twelve-top reservation.

I made it but almost wish I hadn't. It's two a.m. as I write this, and I'm still jazzed on coffee and the little sips of tequila the bartender slipped me for courage. I had forgotten what a nightmare it is to work a Saturday dinner shift. The pace is frantic, the people impatient, the cooks surly from too much partying the night before. I smiled and scurried for six hours without a single pause, and by the time I sank down at the back table to count my bank, I felt as if I had been through a war. I made money, though, over $125 in tips, which I deposited at the ATM inside the Safeway on the way home, so I wouldn't be tempted to spend it.

When I arrived home, every light in the trailer was on, and Jay-Jay and Stephanie sat on the grimy kitchen floor, a vast Lego creation stretching down the hallway as Stephanie relayed a story of her boyfriend Hammie's pizza delivery job.

"...dude says to him he doesn't want to be a pain in the ass but he, like, ordered a super combo with everything but olives and mushrooms and this here is a combo with nothing *but* olives and mushrooms..."

Jay-Jay fit together Lego pieces, a transfixed look on his face. Killer

Bee, who seemed equally infatuated, lay contentedly at Stephanie's feet. I threw down my apron and collapsed on the couch. After Stephanie gave me a rundown on their night, I offered to walk her home. A funny look crossed her face.

"That's okay, Mrs. Richards, I totally just live a few trailers down."

I insisted and waited for her to pull on her coat, which was hairy and tapered down the back like a tail.

"It's late," I grabbed the keys. "Some of the people around here aren't the most notable of citizens." I was referring to the hideous orange trailer over in the far lane that hosted parties so wild the cops had to shut them down. Supposedly the woman cooked and sold meth. Supposedly the man was in jail and came around each time he escaped from the halfway house. Stephanie didn't say a word as she flung an oversized backpack over her scrawny shoulders.

"Got everything?" I said, and then ordered Jay-Jay to lock the door behind us and stick close to Killer Bee. Stephanie shrugged and followed me down the lane, the hardened snow squeaking beneath our boots.

"The next one," Stephanie murmured.

"The orange one?" My voice rose. "Are you sure?"

Stephanie nodded but refused to look at me.

"Well," I stalled. "I never thought—"

"Mrs. Richards, I totally understand your trepidation. But can you, like, imagine it from *my* point of view? I have to live with these people. They're my *parents*. I have a lock on my door this big to keep them from selling my stuff for dope." She spread her arms wide. "Trust me, I know exactly how you feel."

"Well, it's just that..." My mouth hung open, cold aching my teeth.

"So do you?" Stephanie snapped her gum and looked suddenly tough.

"Do I what?"

"Want me to come next week?" Her tone dared me to turn her down.

"No, it's just..." Her shoulders slumped and suddenly I saw her for who she really was: a seventeen-year-old girl who needed to get out of the house as much as possible. "I'd like that very much," I heard my voice say. "Saturdays through at least Christmas."

"I'll totally be there." She stuck her bony wrist toward mine. It hung in the air for a moment before I realized she wanted to shake my hand. Her palm was dry and cold, her grasp firm yet surprisingly tender.

"'Night, Mrs. Richards," she said as she opened the door. The sounds of Van Halen blared out, along with a strong whiff of some really top-notch weed.

PHONE CALL AT 6:03 A.M.

"Carlita, what the fuck?" A vaguely familiar, deep man's voice.

"Francisco?" I pulled myself up in bed and reached for the light.

"Who the hell is Francisco? It's Jimmie. Where the fuck is your order?"

"I can't get the penises right," I said. "They look small and self-conscious."

"Penises *are* small and self-conscious," he laughed. "That's why guys think about sex so much."

I didn't say anything.

"Go buy some smut mags—not *Playboy* or *Penthouse*, they're air-brushed to death. Get something real, with pubic hair and shave marks and pimples."

"Pimples," I mumbled.

"Send everything second-day UPS. I got production waiting. Clear out your calendar, too. You've got twelve orders coming next week for Christmas. Turnaround is short but bonuses are long."

It was hard to imagine that Jimmie had once been a porn star who fucked women while hanging from a flying trapeze bar, but then again, I never imagined I'd grow up to be a waitress who lived in a trailer and cooked clay vaginas in an Easy-Bake Oven either.

LETTER #5

Carlita Richards
202 W. Hillcrest Drive, #22
Anchorage, AK 99503

Dear Ms. Carlita Richards:

We regret to inform you that order #98456 for 11 American Girl doll chests, 5 Retro G.I. Joe crotches and 25 feet of any size, shape, or length cannot be processed due to insufficient credit card funds.

Please submit an alternative form of payment within five working days.

Sincerely,
Big Bertha's Doll Palace
Highway 52
Horseshoe Bend, Idaho

Chapter 8

Tuesday, Nov. 22

THIS WEEK'S OPRAH GIANT LESSON was unbearable. It was about forgiveness.

"You can't heal until you forgive," the Oprah Giant wrote, little butterfly icons floating up through her words for emphasis. "Think of a dirty shirt in the laundry hamper. Wash it all you want, but it won't be clean until you add a stain remover."

We were told to spend the week writing out our stains. It wasn't necessary to actually want to forgive anyone. Merely saying the words would start us on our healing journey.

I thought of all the people I needed to forgive: Mother for being so overbearing, Father for being so distant, Laurel for being so perfect, Barry for being so stingy, Gramma for putting too many dreams inside my head, Jay-Jay for being so vulnerable. Myself for being so flawed. I suddenly felt like crying—I didn't know where to begin, or what I'd do without the hard knot of anger I'd been carrying around for years.

I worked on my doll orders instead. There's something soothing about pounding and drilling, slicing and gluing, and molding clay into small, perfectly shaped boobs. Maybe this is why primitive women pounded stones into beads and molded river mud into pots. It wasn't for the functional use or beauty of the object as much as for the therapeutic value of calming the spirit, of reaching down and finding a beautiful place and communicating it to others.

Gramma understood this. It's why she cooked, why she fussed over recipes and used only certain measuring spoons and never skimped on margarine instead of butter. She never gave a hoot about whether people approved of her or not, but she needed love. She needed to feel that she was part of the community, part of a family. She needed someone to love. Someone to cook for. After Grandpa died, she had lovers, men she called her "gotta go guys," who came over in the evening and left early the next morning. She never hid these men from us, though she didn't share much about them, either. They were just there, musky-smelling older men who left reading glasses and toothbrushes behind in Gramma's dim apartment.

"Was it just sex," I wanted to ask her now, "or did you open up to them, did you figure you had nothing more to lose, that heartbreak was just heartbreak and a few months of misery beat year after year of being alone?"

I'll never know because Gramma died during the second year of my marriage, keeling over in the Kroger grocery store as she reached for a flank steak. Someone at the funeral told us her last words were "Cream instead of milk for thicker—" For the longest time I thought it was a message encoded for me, advice or directions on what to do with my life. I counted the letters, tried different combinations, but it was no use. I realized Gramma simply said what had been on her mind. She was thinking about cooking up a steak with mashed potatoes, so that was exactly what came out of her mouth. There was no magic, no hidden message; probably she hadn't been thinking of me at all.

Wednesday, Nov. 23

"Vanna looks kind of peaked, like she hasn't had sex for years." Sandee was sprawled over the couch watching *Wheel of Fortune* reruns, and she was in that stage of drunkenness right before tears, when the giddiness winds down and the suffering breaks through. In a minute she would clutch my hand and cry about Randall.

I jumped up to show her my latest doll order. The doll's vagina opened with a trapdoor, and inside was a tiny Webster's dictionary.

"You've got to see this," I began, but I wasn't fast enough. Her arm shot out and her hand grabbed mine.

"Oh, Carla, life is just too sad, isn't it?" Then she cried. I didn't say anything—it's one of the luxuries of friendship, being able to cry without explanation. I rubbed my thumb over her knuckles and offered her a wad of paper towels. Finally she wiped her eyes.

"I can't do this any longer," she whispered. "Hand me my purse, okay?"

I reached over and pulled it out from behind the couch. She shuffled around inside and threw a postcard at me. "He's in New Mexico now. Supposedly. The bastard."

The postcard showed horses grazing over a grassy plain, mountains in the background. "Welcome to Ruidoso, New Mexico," was printed across the bottom.

"This has got to stop." Her face was pale, her eyes beady and awful.

"Don't read them," I suggested. "Throw them away. Have someone else get your mail."

"I would, but..." I allowed her her excuses—how could I not, when I had so many of my own? I hadn't been putting much effort into my painting lately. I told myself I was too tired or too stressed, too hungry or too emotionally detached. Really, I was too afraid. It takes guts to paint, and lately I haven't been feeling very brave. My porno dolls are safer. It's all surface; I don't have to dig in and reveal parts of myself.

"...didn't know if I should forgive him for...," Sandee was saying.

"Forgive?" I interrupted, thinking of last week's diary lesson. "Listen, did you ever try writing?"

"I don't have his address."

"Not to Randall. To yourself."

Sandee stared at me quizzically.

"Like a diary," I said. "Or hey, maybe a letter." I leaned forward. "What would you write to Randall in a letter? What would you say?"

Sandee sat silent for a moment.

"You wouldn't have to send it. We could, I don't know, have a ceremony. Burn it, or drive out to Beluga Point and throw it in the inlet."

"Can I do it in the bathroom?"

"I-I guess so."

"All that enamel will make me feel safe."

While Sandee shuffled off to the bathroom with a notebook and pen, I sketched a quick watercolor draft for my next *Woman Running with a Box* painting, dabbing with a tissue to give it a muted, faraway feel. The woman's hands were clenched in a running pose, her knees bent, her bare ankles surprisingly thin and delicate. How would they ever hold her up? Her high-heeled shoes had been replaced with a pair of sturdy Nikes, and on the ground behind her was a towel with the Holiday Inn logo and a box of Sleepytime Herbal Tea. I was shading out the bottom of her ear when Sandee returned.

"Here." She handed me two notebook pages of writing. "I printed so you'd be able to read it better."

"You sure?" I put down my brush and wiped my hands over my pants, black and purple paint smearing across my thighs. "Isn't it kind of personal?"

"Not any longer." She sat at the kitchen table and stared at my painting. "This is wildly bizarre," she said. "It's every woman, isn't it? Every woman running, a metaphor of sorts."

"I'm not sure," I said. "I think it has something to do with my grandmother."

The minute I said that, I knew it was true. The woman looked nothing like my grandmother, yet I knew she was in the painting; I could feel her there, breathing around the edges.

"Can I sleep on the couch?" Sandee asked. "I don't feel like driving all the way home tonight."

"Blanket's in the closet."

"Wait until I fall asleep to read the letter." She lay down on the couch and pulled the blanket over her shoulders. "And listen, can you read it in the bathtub?"

I shook my head yes.

"Promise?"

"Sure."

"It's just one of those letters that needs to be read in the bathtub."

After she fell asleep I sat cross-legged in the dry bathtub and read the letter. I cried at the end. I couldn't help it. It made me feel so soft inside, not just for Sandee but for myself, too.

Dear Randall:

It snowed yesterday morning, sticky flakes falling down across the backyard and covering the old toilet you dragged back there the year before you left. We took pictures of each other sitting naked upon it, remember? I looked for those pictures but I can't find them. You must have taken them. Or maybe I threw them out when I finally realized you weren't coming back. I threw out so much! Now I want it back. I want back the Washington Redskins football jersey you used to wear when you chopped wood. And that old shaving cup you said came from your grandfather, even though it had a Kmart price tag peeling off the bottom. The Kmart is gone now, can you believe it? No more blue-light specials, no more cheap tube socks. I cried when I heard, cried harder than when you left. It's easier to cry over stores than people, you taught me that. Stores don't have to do anything. They squat there looking all smug and satisfied and still we visit them.

I wish you would call. I want you to call so I can hang up on you. I want to hear your voice, hesitant and low.

"Sandee?" you'll say. "Sandee-bean?"

I'll hold the receiver tight, I'll be so happy to hear your voice!

"Listen," you'll say. "I made a mistake. I'm coming home."

That's when I'll slam the phone down, Randall. I'll hold it high above my head and let it crash down. I want you to hear my anger. I want it to ring in your ears for hours and days and weeks.

My anger is all I have left of you. It's eating me up inside. It's like cancer, only worse, because you can fight cancer, you can cut and slice it out, you can zap it with radiation, kill it with chemicals. I can't do anything with my anger except hide it. I tuck it down below my breast, right next to my belly. Every time I eat, I'm feeding my anger. I'm feeding you, you bastard, you fucking spineless coward. I'm feeding you and feeding you and I'm hoping if I eat enough I'll push my anger down and it will finally push out of me. Like a birth. Like contractions. Like labor pains, not of love but of hate. Because you can't hate someone unless you love them, I found that out after you left. You did that to me. You gave me that gift. But I'm not going to thank you. I'm not going to say anything except that I hope that you're lost somewhere and you're so thirsty you can't stand it. When you finally reach a glass of water, you can't even remember the word, you reach for it and what leaks out of your mouth is my name.

Drink me, Randall. Drink me and choke.

Thursday, Nov. 24

Laurel invited Jay-Jay and me over for Thanksgiving. Junior was out of town on a business meeting and she was "cooking light." I envisioned turkey, stuffing, and pumpkin pie. Instead, she served two kinds of potatoes and two kinds of beans. That, along with a basket of Parker House rolls, was our Thanksgiving feast. Laurel sat at the head of the table. Her hair was dirty, and she wore a shapeless yellow dress that made her look like an oversized lemon.

"Where's the rest?" Jay-Jay strained his neck hopefully toward the kitchen.

"The rest?" Laurel asked absently.

"The turkey." Jay-Jay was getting impatient. "You know, with the gravy and the fancy stuffing and the salad with the nuts."

Laurel took a bite of mashed potatoes and stared at her reflection in the fork handle.

"I've never liked nuts, remember, Carla? Remember how I never liked nuts and Mother always made me eat them?"

I remembered no such thing, but I nodded and chewed a particularly obstinate strand of green beans. The other beans were lima, and the potato scalloped, the top crust unbroken. None of us liked scalloped potatoes, not even Laurel, which said a lot for her mood. Halfway through the mashed potatoes, she started bitching about the weather. Wasn't the forecast a load of crap? It was supposed to be sunny. I glanced toward the window. We were in the midst of a snowstorm, the roads clogged with stranded SUVs, the sky the shade of a dirty aquarium.

"But don't worry, Hank says the sun will be out tomorrow." Laurel's voice was hard. "He says that the skiing conditions are great, a soft, powdery snow that makes for fast speeds."

"I didn't know you skied." I glared across my plate of beans.

"I don't. Hank was supposed to teach me." She jabbed a slice of scalloped potato with her fork. "'Supposed to' are the operative words."

"Where's Uncle Junior?" Jay-Jay interrupted. "Isn't he supposed to be here?"

Laurel stopped in midsentence, the potato frozen in front of her mouth. "He had to go down to Seattle for work," she said. "But I'll save a plate of leftovers."

"Does *he* know about this Hank guy?" Jay-Jay's voice was stern. "Does *he* care about all this weather talk?" Jay-Jay stared challengingly at Laurel. Even though Junior has the personality of a gerbil, he and Jay-Jay have always been close. They play computer games and are designing a robot out in the garage.

"Why...," she began, her face flushing. "Why, of course your uncle Junior knows Hank."

"This meal sucks!" Jay-Jay bolted from the table. "It's supposed to be Thanksgiving! Turkey and cranberry sauce, *not* Hank and beans."

Jay-Jay ran upstairs and slammed the bathroom door. Laurel looked at me helplessly.

I shrugged. "He likes Junior. You can't blame him. They do a lot of stuff together."

She pushed back her plate, threw her head on the nicely ironed table-cloth, and sobbed.

"What am I going to do, Carly? My life is a mess." She sniffed and wiped her nose on the edge of the tablecloth. "I think Junior knows. He hasn't said anything but he looks at me all squinty-eyed, like he's trying to see inside my head."

I murmured and patted her shoulder.

"He left last night without saying good-bye. He just walked out the front door. He's supposed to be home Saturday, but what if he doesn't come back, Carly? He hasn't even called. It's like he's purposely ignoring me."

I didn't mention that Laurel had been ignoring Junior for months. I kept up my pats and murmurs while upstairs, Jay-Jay flushed the toilet over and over again. Finally, Laurel rubbed her eyes, sat up, and let out a groan.

"I'm going to be sick again." She rushed for the downstairs bath-room. When she came out her hair was damp, her mouth naked and vulnerable without lipstick. "The flu," she said shakily, as she sank down on the couch. "Can you hand me the afghan?" I covered her up and cleaned off the dining room table. By the time I finished putting away the leftovers, Laurel was asleep. I moved the coffee table closer to the couch, added a glass of water and a handful of napkins, and called for Jay-Jay. He clomped down the stairs with his hair slicked back and a wad of toilet paper wedged in his sock.

"Get on your coat," I whispered. "Laurel's sick."

"Hank's a stupid name," he complained on the way home.

"It is," I agreed, keeping watch for an open restaurant or a fast-food joint. I was starving. I needed protein.

"Mom, don't get mad, okay, but Uncle Junior has dirty magazines in the bathroom," Jay-Jay said excitedly. "Under the good towels."

"You should have stayed downstairs." I pulled into an espresso stand and ordered two sandwiches, hot chocolates, and banana muffins. I rummaged around my purse for money but found only Kleenex and a hunk of Killer Bee's chew bone.

"Aunt Laurel had clothes all over the place," Jay-Jay said. "And a shoe in the sink. A blue shoe, Mom. In the *sink*."

"That's why you stuffed toilet paper in your sock?" I wrote out a check I knew I couldn't cover.

Jay-Jay shrugged and rooted around the bag for his share. "It made me feel better."

I handed my tainted check to the unsmiling woman and as we drove away, I imagined toilet paper stuffed inside my own socks. The rustle of paper against my ankles would be reassuring, like an itch or a scratch. Like someone touching me when I didn't realize I needed to be touched.

Monday, Nov. 28

"Charity isn't about giving money to the poor as much as giving to others," the Oprah Giant wrote in today's blog. "When you give what you have the least of, you are giving the most."

This was a relief to me, since I didn't have much to begin with. I was busy listing the few good deeds I had done over the years when Laurel stormed in.

"Aren't you supposed to be at work?" she demanded.

"I have a dentist appointment later this afternoon."

"I'll just leave you a Post-it note then." She shuffled around the junk drawer. "Don't you at least have one goddamned Post-it?"

I gawked at her in amazement. Laurel never swears; she says it shows poor taste. "Can't you just tell me?"

She sat down at the table and mumbled.

"What?" I covered my diary with my hand so she couldn't peek.

"The clinic," Laurel said. "I need the name."

I kept writing; I had no idea what she was talking about. "In Arizona," she continued. "The one—"

"The abortion clinic?" I was incredulous. "You're pregnant? But you're a Republican."

"I *know* that," Laurel sobbed.

"But..." I couldn't imagine Laurel doing anything as messy as having an abortion. She wouldn't have the strength to push her way through the protesters. "Are you sure?"

"Yes, I *am*. I'm late. Two weeks." She sounded offended. "A woman *knows* these things, Carla."

"You need to get one of those testers," I told her. "They have them at Carrs and Walmart."

She looked up at me, her eyes wide. "Oh, Carla, could you get one for me. Please?"

I ran into a man who looked like my high school biology teacher as I waited in the Walmart checkout with Laurel's pregnancy test. He glared as if about to ask if I still cheated on homework assignments, but luckily another line opened up and I escaped. When I got back home, Laurel was huddled in my bed. She stayed there all afternoon and only came out for supper.

We were eating microwaved pancakes, microwaved eggs, and toast with Smucker's grape jam because Laurel said breakfast food was the only thing she could stomach.

"You look funny," Jay-Jay said, examining her.

"I have a terminal illness," Laurel said.

"Jennifer P's mother has cancer," Jay-Jay said. "She's bald and wears hats from Ecuador."

"I'm not dying," Laurel said. "I'm just getting fat."

"Oh." Jay-Jay lost interest. "What's for dessert?"

After we finished I threw the dirty dishes into the sink with a sprinkling of laundry soap, since we were out of dish detergent, and followed Laurel into the bathroom.

"Read the directions again," she said.

I read them slowly; then I handed her the plastic tester and started to leave.

"No!" she shouted. "Stay with me."

I pulled out last month's *Oprah* magazine from the pile by the toilet, plopped down on the edge of the bathtub, and reread Dr. Phil's column. His bald head shone benevolently from the glossy pages.

"I can't pee," Laurel moaned, her pants sagging around her ankles. "Nothing's coming out."

I ran the water, but that didn't help.

"Stand out in the hall," she demanded.

I stood out in the hall and waited.

Finally she called me in and handed me the tester. Pee dripped over the rug as I carried it to the sink. Laurel sat on the toilet, eyes clenched.

"Don't tell me if it's bad, promise?"

I watched the little plus sign slowly darken. I didn't say anything.

"Say something!" she shouted.

"I, well, I, I mean it might not be..." My voice trailed off.

"Just say it. Spit the fucking words out."

"You're pregnant."

Laurel collapsed on the floor. Her shoulders shook. "Junior is going to kill me. I'll have nowhere to go." She looked up at me, her face drained of all color. "You'll let me stay here, won't you, Carla? When Junior kicks me out?"

"That's not going to happen," I said. "He'll be happy to have a child, once he gets used to the idea. I mean, he and Jay-Jay get along so well, and—"

"You don't get it, do you?" Her voice was deadly, horribly calm. "It's Hank's."

"Junior doesn't have to know." I was shocked by what I was saying, but my words wouldn't stop. "They look a lot alike, the same coloring and hair. What difference does it make? You'll be the one doing all the work."

"Junior will know." She laughed hysterically. "He'll definitely know. Junior can't have kids. He had testicular cancer when he was young. He's totally sterile."

"Oh."

Laurel crouched on the floor and cried and cried. I patted her back, and when that didn't help, I did what I used to do with Jay-Jay when he was inconsolable. I led her to the rocking chair in the living room, took her in my lap, and rocked her back and forth, back and forth, her head on my shoulder, her tears wetting my neck.

"There, there, it will be okay," I murmured in my mother's voice. "Shhh, now, shhh, honey, it's okay, it's all going to be okay."

Words of comfort, lies, the things we want to hear, but it worked. Laurel relaxed, her body growing heavier and heavier. Her hair smelled of lavender shampoo, and her chin dug against my collarbone, but I didn't stop. I kept rocking.

Wednesday, Nov. 30

Gramma would have loved Alaska in the winter. She loved the nights; she said the dark was for secrets, that we all had something we were afraid or unwilling to share.

"Every secret a lie," she said. "You keep them in your pocket, you don't show nobody. That make it a lie."

I had many secrets: That I wanted to be an artist but was afraid to try. That I wanted to quit my job but was afraid there was nothing better for me out there. That I wanted to be touched but was afraid to let anyone get close enough to try. I wanted a man (Francisco?) to walk up to me, slip his hand across my back, and smile, like a scene from a sappy movie. I wanted to lay my head against his chest and smell his familiar smells. I wanted the security of knowing that I would be touched, not fucked, like what Barry and I did, but touched in a way that said my body was sacred to one person on this earth.

Late at night Gramma used to tell stories of her sister who had been lost in the war.

"She just fifteen," Gramma said, wiping tears from her eyes, and for some reason I imagined an empty toy store, dusty racks and shelves stretching on forever as her sister wandered by herself, her socks falling down, her dress torn and damp like the character from the *Little Match Girl* movie we watched every Christmas.

Gramma made sad pastries when she told her late-night stories, rolling out the dough and cutting big circles with the rim of a metal cup, then folding over the dough and pinching it closed with the edges of a fork. She usually cried when she made these; she talked about her sister and wiped her eyes on her apron and kept right on baking. She insisted that the tears were what made the pastries so light and sweet.

"The tongue," she said, "needs a taste of sadness to keep it from falling out."

GRAMMA'S SAD PASTRIES

- 1 cup flour
- Pinch of salt
- 1⅓ tablespoons sugar
- 3 tablespoons butter/margarine
- 1–2 tablespoons cold water (for consistency)
- Jam, jelly, or preserves (for filling)
- Melted butter
- Small bowl of sugar

Preheat oven to 350°. Mix dry ingredients together, except the small bowl of sugar, and slowly fold in butter. Add cold water for consistency. Knead until soft. Roll out across the counter, cut into small circles, spoon in filling, crimp closed with fork. Brush with melted butter, sprinkle with small dabs of sugar, and prick tops with a fork. Cook at 350° for 20–25 minutes. Eat late at night after a good cry.

LESSON FOUR

The Things We Carry

By now you are thinking, *I don't want to know any more about myself.* Don't worry, the worst is almost over. But first you must list your faults. Start with the petty ones: You didn't make your bed, you lied to your boss. Slowly make your way toward the tougher stuff: You aren't as happy as you pretend, you wish you were in better shape. If you are truthful and very brave, you will learn who you are not. This, you will come to find out, is much more important than who you are.

—The Oprah Giant

Chapter 9

Sunday, Dec. 4

JAY-JAY ATE GENERIC CORNFLAKES while reading from his school report on Egyptian mummy facts.

"...hook up the nose and then they pulled the brains out." He slurped cheerfully. "They had to be real careful or they'd mess up the face. And Mom?"

"Yes?" I gritted my teeth and scrubbed a dish with my fingernails.

"They used natron to dry out the body. It's this kind of salt that sucks all the moisture from the skin." He made a loud sucking noise with his mouth.

"That's nice." It had been a rough morning. I finally gathered the courage to open last week's mail only to discover that even after the extra push from my Saturday night shift, I was *still* behind on the electric, phone, and car insurance bills. To top it off, there was a pale yellow envelope from Mother. I haven't written about my mother much. I suppose I've been avoiding it. She sends letters every few weeks, badly typed and reeking of Lysol air freshener. This letter was typical in that it both saddened and infuriated me.

My little Carlita:

Did Jay-Jay get the dental floss I sent? Flossing is so important to a young boy's hygiene. I remember when you and Laurel were girls, you had the most perfect teeth. I was so proud. Neither of you had cavities until you were out of the house and your eating habits went to hell.

Please write your father. He is still fretting over Fido's death. I think he loved that gerbil more than he loves the rest of us and he's taking it hard. "What do you expect, letting him run loose with three cats in the house?" I want to scream. But I hold my tongue. That's what marriage is about. If you had held your tongue you and Barry would still be together.

I sent your Christmas gifts out yesterday. I can't believe that both of my little girls live so far away! When you were young all you wanted to do was stay close. "I'm never leaving," you used to say. "I'm living here with you forever."

Gene is here at least. He brought his new girlfriend to dinner last week. She's tall and pleasant enough but slouches when she walks.

Love, Mother and Father

P.S. Jay-Jay sent a picture of the two of you at Halloween. Have you gained weight?

My stomach hurt after reading this. Why weren't we going home for Christmas? Couldn't we have given Mother this one small thing, the gift of our presence? Of course, I hadn't the money to head home and even if I did, I would end up regretting it. Mother always gets drunk around the holidays, not a slamming-down-the-house drunk but a mournful, soft drunk that leaves her melancholy. It's the only time she openly drinks; the rest of the time she hides her bottles in the cupboard behind the cat food bags.

I clutched the letter in my hand, debating how to answer, when the phone rang. "Can you get that, sweetie?"

Jay-Jay slurped the last of his cereal and ignored me. The phone rang a third time, and then a fourth. "Everyone I know texts," he said. "Only old people use the phone."

The answering machine whirled and a deep voice entered the room. "Carlita? It's Francisco. I think this is you. I have, let me see, four, no, five, calls from this number and I thought: Who would call and listen to me breathe? For some reason I thought of you. Plus you look like someone who would have a kid named Jay-Jay and—" *Click!* The machine mercifully cut him off in midsentence.

"Francisco?" Jay-Jay squinted at me with sudden interest. "A guy's calling you? Guys never call you."

"He's just a customer from work. He orders, uh, verde enchilada with extra pico de gallo sauce." I couldn't stop talking. "Sometimes he gets a side of whole black beans, but not usually."

"Oh." Jay-Jay stared at me closely. "Your face is all splotchy."

I held up the letter. "Grampa's gerbil died."

"He e-mailed me. Gramma wrote too but kept calling me Gene. I think she was drunk."

"She means well," I said quickly. "She loves you more than—"

"Can I go over to Alan's? We're making a duct-tape semiconductor."

"Brush your teeth first," I said, but he was already out the door. I reached down and stroked Killer's bony head and thought about calling Francisco and actually speaking, but knew I wouldn't. The next time he came into work, I'd trade tables with Sandee. I couldn't wait on him now. I felt exposed, as if he knew how lonely I was inside, how needy and weak and scared.

Naturally, the Oprah Giant picked today to blog about love. "Think about having all the love you want," she wrote, and the type was pink, with little hearts at the end of each sentence. "How would that feel?"

"Like shit," I answered. I wasn't sure I wanted love. Or happiness. My misery was my comfort zone, as safe and bland as vanilla pudding. Which is what I'm eating as I write this entry, Pudding Pals, a generic offshoot of Jell-O Pudding Cups, which I can't afford. I can't afford love, either. Thinking about love makes me want to go shopping. There is so much I need! Sexy underpants and push-up bras, skirts that swish against my thighs and gold chains that draw attention to my collarbone.

Of course, the giantess didn't mention lingerie or toenail polish; she was talking about deep love, the kind where looks don't matter and cotton underwear works just fine and you don't have to shave your legs every night because what you're after is the shape of each other's souls.

"Real love is sharing the ugly, selfish parts of yourself without shame," she wrote. "It's less about the red nightie with the matching G-string and more about the dirty smells leaking out of the laundry hamper."

I don't think I could handle a love like that

I think I would run from a love like that.

Monday, Dec. 5

"Laurel's pregnant," I said to Barry after he brought Jay-Jay back from an ice-fishing jaunt, both of them dripping over the kitchen floor.

"Fat guy hogged the good spots," Barry interrupted. "Didn't catch a nibble. Jay-Jay says, 'Why don't we set up right next to him?' but I say that ain't good etiquette."

"I *said* Laurel's pregnant," I repeated.

"I'm not deaf."

"Well, you could have answered. You could have at least nodded."

"My ears are cold."

"It's not Junior's." I stamped my foot like a child. "Do you get it now?"

"Okay." His voice was slightly high, the way Jay-Jay's gets when he's feeling defensive. "Your sister's knocked up."

I didn't say anything.

"The radio announcer?"

"TV weatherman."

"Shit." Barry whistled. "Got any Wheaties? I got me a craving."

Suddenly, eating made perfect sense. I quickly washed out two bowls (the dirty dishes had stacked up again) and poured us each cereal. I added milk and sat down across from him. "I don't know what to do," I said. "I mean, Laurel with a baby, can you imagine?"

Barry slurped in agreement, so I continued. "Junior's sterile, that's what Laurel said. There's *no* chance it could be his. None. Jesus, how would you tell someone something like that?

"You don't." I slammed my hand down on the table before he could answer. "You can't. You leave instead." Barry eyed my bowl so I pushed it toward him. "Or else you make the other person so miserable that they leave. They can't stay together now, that's for sure, though I can't imagine them apart."

I leaned forward until I was practically breathing on Barry. "What would you do if your wife came home pregnant and you knew it wasn't yours?"

"I ain't married," Barry said.

"I *know* that. But say you were. Say we were still married and we hadn't had sex for months and then I come home and say, 'Surprise, I'm pregnant and it's not yours.' Would you hit me?"

"Christ, Carla, that's a hell of a thing to ask." He cupped the cereal bowl in his hands and slurped the remaining milk.

"Well?"

"Well what?" He wiped his mouth across his sleeve. "Jesus, I don't know. Maybe. But we got ourselves Jay-Jay, see. We know what a kid's like, how it don't matter who they belong to, they gradually become yours. Laurel and Junior, they don't got that knowledge. But I seen him with Jay-Jay and I thought, 'There's a guy that needs a child.' Maybe this is gonna be his only chance."

"So you'd forgive me?"

"Yeah, I suppose." He scratched his armpit. "But it ain't about for-giveness when you need something like that."

LETTER #6

Ms. Carlita Richards
202 W. Hillcrest Drive, #22
Anchorage, AK 99503

Dear Ms. Carlita Richards:

Imagine our excitement when we finally received a check to cover your Aug. 6 balance.

We were overjoyed! Until we noticed that the check was made out to "Fifty-six dirty dolls" instead of dollars.

We are intrigued. Clue us in on what this means, and we will forgive $10 from your account.

Sincerely,
Dr. Jack Jennison and Dr. Emelee Harrison
Northern Lights Eye Care Center
"We only have eyes for you"

Wednesday, Dec. 7

"He had a gap between his front teeth and ordered a bottle of wine, de-cent vintage but not too pricey, that would have been tacky."

Sandee and I stood in the Mexico in an Igloo pantry pretending to wipe down trays. We had fifteen minutes before opening and were try-ing to look busy so Mr. Tims wouldn't assign extra work.

"I was wearing new lipstick," she continued. "Cranberry Morning, isn't that a hopeful name? The beginning was good. He took time to ask me questions. And he had on sandals, Carla, in the middle of winter. His toes were chubby and friendly. I dropped my napkin twice so I could get a better look."

Sandee had a theory you could predict a person's character by the shape of their toes.

"He invited me back to his place and I thought, why not, he seemed nice and he works for fish and game; they do background checks, you know. We were sitting on his sofa drinking diet soda, all that carbonation was making me feel tipsy but I was trying not to show it. I could tell he wouldn't appreciate a slatternly woman. He goes over his history briefly—he was married seven years ago but seems over it by now—and then I wait for him to start the moves. Nothing happens, so I go over *my* history, muted of course; why scare the poor man off.

"When he got tears in his eyes talking about the baby moose he had to put down last winter, I couldn't stand it. I grabbed him by the collar and kissed him hard. He kissed me back and it was nice, he didn't cram his tongue into my mouth or yank my breast to pieces. I tingled all over. I don't think I've ever been so swept up by a kiss.

"The next thing you know I'm taking off my dress and standing in front of him in just my bra and panties, good ones too, Nordstrom's but on sale. I'm waiting for him to admire me but nothing happens. Finally I squint open one eye and he's staring at me sadly.

"Put your dress on, honey," he says. He helps me slide it over my head; I feel like a child being dressed by my mother. His hands were warm and tender. I started to cry, I don't know why, but I sat on the floor and cried and cried. He didn't ask what was wrong, he..."

Sandee looked at me intently. Her hair was dirty, and she had accidentally put in the wrong contacts, so one eye was blue and the other green.

"He cupped his hands around my head and held them there. Every so often he gave me little pats. It felt, I don't know. Tender."

Her lower lip trembled and I grabbed her hand and squeezed. "I think I love him," she said. "I can't remember his last name so I can't love him, can I?"

She needed me to tell her no; I could hear it in her voice. I wanted to say that, too. I didn't want to believe love could be so easy, so simple. But I think that maybe it is. I think we make it more complicated than it was ever intended to be.

"Maybe," I began.

"Carla," Sandee warned.

I coughed because I had to do something to fill the silence, which was thick and anticipatory, the way it often gets when two people try to talk about love.

Thursday, Dec. 8

"You haven't told anyone, have you?" Laurel demanded on the phone earlier tonight.

"No." It wasn't really a lie since I had only told Barry.

"I made an appointment. At the clinic. Over by the hospital. For next week. Ten days before Christmas." Laurel laughed harshly. "What a way. To welcome in. The Christ child." She seemed unable to talk in complete sentences.

"When?"

"I just said. Next week." Her voice was tight.

"I meant what time?"

"You coming?" It was more of a challenge than a question.

"You're my sister," I said. "Of course I'm coming."

"Oh, Carly." Laurel was crying again. "You'd do that? For me? Really?"

By the time she hung up I was exhausted. I thought of my own abortion over eleven years ago, how I sat in the waiting room unable to meet anyone's eyes. The room had been clean, almost sterile, with a water fountain in the corner that gave off the smell of chlorine. I almost bolted. Now I wonder if I should have. What would my life be like if I had an almost twelve-year-old little girl beside me, legs long like a colt's? Her hair in pigtails, her fingers dirty, her sneakers colored with green and pink magic markers. Would I be happier? Would I be married, have a better job, be respectable?

But then I wouldn't have Jay-Jay, and that thought is unbearable. It's impossible to think of Jay-Jay not existing; he fills all the holes of my life. Yet he came with a cost, and that was the abortion. Maybe everything good comes with a cost; maybe every gift is filled with a trail of hard choices. I wanted to call up Laurel and tell her this but knew she wouldn't listen. She was caught in the present and I was speaking from the past—the language barrier was too immense.

I picked up the doll I had been working on, a G.I. Joe fashioned into Superman with a thick dick that came with its own cape, which doubled as an emergency condom. As I spiked up Superman's hair, I gave him a couple of tattoos and chiseled out his ass to give it more definition (maybe this Superman swung both ways—and, really, who could blame him?), all the while wondering why Laurel hadn't been using birth control. It was almost as if she wanted it to happen. I was fattening up Superman's lips when Stephanie rushed through the door.

"Mrs. Richards!" she yelled. "Can I, like, borrow the living room? My mother's totally having another party and I need to write a paper." She heaved a stack of books on the table and picked up the Superman doll.

"Oh-my-god, this is totally awesome." She traced his dick with her fingers. "The cape works but it needs something. I know! Doesn't this dude, like, wear glasses?"

"Well, his Clark Kent persona is a reporter and—"

"Then his dick needs to wear them too. You know how guys are totally sure their dicks are the greatest things in the world? If you put glasses on it, it would be this exacting spoof. Like saying, which one is my real brain? Which one am I totally using to see?"

I stared at Stephanie. She had six earrings in each ear and wore a T-shirt that said, "If I'm trying to find Jesus does that mean he's lost?" She looked punkish and tough and very, very young.

"You just hit upon something brilliant," I said.

She shrugged, sat down across from me, and petted Killer Bee. She didn't ask what I was doing or why I had hacked-off doll parts across the table or if I had a good reason for trying to attach a large penis between Superman's legs. The smell of melted plastic filled the kitchen. A moment later she wandered out to the living room, Killer Bee following behind. The TV blared on, followed by the crinkle of papers as she settled down to work. Every so often she snapped her gum. It was a companionable sound, and I nodded along with it as I fashioned miniature glasses from bobby pins. I was gluing the frames to the back of the penis, which I had modeled after a small Vienna sausage, when Stephanie rushed into the room.

"Mrs. Richards!"

Her face was flushed and she cradled a piece of paper to her scrawny chest. "I totally wrote the most awesome poem about David Letterman's hair."

I put down my glue gun and rubbed my eyes. I had forgotten all about her.

"And get this, I said his hair is as bland as the letter *K*, isn't that the best thing?"

I said I supposed it was. "But why *K*?"

"Think about it. All the loser states have a *K*: Kansas, Kentucky, Oklahoma. No one really *comes* from those states. They're just there. Like Letterman's hair, see? It's totally illuminating."

I hadn't known Stephanie was a poet, but it made sense. She was bizarre yet sweet, the kind of girl who could bravely march past whistling construction workers one minute and collapse in tears over an old lady feeding birds in the park the next.

"I'll make up the couch. You can stay here tonight." I pushed back my chair. "You need to take a bath first?"

"Nah, I'm retro." I watched her walk down the hall. The back of her pajamas had "School Sucks" embroidered over the ass, and her T-shirt bagged out at the hips. She was so thin, so defenseless; her wrists were barely thicker than a pencil. I wanted to take her in my arms and tell her that high school was just a phase, that better things waited on the other side, but I stayed at the table working on my dolls. Before I went to bed, I walked out to the living room to turn off the lamp. Stephanie slept curled tight, her arms wrapped protectively across her chest, one foot wedged between her legs like a barrier. Was this how she slept at home, how she kept herself safe among the drug dealers and partiers and god knows what else was over there? I leaned down, pushed the hair off her face.

"Sweet child," I whispered. For a moment, even though the age difference didn't match, I imagined that she was my daughter, the one I had aborted. That this was who she would have grown up to be.

Chapter 10

Friday, Dec. 9

I WAS SO CAUGHT UP in the drama of Laurel's pregnancy that I hadn't given much thought to Francisco, but there he was sitting in my station during today's lunch rush.

"Carlita!" he said heartily. "Long time, no call. Or should I say, no breathe?"

I rushed back into the pantry. "You've gotta help," I said to Sandee, who was arguing with the cooks over the enchilada sauce.

"I'm busy," she snapped. "My orders are fucked and Judge Thurman's in my section." Judge Thurman was notorious for being difficult plus a bad tipper. Still, he was in charge of traffic court, and we all feared we might one day face him over a speeding ticket.

"It's Francisco." I tugged on her apron. "He's out there. You've got to help."

"The god dude?" She piled plates of fajita setups onto her tray, added two containers of salsa and a side of guacamole. "Thought you *wanted* to see him."

"That was before," I whispered. "You know, the calling and breathing and hanging up."

"Listen, Carla, I hate to be the one to tell you this but...hey, that was a chicken burrito, not beef," she yelled to the kitchen, pushing her plate back for a remake and then turning to me. "You have to get over this fear of dating. It's crippling you. Plus, look at it this way. He knows you called and hung up and he still wants to see you." She pulled a new plate from the window and rearranged it over her already loaded tray. "Where's my side of jalapeños?" she yelled as she wiped her hands over her apron.

I mustered up my courage and slowly approached Francisco's table.

"Ready to order?" My waitressing tablet half-covered my face.

"Any specials?" He seemed in an extremely good mood. "I'm celebrating. Hear about the find up toward Barrow?"

I shook my head and lowered the tablet to my chin.

"Remains of eleven sled dogs and a partial harness, looks like it dates over seven hundred years, some woman found them buried beneath her house." He rubbed his hands. "I'm heading up there next week. Hope the weather holds. It's thirty below right now, that's my limit; anything colder and my gums bleed."

I stood there in my ridiculous waitressing uniform feeling more and more insignificant. He tossed his menu down and smiled up at me, a wide, opened smile. I smiled back without thinking.

"Now, write this down. Ready?" I nodded. "Two cheese enchiladas with the hottest peppers you've got, a side of rice, and a couple corn tortillas. And, let me see, a large iced tea with two lemons." He grinned. "I'm going all out, huh? Okay, wait, a small salad with ranch on the side. And dinner, say, at about sixish, is that too early?"

"Six," I repeated dumbly.

"Okay, make it seven, that works for me actually..."

"You're asking me to dinner." It was a statement, not a question. "Why?"

"Because I'll be hungry later."

"I'm busy," I told him.

"What about the following night? Or the night after that?"

I looked at his pleasant face, his wonderful hands and shook my head. "Sorry," I said. "I just...I can't."

"Sure." His face closed over and he tried to smile. "Whatever."

Suddenly my mouth opened and it all spilled out. "You don't understand," I heard myself say. "I'm a waitress, this is what I *do*. I live in a trailer and my sister is pregnant with the weatherman's child." I paused for breath.

"The guy with all the teeth?" Francisco whistled. "The one that never gets the forecast right?"

"There's more." I leaned closer, almost knocking over a dish of mild salsa. "My finances are a mess, I haven't shaved my legs in weeks, and the dog ate my last pair of decent underwear. I have nothing to *wear* on a date!" My voice rose, and the man at the next table jerked his head our way, alarmed.

"I like hairy women," Francisco said. "I have two dogs."

"You don't get it." I lowered my voice. I was so near I could smell his hair, a musky, outdoorsy smell. "I used to be an artist, and know what I do now?"

Francisco stuffed a corn chip into his mouth and widened his eyes, as if to communicate that I should go on. "I make dirty dolls. For an adult website. Nothing sleazy—it's actually one of the better ones—but think of it. While other women are having intelligent conversations I'm drilling vaginas into plastic dolls."

I looked up, suddenly embarrassed. Across the dining room, Mr. Tims waved frantically toward the kitchen. "I have to go, my food's up."

I sprinted toward the kitchen. I felt purged. I had gotten all of the dirty, ugly stuff out right up front. Now I could go back to being a waitress and Francisco could go back to playing with bones or whatever the hell he did. The expediter took out my orders so I didn't see Francisco again until it was time to drop off the check. "Everything okay?" I asked.

"There was a hair in my enchilada but I think it was from my dog. Probably fell off my shirt." He squinted at me. "So how does a guy ask a woman who works as a waitress, lives in a trailer, has a sister knocked up by the weatherman, and does dirty things with dolls out to dinner?"

I didn't say anything.

"It doesn't have to be eventful." He took his Visa card out of his wallet, which was old and cracked, the seams peeling, the leather so worn you could almost see through. "Okay." He sat back and relaxed. "I'll play fair. Here's something about me you probably don't know: I dropped out of Yale to hitchhike around Thailand, my father disowned me, and before we could make things right, he was shot in a liquor store robbery. He died holding a bottle of thirty-five-dollar wine." He was quiet for a moment. "We all have our stuff. Now will you do dinner?"

I felt tender inside, and soft and liquidy. I couldn't talk so I nodded instead.

"Tomorrow or the next day," he said. "I'll call you. Answer this time, okay?"

He signed his credit card statement, squeezed my shoulder, and left. I began clearing his table when the man from the next both motioned with his arm.

"Pssst, over here," he called.

"Can I get you anything, sir?" I hated when customers waved me down or snapped their fingers.

"Just wanted to see you up close." His face scrunched with excitement. "So you're the one who makes those dolls. I thought you'd live in California or Florida. Someplace hot."

"I-I don't know what you're talking about." I felt dizzy and flushed—how much had he heard?

"I'd be honored if you signed my napkin." He pushed it toward me. "My name's Fred but everyone calls me Charlie."

"You must have misunderstood," I protested. "You've mixed me up with someone else."

"Heard what I heard." He shook his head up and down. "You're just being bashful. Must be tough being a famous artist. People fawning over you all the time."

"Where are you from?" I leaned down and touched the napkin, as if it might tell me what to do.

"Billings. Came up for the daughter's birthday. Colder here, but sky isn't as clear."

What the hell, I thought, leaning down and scrawling my name over the napkin. "Just don't tell anyone," I said. "I'm not supposed to reveal my identity."

He picked up the napkin as if it were a holy object. "Oh, oh, oh," he breathed deeply. "The guys back home aren't gonna believe this. I got the Patty Please Me and Willie Working His Wonker dolls." He held the napkin to his mouth and gently kissed my signature as I booked the hell out of there.

"What was that about?" Sandee asked when we finally squeezed in time for a cig dig.

"Just some tourist needing directions," I lied.

"No, I meant the god dude."

"We're going to dinner, I guess." I sighed.

She sucked on her unlit cigarette and eyed me. "The shit never ends, does it? Joe, the good-looking toe dude, texted me three times today. I read them all, too, the minute they came in."

We fake-smoked and shivered. Around us, the sky was gray, the mountains rising to the east with a white fury.

"A moose got hit on the Glenn Highway, that's why the texts." Sandee tucked her cigarettes back in her apron. "They found a leg stuck in the windshield. The moose, not the driver. Joe said it screamed, over and over, high-pitched and awful until they put it down. Then there was just silence."

I waited.

"I think I've been screaming inside since Randall left," she said. "I want that silence."

"So go shoot something."

She looked at me, her eyes fierce. "You mean it?"

I nodded. I was a fairly decent shot, having trudged behind Barry on hunts for so many years.

"Yeah, okay." She tightened her ponytail and looked off toward the mountains. "Maybe I need to start thinking like a man. Maybe I need to shoot the hell out of something."

Saturday, Dec. 10

My dinner with Francisco was a disaster. It started off okay. Stephanie arrived to babysit, plopped down on the couch, and began texting her boyfriend, Hammie. I asked if I looked okay.

She nodded without looking up.

"No, I mean really." I had spent over fifteen minutes on my hair, which was twisted in a complicated knot that prevented me from turning my head too quickly.

Stephanie finally glanced up. "You look okay," she said with disinterest.

"Only okay?"

"For an older woman going on a date, sure."

I kissed Jay-Jay good-bye and grabbed my purse.

"Your hair looks stupid," Jay-Jay complained. "Dating is stupid. *Dad* doesn't date."

I kept my mouth shut and squeezed out the door. Francisco had chosen Moose's Tooth, a popular restaurant in midtown that caters to young professionals but also welcomes grandmothers and families with small children. I parked next to a dented green truck, hurried through the crowded lobby, and looked around—I didn't see Francisco anywhere.

"Do you need a table?" the pretty young hostess asked. Her teeth were overly white, her mouth coated in bright purplish lipstick.

"For two," I said. "I'm waiting for someone." I sat in the small lobby area with the strange plastic pager that would buzz when my table was ready. Across from me a young couple nuzzled together.

Ten minutes later, the pager buzzed and the hostess led me to a small table against the side of the room. "Enjoy your dinner," she said with a toss of her pretty head. I ordered Diablo Bread Sticks from the hurried waiter and skimmed through the menu. The salads were always a good choice, but I didn't want to worry about lettuce sticking in my teeth.

"Ready to order?" the waiter asked when he set down the breadsticks. I shook my head. "I'm waiting for someone."

"Good for you." He winked as he charged toward the next table. I munched on the breadsticks, intending to only eat half, but before I knew it they were all gone and Francisco still hadn't arrived. I called him on my cell and left a message. Ten minutes later, I called again; still no answer. I was pissed. I had been waiting over forty minutes.

I told the waiter I was ready for the check. He nodded and placed it gently on the table, as if understanding how fragile I felt. I left a massive tip and walked past table after table of happy diners as I headed toward the door. I felt humiliated and used, as if everyone in the restaurant knew I had been waiting for a man who had never shown. As soon as I reached the car, I pulled out my cell and rechecked the messages, but there were none from Francisco. Finally I called Sandee in the middle of her dinner shift.

"He stood me up," I said, my voice breaking. "I waited over an hour and he never showed."

"Who's standing?" Sandee shouted above the roar of Mexico in an Igloo.

"He. Stood. Me. Up," I enunciated slowly.

"Fucker." There was a loud bang in the background, followed by a door squeaking closed. "Okay, I'm in the bathroom. What happened?"

"Nothing happened, don't you get it? He never showed. I put on makeup. I wore heels." I was trying not to cry.

"Listen, this is what you do." Sandee's voice was comforting and firm. "Drive home and send him a text. Tell him that you're sorry you missed him but an emergency came up. Make him think that you stood *him* up."

"That's genius, really, I mean—"

"He'll call you the next day," she interrupted. "I've done it a thousand times. Nothing gets to a guy like a woman turning away."

"I don't want to see him again."

"Exactly! That's my point...Shit, my order's probably up. Promise you'll do what I said?"

"I'll try," I said unconvincingly, but it didn't matter because she had already hung up. I sat in the car feeling sorry for myself, not so much because a man I barely knew had turned out to be a loser but because I had allowed myself to hope.

"Well, Mrs. Richards, what did you totally expect?" Stephanie said as she fixed me a cup of Sleepytime tea. "Men don't know *how* to communicate. They're trapped inside the urges of their penis. My friends and I totally call it 'penis participation.'"

"He's not a teenager," I snapped. "He's almost forty. Plus you don't need to converse to leave a message."

"Maybe not to *you*, but guys' brains are totally different. They can't *think* the way we do. It's sad when you think about it. They're so stunted. It's almost as if they're deformed." She snapped her gum for emphasis.

"You're only seventeen," I told her. "You're supposed to be more optimistic."

She shrugged. "I can't help it. I had to grow up when I was, like, five."

I grabbed an old stack of women's magazines and wandered into Jay-Jay's room. He was still awake, so I sat on the floor and read up on ways to improve myself.

"Dad called," Jay-Jay said without looking up from his book. "I told him you went to meet some guy but didn't tell him about your hair."

"Thanks." My hair had fallen out of its knot long ago; it lay bunched and fallen around my shoulders. Jay-Jay scrambled off the bed to go say a second good night to Stephanie, Killer Bee stumbling behind him. I sat pressed against a box of Legos and skimmed an article about reclaiming one's inner childhood joy.

"Some guy's on the phone." Jay-Jay's head appeared in the doorway. "He's leaving this super-long message, and Mom, he used the word *mulligrubs*, isn't that cool?"

"Delete it." I opened a new magazine.

"But, Mom, he said that he hoped you didn't have the mulligrubs after today's misunderstanding. How can you delete something like that?"

"Easily." I threw down the magazine and picked up another. "Mulligrub guys are a dime a dozen."

I knew that they weren't, though, and apparently Jay-Jay did also, because he didn't delete the message. I listened to it after everyone was asleep, leaning over the answering machine with a towel over my head to muffle the sound of Francisco's voice apologizing for not being able to reach me. He had to catch a last-minute flight to Barrow and cell reception was down. He was stuck inside a motel with polka-dot curtains. "Please don't be besieged with the mulligrubs," he said, and then he laughed. I started to laugh and then pressed my hand tight against my mouth as if to hold it all in, because I suddenly realized that I was being given an out. Fate had handed me the perfect excuse to stop whatever might happen with Francisco before it had even begun. It was almost too perfect. I closed my eyes, poised my finger over the Delete button. *Just one tiny press,* I said to myself. My hand wavered in the air. I stood there for a long time, unsure of what to do.

Sunday, Dec. 11

Sandee and I walked along the frozen beach out by Point Woronzof, Jay-Jay's BB gun swinging against my chest. The wind blew damp and cold, and large blocks of ice littered the beach. We moved slowly, due to snow pockets that plunged us down past our knees.

"Did we have to come this far?" Sandee stumbled and caught herself on a jagged iceberg shaped like a huge breast. "Couldn't we have shot cans in the yard?"

"It's illegal to shoot in the city."

"It's a BB gun, Carla. We're not using real bullets."

"I didn't want anyone to see us," I admitted. "It felt, I don't know. Private."

Sandee nodded and kicked snow off a log, clearing it off so that we'd have a place to sit. "Should we shoot into the water or the bluffs?" We were on a narrow strip of beach that curved around the Earthquake Park, the inlet on one side and bluffs rising above our heads on the other. No one else was around; it was silent except for the wind and the water bobbing against the ice. I took the cans out of my backpack and arranged them facing the water. Sandee and I had decorated them earlier, hers covered with photographs of Randall and mine with blond-haired models that reminded me of Francisco. We stacked the cans three high and then moved back toward the bluffs. "You first," Sandee said.

I pumped the gun, which was modeled to look like a rifle though it was much lighter, held it up to my shoulder, took aim with one squinty eye, and pulled the trigger. The shot cracked and two cans flew through the air.

"Wow, I didn't think you'd actually hit anything," Sandee said.

"Thanks."

"No, I meant it as a compliment." She raised the gun, shimmied her hips, shot and missed. "Fuck," she whispered, and tried again and again. "Help me out here, okay? I refuse to embarrass myself in front of Randall's photos, the bastard."

I showed her how to position the gun, how to sight her target, how to hold her breath the moment she pulled the trigger. "Don't aim directly at what you want to hit." I tried to remember what Barry had told me when he first took me hunting years ago, back when he still harbored illusions of turning me into a rugged Alaska outdoorswoman. "Aim very,

very slightly to your dominant side. See, watch me. See how I lean into my right a few seconds before I shoot? So I aim a little past my target to the left, to compensate." I couldn't remember if this was what he had actually said or if I was making it up, but it didn't matter.

Sandee hunched over the BB gun, pulled the trigger, and missed again. "Fucking bitch," she yelled. "I won't let you do this to me, Randall." She moved closer to the targets, missed again, moved closer and finally hit the edge of a can with Randall's picture. It slowly toppled over. "Wow!" she smiled over at me. "That's super intense, isn't it? It's almost sexual." She pumped the rifle, raised it, and blew two cans away. "Did you see that!" She danced around the snow in her heavy winter clothes, looking carefree and ridiculous.

After we obliterated the cans, we gathered the pieces in a plastic shopping bag and headed up the bluff path to the car. "I feel like I'm on a high." Sandee shoved the can remnants inside a bear-proof garbage can with a complicated lid. "Like I'm invincible. No wonder men are so arrogant. I would be too if I grew up shooting."

"Well, there's probably more to it than that." I started the car and headed toward the grocery store. "I think it has to do with testosterone levels."

"Probably," she said. "I'm starving, what about you? I feel like a banana split. I haven't had one in years."

"Yeah, me too." My teeth were ready to rip into raw meat, into a live animal, though we ended up buying twenty dollars of sugary carbohydrates. We made banana splits for everyone, and after we finished I lured Sandee over to the answering machine to help analyze Francisco's message.

"What do you think he meant?" I sat on the floor, the carton of Safeway chocolate ice cream between my legs. "You think he's telling the truth? You think he's worth seeing again?" I sprayed whipped cream on my fingers and ate it.

"You can't believe him." Sandee spooned ice cream from her bowl. Her lips glistened with chocolate sauce. "Maybe everything he said was true, and probably it wasn't, but let's just say it was. It doesn't matter, you know why?"

I swallowed and waited.

"Because he didn't call you first. How many messages did you leave, three? Four? It was his duty to call and leave a message first, since he was the one in the wrong. And yes, I realize that he was in a hurry, but a phone call takes less than a minute. But that's not the point, either."

"So what *is* the point?" I was getting cranky from too much sugar.

"He didn't take time for you. It sounds like a small thing, but it's not. If I had been smarter, I would have noticed the same thing about Randall and saved myself a lot of anguish." She squirted more whipped cream over her sundae. "Maybe I should have shot him. Has anyone mentioned that? Tell me the truth, okay? Do people think I killed my very own husband and buried his body out in Vegas? Is that what they said when he didn't come back?"

"No one thinks that," I reassured her, though of course people had wondered exactly that. "They just thought you were, you know, a woman who couldn't keep a man."

"I've been called worse things." She dipped her fingers in the ice cream and scooped out a handful. "But it would have felt good to shoot him."

"Yeah," I agreed. "It probably would have."

WHAT'S ON MY KITCHEN TABLE

Electric bill: DUE
MasterCard bill: DUE
Gap credit card: DUE
A tattered copy of *Loving the Right Men for the Wrong Reasons*
Six Barbie hands, cut off at the wrists

Chapter 11

Monday, Dec. 12

"I'M STAYING HERE."

"Wh-what?" I opened my eyes early this morning to Laurel standing above me eating crackers, the crumbs falling across my arms. "How'd you get in?"

"You gave me a key, remember?" The side of the bed shifted as she sat down. "You shouldn't keep the house so cold. It's bad for the digestion." She stuffed another cracker into her mouth. She slid into bed next to me, her feet cold when they brushed my bare leg.

"Junior came back from Portland yesterday, but he won't notice I'm gone. I made apple crisp for breakfast, with whole wheat crust. As long as he gets his fiber he'll be okay." She turned over, fluffed her pillow, and was asleep within minutes. It was odd having someone in bed with me. Barry occasionally fell asleep after our sad little bouts of sex, but I couldn't remember the last time I lay awake beside someone in the dark without feeling burdened or heavy. It must have been when Jay-Jay was smaller and crawled in beside me, his back tucked up against my hip, his lips sucking as if even in his dreams he was aware of me as mother, supplier of milk.

"Carly?" Laurel was suddenly awake, or maybe she had never been asleep. "We're out of crackers, but don't get the Keebler brand, promise? I keep imagining my baby morphing into one of those elfy creatures from the commercials." She shivered and yanked the quilt over toward her side. "What would I do if I had a something like that?"

"I thought you were having an abortion."

"I *am*, Carly. Just get another kind of cracker, okay?"

Tuesday, Dec. 13

I didn't expect Laurel to get up for breakfast but there she was, sitting at the table in front of a pile of unpaid bills when I came in from walking Killer.

"What took you so long?" she said crossly. "I'm starving."

I fixed scrambled eggs and toast while Jay-Jay complained about the powerlessness of childhood.

"It's not so great," he said. "You don't get to choose what to eat or when to go to bed."

"If someone had told me when to go to bed I wouldn't be in this trouble," Laurel muttered. Jay-Jay ignored her.

"It's a monarchy," he said in that smug tone he's been using a little too often lately. "Kids are serfs and the parents are feudal landowners. That would make Killer, let me see, a..."

"Where did you learn about monarchies?" I interrupted.

"Mr. Short. He says true monarchies seldom exist. Most are imitation, like processed cheese slices."

He took a gulp of orange juice and burped. Laurel didn't say a word. He burped again, louder this time, and she sat quietly and played with her eggs.

"What's *her* problem?" he asked.

"I'm going back to bed." Laurel said. "I feel a little woozy." She rushed across the room and threw up in the sink. Jay-Jay was horrified.

"Mom," he whispered. "Do something, okay?"

I followed Laurel to my bedroom and helped her off with her blouse. Her bra was yellow with tiny orange flowers printed across each breast. This made me incredibly sad.

"Tuck me in?" she said in a small voice.

I smoothed the comforter and tucked it around her shoulders.

"Now say 'Good night, sleep tight.'"

"It's morning," I stalled.

"I *know*. It's just something to say."

"Goodnightsleeptight," I said quickly, hoping to get to the door before she started crying.

"Carly." She clutched my wrist. "Will it hurt?"

I didn't know how to answer. My abortion hurt for a few hours but I knew she wasn't talking about physical pain. Emotionally, it hurt for a long, long time. Pain still flares up unexpectedly.

"They don't use machines any longer," I stalled. "They have a shot now, it's more like a miscarriage, you don't even have to—"

"Mom! I'm going to be late," Jay-Jay yelled.

"Call in to work for me, okay?" Laurel burrowed deeper beneath the covers. "I feel so heavy. My lips are too tired to talk."

"Laurel is staying with us for a while," I told Jay-Jay as I drove him to school; we had missed the bus again. "She isn't feeling well."

He played with the carabiner clips hanging from his backpack. "We might have to keep it quieter too, especially Thursday. She has to go in the hospital and well, it's nothing to worry about really, just day surgery, not even day, more like an hour or two." I laughed nervously. "I'll take the afternoon off, stay with her, be back by the time you get home from—"

"Did you remember lunch money?" Jay-Jay interrupted. "You forgot yesterday and I had to eat Josephine's sandwich and, Mom, it was organic. I almost puked."

"Oh shit." I had forgotten. "Listen, I'll swing by the cash machine. It'll only take a minute."

"You can leave it at the office."

"No, honey, I'll bring it to your classroom to make sure you—"

"Mom!" Jay-Jay hissed. "You have on *shorts*."

"So?" I looked down at my legs, pale and chapped and partially covered by my long winter coat.

"Forget it." He reached for the door handle. "I'd rather starve."

"Fine!" I snapped.

The door slammed and Jay-Jay ran up the school steps, his ridiculous green knapsack bumping against his shoulders so that he resembled an oversized praying mantis. I wished I could follow him. I didn't want to return home and hear Laurel snoring from my bedroom. I felt guilty about her pregnancy and slightly ashamed. If I had paid more attention, listened more carefully, not necessarily to what she said but what she hadn't, I might have picked up on her state of mind, realized she needed help, an ear to listen, a shoulder to lean on. But I had been too involved with my own life, my own problems. Now I wanted to lay my hand on her shoulder and say, "Bless me, sister, for I have sinned," the way we used to say to the priest before confession, before we bowed our heads and waited for penance, all those tedious Hail Marys and Our Fathers, which we cheated by praying only half of. After church, Gramma took us to eat at the Swedish smorgasbord out by the highway. She didn't particularly like the Swedes, since she considered them sissies for not involving themselves more in the war, but she did appreciate their attitude toward food. She was sure that all-you-can-eat buffets originated in Sweden. I don't know how she came up with this, but she believed it to the point that she taped a map of Sweden to her refrigerator. It made her happy, she said, to think of all those people eating as much as they wanted, beverage included, for one small price.

MESSAGE ON MY CELL PHONE AT 2:32 A.M.

"Hello, Carla? It's me, Francisco. I'm still up in Barrow but I'll…" He paused and cleared his throat. "I'll be home by this weekend. I guess you're, uh, still mad about the restaurant." He cleared his throat again. "I should have called. I just, well, I just...this is all so damned hard, isn't it? I just think that maybe we should, I don't know, maybe just...Damn it, I'll call when I get back." He cleared his throat but didn't hang up. He stayed on the line breathing until the machine finally clicked him off.

Wednesday, Dec. 14

It's three a.m. and everyone is finally asleep. It's been a long night, all of us frayed and stressed except Jay-Jay. Laurel wanted Spam for supper, an unusual request since she rarely eats meat, though Spam probably couldn't be classified as real meat. She demanded I fry her up some as soon as I got home from work. I mixed it with potatoes, added onions and peppers, Gramma's old hash recipe, and as I fried up that stinky meat product, Jay-Jay quizzed us on Spam facts.

"Guess what state eats the most Spam? Oklahoma, Washington, Alaska, or Hawaii?"

"Alaska." I was sure I was right. Where else could you find enough people willing to eat what was basically dog food?

"Nope. Hawaii. Okay, next question: if you took all the Spam ever eaten, how many times would it circle the globe?"

"Oh-oh-oh, I know," Stephanie yelled from the living room; it seemed she was staying with us again. "It's totally eight."

"Nope, ten! Okay, last one. Think hard, you guys, you're batting zero. Name one state where Spam is made. There are two, but you only gotta answer one."

"Texas?" I asked.

"No."

"Virginia," Stephanie said.

"Nope."

"Wait," Laurel yelled. "It's Ohio, isn't it? Cleveland?"

"Think harder, okay? It starts with an *N*."

"North Carolina," Stephanie called out happily.

"N. E. B."

"Nebraska," Laurel shouted. "What's the other one?"

"Minnesota."

"No way. You sure?"

"Yep." Jay-Jay was already bored with this game.

After our crappy supper, Stephanie left to meet Hammie and I hunkered down at the kitchen table to catch up on my bills, which for once were only overdue and not delinquent; I took this as a sign of progress. I was deliberating on whether to save the Gap credit card bill for next month or send in a bad check when Laurel called out from the living room.

"Did you remember my blouse?"

"Can't you wear one of mine?" I signed my name to the Gap check and tidily licked the envelope.

"I can't believe you didn't remember. My lucky blouse? The one I've kept all these years? I wore it when I took my SATs, and the night Junior proposed."

"So?" I was on a bill-paying roll. My endorphins were flowing, as if I had been jogging. I was almost high.

"You promised to get it for me, remember?"

I pounded stamps over the bills and spread them out in front of me: Visa, Paid! MasterCard, Paid! Electric, Paid! Gas, Paid! Gap, kinda/sorta Paid! I wiped my sweating hands over the dish towel. "What am I supposed to say to Junior?"

"You don't have to say anything. Pick up the blouse and get out."

I couldn't do that, though. My loyalties lay with Laurel, but Junior has been in the family for over a decade. Last year he bought Jay-Jay an acre of land on the moon for a birthday present, something Jay-Jay still talks about. I grabbed a handful of pretzels, called for Killer, and headed out to the car. Gramma always said that chewing got her brain working and I was hoping for the same as I drove south to the Hillside section of town, the roads becoming slipperier and less crowded the farther I got from town. I parked in the driveway and shut off the engine. Without the intrusion of streetlights, the sky was clear, the stars spreading out, the moon a round ball that reminded me of a pregnant woman's belly. Junior answered on the first knock. He looked terrible. His pants were wrinkled and there was a stain on his shirt.

"So," he said as he closed the door behind me. The smell of take-out pizza filled the air. "How's Laurel?"

I kicked off my boots.

"Look, I'm not stupid, I know she's there. I see her car in the driveway. I drive by every night before bed, just to make sure she's still there."

"Oh." I didn't know what to say. I hoped he wouldn't start crying.

"You want some pizza? It has anchovies but you could pick them off."

"No thanks, I can't—"

"I know she was seeing another man. I'm not dumb. I almost stayed in Portland last month. Then I stopped at a light downtown and a family walked by with two little girls. You could tell they didn't have much money but they held hands and laughed; they looked so happy. That's when I understood what's been missing between us: a child."

"Wh-wh-what?"

Junior kept right on talking. "She's probably told you I can't have kids. I'm not proud of the fact. But we can adopt, and if she wants to do the whole pregnancy experience I'm willing to go the artificial insemination route. We can pick an educated donor, someone with strong genes."

I could feel laughter in my throat, that hysterical, inappropriate laughter that descends during funerals or long church services. I coughed instead, and Junior looked at me dully.

"She's a difficult woman, I'll admit, but I've never met anyone like her." He slumped back against the couch cushions.

"Excuse me, I need to get something." I rushed up the stairs. The bedroom was neat; it didn't look as if Junior had been sleeping there.

Downstairs I could hear the TV, the volume turned up too loud. I opened the closet door, walked to the back, and pulled down the last black blouse on the rack. I escaped a few minutes later, Junior following me to the door and urging me to stay and watch *Law & Order* reruns with him. His voice was pleading, his ankles pale and bony above his slippers, which were on the wrong feet.

After everyone went to bed, Laurel clutching the blouse like a blankie, I struggled with a double-penis military doll order but couldn't decide if it should have four testicles or two. Would an extra penis automatically mean extra balls? And if so, one more or two? I tried attaching extra balls but they looked cumbersome and crowded, swinging between poor Ken's legs like tiny balloons. I finally gave up and ate. I devoured two peanut butter sandwiches and half a bag of stale marshmallows, my teeth stinging from the sugar. I didn't stop there. I ate a can of cold cream of mushroom soup and the leftover spaghetti from Sunday night that may or may not have been going bad. Hunched over the table shoveling food into my mouth, I suddenly imagined the woman running through my paintings doing the same, both of us pigging out together. Even though this woman didn't exist, I suddenly missed her company. I imagined how it would feel for her to sit next to me, her presence soft and comforting, her breath reeking of garlic like Gramma's. Without thinking about it, I reached out, grabbed the phone, and dialed Francisco's cell. It rang six times before he finally answered.

"Hello?" His voice was sleepy and vague. "That you?"

I didn't say anything. I clutched the phone to my ear and breathed. He breathed back, steady and slow.

"Francisco?" I whispered; it was the first time I had ever said his name to him. "My sister?" My voice cracked. He didn't say anything. He kept right on breathing. "My sister's having an abortion tomorrow," I whispered. And then I hung up. Softly.

Chapter 12

Thursday, Dec. 15

WE GATHERED AROUND the kitchen table earlier this morning, our sad little version of the Last Breakfast. We even wore robes like the apostles, though we weren't eating fish but Safeway brand cornflakes. Laurel looked especially tragic, with her unwashed hair and ratty night-gown, and even Stephanie was subdued, her '50s-style poodle bathrobe slumped dejectedly over her shoulders. We ate in silence. The only sound was our chewing.

Halfway through our stilted meal Jay-Jay appeared. He had on the never-before-worn khaki pants Laurel had given him for his birthday, along with a wrinkled oxford shirt that looked vaguely familiar. He held typed papers in his hand and his face wore a hopeful, expectant look. I knew what was coming. I watched as he sat down and began distribut-ing the pages.

"My Christmas list," he said proudly. "The Really, Really Wants are highlighted in red type at the top. The Really Wants are in green, and the Wants But Don't Have to Haves are in basic black."

Laurel sucked in her breath but Jay-Jay didn't notice. "I've itemized according to price, store, and website. This way you won't waste time looking for something at the wrong place."

"Well," I began. "This seems very industrious—"

"Or you can just give me money and I'll buy the stuff myself. Gift cards work, too—as long as they're not stingy."

No one said anything.

"But wrap them up, okay? I want to see presents under the tree."

We tried, Stephanie and I, to act interested in Jay-Jay's spiel. We asked questions, we nodded, we fake-laughed. By the time he caught the bus, even Stephanie looked frayed.

"My mom would totally light a joint right now," she said. "Just to, like, get the edge off."

When it came time to drive Laurel to her appointment, Stephanie was nowhere to be seen. I was disappointed. I needed her to pat my back and tell me that everything was going to be, like, totally okay. I put on my boots, zipped my coat, and waited in the trailer's arctic entryway, thinking of the holy water in church and how we dabbed it on our foreheads as we entered. Gramma stuck in her whole hand and splashed it across her face. She believed in stocking up on good fortune. She also didn't like the taste of the communion wafers and once took it upon herself to improve the recipe, rolling out dough over the kitchen table and cutting small circles with the cap from Mother's face cream. After seasoning to her liking and baking on wax-papered cookie sheets, she tucked them inside a Tupperware container and carried them proudly to Mass. The priest blushed when she presented them to him, stammering that only those appointed by god had the authority to make the communion wafers. Gramma snatched her wafers out of his hands and sat out the rest of Mass in the bathroom.

"What a big *dupa*," she huffed, as we filed out to the car. "God need to find a better cook."

We ate those wafers on the drive home, and they were light and subtle with a small flavor of cinnamon, followed by a kick of licorice. We held the flavor against our tongues, closed our eyes, and swallowed these blessings not from god but from our fat and sweaty grandmother.

"Ready?" a shaky voice said. I opened my eyes to my sister standing in front of me dressed all in black, as if in mourning. I followed her out to the car.

"Laurel—," I began, but she held up her hand.

"Don't. Please. Just drive, okay?"

We waited silently through two intersections, and then we were there. It was a Thursday morning, a nothing day, temperatures in the low teens, yet more than twenty protesters stood in the parking lot waving signs with pictures of screaming fetuses and tiny fingers blown up to giant proportions.

Laurel blanched. I reached over and squeezed her hand. "We can do this," I said, but my voice wavered. The protesters surged toward the car.

"Save your baby, don't kill your baby," they chanted, their signs bobbing and swaying. A camera went off.

"Carla!" Laurel clutched my arm and I hesitated, my hand poised over the doorknob.

"One, two, three," I counted, and then I opened the door. The crowd swarmed.

"Jesus wants your baby to live," a fat woman cried. "He sent me here to help you." Her breasts pressed against my chest. The door to the clinic was only twenty-five feet away but it might as well have been another country. We were packed tight; we couldn't budge. Laurel's knees buckled and she fell against me. I gritted my teeth and pushed hard.

"Move," I yelled, as I flailed against the fat woman. She refused to budge. "Move, damn it!"

They packed tighter, an array of jackets and faces and hats, their breaths stinking of coffee and righteousness. Laurel's teeth chattered in my ear.

"Let us through," I cried, pushing harder. "Let. Us. Through."

"Pray to Jesus," the fat woman continued. "Get down on your knees and pray—"

Her head snapped back.

"You heard her," a female voice sang out, followed by a familiar snap of gum. "She totally said to get the hell out of the way."

"Stephanie?" I asked.

"Don't worry, Mrs. Richards," she yelled, as she yanked the fat woman's ponytail harder. "I'll get you out of here in, like, a minute."

She was dressed in camouflage tights and skirt, an oversized army coat hanging almost to her ankles. She looked tough and ridiculous as she tugged the woman by the hair toward the clinic door. The protesters parted like the Red Sea.

"Fucking freaks," she muttered, expertly punching a man in the gut as he barreled down upon us. She leaned over and wiped a strand of hair out of Laurel's face. "A few more steps and we'll totally be there."

A moment later we were at the door. I placed my hand over the small of Laurel's back, her spine pressing my palm.

I helped her through.

Sometimes my grandmother's ghost visits me. This has happened twice before: on the night Jay-Jay was conceived and during the worst of my labor, when I was wet with sweat and howling for god to please, please, please put me out of my misery. Instead he sent my grandmother, who appeared before me in her faded red-and-blue-flowered dress, her stockings rolled down, the toes of her shoes cut to give her bunions room to breathe. She held my palm and recited recipe ingredients: two cups of sugar, a pinch of cinnamon, three egg whites. By the time Jay-Jay's head appeared, I had been through half the cookbook. Today Gramma appeared in the clinic bathroom, the one right off the waiting room filled with empty urine specimen cups and surplus paper towels. I was drying my hands when I caught a glimpse of her in the mirror.

"Gramma?" I said. She had on a horrid green dress and sturdy Reebok sneakers, and she was fiddling with one of the specimen cups. "What are you doing here?"

"*Ach*, it cold outside," she said.

"Did you come to see Laurel?"

"Such a clever cup." She lifted it toward her mouth and I reached over, snatched it before it hit her lips.

"These are urine sample cups," I hissed, feeling as if I were talking to Jay-Jay when he was young. "You aren't supposed to drink out of them."

"*Nie*, not Laurel," was all she said, looking at me with her blue eyes, layers of sadness in the shadows, small flicks of hunger: Polish eyes. "I come to see you."

"Did it have to be in the bathroom?" Gramma never gave a hoot for privacy and used to pee in a plastic bowl if one of us was using the bathroom when she needed it. She'd dump the contents in the toilet as soon as it was free, wash her hands, and store the bowl beneath the kitchen sink. No one dared breathe a word of this to Mother.

"Once, when I still young, I lost my baby," she said. "It so small, like a teeny fish."

"I know," I interrupted. "Mother told us."

Gramma stared at me with her blue, blue eyes. "You know nothing," she said. Her voice was surprisingly harsh. "Sit. There not much time."

I closed the toilet lid, plopped down, and folded my hands as if in church. I had the feeling that whatever came next wasn't going to be pleasant, and in a way I was right. In another, I was very, very wrong.

"After the war, we move to Podlaskie, before we live near Warsaw," my grandmother began. "That is after I marry Dionizy." Gramma sighed. "I never love him, but what the so, eh?"

I glanced nervously at my watch. Leave it to Gramma to pick the worst possible time to tell her story. Growing up, she didn't talk much about Poland. It was over and done with, she used to say. Then she'd bake a strudel or cream puffs and spend all day in the kitchen as if in penance. "I should check on Laurel," I said. "She probably needs—"

"*Nie*, she waiting for them to jab her blood."

"Blood work," I corrected.

But Gramma ignored me and continued. "The Russians ain't as bad as the Nazis. It hard to get meat but we do okay. Momma and Poppa and Lizzie follow a couple of months later. It take all Poppa's money to bring us all there." She sighed again. "I not sure why he don't smuggle us from Poland. Maybe it too hard to leave. We there almost a year and there is a knock on the door late, *ach,* June 15, 1941, I never forget that date." She spit over the floor. "Soldiers come for Poppa and Dionizy. They say they only need to ask question. Dionizy forget his hat. I still see it on the floor by the door. It brown and yellow. I still hate that hat."

Gramma stared at her hands. "That the last we see of them. Momma learn the next day they on the transport. She think we are next so she send me and Lizzie to the country. 'Watch your sister,' she say. Lizzie is eight year younger. We stay with friend of cousin. Momma get taken three days later. I don't say this to Lizzie but she find out. One night she gone. 'Left to find Momma,' she write and that is all. I never see her again."

I squinted at Gramma as if seeing her for the first time. "But the Russians were on our side," I said. "They were the good guys."

Gramma spit again. "*Kurwiec.* They want Poland for themselves, all of us out. I never see Poppa or Lizzie again. Momma make it to Siberia, I get some letters, then nothing. Dionizy the only one who live. After he come back we have a baby, a little girl, she have yellow hair like the dandelions. I name her after Momma. I am already in love with Manny then, he from far away but a good man. Maybe the girl is his, I not know. She die four months old. Dionizy pry her from my arms when I sleep, I cannot give her up. As soon as the war over, I leave and come here. I steal money from Dionizy's store, get on the boat, leave. I have no reason to stay.

"I get letter from Manny, 'Meet me in Chicago.' I go but he ain't there. I stay months and he never show up. Maybe he get lost or change his mind. A few while later I marry your grandpoppa." Gramma sighs. "Too many girls die."

"Maybe it's a boy." I knew right away she was talking about Laurel.

"No, it a girl," Gramma said, placing her moist hand against the side of my face for a moment. "*Do widzenia,*" she said, and then she was gone.

"Jesus," I whispered to myself as I washed my hands over and over, and then went back to the waiting room, where Stephanie read magazines and Sandee, dressed in her Mexico in an Igloo uniform, checked messages on her cell. She had taken off the early part of her shift to be with us.

"You look awful," she said, handing me a cherry Life Saver. "Your face is damp and sweaty."

"I'm fine." I laughed harshly, then covered my mouth with my palm.

"Mrs. Richards." Stephanie's head popped up from the magazine. "Listen to this. Tobias Wolff, the writer? He says that he sometimes rewrites a story five times."

I popped a Life Saver into my mouth, the flavor flooding my tongue with memories of elementary school and the promise of recess.

"I'm thinking of applying to Stanford," Stephanie continued. "It would be totally awesome to study with Tobias. He wouldn't have to like anything I wrote. Just knowing his bald head was in the same room as one of my stories would be enough." She snapped her gum happily.

I picked up an old *People* magazine. Reese Witherspoon stared back at me with her pretty hair and pointed chin. "We have to stop her," I said. "She can't do this."

"Well, that's really not up to us," Sandee began. "It's her body, after all, and what she does with it is her choice."

"But she's my sister."

"If I got pregnant my mom would be ecstatic," Stephanie said. "One more person on our welfare check. Not that I'd raise it in that house. I'd run away and, like, go into foster care."

"But you'd have it?"

"Oh sure," Stephanie said. "Why not?"

"What about college and Tobias Wolff?"

Stephanie shrugged. "He'd totally have to wait."

"Thank you, Stephanie." I set the magazine down.

No one stopped me as I walked down the back hallway and through the first door. A young girl sat on an exam table wearing nothing but a pair of Scooby-Doo underpants.

"Sorry," I said. She didn't even look up. Three doors later, I found Laurel huddled against the back wall of an examination room wearing an ugly pink hospital smock. When she saw me she let out a muffled sob.

"I couldn't do it, Carly," she sobbed, gripping my hand so tight I let out a little yelp. "I'm sorry, I'm sorry, I couldn't do it."

I hugged her hard, spit running out of her mouth and across my shirt. "Sorry," she cried over and over. "So, so sorry."

"Let's get you out of here," I said.

"The doctor," she began, but I gathered up her clothes and shoes and pushed her toward the door. "I need to sign—"

"You don't need to sign anything." My voice was harsh and deep, and Laurel looked at me in surprise. I pushed her down the hall and into the waiting room.

"We're leaving," I said. Sandee and Stephanie dropped their magazines and rushed over.

"Cool top." Stephanie yanked Laurel's smock down over her back. "Can I borrow it sometime?"

We hurried Laurel out the door and past the reception area where a girl with pierced eyebrows yelled that we needed a doctor's approval before leaving. The protesters cheered as Stephanie helped Laurel into the backseat. Sandee drove behind us the whole way, and it was comforting to look out the rearview mirror and see her dusty Subaru. Laurel slumped in the backseat, Stephanie's hand tight on her arm. No one said a word. The only sound was the persistent and steady snap of Stephanie's gum.

GRAMMA'S COMMUNION WAFERS

- 6 cups white pastry flour
- 1⅛ cup butter/margarine
- Pinch of salt
- ½ cup sugar
- 2 teaspoons cinnamon

- 1½ teaspoon anise (ground or liquid)
- 3–6 tablespoons cold water (for consistency)

Preheat oven to 350°. Mix ingredients in a large white bowl; use your hands, the way the priest uses his hands to make the sign of the cross. Roll dough out until it is very thin. Cut circles out using a small jar or cup. Bake on ungreased cookie sheet for 7–10 minutes, depending on desired consistency. Eat with dark red wine. Close your eyes and swallow. Know you are blessed.

Saturday, Dec. 17

"I'm going to be an aunt," I told Barry. It was past midnight, and we sat up in Jay-Jay's tree house, naked except for blankets wrapped around our flushed bodies. It was two degrees outside, the sky clear, the stars glittering cold. Beside us, a small camp stove gave off sputtering flicks of heat.

"Didn't think she'd go through with it." Barry grunted and rubbed his foot.

"Yeah, well, now she's talking about a home birth. In *my* bedroom." He handed me a joint and I inhaled and coughed, inhaled and coughed. "Laurel's moved in, Stephanie's on the couch, and Sandee stops by every other night to complain about Joe. Do you know him? The fish-and-game guy?" Barry shook his head no, so I continued. "I can't paint or work on my dolls; I can't even use my own bathroom. It's almost Christmas and I've barely gotten Jay-Jay anything."

"Thought we was getting him a laptop." He grabbed the joint from my hand and expertly inhaled.

"Yeah, it's on order." I closed my eyes, colors flashing behind my lids: carmine, violet, a bismuth yellow the exact shade as the ribbon tied around the secret box that kept appearing in my paintings, which I hadn't gotten around to finishing. I swallowed glumly. "Have I ever finished anything?" My voice was far away, the way it gets when I'm high. "In my whole life, tell me, have I ever finished one thing?"

"I dunno." Barry stared down at his penis, as if expecting it to perform tricks.

"I barely finished high school, I never filled out my college applications, and I didn't finish our marriage." I was getting more and more depressed. Pot did that to me sometimes, took me down before flying me up. "I've never lasted at a job longer than three years."

"You had Jay-Jay, that's something."

"I didn't have much of a choice."

"Always a choice."

"I guess." I sighed and picked at my cuticle. "I shouldn't have given up so easily." Barry's edges were starting to fuzz. "Don't act like you know what I'm talking about when you don't," I yelled before taking one last hit; I held that sweet smoke deep inside my lungs. "It's painting, okay?"

"I seen you paint."

"Not seriously." I laughed an ugly laugh. "Not like it was what I was meant to do. I want..." I couldn't think clearly, couldn't put into words the ache inside me, the loneliness, the need. "I want...more."

Barry nodded and grabbed the joint. "So get more," he said, his eyes dulling.

"I don't know how." I was beginning to relax now, to go with the flow. I lay back and looked up at the rough plank ceiling.

"Nobody knows cow, I mean how," Barry slurred. "You just gotta moo, you know? Moooovvvvve forward."

I giggled and closed my eyes, colors swishing by. Barry woke me a few hours later, the stove out, my nose so cold I couldn't feel it.

"It's past three." He pulled on his pants and groped along the rough planks for his socks. "Ouch!" He sucked on his finger. "Got me a splinter." He held his hand in front of my face but it was too dark to see.

"I'll get the tweezers," I said wearily. The night was heavy and cold, and climbing down the ladder felt claustrophobic, as if I were moving inside a huge freezer. I led Barry into the house, creeping past Stephanie on the couch and Jay-Jay sleeping in his room. Barry paused and stuck his head in the door.

"He looks good sleeping," he whispered. "Some kids get all dopey-faced but Jay-Jay looks like he's figuring things out." He laughed softly, and Jay-Jay rolled over in his sleep, as if following Barry's voice. I turned on the bathroom light and we both cringed. Then I got out the rubbing alcohol and tweezers and set about pulling fibers of wood out of my ex-husband's palm. It reminded me of that story of the lamb pulling a splinter out of the lion's paw. I told this to Barry, and he grunted.

I put the rubbing alcohol away and started brushing my teeth. Barry leaned toward the mirror and picked a small pimple on his forehead. Our eyes met in the mirror and we looked away guiltily.

"We've got to stop." I sat down on the closed toilet seat. "Look at us, it's like we're still married. This can't be normal, can it?"

"Dunno." Barry sat on the edge of the tub, his large knees hunched against his chest. "Normal for us, maybe."

"I met someone," I blurted as I got out the dental floss, breaking off a strand and handing the container to Barry. "We had one date but he never showed. He said he was in Barrow. Sometimes I call him at night just to hear him breathe."

Barry didn't say anything.

"Do you really *want* to do it again?" I waved my dental floss through the air. "The beginning so good and then the middle kind of sagging and before you know it, the ugly, cold ending? You really want to try all that?"

"Yeah, I do." His voice was firm.

We flossed in rhythm, our elbows moving in time. It was comfortingly familiar yet vaguely shameful, the way I sometimes felt after I masturbated, satisfied yet hollow, as if I had stroked myself to pleasure in all the wrong places.

Chapter 13

Monday, Dec. 19 (early, early, early morning)

I SPENT THE WEEKEND cramming the last of my holiday doll orders, staying up through the night fueled by chocolate, coffee, and the clever caffeinated lip balm I bought on Jay-Jay's favorite website. Six dolls in two days was too much, and frankly, it showed. These definitely weren't my best, and the Whip Me, Sip Me, Flip Me doll ended up with lopsided balls, but as Stephanie pointed out, it lent a more realistic appearance.

She picked up a brown-skinned Barbie and gave her a butch haircut. "To make her, you know, look like she's tougher than sex. Like she doesn't need it but wants it. I think that's totally what makes men hot."

I stared at Stephanie. How could someone from such a broken home, with no parents to speak of, someone who has practically raised herself—how could someone like that be so wise? "Steph?" I said. She turned and looked at me. Her blusher was the wrong shade and her eyes, beneath their purple makeup, were so trusting and open that I couldn't go on. "Wanna help?" I asked instead.

"Oh, Mrs. Richards, you mean it?"

"Totally." I pushed over supplies and explained the orders. She chose Tie Me, Tickle Me, Teach Me, a submissive forced to walk on all fours like a dog.

"This is totally the best thing that's happened to me," she gushed. "I mean, think of it. Some guy is totally going to be jerking off to something I made. That's, like, well, that's almost like being famous or something."

"I worried that I was a bad influence, that I could be arrested for including a minor in the design of one of my porno dolls. "How old are you again?" I asked Stephanie.

"Seventeen," she said. "But don't worry, Mrs. Richards. With the stuff I've seen over at my house, a few fake dicks aren't going to warp my mind. I'm, like, an old soul. It takes a lot to faze me."

We worked for two hours straight until Jay-Jay came home from his friend Alan's house. Stephanie fed him a grilled cheese sandwich, ordered him to do his homework, and returned to her doll. The longer she worked, the more cheerful she became. She hummed and tapped out songs with the toes of her high-topped sneakers.

"Hey, Mrs. Richards," she sang out. "Name this tune, okay? See if you can get it in, like, ten notes, okay?"

I played along. I even devised my own tunes, which I tapped out with the toes of my old slippers. We were deep into a country-western round, our hands covered with cuts, burns, and scratches, when Laurel straggled out of bed for the day. It was past five, almost dinnertime.

"God," she said, sweeping into the kitchen like an old-time movie actress. "I feel so woozy. My stomach won't let me eat a thing." She glared as if this were my fault. Then she caught sight of the Dora Do Me Both Ways doll I was working on. "What's *that*?" She tittered and then covered her mouth. "I'm going to be sick again." Her feet pounded toward the bathroom.

"She won't make it," Stephanie said cheerfully.

She made it, but barely. "It's the oddest thing," she said a few moments later as she slumped down in the chair across from me. "My throw-up keeps tasting like Bugles. Remember? Those corn-tasting crackers Mother served with tomato soup?"

I measured a dildo against the doll's butt.

"I wonder if they still make those." Laurel picked up a naked doll and peered between its legs. I waited for her to ask me why I was drilling vagina and butt holes into dolls but she was too involved with her own suffering to care. "I feel like beef stew," she said. "Got any? It's the only thing that sounds remotely edible."

Beside me, Stephanie hammered a piece of wire. I had no idea what she was doing but trusted her instincts.

"Not Dinty Moore, though," Laurel continued. "The Safeway brand. It's less salty and the vegetables are soggier. Soggy is the only thing I can cope with right now."

"My mom totally ate marshmallows when she was pregnant with my sister," Stephanie said. "Everyone says that's why she's so pale and puffy." Stephanie's mother weighed over three hundred pounds and had four kids by four different men. "She hates marshmallows now, though. It's the only food she won't eat."

Talking about her family seemed to depress Stephanie, and she bit down on her lip and got to work attaching a spiked dog collar (which she made from the tops of thumb tacks and an old piece of leather) around the doll's neck. She added a leash printed with tiny fish.

Laurel squinted across the table. "Are those lobsters?"

"Crayfish." Stephanie snapped her gum.

Laurel looked around as if for the first time. "What exactly are you *doing*?" She spread her arms and knocked over a pile of penises. "Is this a *penis*?"

"Yes," I said proudly. I had finished the penises last week and was pleased at how realistic they looked, especially the crooked veins I had painted down each shaft.

"Well," Laurel huffed, sounding like her old self again. "This certainly doesn't look like something a woman with a small child should be doing. I know you won't like hearing this, Carly, but it looks—"

"Those are for Mom's porno dolls," Jay-Jay interrupted from the hallway. Everyone froze. "It's no big deal," he said. "It's not like I'm going to grow up and chop people into pieces because there were dirty dolls in my house."

My face turned red with shame. "Well, honey, it's not exactly porn. More along the lines of erotic art."

"Whatever," he said with a shrug. "Do we have any Goldfish crackers?"

"Nope."

"Regular crackers?"

"Nope." Laurel was eating us out of house and home.

"Toast?"

"I'll totally make it for you." Stephanie jumped up and rustled Jay-Jay's head. "With jelly on the bottom of the peanut butter, right?"

"I sell them on a website," I explained to Laurel as Jay-Jay headed to the living room with Stephanie. "It's a classy site. Some of their articles have been reprinted in the *Village Voice* and ..."

Laurel picked up a doll and peered at the half-finished labia. "Are vaginas ugly or amazing?" she said. "I can never figure it out. One minute they look ugly, the next mysterious and forbidden." She held up another doll. "These aren't bad, actually. That snobby art critic from the paper would probably say they're scathingly honest."

"Well, I don't think he'll ever see them, so I doubt—"

Laurel burped. "Listen, I really need some beef stew. Can you get me some, Carly?"

"I'm kind of busy." I etched a sunflower tattoo over a doll's buttocks. "Can't it wait?"

"Well, of course it *could* wait," Laurel said sarcastically. "I could keel over and *die* and then you wouldn't have to bother. Or I could sit here and throw up all over these *dirty dolls*."

I slammed down my doll, got my keys, and headed for the door.

"The Safeway kind," she yelled after me. I drove through the snow to the store, bought four cans of beef stew, warmed one up in the microwave, and served it to Laurel, who sat playing with a Ken doll's newly fashioned boobs.

"I wish I could take my breasts off and fold them in a drawer like a sweater," she said. "I'd never have to worry if they're bouncing or my nipples are showing." With that she attacked her stew, gobbling it up so fast she barely had time to chew. I watched in amazement—Laurel had always prided herself on impeccable manners.

"How would you reattach them?" I asked. She raised her head; a piece of carrot was caught in her teeth.

"Snaps," she said. "Over my chest." She took another bite. "I wonder why clothes no longer require snaps."

With that she went off to watch TV in the living room. The old Laurel had rarely watched TV. The new Laurel had a whole lineup of reality shows she couldn't miss: *The Amazing Race. Survivor. America's Next Top Model.* Although she was more easygoing now, I wasn't sure if it was good for her to be so lax. It was like watching a species trying to defy its genetic heritage, like birds flying north instead of south each autumn.

After a taped *Survivor* episode blared on, I returned to my doll orders. Stephanie had a paper to finish for school, so I was on my own until Sandee stopped by after work to complain about Joe. I immediately put her to work sanding down butts.

"Joe wants to take me to Seldovia," she said. "He wants me to meet his mother."

"Really?" This cheered me up. "He said that?"

"We haven't even slept together." She was clearly depressed. "I'm not ready to meet his mother."

"Ever find out his last name?"

"Don't laugh, okay? But it's Smith."

"Joe Smith?" I was incredulous. "That was the name you couldn't remember." I leaned forward. "I know you don't want to hear this but if you can't remember Smith, you're doomed. You're definitely in love."

"I know," she said angrily. "Don't you think I fucking know that?"

I was jealous. I wanted to be in love and miserable. I told her so.

"So call the god dude," she snapped.

After she headed home, I continued through the night, shipping everything off early in the morning at the Airport Post Office. As soon as I returned home, I started writing this. More than an hour has passed and I'm still writing. My hands ache and a blister is forming on my index finger, but I can't stop. Now that my dolls are finished until spring orders, what will I do with myself?

You'll finish your real work, a voice in my head replied in a calm, clear tone that couldn't possibly belong to me.

LETTER #7

Ms. Carlita Richards
202 W. Hillcrest Drive, #22
Anchorage, AK 99503

Dear Carlita Richards:

We were so excited to receive payment for your long overdue library book, How to Save Your Own Life *by Erica Jong, that we've named you Redeemed Library Patron of the Month.*

Please send a photograph of yourself by the end of the week so that we may include it on our main bulletin board, along with our announcement. A short bio on your reading habits would be much appreciated.

Congratulations on finally settling your bill, and welcome back to Anchorage Community Libraries.

Sincerely,
Margaret M. Miller
Anchorage Community Libraries

P.S. Have you saved your own life yet?

Friday, Dec. 23

"Joe keeps staring at my fingers." Sandee cut lemons into furious slices. "I think he's getting me a ring for Christmas."

"It's kind of sweet." We were finishing up our morning side work in the Mexico in an Igloo lounge. "Barry gave me a weed whacker our first year together."

Sandee shook the knife at me. "Better than a ring."

"Yeah, right." I took the knife from her hand and finished the lemons. "I've been thinking." I glanced at my watch. I had a feeling that once I started I wouldn't be able to stop. "We're both being ridiculous, don't you think? Overly cautious. We've reverted to born-again virgins, love-wise. Women who can fuck but can't open their hearts."

Sandee slumped against the counter. "It's almost Christmas. Why would you say something like that when it's practically a holiday?"

"I don't know, I just..." I put the lid on the lemons, wiped my hands over my skirt, and attached the Feliz Navidad pin shaped like a baby Jesus that Mr. Tims wanted us to wear. He wasn't religious, but the pins came for free with the tequila and he figured it would keep the church crowd happy. "We're playing games, don't you think? Acting like we're still in high school?"

"You wouldn't say that if Francisco came in," Sandee challenged. Her baby Jesus pin sagged at her breast, as if it were nursing.

"Would too." I wasn't being particularly brave; Francisco was spending the holidays up in Fairbanks, or so I thought. Right past noon, amid the horrid Spanish holiday music and the throngs of last-minute shoppers, with the kitchen backed up, the bar out of limes, and Mr. Tims in a frenzy, Sandee tugged at my ponytail.

"Time to play games," she said as I loaded my tray with taco salads and chicken fingers shaped like sombreros.

"He's here?" I looked around, as if Francisco might be in the kitchen. "You sure it's him?"

"Swedish hair, big feet, smells like dog—should I go on?"

"He's supposed to be in Fairbanks."

"What were you saying this morning?" Sandee repositioned the plates over my tray. "That we have to stop being overcautious about love?"

"Stop the hissy fight, food's dying." Mr. Tims swung a towel at my butt so I lifted my tray and adopted the swaying type of walk necessary to balance ten plates of Mexican food over my head. I noticed Francisco right away. He had tinsel stuck to the back of his neck and wore an ugly sweater with reindeer prancing up the sleeves. I was horrified.

"Carla!" he said as I passed, but I didn't answer. I snapped the tray jack open with my right hand and expertly lowered the tray; I felt his eyes on me as I served and it made me so nervous that I half-clobbered an elderly woman with a tamale plate.

"Sorry," I murmured, but she just giggled and sipped her Midori Christmas margarita. After all the plates had been distributed and the second round of drink orders taken, I stalled beside the table, fidgeting with the hot sauce dishes and water glasses.

"Be a dear and scoot," the elderly woman scolded, so I picked up my tray jack and scooted. Unfortunately, I had to pass Francisco's table on my way back to the pantry. I blushed and stared down at my ugly, thick-soled waitressing shoes.

"Car-lita," he sang, drawing out a fake Spanish accent. "*Feliz Navidad*, my Mexican friend." He raised his water glass to me and then set it down and patted the booth next to him. "Take a load off those feet, honey." He grinned. He seemed in especially high spirits.

"I can't sit with customers." I leaned across the table from him. "Mr. Tims would have my ass."

"And what a fine ass it is." He leaned forward. "I'm drunk but don't tell anyone, okay? The office party got out of hand."

"I thought you were up north."

"We celebrated on the plane down from Barrow. I was supposed to get off in Fairbanks."

"So why didn't you?"

"Scenery's better down here." He laughed and handed me his menu. "Know what I'm in the mood for? A tuna melt with Velveeta cheese, like my mom used to make. With dill pickles."

"Closest thing we've got is shrimp fajitas. Should I order—"

"Pickles!" He smacked the table with his palm. "I forgot to ask what happened to your sister." He lowered his voice. "Did she go through with it?"

"No, she's having it." I began to move away; Table Eleven was waiting impatiently for its check, and Table Nine needed more drinks. "I have to go. Do you want anything?"

"Nah, I have to get back to the airport. I'm on standby. The place is packed, but I have Gold Wings status."

"See you." I turned and dropped off the check at Table Eleven, pulled the empty glasses from Table Nine, and headed for the bar. I never made it. Francisco grabbed me, pulled me past the hostess station and out the front door. Snow blew across my face and my skirt flapped against my hips.

"There's my cab." He pointed toward a taxi idling across the street, then grabbed my shoulders and stared at me hard. I was terrified that he would kiss me but he traced my cheek with his finger. His touch was surprisingly gentle. "You have the damnedest bones," he whispered. His breath smelled of alcohol and mints, and I closed my eyes, tilting my face up toward him. "Such nice bones," he murmured. My knees wobbled, my throat tightened. When he finally kissed me, it wasn't a kiss so much as a flutter of his lips against mine, so soft and fleeting that it reminded me of holding a hurt bird in my hand as a child, how light the wings had felt, how delicate and warm and fragile.

"Merry, merry," he whispered against my hair. I watched him run across the street in his ridiculous sweater. He was slightly pigeon-toed, his left leg kicking back at an awkward angle, and this caused my throat to choke up. Part of me wanted to run after him, take a chance, be brave, but I was saved by Mr. Tims.

"Table Twelve's bitching about the red sauce and the woman on Table

Nine says the halibut's off," he yelled, holding the restaurant door open for me. "Christ, you're all wet." He brushed snow from my shoulders. "Fucking Christmas," he said, and I followed him back to the dining room.

"What did he say?" Sandee asked when we met in the bathroom at the end of her shift. "Did he kiss you?"

"Sort of." I couldn't meet her eyes.

"Ha! Now you know how it feels. Here." She fished a cigarette out of her pocket and handed it to me. "Marlboro—unfiltered, too. A guy at the bar brought them up from Texas."

"Thanks." I held the unlit cigarette against my mouth, the sting of tobacco puckering my lips.

"No problem." Sandee shrugged sympathetically. "You would have done the same for me."

Chapter 14

Sunday, Dec. 25

IT'S PAST MIDNIGHT and everyone is asleep: Jay-Jay, Laurel, and Stephanie. I'm sitting at the kitchen table, Killer curled across my feet. I can see the Christmas tree lights flashing in the living room, cheery smears of blue and green, the colors Jay-Jay insisted upon this year.

It was a good day, and it all began with the Oprah Giant's Christmas message.

"The holiday season is about giving," she wrote, and this time it was in red-and-green script with candy canes dancing about the periods. "Most of us think we are giving, but we're not. We're merely going through the motions."

She asked us to list everything we planned on giving this year and then list them in correlation as to how hard it was to give. I jotted down all the gifts I had bought, and I had to admit that beside the financial aspects, everything was lightweight. Nothing altered anything inside of me or made me feel as if I were changing a life, which the Oprah Giant said was the true meaning of giving.

"The hardest gifts are the ones that take away a piece of ourselves," she said. "Not a monetary debt but a debt of our psyche." She challenged us to give at least one such gift. "It might hurt," she warned. "You might feel sad or even resentful, but don't worry. The beauty of the universe is that when you give freely from your heart, you receive back more."

I was busying pondering this message when Laurel snuck up beside me.

"Do you remember those purple mittens I used to have?" She sat cross-legged on the living room floor, where I had been sleeping on Barry's old camping mat, my usual bed, now that Laurel had claimed my bedroom.

"Shhhh," I whispered, pointing up to where Stephanie snored happily from the couch.

"Soft purple, not that hard shade they have now. Muted like a heartbeat. I wore them with my yellow coat, remember?"

I nodded; I remembered no such thing.

"That's what I want for Christmas."

"Mittens from your childhood?" The idea appealed to me. Maybe this was what the Giant had meant. I could run to Fred Meyer tomorrow morning and buy a pair, check my good deed off the list, and be rewarded with instant karma.

"Listen." Laurel scooted closer until her butt nestled against my hip. "What would you do if someone said you could go back in time and change one thing? Would you do it?"

"Jesus, I don't know."

"But here's the catch," she continued. "You might not end up where you are today. Changing that one thing might make it impossible to get back to where you are now. But wait, you might end up somewhere better, the place you've always dreamed of." Her voice rose, and she waved her hands excitedly.

"Mom?" Jay-Jay called from his bedroom. "Can I get up now?"

We have a rule that no presents are to be opened until seven a.m., though we never manage to stick to it. "Might as well," I called back.

Laurel tapped my shoulder. "Could you give up what you have now for the chance of meeting your utopia?"

I stared at her dumbly. All I could think of was Insectopia, from the *Antz* movie. The ants' paradise turned out to be the crumbs of a human picnic. I was explaining this to Laurel when Jay-Jay raced into the room, his face flushed, his pajama top turned inside out.

"Time to organize the presents," he yelled. Stephanie muttered but slept on. "Mom, you get the medium ones, Aunt Laurel the small ones. Me, I'll grab the big guys. They're probably for me anyway."

We grabbed presents and stacked them in piles according to the name tags. Jay-Jay's pile was the biggest, of course; Christmas is for kids, after all. But Stephanie's was nothing to sneeze about, either. Laurel, concerned about Stephanie's welfare, had dragged herself out of bed last week to buy two hundred dollars' worth of "top-notch teen clothes" at the Gap. I imagined Stephanie pairing a Gap T-shirt with a skirt made from old bath towels, or expensive low-slung jeans with a halter stitched from kitchen curtains.

"Okay," Jay-Jay shrieked, Killer dancing around him. "One-two-three: open!"

He grabbed the first package, a medium-sized box from Laurel. "Wait! You gotta wake Stephanie. Everyone *has* to be up. It's the tradition."

I reached over and shook Stephanie's arm.

"Huph?" she groaned. "Umpf."

"You need to sit up and open your eyes," I told her. "Apparently it's the tradition."

"Oh-my-god, it's Christmas." She flew off the couch in her men's boxer shorts and sweatshirt that said, "Reindeers do it with red noses." Her skinny legs were covered with inked fragments of poems she often wrote across her skin before falling asleep. "This is totally going to be the best holiday ever." She sat down happily next to Jay-Jay, the Christmas lights flashing across her red-and-green-streaked hair.

"Yours are over there." I nodded with my head and Stephanie squealed.

"Oh—Mrs. Richards, you shouldn't have. You're a single mother. You're totally at the bottom of the economic infrastructure."

And so we commenced to open. We thanked and remarked and complimented and appreciated. Even Laurel seemed genuinely pleased with her gifts, most of which were for the baby, the sex of which was still undetermined, though Gramma had insisted it was a girl. Jay-Jay gave me the framed mathematical code he had fashioned out of macaroni, Laurel gave me a gift certificate to Safeway, and Stephanie handed me a book of self-published poems titled *seals and smells of water*. It was cheaply put together and didn't contain any capitals; tears came to my eyes as I browsed through it.

"I'm totally in love with E. E. Cummings this month," she said with a blush. "Last month it was Adrienne Rich even though she's, like, super old."

Jay-Jay made out with the laptop Barry and I got him, plus computer gadgets, video games, and a horrid brown sweater from Laurel that he immediately pulled on over his pajama top. Jay-Jay is like that, considerate of others' feelings. Later, he'll complain about this sweater, but he'll never let on in front of Laurel.

Hammie and Sandee showed up for dinner, though Barry wasn't able to make it. We normally shared half days on holidays, which usually meant we ended up spending them together; it was easier that way. This year he had headed back to see his folks in Idaho, and his plane had been delayed in Seattle.

"I'm afraid of what Joe got me," Sandee said, as we relaxed around the table with red wine after dinner. Jay-Jay was out in the living room playing *Paper Mario* with Steph and Hammie.

"Men aren't the best shoppers," Laurel agreed. She was drinking grape juice with seltzer water and let out a soft burp every now and then. "Junior once got me a book on sailing and I don't even own a pair of deck shoes. Can you imagine?" She swilled half the glass before slamming it down. "Well, fuck it," she said. "Fuck them all." She smiled bravely with grape-stained teeth.

Barry called a few hours later and asked if I could pick him up from the airport. His voice sounded shaky; turbulence had been bad.

"Guy across from me shot his drink right out of his hand, all over this fat lady sitting next to him," he said when I met him at the baggage terminal. His face was pale and he needed a shave. "Next thing you know, they was cozy and laughing. Heard him ask her out."

He grabbed his suitcase, which was duct-taped across the front. "How's your mom and dad?" I asked.

Barry sighed. "Good as can be. Dad's thinking of retiring."

"He says that every year."

Barry grunted. Outside, the wind was sharp, the sky clear, the stars opaque in the city lights. By the time we got to the car the windshield had frosted over.

"Gonna come over?" Barry asked.

Another holiday tradition was that Barry and I always fucked on Christmas, during the long lull of the evening after the presents had been opened and our stomachs were bloated from too much rich, sugary food. I gripped the steering wheel and drove slowly over the icy roads until we hit the turnout area for Earthquake. I pulled in and turned toward Barry.

"We have to stop," I said.

"I know." This was his usual reply. I took Barry's face between my palms, the face I knew so well, the one I used to trace with my tongue, the face I used to love to wake up to each morning, a lifetime ago when we were different people who wanted different things.

"I'm stopping," I said, leaning forward and kissing him on the mouth. His lips were chapped, and I drank in everything I once loved about him, everything that I once hated. Then I pressed my lips harder and gave him back the parts of myself that cherished him: I gave him back my adoration, my love, my belief in his stumbling goodwill.

"But it's Christmas." His voice was slightly whining, with an edge of disbelief.

"That's why," I said. I didn't say more. Maybe I would tell him later, when we were older and Jay-Jay was grown and we were both married to other people. I'd tell him how leaving for good, stopping all traces of sex between us, was my gift to him. It was the one thing he needed me to do, the one thing he couldn't do himself, so I gave him his freedom and with that the possibility of finding someone who loves him the way he deserves to be loved, fully and completely, with no holding back. I couldn't do that when we were married. I don't know if it was because I didn't have it in me at the time or if he was never the man for me. It's almost as if we were children together, and once we grew up, we looked around and wondered how in the hell we had ended up together.

"We'll still see each other," I said stupidly. "We just won't, you know. Fuck."

Barry didn't say anything. His jaw was rigid and terrible.

"Say something, damn it," I yelled.

He reached out and traced my cheekbone with the tip of his finger, almost the same gesture Francisco had made.

"Remember them peanut butter cookies?" Barry said.

My stomach lurched with grief, and suddenly I understood that this was a real gift, the kind the Oprah Giant had been talking about.

"Yeah." I wanted to reach out and take his hand, but I didn't. "Those were the best cookies."

And they were. Because here's a shameful secret, one shared by no one but Barry and me: I almost didn't have Jay-Jay. I almost had a second abortion. We weren't in a good place in our lives. We had no money, we were living in a roach-infested apartment, and I was terrified of having a child. Barry was the one who saved me. Barry, who had never stuck to anything in his life, who was the king of noncommitment. He rubbed my feet when gas pains tore through my belly, carried the TV in from the living room on those days when the nausea swirled my head and I felt marooned to my bed. He soothed me with navy bean soup and Parker House rolls, vegetarian lasagna and garlic biscuits, and later held my hair back away from my face when I threw up those very meals he cooked with such attention.

My morning sickness never subsided after the first trimester, the way all the books promised it would, and the doctor, a cheerful young woman from Georgia, simply shrugged her shoulders and said that it happened sometimes. I quit my waitressing job, stayed home, and read romance novels with covers of brooding dark men chasing women whose boobs were about to bounce out of their dresses. I touched myself and imagined old lovers with a yearning that bordered on the obsessive.

Meanwhile, Barry worked two jobs to save up for the baby. He had become an almost model employee, showing up on time and not hiding out in the bathroom during the more tedious chopping and dicing that took place in the beginning of each shift. He worked banquets and large weddings and volunteered for the governor's banquet even though he wasn't a Republican.

At night when I felt lonely and scared and woke Barry and asked him what he would do if I died in childbirth, he said all the right things, explaining how he would have my body cremated and scattered over the beach down in Homer, and how he would tell our daughter or son all about me, and that while he might marry for the child's sake, he would never, ever love anyone as much as he loved me. Right before I'd fall back to sleep he'd put on his bathrobe, clomp on down to the kitchen, and take four peanut butter cookies from the freezer, microwave them for fifteen seconds, and bring them up to me with a mug of milk. Barry made these cookies on the weekends, and they were sweet and rich with chunks of almonds and walnuts and just the faintest twinge of banana extract. I'd wake hours later to the smell of peanut butter against my nose, reach out my tongue, and lick the crumbs up in the dark.

BARRY'S PEANUT BUTTER COOKIES

- 1 cup margarine
- 2 tablespoons plus 1 teaspoon vanilla extract
- 2 eggs
- 1½ cups crunchy peanut butter
- 1 cup whole wheat flour
- 1 cup white flour

- 1 cup brown sugar
- 1 cup white sugar
- 1 teaspoon baking powder
- 1 teaspoon baking soda
- Pinch of salt
- ¼ cup chopped walnuts
- ¼ cup chopped almonds
- ¼ cup chopped peanuts
- Splash banana extract

Preheat oven to 350°. Mix margarine, vanilla, and eggs, slowly folding in peanut butter. In a separate bowl, sift together flour, sugar, baking powder, baking soda, and salt. Slowly add to the wet mixture, along with the nuts. When the dough is smooth, roll out small balls, crisscross with a fork, and place on an ungreased cookie sheet to bake at 350° for 10–12 minutes. Eat while still warm and then sit back, fold your hands over your stomach like a smug little Buddha, and smile.

LESSON FIVE

Loosening the Load

It's time to clean out your emotional wardrobe. That cowl-necked resentment from the '80s—good-bye! Those high-rise ambitions that pinch your waist—so long! That flirty boyfriend with last year's hemline—good riddance! Girlfriend, don't stop now! Those stodgy self-concepts, those self-pitying accessories, those unbuttoned morals—gone, gone, gone. The next time you dress, your emotional self will finally match the well-groomed person you see in the mirror.

—*The Oprah Giant*

Chapter 15

Tuesday, Jan. 3

"YOU GOT SOMETHIN' UP FRONT," the hostess told me, as I hurriedly slammed side salads onto my tray. "That blond guy? He says to give it to you 'fore you left."

"Francisco? He's supposed to be in Fairbanks."

"He came when you were serving that big table." She plucked a crouton off one of my salads and plopped it in her mouth. "Wanna see?"

I followed the hostess as she weaved her way back up to the lobby. She leaned behind the hostess stand and retrieved a box. It was covered in red tissue paper, with the words "Adidas Trainer" pushing up through the thin wrapping.

"Did he say anything else?"

"Nah, he looked in a hurry." She stared at the box. "He got big feet though, size twelve. That ain't nothin' to sneeze at."

I wanted to open the box, which thumped deliciously when I shook it. At the same time, I didn't want to because I was certain it would be a disappointment: a fruitcake or an ugly pair of socks. Probably he regifted something from his office Christmas party and gave it to me to start the New Year off fresh, no blights or misdeeds by his name. I jammed the box into my work locker and tried to forget about it, but I couldn't. Throughout the rest of the afternoon, as I carried out plates of steaming enchiladas and pollo fundidos, I could feel the box waiting in the dark, nestled cozily beside my boots and winter coat.

I still hadn't opened it by the time I picked Jay-Jay up from school.

"Oh wow, another present." He grabbed it from the backseat and gave it a hearty shake. "Who's it from, that Mr. Tims guy?"

"It's not yours, it's, well, mine." I felt myself blushing. "From someone at work, a customer to, uh, thank me."

"Oh." He lost interest. "Did you know that Mark Twain was born and died in the year of Halley's Comet? That's, like, practically impossible."

"I suppose it is." I eased my foot on the brake and slowed down as a police car pulled up in the lane beside us.

"His real name was Samuel Clemens. That's a dumb name, huh?" He tapped his fingers on the box. "Can I change my name when I'm older?"

"Why would you want to do that?"

"I'm the only one in the *whole* school with a hyphen in my name, except the divorced kids." He glared at me as I signaled to turn on Spenard Road.

"So take out the hyphen," I said.

"Jay sounds dumb, like a baseball player."

I pulled into the driveway and shut off the engine. "Here." Jay-Jay shoved the wrapped box into my hands. "I'm not carrying in *your* stuff." He ran up the steps, his backpack bopping up and down. I stuffed the box under my coat and hurried past Laurel and Stephanie, who sat in the living room cutting pictures out of magazines.

"Well, don't bother asking how *my* day was," Laurel yelled as I passed. "It's not as if I've been sitting on my ass doing nothing the whole time."

I veered into the bathroom, locked the door, and climbed inside the dry bathtub, which smelled comfortingly of damp soap and dirty feet.

"You going to be long?" Laurel yelled again. "I'll need to pee again in about, oh, five minutes."

I counted to three and tore off the wrapping paper. Inside was an ordinary shoe box with a Sports Authority price sticker on the side for $109.99; obviously Francisco favored expensive athletic shoes. I placed my hands on the top and was ready to lift when I realized that I was living out the scene from one of my *Woman Running with a Box* paintings. I was getting ready to open the box! I sucked in my breath and slowly lifted the lid. Inside was more tissue paper, green this time. I paused for a moment, not sure I really wanted to continue, but of course I did, so I pushed the paper aside and gasped, my elbow knocking over a shampoo bottle. There, tucked inside the box, was a thick white bone, a red ribbon tied jauntily around the middle. It was gruesome, bizarre; I didn't know whether to be offended or moved. After all, Francisco was an anthropologist; bones were what he did, so in that sense he was giving me a part of his life. I picked it up. It was smooth and polished, beautiful in an odd sense. I was fairly certain it was a femur, since there was a rounded knob at the top that resembled the head of a penis. I folded the tissue paper and placed the bone back in the box. I had no idea why he had given me this peculiar gift. Still, he had made a move, taken a chance. It was brave, like a lone voice calling out, not sure if anyone would answer.

"Are you done yet?" Laurel's own voice yelled out. "I have about a minute before my bladder explodes."

I flushed the toilet and ran the water, and right before I left I tucked the box in the linen closet behind the extra towels, giving it a little pat before I closed the door.

"What took you so long?" Laurel demanded when I finally emerged, blinking in the flashing lights of the Christmas tree I still hadn't taken down. "I thought I'd have to use a bowl." She pushed past me and slammed the bathroom door.

Wednesday, Jan. 4

"It looks like we're finally going to *do it* this weekend." Sandee and I stood at the Mexico in an Igloo bar separating coffee filters and watching *Judge Judy* on the large-screen television. We had a few minutes before Mr. Tims opened the door and Sandee was using it to brief me on her latest Joe update. "He sent me flowers with a key attached to the note: Dimond Center Hotel, with little kiss marks across the bottom."

"Roses?"

"Worse, dried violets and wildflowers. He picked them himself last summer." She smacked an obstinate bundle of coffee filters against the bar to loosen them up.

"He didn't know you last summer."

"That's what I said, but he just shrugged and clicked his tongue against the inside of his cheek. It's what he does whenever he's feeling unsure, and damned if I don't start clicking my tongue along with him."

My tongue involuntarily clicked against my cheek.

"Stop that!" Sandee grabbed the coffee filters out of my hands. "When I think of sleeping with him, my stomach hurts."

"In a good way?"

"What's the difference?" I followed as she marched out to the pantry and shuffled through her locker for her apron and waitressing book. "If your stomach hurts, it hurts. Who cares if it's warning or anticipation?"

"Francisco got me a bone."

"Huh?" Sandee stopped midway from pulling her hair up into a ponytail. "Did you say bone?"

"Wrapped in tissue paper and stuck in a box. I haven't told anyone, not even Laurel."

"Wow, is it human?"

"I don't know. He's an anthropologist, so it's possible."

"That's creepy." Sandee looked interested in me for the first time all morning. "Was there a note?"

"No, but it was clean."

She finished with her hair and then helped pull mine back. "You need to thank him but not too much. You can't act too interested until he reveals his intentions. For all you know, he has another girlfriend or even a wife stashed somewhere. Trust me, I've seen it all these past couple of years."

"Thanks." My hair was pulled so tight it hurt to move my mouth.

"Maybe we should get makeovers or haircuts." Sandee examined her face in the mirror behind the pie case. "Something sleek and expensive. Think it would make us feel better?"

"No."

She sighed. "Probably we need to go out and shoot again. I can see how these things evolve, first cans and then small animals, birds, and finally large mammals."

"With a BB gun?"

"I'm just saying . . . Damn it, he's going to win, isn't he?"

"Joe? Well, you could end up winning, too."

"Yeah, right." She slammed a ladle into the salad dressing and turned so fast she bumped into me. "Why do we waste so much fucking time talking about men?"

Thursday, Jan. 5

Junior calls every evening and leaves the same message on Laurel's cell: "Laurel, we need to talk. Call me—my cell is always on."

Laurel listens to these over and over before deleting with a triumphant little cry.

"He misses you," I tell her. "He had pizza stains on his shirt when I went over a few weeks ago. He sagged like an old blanket."

"So?" Laurel puts her hands on her hips, tilts her head forward. "Now he's sorry? Now he wants to change?"

I don't mention that Laurel was the one who had the affair. Marriages are complex, and there's never just one perspective or one person to blame. This morning as we watched the first half hour of *The Price Is Right,* crumbs falling over my last clean waitressing blouse, Laurel asked me to make her warm milk. "With a little bit of cinnamon," she added, patting her belly, which was quickly expanding. I got up, splashed milk in a pan, and stirred in cinnamon and sugar. Right before it came to a boil I added a dab of vanilla, Gramma's little secret, then set the mug down in front of Laurel and turned down the TV; I had the feeling something big was coming. Her hands shook slightly as she drank.

"There's nothing like hot milk, is there?" she said. "Maybe it reminds us of our mothers, do you think, Carly? Do you think we crave milk late at night because we crave having someone take care of us?"

"Probably."

"When I married Junior, I thought he'd take care of me." Laurel held the mug up to her face, the steam rising against her chin.

"I told Junior about Hank when I went over to get some of my things yesterday," she continued in a weary voice, and I nodded because I remembered how she looked when she straggled back home, her face pale, her mascara smeared beneath her eyes. "Afterward he thanked me, can you believe that? As if I had just finished testifying in court. 'Thank you, Laurel,' he said in the crisp, professional voice he reserves for work. It would have been easier if he had gotten mad." She set her mug down on the coffee table with a bang. "But he couldn't get mad, that's the big secret stretching out between us." She laughed harshly. "Remember when we moved up here? We didn't come here because of work or because either one of us particularly *wanted* to live in Anchorage. Oh, we lied and pretended we did, but really we came because I insisted. I said, 'Alaska or the door.' It took Junior two days to decide."

"But I thought—"

"I know. That's what we wanted you to think. The truth? Junior was having an affair with one of the interns. An eighteen-year-old who turned out to really be sixteen. He could have been charged with statutory rape; it would have been a death sentence for his career, but the parents agreed to forget the whole thing if we left town."

"Junior?" I couldn't imagine him capable of grand passions, but then again, you never really know a man until you've slept with him. Energetic men can be the laziest lovers. It's the soft-spoken, intellectual types who often turn out to be the most inventive.

"He wanted to go to California or Washington, but I said Alaska. I wanted somewhere safe, and you were here. I knew that anytime I could have told you, and you would have shrugged like it was no big deal and offered one of your own stories in return."

"Oh, Laurel." I reached out to grip her hands in mine but she fought me off.

"No, there's more. I told Junior about the baby, and he started to yell and suddenly stopped; I could tell he was remembering. It was as if someone had pricked him with a pin and all of his air was leaking out. It was like watching someone die.

"Then he pulled his shoulders back and walked out the door. He didn't even slam it; he closed it very soft, almost gently. I packed up and was gone before he came back. I didn't want to see his face—what could we possibly say? There is nowhere to go from here. Every time he looks at this baby he's not going to see a child, he's going to see all of our mistakes stretching between us."

Laurel clutched her belly and sobbed, mascara leaking across her face. She made no move to wipe it off; she sat there and offered me all of her sadness and pain, and how could I possibly accept it when I had so much of my own? Yet I did. I took her too-straight shoulders in my hands, leaned over, and kissed her on the mouth. Her lips were soft and tangy and so much like my own it was as if I were kissing myself, kissing away my own pain and troubles, the ugliness and brutality I knew I was capable of.

She wiped her mouth and gave me a shaky smile.

"Love is a terrible thing, isn't it?" she whispered. "An awful, horrible thing."

I didn't tell her what Junior had said about wanting a baby the night I had gone to the house to look for her blouse. Maybe I would tell her later, or maybe I would wait and see if he had the guts to tell her himself. I turned up the TV. A fat woman got ready to drop her last Plinko chip. The first two had fallen into the zero slot, and for some reason this cheered us up. I smeared peanut butter over two more crackers and handed one to Laurel. We bit down at the exact same time. I grunted contentedly.

Friday, Jan. 6

This week I'm supposed to keep a gratitude journal, that's what the Oprah Giant called it. "The only way to truly appreciate what you have is to give it a name," she wrote. "This is the beginning of grace."

I don't know about the grace part: what, exactly, does that mean? The only Grace I ever knew picked her nose and sat ahead of me in fourth grade. Nevertheless, I've been jotting notes on Post-its and Jay-Jay's old spelling tests, my gratitude splayed across the house on grubby scraps of paper.

"Jay-Jay's wit," I wrote over the electric bill, which I still haven't remembered to pay. "Laurel's car," I wrote the morning my own car refused to start in minus-twelve-degree temperatures. "Stephanie's poems. Sandee's soft breasts when she hugs me. Barry's dumb optimism. Killer Bee's lopsided nose."

Probably I should be casting about for grander graces and writing about how my needs are miraculously being filled, my old hurts from childhood suddenly soothed. But many of my needs haven't been met and parts of my childhood can still reduce me to tears. I *am* grateful for Jay-Jay and Laurel, though, and Stephanie and Sandee, Barry and even Francisco, whom I'm afraid to know but still appreciate.

I am grateful. At least some of the time. All of the time?

Some of the time.

Thinking of this made me so melancholy that I poured a shot of Baileys Irish Cream into my tea, and then I went back for a second shot, and a third. I paced the house, eventually wandering into the bathroom, where I felt behind the towels for Francisco's bone. The minute my fingers grazed the cold surface, I became furious. Who did he think he was, giving me a bone? A bone! Did he think I was a fucking dog? I swigged Baileys straight from the bottle and fumed. By the time Stephanie and Jay-Jay returned from the high school basketball game, I had reached that state of drunken self-pity.

"We lost again," Stephanie interrupted as she and Jay-Jay slammed into the house.

"There was a fight during halftime. Between two *girls*." Jay-Jay's face was smeared with chocolate. "The tall one got a bloody nose. It was so cool."

"Two cheerleaders," Stephanie explained. "One had totally been two-timing with the other's dude. The principal tried to break it up and they scratched him across the face."

"How come I always miss the good stuff?" I hiccupped, covering my mouth so they wouldn't smell the sweet Baileys' fumes. "It's after ten, mister," I told Jay-Jay as I squinted at the clock, which swayed back and forth. "School will be here soon."

"Your voice sounds funny," he complained as he headed off to the bathroom.

"My voice *feels* funny," I yelled back.

"Chill, Mrs. Richards." Stephanie snapped her gum. "You're totally wound tight."

"That's it!" I pounded the table. Stephanie jumped. "Get your shoes, I need a chauffeur."

"You're drunk." Her voice was disapproving.

"It's just a few miles," I insisted. "Laurel's here in case Jay-Jay needs anything." I jammed my boots on the wrong feet. "How do I look?" My coat was inside out, my sweatpants stained with hot chocolate.

"Okay, I guess." Stephanie picked up the keys. "But I'm totally not going to a liquor store."

"Francisco's," I said as I followed her to the car, the cold air causing my head to ache. "Over past Earthquake Park."

"I don't think that's a good idea, Mrs. Richards." Stephanie started the car as I fumbled with my seat belt. "You're sloshed and he'll be, like, who is this woman? He'll totally lose respect for you."

"Good!" I haltingly gave the directions I had memorized from MapQuest during a melancholy lull last week, and a few minutes later Stephanie pulled up in front of a pinkish-orange house with trees cluttering the yard.

"Ugly color but gutsy," Stephanie said. "Think he's married?"

"I don't know." It was an awful thought.

"Want me to come in for, like, support?"

I thought of her punching the guy in the belly at the abortion clinic but shook my head no. "Oh, shit!" I cried as I opened the door. "I forgot the bone."

Stephanie cleared her throat nervously. "I'll just wait here for you, Mrs. Richards. Just don't make it long. You only have a quarter of a tank."

I walked up the driveway feeling strong and vengeful. I pounded the door. Francisco answered on the third knock wearing a black T-shirt and a pair of pajama bottoms printed with Scottie dogs.

"Carlita," he said, surprised. I staggered against the doorframe and waited for him to invite me in. We peered awkwardly at one another.

"A bone," I finally said. "What the hell was that supposed to mean?"

"Oh," he laughed. "It was, well." He didn't say anything else. He had his glasses on and his eyes were greener than I remembered. I glanced down at his feet, which were bare and looked cold, and I started to cry.

"Don't," he said, his voice gentle. I wiped my nose on my coat sleeve, mortified. I knew I should leave but I couldn't move. "Want to come in?" he finally asked. I nodded and followed him into the book-lined living room littered with driftwood, bones, and colored glass. "I like to collect things from the beach." He shrugged, his face reddening. "Most of it came from down around Homer. That raven wing there? That was outside of Hope; I had to fight another guy for it. Ended up costing me forty bucks and three beers."

"Why?" I asked.

"I thought it was beautiful, lying there in the middle of the road like a—"

"Not that." I stomped my foot. "The phone calls, the breathing, the asking me out and not showing up, and now a bone? What the fuck kind of game are you playing?" I could smell the alcohol on my breath. "I'm not drunk," I said defensively.

Francisco ran his hand through his hair. "I wanted to get to know you better." He looked at me hard. "I've had a rough time. This isn't easy for me, either."

I looked frantically around. "I thought you had dogs." My voice was accusing.

"In the backyard," he said, moving toward me. I looked around in alarm. The room was small and cluttered; there was nowhere to run.

"I have to go." I zipped my coat and turned to leave, but then I thought, in my blurry, drunken haze: what would the Oprah Giant do? I doubted that she would walk away from a man like Francisco, especially when he had such a goofy, lovesick look on his face. I felt my legs moving forward, heard my grandmother's voice counting in Polish: *Jeden*, and I took one step forward. *Dwa*, and I took a second step. *Trzy*, and I was standing in front of him. *Cztery*, and my arms reached out to him. *Pięć*, and I was in his arms. *Sześć*, and we were moving across the room in a clumsy, awkward dance, my face pressed against his neck, the heat of his breath tickling my hair. *Siedem, osiem, dziewięć*, and we were in the hallway. *Dziesięć*, and we waltzed in our hideous way toward the bed. *Jedenaście*, and my shirt was off, and we were no longer dancing. I pulled his shirt off, too, and his chest was smooth and warm. "Stephanie's out in the car," I whispered, as he traced the curve of my spine.

"I know," he said. "I peeked from the window. You almost stepped in dog poop on the way in."

Hearing him say that caused tears to come to my eyes. It was the most romantic thing anyone had ever said to me. We held each other like that, on his bed, our bare chests pressed together, the beat of our hearts thudding away the seconds.

"Sorry," I said to Stephanie when I finally made it back out to the car. She was reading a poetry book called *the fever almanac*, which had a woman's nyloned leg over the cover. She looked up and shrugged.

"It's retro. You totally needed to get laid." She fastened her seat belt and jerked the car into drive.

"I didn't," I said. "Just, you know, touching."

"Touching is totally the best part," Stephanie agreed. I looked out the window and watched houses and snow-covered yards flash past, my belly doing happy little flip-flops, my nose still filled with Francisco's scent. When we stopped for the traffic light on Minnesota Drive, I looked over at Stephanie. She sat straight, her shoulders relaxed, her pleasant face opened and vulnerable. I could imagine her twenty years from now, older but still as strong, still making it through on guts and good nature.

"You're going to make it, you know? I mean in life. You're going to do okay, Stephanie."

"Oh, well." It was the first time I had ever seen her blush. "I'm totally . . . it's just, Mrs. Richards, I have been working my ass off for, like, my whole life trying to rise above the family fiasco. It's totally exhausting. My soul is wrinkly and aged from such unflinching effort."

I didn't believe it. If anything, Stephanie's soul shined brighter than anyone's. I wanted to tell her this, but it would have embarrassed her and besides, I think she already knew.

Chapter 16

Saturday, Jan. 7

"Jesus, look what the sled dog dragged in," Mr. Tims said to Sandee as he whipped ranch dressing and horseradish sauce together for tonight's prime rib special. Sandee looked awful, her skirt wrinkled, her blouse splattered with a couple of days' worth of grease, and instead of the perky high-heeled shoes she always wore, she had on a pair of scuffed hiking boots. Her feet looked enormous and ungainly as she clomped around the pantry picking up her order.

"I haven't been sleeping well," she admitted, slamming a beef burrito onto her tray. "Not that it's anyone's business. Damn it, where's my pico de gallo?" She hefted her tray to her shoulder and lifted it above her head; there were sweat stains beneath her arms, but I kept my mouth shut and followed her out to the dining room with the missing salsa.

"There you go. Doesn't that look good?" Sandee's voice was high and fake as she served the plates, enchilada sauce splashing a fattish man's lap. "Sorry, honey." She pulled napkins from the extra supply she kept tucked in the bosom of her blouse. "Some days it's all shit."

"Isn't that the truth," the man replied a little too heartily.

"Cig dig," I hissed. "Five minutes."

"Yeah, yeah," she muttered. A few minutes later we crammed together in the far handicap bathroom stall, since it was too windy to stand outside. I let Sandee sit on the toilet, since she was the worse off, while I leaned up against the sink.

"So what's up?" I asked

She tapped the heels of her hiking boots together three times, like Dorothy in *The Wizard of Oz*. "Nothing," she said defensively.

"This is about what happened at the hotel Saturday, isn't it?"

"I said, nothing happened."

"Nothing?" My voice raised in disbelief.

"We curled up in bed and watched a foreign movie without subtitles, and then he fell asleep. He snores, though not consistently. More like a stutter."

"You sure?" Sandee wasn't the kind of woman men lay beside in bed without initiating sex. She was too ripe, too lush. Seeing her in a bra and panties was like seeing a fuller-figured version of a Victoria's Secret model. She had that kind of sexual presence.

"It was a relief to lie there and hold hands and not worry if my stomach was too fat or if I should act less experienced than I really was. I slept so well. I don't think I've ever slept that way with a man before, not even Randall." She kicked at the toilet paper littering the floor. "It isn't good, is it? Lying there with him like that?"

"Probably not." I thought of how I had felt holding Francisco on his bed, how warm and safe it had felt, yet also scary, the way I had so quickly left my defenses behind. "I saw Francisco without his shirt on," I offered.

Sandee picked toilet paper off the bottoms of her hiking boots. "How was it?" she finally asked.

"We just held each other. Sort of like what you guys did." I felt momentarily ashamed, as if we had both failed to properly entice our men. Yet while I couldn't speak for Sandee, those few minutes of touching Francisco had been more intimate than any sex. "Maybe," I began hesitantly, "Maybe we're both falling in—"

"Don't!" Sandee held a sheet of toilet paper up like a shield as she pushed past me and stormed out of the stall. I caught up with her in the bar bumming a cigarette from a table of half-sloshed secretaries. It took three tries but she finally managed to light it. She inhaled and choked. "I'm going to marry him, aren't I?" Her eyes were hard and fierce. "I'm going to end up with a fish-and-game warden. We'll eat caribou steaks while dead animal heads watch us from the walls."

"I think you'll be h—"

"Happy?" She shouted. Heads turned. "Who the fuck ever said I wanted to be happy?"

Monday, Jan. 9

"Mom." Jay-Jay interrupted my nap by shaking my shoulder, but my eyes refused to open. "Wake up. There's something outside."

"Moose?" Last winter a moose got tangled in the neighbor's Christmas lights and the fish-and-game department had to tranquilize the poor thing before they could cut the wires from around its belly. I wondered if Sandee's Joe had been one of the bearded guys who had shown up with tranquilizer guns and nylon netting.

"Mom! You have to look." I popped open one eye. Jay-Jay stood before me with a peanut-butter-smeared face and wearing one of Stephanie's shirts with a picture of Santa Claus and the caption "Never trust a fat man."

"What?" I pulled the covers over my face, but Jay-Jay tugged them away.

"It's some kind of bone, I think from—"

I was out of the sleeping bag in a second, Jay-Jay and Killer following as I sprinted for the door.

"See?" Jay-Jay pointed to the snow-covered porch chair I had neglected to bring in. "There's a note but it's all soggy, something about—"

I snatched the note from his hands and stuffed it down my bra; the paper crinkled deliciously against my breasts. "Give me the bone." I held out my hand.

"But, Mom, it's a clavicle. See how it curves? Doesn't it look like a dragon wing?" Jay-Jay carried it inside and carefully set it on the kitchen table. "Maybe it's part of a secret code." He rubbed his hands excitedly. "We have to put it together to decipher the message. It could even be from the CIA."

"It's not the CIA," I said, removing the note from my bra and smoothing it over the table. "It's from Francisco." I skimmed over his slanted handwriting. "He's headed down to San Diego for a forensic anthropology conference."

"That guy from the phone?" Jay-Jay's voice rose. "Does Dad know?"

"There's nothing to know. He gave me a bone, that's all."

"I don't want to see it." Jay-Jay pushed the bone toward me. He looked upset.

"Honey, I know you love your dad and it's okay. I love your dad too, just not in the right way."

"You could try," he insisted. His voice trembled. "You could both try."

"It's too late." My voice was gentle.

"Growing up sucks." Jay-Jay slammed the clavicle on the table.

"It does," I agreed, wondering for the hundredth time how the divorce had affected Jay-Jay. There's no way he could have come out of it undamaged, though we tried to shield him from the worst of it.

The night Barry left for good, Jay-Jay was over at Laurel's. When she brought him back he raced through the door and stopped in the middle of the living room. "Dad?" he yelled, his face white, his heels raised as if to make himself taller. "Dad! Dad! Dad!"

I pulled him toward me. He was four at the time, his face round with the last of his baby fat. He kicked and punched, bit my arm, screamed and cried until I gathered him up and carried him to the rocking chair, where I rocked and smoothed his hair as I murmured, promising him things I had no right to promise. When he finally settled down, I carried him to bed and slept next to him the rest of the night, his chest shaking every so often as if even in his dreams he was fighting off loss.

Thinking about this made me so sad that I decided to make *kolachkes*, a Polish cookie Gramma whipped up when she was hit with the lonelies. As I cut the butter into the flour I missed Gramma so much my knees shook. I wanted her near; I wanted to smell the oniony reek of her sweat and feel the comforting pat of her paw-sized hands across my back.

After I filled each cookie with fruit, I wiped my face with the dish towel. "Let's take Killer out," I yelled to Jay-Jay, who was in his room doing homework.

It was a cold and quiet night. The snow drifted high against the trailers as we headed for the lagoon, Jay-Jay pulling his sled behind him until we reached the big hill across the street from the high school.

"Push me, Mom, hard," he ordered, and I pushed against the orange plastic sled until he was flying down the hill, Killer chasing after him and nipping at his jacket.

"Okay, now it's your turn," Jay-Jay said after his third trip down the hill. I situated my ass on the very small seat, tucked my legs across the narrow strip of plastic, and held tight to the sides. From a sitting-down position, the hill looked very big and very steep.

"Are you sure this is—," I started to say, and then I was zooming down the hill, picking up speed and jolting over bumps. I couldn't help hooting and hollering because there was something so benignly dangerous in the slap of the wind across my face and the scratch of the sled scraping ice. I veered to the left before I reached the bottom and crashed into a rock, my nose leaking blood over the snow.

"Wow, Mom, you're bleeding." Jay-Jay was impressed for once. He handed me his mitten, and I pressed it to my nose as he gathered the sled, called for the dog, and started for home. I followed his small back as we slipped and slid up the hill. Every so often he turned and patted my arm as if for encouragement.

"It should stop soon," he said. "Unless you have hemophilia, then you'll probably die."

I nodded and walked behind him and it was strange, almost as if he were taking care of me. I wanted to cry, not because I was sad but because I felt so full of the night, and the cold, and Jay-Jay's solid neck as he turned and shouted, "Mom, hey, Mom, let me know if you want to slow down, okay?"

Oh, children will break your heart, the way they leave, a little more each day, pulling and pulling, and no matter how much you long to pull them back, you have to let them go. You have to follow them until you know the shape of their shoulders, the set of their knees, the way their feet turn inward or outward as they move confidently away from you.

GRAMMA'S KOLACHKES

- ¼ cup yogurt, fruit or regular
- 1 package yeast
- 1 egg
- 1 cup shortening (butter works best)
- 2 cups flour
- ½ teaspoon baking powder
- ¼ teaspoon salt
- Jelly or canned fruit

Preheat oven to 375°. Mix yogurt and yeast together and let set 10 minutes and then add egg. Cut butter in with dry ingredients and roll out dough. Cut into circular shapes and make a thumbprint in the middle of each one. Fill with jelly or canned fruit. Bake 10–15 minutes. Sprinkle with sugar while still hot. Then tuck a napkin across your lap to catch crumbs as you stuff the cookies into your mouth. If you need extra filling, spoon in preserves or canned fruit. Still feel lonely? Have another one. And another. Eat the whole damned batch by yourself.

Wednesday, Jan. 11

Uh-oh.

"Do you know how much you owe on your credit cards?" the Oprah Giant wrote in perky green script in today's blog. "Then you'd better figure it out, girlfriend!" she continued. "Overspending isn't a sign of prosperity; it's a sign of insecurity and a lack of self-respect."

That was easy for someone with three best sellers and a cushy motivational speaker job to say, but I'd bet my ass that even the Oprah Giant couldn't make it on a waitress's salary without going into serious debt. I dumped my unopened mail across the table and tore at the envelopes. I had been paying a good chunk of my Saturday shift wages to lower my balances and they were lower, granted. Still, seeing the numbers in staid black ink was startling: how could I owe so much and still have so little?

I followed the Oprah Giant's advice and wrote letters requesting payment plans to all of my debtors. Thankfully, she had included a form letter to edit (i.e., copy word for word).

The next step was to cut up all but two of my credit cards, one hidden in a hard-to-reach location for emergencies and the other kept in the freezer and thawed out only for essential purchases.

"You'll feel deprived the first few weeks," the Giant wrote. "You might even have a temper tantrum or two because, face it, owing money isn't the most adult decision you've ever made."

I ate three brownies, two cookies, and the chocolate bar Jay-Jay had hidden in his nightstand before spreading my credit cards over the table. Their plastic faces shone in the overhead light, so bright and cheerful! They were like friends, flashing their sixteen-digit numbers and promising me all the things I wanted but couldn't afford. I picked up the scissors, gritted my teeth, and sliced through a Gap card, followed by Capital One, American Express, Old Navy, and Alaska Bank Visa. After I destroyed my stash, I hid my Alaska Airlines Visa in the ceiling tiles above the TV. Then I filled a Ziploc bag with water and placed my Denali Credit Union MasterCard in the freezer, where it sagged forlornly against a bag of Tater Tots.

"Did you remember to get yogurt?" Laurel straggled into the kitchen, rubbing her eyes. It was five thirty at night and she was just getting up. "The kind with the fruit at the bottom, not mixed." She yawned and sat down at the table, totally unconcerned with why I was shoving pieces of hacked-up credit cards into an empty orange juice carton.

"It's so I can't fit them back together and online shop," I explained, but she ignored me and reached for a cookie. "Okay, I owe a little on my credit cards." I threw down the orange juice container and waited for her to reprimand me, but nothing came. Laurel was still in a funk. Two nights ago she had met with Hank to tell him about the pregnancy. He held her hand and said all the right things. Then he promptly changed his phone number and e-mail account and had her name blacklisted at his office. Laurel had told me this story three times already, and I was afraid she was getting ready to tell me again, but she let out a dramatic sigh and reached for her laptop instead. I sat down across from her and browsed the University of Alaska art brochure I had picked up at the college.

"I met this guy," I heard myself tell Laurel. "He's this customer at work, an anthropologist with the most amazing hands. He touches me as if I were an artifact, like I'm worthy of praise." I paused for a moment, embarrassed at my level of intensity, but she was busy tap-tap-tapping away at her laptop, so I continued. "I went out with him but he never showed; the evening was a disaster so I thought, okay, that's that. But then he gives me a bone, a femur. Then we necked on his bed, but nothing more. Until a few days ago, and then a clavicle appears on my doorstep. Is that creepy, do you think? Or would you say it was more—"

"How do you erase tabs?" Laurel interrupted.

"Did you hear anything I said?"

"You got a bone, and then another. Now can you help me erase tabs?"

"Don't know how."

She pounded a couple more keys and turned the computer screen toward me. A spreadsheet filled the page, each column a different shade: yellow, black, red, brown.

"I'm charging the bastard," she said. "Right here, see? That's for sexual encounters. Over here I've detailed positions, approximate length of time, variations, etcetera."

I stared at the lists: missionary, me on top, me on my side, doggy style, me over the kitchen table, me in the car.

"Laurel?" I said. "How long did you—"

Stephanie slammed in the door at that moment, bringing a draft of cold air. "The roads are a total mess," she said. "Hammie could barely make it up C Street and he was like, work is totally gonna suck tonight and I'm like, keep your mind on the road...Whoa, what's this? Doggy style? Me over the kitchen table? Mrs. Richards, are you totally writing erotica?"

"It's mine," Laurel said smugly. "I made a spreadsheet of sex with Hank."

"Wow, four hours." Stephanie said. "That's awesome for an old guy."

"I'm not sure how much to charge," Laurel said. "I don't want to make myself look cheap and charge too little, but I don't want to make it look like it was a big deal, either."

"Google it." Stephanie leaned over and typed in "Prostitution rates" and "Alaska." Over 549,000 hits came up. "Find the lowest and the highest and then figure out the, like, median average. Jay-Jay could totally do that in a minute."

"I don't think this is something we should involve Jay-Jay with," I said.

"Chill, Mrs. Richards." Stephanie popped her gum. "I was just, like, stating an undeniable fact."

We settled on prices—$85 for a blow job, $100 for basic sex, $150 for extras such as multiple positions, and $500 for the few times they managed to spend the night together. I got up and slid two large flour tortillas filled with cheese, onions, and peppers into the oven for quesadillas.

"This is just the beginning," Laurel said.

"Beginning?" I asked stupidly.

"Of all the stuff I'll need: child support, health insurance, day-care expenses." She ticked them off on her fingers. "Private school, sports activities, braces, and a private East Coast college. Then of course he'll have to pay for the wedding."

"It's a girl?" Stephanie asked.

"Of course it's a girl," Laurel snapped. "Do you think I'd consider bringing another man into this world?"

Chapter 17

Friday, Jan. 13 (bad luck for all!)

TODAY IT WAS THREE RIB BONES mailed in an overnight delivery box from San Diego and waiting by the mailbox when I got back from Killer's morning walk.

"Cool, rib bones!" Jay-Jay said when he came out for breakfast. "Can I take them to school?"

"They might be important artifacts," I said as I stirred oatmeal; I wanted to keep the bones for myself.

"Soon we'll have a whole skeleton." Jay-Jay chewed on toast. "This guy is weird, huh? Did Dad bring you bones?"

"He killed animals and brought them home, so, yeah, I guess you could say so."

"On TV guys bring flowers, but that's not Alaska, huh?"

As soon as he left for the bus stop, I pulled my easel out from the kitchen corner for a quick hour of painting before work. My latest *Woman Running with a Box, No. 7* peered out from the canvas with my grandmother's face but my eyes and mouth. Her blouse unraveled, and she cradled the box possessively against her chest, the lid loose, the ribbon tattered and torn. Both the box and the woman looked as if they had been through tough times. I worked fast, instinct taking over. When the alarm alerted me that it was time for work, I shook out my arms and stepped backward, catching the painting in full light. I gasped and quickly made the sign of the cross, the way Gramma used to whenever her cooking creations flopped. My Woman Running knelt on the ground in front of the white box, which had ripped open, an assortment of my dirty dolls climbing out. I recognized them immediately: Oral Me into Oblivion Oscar, Spank Me Silly Samantha, and Boob-a-Licious Billie, all of them outlined in the garish yellow of highlighter markers. They looked dangerously seductive yet strangely childlike, as if unaware of how much they needed protection. I peered more closely and noticed tiny messages scrawled over their arms and legs: *Free Me. The rabbit vibrator stimulates the G spot. According to the Pope, birth control is a sin.*

"Wow!" Stephanie whistled from behind me. She had snuck out of school for third period, which was gym; this week they were playing Nerf dodgeball. "Mrs. Richards, that's, well, I totally don't know *what* it is, but it's visceral. It totally bites my mind."

She was right. The longer I looked, the more I had to admit that it was good, very good, perhaps the best thing I'd ever done. I had caught the woman in suspended disbelief, in that moment of recognizing that something isn't what it should be but still hoping the signs have been misread.

"You've got to send that out." She searched the cupboards for a mid-morning snack. "It's a message, you know? It's a voice you can't, like, put into words." She grabbed a package of saltine crackers and headed back to the living room. I washed out my brushes and covered the canvas with a clear gloss sealant, and right as I slipped my waitressing apron over my head (hoping that no one would notice the bright yellow paint embedded in my knuckles), the phone rang.

"Hello," I yelled into the receiver.

"Mrs. Richards?" The woman's voice was familiar, but I couldn't place it. "You need to pick up Jay-Jay."

"Is he sick?" My heart sank: it was the principal of Jay-Jay's school, a short woman who wore suits so sharp I had to resist the urge to salute.

"He's exhibiting undesirable behavior."

"I-I'm not sure what that means," I stuttered.

"Can you be here in twenty minutes? I'll schedule a meeting with Mr. Short to see if we can clear this up."

I hung up, called work, and left a message for Mr. Tims that I had a family emergency, then hightailed it to Jay-Jay's school. Inside, the air smelled of disinfectant and sweaty feet. I sat in a chair in the office and watched the secretary eat M&M'S candies. Finally Mrs. Clampsen called me in.

"Sit." She pointed to a chair. "Mr. Short and Jay-Jay will be here shortly. I wanted to talk with you first." A faint mustache glowed across her upper lip. "Jay-Jay is extremely intelligent, Mrs. Richards, and we're worried he's not getting the correct stimulus at home."

"Stimulus," I repeated.

"He needs to broaden his horizons, attend museum and gallery functions."

"Jay-Jay was at the museum last week," I lied. I wanted to kick her fucking expensive shoes. I didn't have the chance, though, because Mr. Short and Jay-Jay walked through the door.

"Uh-oh," Jay-Jay said when he saw me.

"Jay-Jay, now that you have a parent here, why don't you tell us about the incident this morning?" Mrs. Clampsen's voice was sharp and cold.

"The *incident*," Jay-Jay repeated with emphasis, "was that I gave Julianna a rib bone."

My head jerked up. "Francisco's bone?" I asked.

"It's human?" Mrs. Clampsen clutched her throat. "It belonged to a dead person?"

"All bones belong to the dead." Jay-Jay rolled his eyes.

"It's okay, honey." I reached out and patted his shoulder. "Just tell us why."

"Julianna was crying in the janitor's closet, Mom." He kicked at the wastebasket with the toe of his sneaker. "Her parents are getting divorced, she's real upset, they're fighting over her and everything."

"So you gave her a rib." It made perfect sense. Francisco gave me the ribs to express his feelings for me, and Jay-Jay gave one to a girl to express his feelings for her. It was full circle, like the Oprah Giant talked about.

"Why a bone?" Mr. Short shook his head. He was a burly, short man with a receding hairline and crinkly eyes.

Jay-Jay looked miserable. "She said she felt like she was coming apart. It just seemed . . . I can't explain it. It seemed right. I didn't *expect* her to freak out."

"You did good, honey." I reached over and hugged him.

"Well." Mrs. Clampsen drew the word out between her clenched teeth, and then she sighed, her shoulders slumping. "Jay-Jay, you go back to class. Mr. Short and I need to talk with your mother for a minute."

Jay-Jay glanced nervously from one face to another before heading to the door. There was a stain on the knee of his jeans and his shoes were untied. My heart ached. I wanted to gather him in my arms, never let him go. "Now," Mrs. Clampsen said. "I probably don't need to tell you, Mrs. Richards, that Jay-Jay is smart, extremely smart. He tested off the charts, and his analytical reasoning is higher than anyone we've seen in a long time."

I nodded and tucked my hands beneath my waitressing uniform, which had a smear of dried salsa across the hem.

"He needs to be in a more intellectually driven environment. Colleges are cutthroat these days. He'll need advanced languages, classical literature, and a strong focus on the sciences."

"He's eight," I said.

"Indeed." Mrs. Clampsen's glasses glinted in the overhead light.

"Well, shouldn't we be talking about *middle* school, not college?"

Mrs. Clampsen removed her glasses and rubbed her nose. "Timothy, can you explain? I haven't the patience today."

Mr. Short leaned forward. He smelled like Aqua Velva aftershave and wood chips. "What Mrs. Clampsen is saying is that Jay-Jay has the potential, and drive, to go far. We're afraid he isn't getting enough push at home. We'd hate to see him stunted by his, ah, social situation."

"You mean me?" My hand flew out from beneath my leg and slammed down on the table. Mrs. Clampsen jumped slightly. "You mean that you don't think I'm smart enough to mother my own child." I stood up and pulled my jacket closed. "I *birthed* him. Those smarty-pants genes had to come from someone." I was giving them exactly the low-class scenario they expected, but I couldn't stop. "I may live in a trailer, I may work as a waitress, but at least I have *manners*. I would never insinuate that someone was too dumb to guide her own child."

"Calm down, Mrs. Richards. We were simply stating—"

I cut off Mr. Short with a wave of my hand. "I have to get to work." I leaned over and stuck out my hand. "Thank you for the meeting," I said. It was a tactic I had learned waiting tables. We called it KTWK, which stood for Kill Them with Kindness, and it was amazingly effective. It worked this time, too.

"Don't forget the summer camp forms," Mrs. Clampsen called out as I walked toward the door. "We need everything by the beginning of February."

"Camp?" It was the first I had heard about it.

Mr. Short walked me down the hall. "Gifted camp, with an emphasis in mathematical studies," he explained. "At Berkeley this summer. The competition is fierce, but we feel Jay-Jay has a good chance. Less than 2 percent of applicants are accepted. The essay is of particular importance."

"Listen." I stopped by a locker covered with Hannah Montana stickers. "Is it just me, or isn't camp supposed to mean marshmallows and bee stings?"

Mr. Short laughed, as if I had told a joke. "Don't worry, Mrs. Richards, Jay-Jay will have more than enough opportunity for fun after he brushes up on the basics."

"How much?" I hated the edge in my voice. "For the camp, how much?"

Mr. Short squirmed. "There's financial aid, of course, and partial scholarships."

I waited.

"Three thousand for one week, forty-five hundred for two."

"Holy shit." I slumped against the locker. "My trailer is barely worth that much."

"Mrs. Richards, we must be brave." Mr. Short patted my shoulder awkwardly.

On the way home, I was so upset that I missed a stop sign and was pulled over by a good-looking cop.

"Any reason why you decided not to stop?" His crotch was at my opened window, staring me directly in the face.

"My son is applying to Berkeley summer camp and I live in a trailer," I said.

"The last lady had a dying grandmother." He scribbled something down. "License and registration, please."

I handed him my driver's license and groped around the glove box for my registration, praying that it was current. It wasn't.

"Says here that you're five foot eleven." He peered inside the window. "Unless you've got really long legs, that's a lie."

I fiddled with my seat belt, which suddenly felt too tight. "It's so I can weigh more." He stared. "You know, the taller you are, the more you can weigh. According to those charts in the doctor's office," I added.

"Registration, please" was the only thing he said. I gave him my expired card.

"Did you lie on this, too, or is it really expired?"

I flushed. "No, it's expired."

He didn't say anything. "I'm waiting for your excuse. I figure it's gonna be a good one."

I took a breath. "I haven't gotten to that part of the Oprah Giant's diary yet, you know, the organizational skills. I'm still straightening out my finances, which have gotten better, by the way. And I'm painting again, though—"

He raised his hand. "Stop, please. I'll just be a minute." He left to return to his patrol car as I fiddled with the radio and worried how much the ticket would be: A hundred fifty dollars? Two hundred? I had never gotten a ticket before, not even the time I was stopped outside of Healy and the whole car reeked of dope. But my luck was changing, I could feel it. This was going to be the Year of the Ticket. Still, the cop did have a nice crotch. I wondered if I could use him as a dirty doll model. Would he pose for me if I asked discreetly? Men were vain about their cocks; they didn't hesitate to show them off. And putting one in a painting, why, that was akin to immortalizing it, every man's dream. I was wondering if this cop's dick was straight or hooked to the right like an apostrophe when he appeared in the window.

"Carlita Richards?"

"Yes." I sat up straight. "That's me."

"Says in public records that you're divorced."

"Yes, that's right." Was I about to be propositioned? Had he somehow picked up on my vibes?

"A single mom to this kid who wants to go to camp at UCLA?"

"Berkeley," I corrected.

"Tell you what I'm gonna do." He leaned over until he had practically shoved his way into the car. "My momma raised three kids by herself, worked two jobs. It's tough. But you still got to obey the law." He straightened up. "I'm issuing a verbal warning for failure to stop and a thirty-day notice to get your vehicle registered."

"Th-th-thanks," I stuttered, close to tears.

"I'm not always this nice. If I see you driving so much as an inch over the speed limit, I'm gonna nail you. Now get out of here before I change my mind." He slapped the roof of my car and strutted away. I watched his ass, appreciating the way the dark pants flattered his hips and thighs, imagining him bent over, his ass enlarged and shining like the moon: Carnal Cops, I would call it, or maybe Pull Me Over and Pull It Out.

I was so distracted that I almost missed the next stop sign, too, but luckily the cop was long gone by then.

ME, EARLY IN THE MORNING

Early this morning before anyone woke I snuck out with Killer on the pretense of taking a walk. Instead I got into the car and drove out toward Earthquake Park, pulled up in front of an ugly pinkish-orange house, and slipped a manila envelope into the mailbox. I drove back home, made a pot of coffee, and was sitting at the table reading the paper by the time Stephanie and Jay-Jay stumbled out of bed.

"Morning," I said cheerfully, as if trying to hide my guilt. No one noticed anything different about me as they rushed around looking for lost notebooks and stray socks. After the door slammed and I was left alone with Laurel sleeping in the bedroom and Killer sleeping at my feet, I sat and stared at my hands, which are thick knuckled with long fingers, my nails embedded with paint, so that I have to wear dark polish to hide the stains.

The envelope I left in Francisco's mailbox contained three pieces of the *Woman Running with a Box, No. 9* watercolor cut into eight slices, like a pie. I served him one for each bone he's left me. He leaves me parts of a skeleton, which are physical, and I leave him parts of my painting, which are visceral. We are both giving and receiving, though it's far too early to know who is giving the most. I'd like to think that it is me, but he would probably think the same thing. Probably, we always think that we are giving more than we actually are.

Saturday, Jan. 14

I. Am. So. Depressed. Again.

I opened the newspaper this morning to the large, smiling photograph of a woman from my childbirth class. She had published an

award-winning poetry book, and one reviewer praised it as "images filling the tongue like rain." I skimmed through the article. Mari Campton
had three kids under the age of nine, and after her husband died four
summers ago (he had fallen backward over a cliff while photographing
mountain sheep), she decided to put her grief into words. She worked
full-time as an occupational therapist and was getting a master's in
writing—where in the world had she found the time? I worked full-
time, had one child, and was lucky to find a spare hour to paint twice
a week. Yet she had managed not only to hold herself together through
her husband's death but to care for three children, work, go to school,
and write a book.

"I wrote in the mornings before the children woke," she said in the
article. "I carried around a tape recorder and recorded lines that came to
me as I drove to swim lessons and gymnastics. I wrote in the bathtub
and during lunch hours."

It took her almost three years to finish the book.

I ate the crusts of Jay-Jay's leftover toast and read the excerpt. It
was good, really good. I was jealous beyond words: Someone had what
I wanted and, worse yet, probably deserved it more. She had worked
harder to write that book than I had ever with my painting. She found
time in minutes, not hours, and did the best she could. She hadn't given
up or pushed her poems aside or stored them in a closet. She brought
them out, made them part of her life.

Why couldn't I do the same? Well, nothing was stopping me.
Stephanie was available to babysit and Laurel could fold laundry, and
while I couldn't paint while driving or taking a bath, I could free my
mind and start the transition from daily life to painting. What exactly
was stopping me from being who I wanted to be?

"Nothing," I said out loud. Killer barked as if in agreement, and I
threw her a doggy biscuit. Then I snuck into Laurel's room (my room?)
and grabbed her digital camera without waking her. I took photographs
of my best *Woman Running* paintings, hurriedly typed up a prospectus
(shamelessly borrowed from an Internet sample), added a résumé (again,

shamelessly borrowed), printed out fifteen copies, and sealed one of each in manila envelopes. I drove to the Airport Post Office and mailed a packet to every third art gallery in the phone book. I felt strong doing this, and proud and vindicated.

Twelve hours later, however, I feel quite differently. Shame floods my mouth, thick and rust flavored, along with that old voice in my head: *who do you think you are?*

Which is a good question. Who *do* I think I am? An artist? Someone with the talent to net a show in an environment where artists outnumber gallery openings sixty to one?

Gramma always carried herself with such bravado, though much of it was false. "I ain't as fat as I look," she'd say whenever anyone told her she had guts. Then she'd tell the story about smuggling a pig across Poland dressed in baby clothes, its piggy head wrapped in a scarf, nothing showing but its greedy eyes. The train was filled with soldiers, and if Gramma had been caught she would have been shot.

"Or worse," she whispered, and Laurel, Gene, and I huddled together, imagining hideous tortures where our grandmother was flayed with noodles and made to eat sweet cakes until her belly exploded. Before she boarded the train, Gramma drugged the pig with expensive medicine bought from the underground market.

"*Ach*, he sleep like a baby," she said.

When two German officers sat down across from her, she opened her lunch basket and took out hunks of smelly cheese and green sauerkraut to cover the piggy smell. She offered these stinking gifts to the officers; of course, they turned her down.

She got off the train at Krakow, where her sister and mother were waiting.

"It a shame to kill that pig." Gramma clasped her hand around her throat. "But people gotta eat. Still, it make my *brzuch* ache. Maybe I think it really is my child, maybe I do that somehow."

Mother pooh-poohed this story. "She made it up," she insisted. "She got it from some movie."

Probably she did, but we didn't care. We loved this story, loved to think of our fat, sweaty grandmother sitting on a train across from German officers, a pig dressed like a baby cradled in her arms. We loved the comfort it brought, the reassurance, the message embedded in this strange tale that we heard but wouldn't understand until years later: that in a world where pigs can pass for babies, there is always room for possibilities.

Chapter 18

"I'm back," he yawned. "My luggage didn't make it, so I stole one of those airline pillows in my pack. I'll give it back when they give me back my suitcase."

I sat on the kitchen floor and picked dog hairs off the linoleum.

"You there?" he asked.

"Yes," I finally said. "I got the bones."

"Oh." He paused. "Did you like?"

"I-I guess. I mean, I'm not sure what to *do* with them. But they're nice." I didn't want to hurt his feelings. I knew how sensitive men could be. "Jay-Jay took one of the ribs to school and gave it to a girl."

"No way!" Francisco's voice immediately perked up. "Does he like her?"

"Maybe. He got in trouble, though. The principal called; it was kind of a mess."

"Bones can be powerful. They hold the essence of life, even after death. It's mind-boggling, when you think about it." He yawned again. "Listen, I'd better hit the sack. I'll call tomorrow. Let's get together, okay?"

"Um, sure."

"'Night."

I placed the phone next to my pillow. Francisco was no longer on the line, but I liked knowing that I could call anytime, even in the middle of the night, and he'd pick up and let me listen to him breathe.

Monday, Jan. 16

I left work early today and drove home to pick up Laurel for her ultrasound appointment. She stumbled down the steps in a hideous red-and-green-plaid maternity blouse with a red bow tied around the neck.

"Not a word," she hissed, as she slid into the passenger seat and fastened her safety harness. "Mother sent it last week. She's under the mistaken impression that it's Junior's baby, not that I'm about to correct her."

"I was just going to say that you forgot your coat," I lied, as I peeled out of the driveway. Fifteen minutes later we arrived at the Dimond Medical Clinic, where we sat with Dr. Betsy ("That's my last name, not my first. I'm not the Betsy type," she informed us the minute we walked into the room). "Okay, Laurie, feet in the stirrups."

Laurel's eyes widened, but she didn't say anything. It wasn't like her to not give the doctor a piece of her mind for getting her name wrong, though it's difficult to be dignified with your legs splayed open in front of a woman you've never met. The doctor did a quick pelvic exam as I hummed and stared at the ceiling; when I peeked over Laurel had her eyes squeezed tight, the way she used to when we played hide-and-seek.

"Now I want you to sit up and drink this." Dr. Betsy handed her a huge bottle of colored water. "Don't worry, there are no calories, just flavoring." Laurel nodded and obediently began to drink. "You wouldn't believe the gripes I get about the flavoring—women worried that they might accidently suck in fifty or sixty extra calories. As if that would matter. Pregnancy is the great equalizer." Dr. Betsy nodded thought-fully. "Skinny women bloat up like there's no tomorrow, and next thing you know they're in my office crying about how they treated the fat girl back in high school.

"Laurie, you can slip into this robe"—she pointed at a hideous green terry cloth robe with sunflowers climbing up the sides—"and go sit in the waiting room. We have another fifteen or so minutes before the liquid hits your bladder. Don't pee, don't fidget, and don't laugh, got that?"

Laurel pulled the ugly robe over her paper smock and waddled out. I followed with her shoes, and we sat side by side trying to find the hid-den objects in *Highlights for Children* magazines. She sipped the flavored water with a seriousness that brought tears to my eyes. Right as I circled a hair clip hidden in a pony's leg, Dr. Betsy called us back into the of-fice. Laurel lay down on the sheeted table and I stood beside her. When she wiggled her fingers, I instinctively grabbed her hand.

"Warning, this will be cold." Dr. Betsy placed a white knob shaped like the leg of a couch over Laurel's abdomen.

Up on the computer screen grayish shadows vibrated and expanded in a strange tunnel that looked like a light from a late-night-movie spaceship. Then the outline of Laurel's baby swam into view, its froggy head bopping in amniotic fluid, one arm outstretched, the other pressed against its mouth as if ready to whisper secrets.

"It's an active one." Dr. Betsy pressed buttons on the computer and zeroed in on the focus until the baby's head emerged, alien shaped, the eyes overly large, the body tossing back and forth.

"Do you want to know the sex?" Dr. Betsy asked.

"It's a girl," Laurel said. "But go ahead and check if you don't be-lieve me."

As Dr. Betsy maneuvered the knob around Laurel's belly, I remem-bered back to my own ultrasound. I was afraid at the time that Barry would say something dumb or tell off-the-wall jokes, but he stood be-side me, bearded and serious as we waited to see our son for the first time. My eyes filled with tears at the memory of Jay-Jay's face, along with the *whump-whump-whump*ing of his heartbeat, so familiar it was like hearing my own breath.

Dr. Betsy punched more computer keys and the baby's feet kicked toward us as if sending a message. "She's going to be a handful, I can already tell," Dr. Betsy said. "It's the attitude. You might think that if you've seen one ultrasound, you've seen them all, but every so often distinct personalities emerge. One mother suggested that these were the old souls, returning to fulfill a prophecy."

Dr. Betsy printed out photos to take home. Laurel clutched these in her hands and refused to let go, so I helped her pull on her pants and button her blouse. Her face was dreamy, flushed, and she stared out the window on the way home, not saying a word until I turned onto Spenard Road.

"Did you hear what she said, that my baby is an old soul, here to fulfill a prophecy?"

I nodded and zoomed through a yellow light at the Fireweed intersection.

"Maybe that's why...Carly, can I tell you something if you promise not to breathe a word to anyone?"

I bypassed our road and kept driving down toward the lagoon.

"I did it on purpose. Don't say anything, just let me finish." She sucked in her breath and patted the photos against her chest. "I never planned on having kids. That's one of the reasons I married Junior. He couldn't have kids, I didn't want them—it seemed the perfect match. But then about a year ago I started seeing babies everywhere. It didn't matter where I went, to the gym or Kaladi Brothers or the supermarket, it was almost as if they were following me. I was annoyed at first; you know, I've never been a baby person. Then one day as I slid my credit card through the card reader at Fred Meyer, I saw a woman behind me holding a baby, and its legs were so chubby, the skin so perfect and smooth, that I leaned over and kissed its bare foot.

"Well, I was mortified. I apologized over and over but the mother just laughed, said she understood, that babies were the milk of the gods—isn't that a beautiful saying, Carly? The milk of the gods."

I pulled into the lagoon parking lot, put the car in park, and left the heater running on low.

"It was later that week, a Wednesday night," Laurel continued, "which I took as a good sign. Remember how I always did better on tests midweek? We were at the Sheraton, the TV was on; Hank liked to catch himself doing the weather report, it perked him up, if you know what I mean. I got up and went in the bathroom, and I still remember the light, so gold and soft as I watched my reflection pull out my diaphragm and flush it down the toilet. It almost didn't go down but I pushed it hard with a toilet brush I found beneath the sink. I washed my hands, patted lotion across my face, and went back to Hank. I felt the moment it happened, felt the clink of my egg reaching out and grabbing the sperm. I say 'the' sperm because even then I didn't see it as Hank's, only as something that belonged to me.

"The funny thing is that a week later, I no longer cared about babies. I felt no attachment, no desire to touch them, let alone kiss their feet. By that time, of course, it was too late to see a doctor about a morning-after pill. I knew before I took the first test that I was pregnant, though by that time I no longer wanted it. But that must not have been true or I would have gone ahead and had the abortion, wouldn't I? It was almost as if the baby decided I would have it; it picked me as its mother, and that was that."

"Like Jay-Jay," I said. "There's no way Barry and I could have produced such a kid by ourselves. He's either a genetic mutation or a miracle."

"A miracle," Laurel mumbled. "The milk of the gods. My baby is going to be an old soul. I wonder what she will teach me?" She leaned back and closed her eyes. "This is going to be hard, isn't it, Carly? This is going to be the most difficult thing I've ever done."

WHAT'S ON MY KITCHEN TABLE

Dr. Spock baby book
DVD: *Eating for Two without Looking Like Two*
Bank of America MasterCard bill, paid and waiting to mail
Alaska Airlines credit card bill, paid and waiting to mail
A tibia bone

Tuesday, Jan. 17

"I'm getting fat," Barry said over the phone this morning at 5:30 a.m. "Pants don't fit and I got this lumpy thing going on around my belly."

"You look fine," I yawned, trying to remember if this was true. "You're a chef. You're supposed to be heavy."

"I didn't say heavy, I said a few pounds."

I barely listened but Barry didn't seem to mind. Now that we no longer slept together we had become friends, real friends, the way we weren't able to be when we were married.

"... find me attractive?" he said, and I knew this was my cue.

"Women like a bit of a belly on a man," I said. "It's sexy. It says, here's a guy who isn't afraid of his appetites."

"I ain't gonna believe that," he said, but his voice sounded stronger. "Jay-Jay told me about the camp. Says it costs five grand and you wasn't gonna be able to come up with half. So I says, don't worry, I'll figure something out."

"Huh?"

"All that money you think I owe on Jay-Jay's support? I ain't been holding out on him. Maybe I was pissed, okay, I was pissed, but damn it, Carly, a man's got a right to hold a grudge and it's not like you been starving. I would have stepped right in if things got critical, you know that about me."

I held the phone tight to my ear, my fingers cramping.

"I got it all." He let out a long breath and was quiet for a moment. "For college, see, I started this CD, one of them jump-uppers where they let you add quarterly. He got, let me see." I heard the shuffle of paper and the bang of something knocked over. "Six thousand two hundred and fifty-six dollars. That's the last statement, so of course it's up by now."

I didn't know what to say. On one hand I was furious: he had had the money all along! While we ate generic spaghetti and wiped our butts with cheap, scratchy toilet paper! On the other hand, he was right: I always made do and things have been tough, but we never went hungry or cold, and there was always enough for everything we needed.

"You got every right to be mad," Barry continued, "but I always done good by Jay-Jay. He can go to camp if he gets one of them partial scholarships, and later a big-league college."

I didn't have the heart to mention that those "big-league" schools cost over forty-five thousand a year. Instead I said something that surprised us both. "Thank you."

Five hours later I crouched in the lounge on the first cig dig of the shift and told this to Sandee. It was too cold to go outside, and a table of off-the-base soldiers was getting seriously sloshed across from us.

"We finally did it last night," Sandee interrupted. "It wasn't very good. Shouldn't that make me happy, for it to be bad so that I could say, 'Okay, this isn't the man for me,' and then walk away, no obligation, no refund?"

"It isn't always good the first time, you know that. Expectation alone can ruin the experience."

"I don't understand." She sank down into a sitting position, her clumpy hiking boots splayed out in the aisle. "Everything was perfect. He touched me so tenderly, as if I might break, little touches like whispers across my skin." I sat down beside her, the carpet spongy and dirty. "It wasn't bad, don't get me wrong. He knew what he was doing; he tried his best but I just couldn't get there."

"So you didn't come, big deal. Sometimes it takes time to learn each other." I was jealous: I wanted to sleep with Francisco, yet I was relieved that I hadn't.

"I suppose." She was clearly depressed. "He left right after. I found his socks beneath the bed, that's how fast he took off; he didn't even bother grabbing them."

"I thought he didn't wear socks." She looked at me blankly. "You know, the sandals without socks? The first date?"

"Oh, *that*. He was just trying to impress me. Now that he knows he has my interest, he wears socks again."

"He's in love with you." I pulled her up and wiped the dust off the back of her skirt as Mr. Tims veered toward us.

"Now that you girls have finished with your fake cigarette break, can you please get your asses back on the floor? I'm out of Valiums." He ran his fingers through his dark hair. "You *do not* want to get on my bad side today."

An hour later, in the thick of the lunch rush, with all my tables full and a two-page waiting list up front, I turned around and there was Francisco sitting in my section again. His hair was windblown, his face chapped from being outside, his beautiful hands folded over his place mat. He looked so damned good that I couldn't stand it. My mouth opened but no words came out. He didn't say anything, either. We looked at each other.

"I think I'm going to have to put my glasses on for this." He rummaged through his pockets until he pulled out a worn black case, which he opened, and quickly set a pair of silver-rimmed glasses on his nose. "That's better, I can see you now." He gazed at me in a friendly, unabashed fashion, the way a child stares, unself-consciously.

"I just got back from Moose Pass. Someone thought the bone in their root cellar was from a dinosaur—a raptor, to be specific. So I drive all the way down there. The road's a mess, over ten cars in the ditch, and when I get there everyone's sitting around the kitchen table, stoned, the bone painted blue with red polka dots. Artists." He shook his head and then, as if remembering that I was one, smiled and said, "No offense."

"So what was it?"

"It was a pig skull. Don't you love it?" He slapped his thigh and laughed. "Talk about karma." He took a long drink of water, his head thrown back, the underside of his throat exposed and vulnerable. "I got your present, three pieces of painting for three bones." His voice was serious, almost soft. "I've missed your face. Your angles are so odd, as if your skin is new but your bones are ancient."

I felt hot and shaky; I was afraid I was going to throw up.

"Bones are the true history," he went on. "You hold one in your hand and you feel things, not voices, yet you know right away it was connected to a person, that it was once alive." He shuffled his large, sneakered feet beneath the table. "Sorry." He looked down at the chip basket. "Sometimes I go on."

"No." I inched closer. "It was nice."

At that very moment Mr. Tims materialized by my side. "Carlita," he barked. "Orders dying in the window. Scoot." He turned to Francisco. "You know her?"

"Not as well as I want," Francisco said.

"Hmmmm." Mr. Tims rocked back on his heels as I hid in the waitressing station, listening. "She can be stubborn, that's for sure, but here's what will clinch the deal: halibut—and quality, too, not that frozen crap. Cook it with a nice lemon sauce, spicy but not overpowering, or you might scare her away. Her ex is a chef, did you know? Works down at the Hilton and Captain Cook. Temperamental little shit, but what he does to a shrimp could make you weep."

Francisco looked startled, and I slipped off to the pantry, loaded up my tray, and delivered food to three tables before returning. Francisco was playing with the corn chips, lining them up into tic-tac-toe formation and eating the outer edges. "You ready to order?" I asked in my smoothest waitress voice.

"You were married." He said this as a statement, not a question. "Of course I knew that. You have a son. I just never stopped to think of the consequences." He shuffled the corn chips around. "You like food?"

I blushed, as if he were asking me if I liked sex. "Yes," I whispered. "I do."

"Okay, I'll have to make you dinner." He squared his shoulders, as if this were a challenge. "I can cook, you know; my mother taught me. Said that boys would be boys but a good meal would overlook the fact." He stuffed four corn chips into his mouth. "I'll take the soft tacos." Crumbs flew. "Without the onions but extra cheese." He tapped his fingers over the table. "You cook?"

"Bake, mostly. Polish recipes and gooey breads."

"Shit." He wiped his mouth. "This is going to be harder than I thought."

Wednesday, Jan. 18

"It's because I never had to share a cubby," Laurel complained. It was almost dinner and she sat at the table, eating pistachio nuts. "In school I always had my own. No wonder I can't share. I'm selfish, and don't look at me like that."

"I wasn't looking. I'm cooking." I was pleased with the rhyme but Laurel didn't notice.

"It's why my marriage didn't work. I never saw Junior. He was just there, like the lamp shades and towel racks. Remember I told you we were meeting today? He picked Kaladi Brothers. I knew it was going to be bad. A café is where you say good-bye, like that Journey song."

She licked the salt off her lips. "He said he was willing to put it all behind him and move on. That's what he said, 'Move on,' in this horrible stern voice, as if he were trying to convince himself. Then he said that a baby might just be what we needed, that we had had problems, but maybe this was the universe's way of seeing that we finally became a family."

"What's wrong with that?"

"It's not what he said, it's how he said it. I knew he was never going to forgive me, not for having the affair so much as getting pregnant and reminding him that he can't give me a child. If we had adopted it would be a joint decision, something we had both failed at, not just him."

I had never heard Laurel talk so openly. I added rosemary and basil to the sauce and clucked my tongue in encouragement.

"Then he said that we needed to take a time-out from each other, which was what I *thought* we had been doing, but leave it to a lawyer to make everything official. After it was over, he shook my hand and left.

"On the way home I stopped at the bank to transfer money into my checking account." Laurel spat pistachio shells angrily. "The teller came back and said the accounts had been frozen. I could barely look at her, I felt so ashamed. I had to use my personal savings instead."

"He froze your accounts?"

"The joint ones."

"You need a lawyer," I told her. "A woman with shoulder pads and bright red lipstick and—"

"Sometimes I think that if I could just figure out why I slept with Hank and got pregnant and messed everything up, I could fix it again."

"Maybe you didn't mess everything up. Maybe you saved yourself the only way you knew how." I sounded more and more like the Oprah Giant. As I stirred Gramma's tomato sauce, I told the story of how I became pregnant with Jay-Jay. It was purely by accident; Barry and I had decided to wait at least five years to start a family, time enough for him to figure out what kind of chef job he wanted to work and me to dabble in my art while still bringing in enough to help out with the bills. When I missed my period, I barely gave it a thought. Three weeks later, my breasts bloated and sore, I broke down and told Barry I was late.

"It wasn't easy," I told Laurel as I added spaghetti to a pot of boiling water. "But you know what? It was a good thing, making that mistake. It was the best thing that ever happened to us."

E-MAILS #2, #3, AND #4

Dear Artist:

Thank you for submitting work to the Aurora Borealis Gallery. We regret to inform you that your slides/paintings/video proposal didn't make it to the second round of screenings. We wish you all the luck in placing your work elsewhere. Sincerely,

Dick and Tom Grady,

Aurora Borealis Gallery

Dear Artist:

The Northern Scene Art Gallery no longer accepts unsolicited submissions.

Sincerely,

Waverly Wilcox,

Northern Scene Art Gallery

Dear Artist:

Thank you for submitting work to the Anchorage Depot Gallery Spot.

Unfortunately, your proposal doesn't meet our current needs.

We wish you the best in all your artistic endeavors.

Sincerely,

Violet Meadow,

Anchorage Depot Gallery Spot

P.S. The committee was quite amused with the odd little characters shadowing the bottom level of your paintings.

Chapter 19

Friday, Jan. 20

JAY-JAY SAT ON THE BED, meticulously filing my rejection notices in a ledger he had made from an old notebook as I stood in front of my closet trying to decide what to wear on my second first-date attempt with Francisco.

"You're being rejected at a 76.72 percent rate," Jay-Jay told me. "Of course, they haven't all come in yet, so that's just an estimate."

I nodded and pulled out a blue blouse. I was startled by how fast the rejections had poured in. The first one arrived via e-mail two days after I mailed my proposals, which meant that whoever had opened it had immediately judged it unworthy, not a good sign.

"Here's another one that mentions the little creatures lurking around the bottom of the canvas. That's what it says, Mom, 'lurking around the bottom.' Isn't that neat?" He looked up. "Those must be your dirty dolls, eh?"

I threw a sweater across the floor. "I don't know, honey." I kicked the sweater into the closet. "I didn't purposely put them in. It must have been my subconscious."

"Mr. Short says that the subconscious is a myth of modern-day society unwilling to shoulder its own blame." He narrowed his eyes as I pulled an old broomskirt dress off a hanger. "Are you seeing that bone guy again?"

"Yeah." I sat down on the bed. "If I can find something to wear."

"Dad has bones, out in the garage. A bear skull and a wolverine leg."

"I suppose he does." I was quiet for a moment. "You probably don't remember, but when you were little, you found a fish bone on the beach. Your dad took a picture of you holding it up. It was almost as big as you." I laughed. "You tried to eat it and your dad was afraid you'd choke, so he buried it and you cried and cried. Finally he dug it up and gave it back to you."

"I don't remember."

"It was down in Homer. You weren't quite two."

"Oh." Jay-Jay thought about this for a moment. I looked over at him, his winter-dark hair falling over his forehead. I wanted to tell him that I once loved his father so much that it scared me, but I couldn't remember if it was true. I did love him once, though, and I wanted Jay-Jay to know that, wanted him to know that he had been conceived in love, that he had been wanted, that even though he hadn't been planned, he had been welcomed, cherished. Instead I asked if he wanted me to leave money for a pizza.

"Nah, Hammie's stopping by after work with the leftovers. They get to eat *all* of the pizzas no one picks up, and Mom, Hammie sometimes leaves them for the homeless people in the park downtown. Last week some drunk guy threw *rocks* at him, isn't that cool?" He closed the ledger and tucked it against my pillow.

"I hope no one got hurt." I decided on jeans with a T-shirt and sweater. Why bother to dress up when the man had seen me clomping around in a stained waitressing uniform? I brushed my hair, patted blush on my cheeks, and wondered if I should wear mascara. I decided not to, since I didn't want to worry about smears. Once ready, I sat out in the living room with Stephanie and Jay-Jay, who played Rummy-Jummy, a complicated rummy game they had made up, while Stephanie complained about an English teacher who had it in for her since she wrote a poem about Jesus coming back as a moth.

"He gave me a D on the paper and I'm like, whoa, dude, this is a good poem, but he said it wasn't realistic." She slapped down three jacks. "So then I say, come on, is rising up from the dead realistic to you? That's when he totally slammed me with two days detention for being insolent and—"

A knock interrupted her complaint, and Killer charged for the door. A moment later Francisco stood in our shabby living room wearing jeans, a Pompeii survivor T-shirt, and no jacket. I threw magazines and dirty socks off the couch to make room. He sat down and rubbed Killer's smelly ears. "You must be Jay-Jay." He leaned over and held out his hand. Jay-Jay ignored him.

"My dad has bones, too," he said. "Animals, not people. Anthropologically speaking," he added sarcastically.

"Manners, mister," I snapped, and Jay-Jay sighed, held out his arm, and shook Francisco's hand.

"Oh my god," Stephanie squealed. "You have, like, the coolest T-shirt in the friggin' world." She stuck out her bony wrist. "I'm Stephanie. Babysitter and resident teenager. I cook, fold laundry, but totally don't clean."

I pulled on my boots and coat and almost had Francisco out the door when Laurel flew up the hallway, her flannel nightgown streaming out behind her. "Wait!" she cried. "You forgot me." Her hair was in pigtails; she looked about twelve. "You must be Francisco. We've heard so much about you. Do you cook?" She leaned in closer. "I have an overpowering urge for chicken pot pie."

"Um, sometimes." Francisco squinted at Laurel's forehead, which had "Beef Stew" scrawled across it in yellow marker. After we escaped and settled in his car, I apologized for my family.

"I don't bring men home very often," I admitted. "I guess they see this as kind of a big deal."

"Do you?" Francisco turned onto Northern Lights Boulevard.

"Do I what?"

"See this as a big deal?"

I shrugged. "We both have on jeans and T-shirts."

"Not just *any* T-shirt," he said. "I got this in a bar in the Yukon when I drove up from a job site in Colorado. The woman ordered me to wipe my feet before I walked in, and then she comes over with a bucket and scrub brush, gets down on her hands and knees, and scrubs the floor around my feet. Talk about Catholic guilt." He shook his head.

"What were you eating?"

"I was waiting for you to ask." He grinned over at me. "Pancakes, big as dinner plates. No sausage or eggs, just hotcakes and butter."

"Gramma used to make them like that, only she used honey."

He parked in front of the odd orange house. "Here we are. I have to warn you about the dogs. They're hyperactive."

"Figures. Mine is about the same." That was a lie; Killer wasn't so much hyperactive as hyper-confused.

"The big one is Abraham Lincoln. I'm sorry, that's his name. You'll understand when you see him. He's got that regal air. The smaller one is Mamie Eisenhower."

"I didn't know you were political," I said, as a yellow Labrador retriever flung itself into my arms, wiggling and yipping as if he had missed me for years.

"Down, Mr. Lincoln," Francisco ordered, and Lincoln tucked his tail between his legs and hid beneath the table. Mamie stood in front of me, her head half-cocked. She was one of the clumsiest-looking dogs I had ever seen.

"Have a seat." Francisco motioned to the chairs and I sat down. The legs wobbled.

"Just like home," I said happily. Francisco smiled at me, and I smiled back.

It was that easy.

* * *

After a dinner of baked salmon with an unusual lemon sauce that kicked life up through my mouth and into my nose ("horseradish," Francisco had said when my eyes teared up), we sat on the couch with mugs of blueberry tea, and Francisco told me about the whale jawbone he had photographed up in Barrow. "It was over a thousand years old, in fairly good condition with scrape marks along one side indicating..." He shook his head, reached over, and traced my cheekbone lightly, a mere flutter, so that it felt like moths, like wings brushing my skin. "You've got the best damned bones in your face," he said, his voice husky. "Listen, why don't we—"

At that moment, my cell rang. "Shit." Francisco removed his hand from my face and sat up straight. "Is it the pink-haired babysitter?"

I pulled my cell from my pocket, looked down to see Barry's name lit up. "No, it's someone else. Give me a minute, okay?" I walked over to the window and said hello. Barry's voice was frantic.

"Carla. I need some help." He laughed too loud. "Seems I got myself locked in."

"I'm in the middle of something," I hissed. Behind me I could feel Francisco tense up, listening.

"Tried to get out but the damned door's locked up. Got enough food but nowhere to cook, that's the thing." He laughed, higher pitched this time.

"Just tell me straight. I'm not in the mood for games."

I soon learned he had accidentally locked himself in the dry storage pantry at the hotel while checking ingredients for next weekend's banquet.

"Door shuts behind but don't normally lock. Think the security guards must have locked it while I was in the back." His voice was shaky; Barry tends toward claustrophobia. "Was gonna call 911 but didn't want to be in tomorrow's paper, might lose jobs if people think I'm scattering." He paused a moment. "Can you come let me out,

Carla? Here's the back door code. Write this quick 'cause my phone's dying."

I motioned to Francisco for a piece of paper and wrote the numbers down. "I'll be there shortly," I said, hanging up and turning toward Francisco. "I have to go rescue Barry. He locked himself in the dry storage at the hotel and he's falling apart, he's claustrophobic big-time. Can you drive me home and I'll pick up my car?"

"Your ex-husband?" He pulled on his coat, a rumpled jacket with a torn hood. "I'll take you. Lincoln and Mamie could use the drive."

On the drive downtown, neither of us talked. I didn't know if he was angry or disappointed; I was both. I was also curious to see how flexible he was, and how he'd react to the messier aspects of my life. We parked on the side of the street, walked around to the back door, and punched in the key access code. Inside it was dim, with only the safety lights on, and smelled of onions and chicken, a comforting smell from my childhood. I led Francisco down the long hallway and through the doors to the main kitchen. The pantry was in the back; I knew this from having occasionally served banquets. I knocked on the door. "Barry? We're here. I'm opening the door now."

It wasn't locked but the latch was stuck. "Can you get it?" I asked Francisco, and he gritted his teeth and pulled until the door swung open. Barry sat huddled against a hundred-pound bag of rice, his forehead lined with sweat, his chef's hat bunched in his hands.

"Pitch-dark in there, not a bit of light 'cept the small stream coming through the door," he said, as he stumbled out, blinking in the harsh overhead lights we had turned on. "Makes you wonder about things, being in the dark so long." He wiped his mouth on his sleeve and blinked, noticing Francisco for the first time. "You must be Carla's new guy." He held out his hand to shake. "I'm Jay-Jay's dad, you meet him? He's quite the kid." Barry laughed and hiked up his pants. "Need to find me something to eat, sweet but not too much. Maybe a fruit tart." He disappeared into the walk-in refrigerator. "You two have dessert?" he yelled out.

I glanced at Francisco and shrugged. I wanted to be alone with him but also wanted to see how he'd treat Barry, if he'd be able to see through his bad grammar to the loving, kind, genuine person hiding within. "No," I said, "we haven't."

"Good." Barry emerged, his arms loaded down with pans. "Just gimme a minute. Made some cranberry-lemon tarts the other day, heavy on the ginger but ain't too rich."

Francisco and I pulled up chairs to the prep table while Barry heated up the tarts, which he served with homemade whipped cream flavored with rum and cinnamon. The crust melted in my mouth, followed by a rush of sourness, and just when my tongue began to pucker, the sugar came through with a light, sweet promise.

"Wow," Francisco whistled after taking a bite. "I heard about you up in Nome after the Iditarod. This musher's wife raved about your scallops in red wine sauce. Said it was better than sex."

"Cooking's just mixing and measuring," Barry murmured, but he added another piece to Francisco's plate. As Barry and Francisco talked about hunting up in the Brooks Range, I ate a second tart and thought of how everyone I loved shared food with me at one point or another, how even Jay-Jay sometimes cooked for me when I was sick. There's something undeniably tender about a man making a meal for a woman, those large hands chopping and stirring. It's sensual and slow, like sex, with the reward at the end, after the slow and delicious buildup.

"Eight-point buck but couldn't shoot him. He had this look on his face, like he shoulda been wearing glasses," Barry was saying, and Francisco reached beneath the table and squeezed my knee. They genuinely seemed to like each other; they even had similar mannerisms, both of them leaning forward and waving their hands when they got to the good part of a story. I sat between those two odd and wonderful men, and I licked sugar from my lips.

Monday, Jan. 23

Laurel returned to work today after having used up all of her sick and vacation days. She emerged from her bedroom at 7:45 a.m. and sat down with the rest of us for breakfast wearing her usual work blazer and blouse, the buttons straining across her growing breasts, and instead of a designer skirt she wore a pair of casual pants bought on clearance at JCPenney.

"I'll take two eggs but no toast," she said. I sat at the other end of the table reading a *Runner's World* magazine, though I wasn't a runner.

"I'm not cooking." I didn't even look up. "It's a Monday, oatmeal day. There's some left in the pan, and strawberries in the fridge."

"You go on one good date and look what happens: oatmeal for breakfast." Laurel sighed. "I'll have to fight my protein cravings until lunch." But she got up and spooned herself a huge portion, plus she popped two slices of bread into the toaster. "Where's Jay-Jay?" She looked around, as if noticing us for the first time. "Shouldn't he be up by now?"

"Barry picked him up early and took him out for breakfast. He invited us all, but I didn't feel like getting out of my pajamas." I yawned and went back to the story I had been reading, about a seventy-four-year-old marathon runner who ran thirteen to twenty miles on the same half-mile stretch of beach, back and forth and back and forth. Would that equal insanity or dedication?

"Well, I have to get going. How do I look?" Laurel stood before me in her expensive blouse and cheap pants, her hair styled only in the front, her stomach poofing out against the blazer so that she looked like a middle-aged housewife getting ready to do the weekly shopping.

"You look great," I lied, neglecting to mention the smear of strawberry down the side of her pant leg.

"Wish me luck." She waved her hand and marched out the door in a pair of my heavy Sorel boots.

I cleaned up the kitchen, took Killer for a quick walk, and headed into work early, since I had a twenty-top reservation at eleven a.m.

Sandee was already there, hacking tomatoes for side salads, seeds flying every which way. She still wore her hiking boots, along with an ugly flannel shirt in place of a blouse.

"You look like a lumberjack," I told her as I tied my apron around my waist and got ready to prep the salad dressings and desserts.

"Good!" A tomato quarter flew across the room and smacked into the wall. "I'm becoming a nun," she said. "One of those orders where you aren't allowed to speak. Do they still have those, you think?"

I rolled balls of ice cream through a mixture of crushed cereal and spices for the fried ice creams. "What'd Joe do this time?"

"Nothing. I haven't heard from him in over a week."

"He's probably down in Seward. A bear woke up from hibernation and got its foot stuck in a toilet in the harbormaster's bathroom. I saw it on the news."

"Didn't you hear me? I said I haven't heard from him. That means no text or phone calls."

"Doesn't sound like Joe."

"He's a guy, get it?" Sandee's voice was awful. "It's all about sex or not having sex or having too much sex." Her voice trembled, and she put down the knife and took a breath. "It's not about sex at all. It's Randall. Joe says that as long as I'm still married, then we're committing adultery. He actually used that word, as if he were a preacher."

"You should have him legally declared dead," I suggested. "Put an ad in Vegas newspapers and if you don't hear from him, that's that. Or hire a private detective. He could have an address and phone number in a couple of days. Call Randall, tell him you want a divorce, and cut the cord, for once and for all."

Sandee stopped chopping. "You'll go with me? To the detective's office?"

"Sure." The idea frightened me for some reason. "Make an appointment and we'll drive over together."

After the worst of the lunch rush was over and I was wiping down the pantry counters, Sandee handed me a business card. "Toodles O'Brien,

Private Investigator," it said, and had a photograph of an unsmiling Native woman.

"A customer left this—it must be fate. We're meeting her at four fifteen. She doesn't normally do same-day appointments, but she had a cancellation and said to come on in. I'm heading home to pick up a photograph of Randall plus his Social Security number." Sandee picked dried food off her apron with her fingernails. "Can you believe I'm finally doing this? You can come, right? Please tell me you can make it."

I had grocery shopping to do and overdue movies to return, plus I needed to stop at OfficeMax to pick up a new printer cartridge so JayJay could print out his essay for Berkeley gifted camp, but I agreed nevertheless. Then I texted Stephanie that I would be home late and could she please defrost the chicken in the freezer.

A little before four p.m., Sandee arrived. I almost didn't recognize her. She wore a stark black blouse with a high collar and an ugly floorlength pleated skirt, and she had her hair in a fussy bun that gave her face a sharp, prim expression.

"Jesus, what did you do to yourself?" I asked.

"I don't want her to think I'm a slut."

"You're not a slut," I said as I refilled ketchup and Tabasco bottles. "You've just been experimenting with single life."

We drove over in her car, which was neater than mine, so neat that I marveled over the uncluttered dash and sole coffee cup in the cup holder. Sandee pulled into a house tucked behind the Park Strip. Wind chimes hung from every tree branch so that walking up to the front door we were serenaded with rings and soft clicks.

A thirty-something woman opened the door before we reached it. Her hair was twisted into four thick braids, and she had her eyebrows, nose, and chin pierced.

"I'm Toodles." She reached out her arm. A wolf tattoo circled her wrist. "Brother wolf," she said, noticing my stare. "He protects me. Sweets, you don't have to take off your shoes," she said to Sandee. "Anyone want coffee or tea?"

"Tea," Sandee and I said in unison, and Toodles sized us up with her dark, beautiful face. "Devil's club and rose hip," she said, motioning for us to follow her out to the kitchen. "I don't usually work at home, but I didn't feel like putting on my boots and walking to the fucking office. Sorry about the language. I'm an Aries, which means I swear a lot. Actually, I'm not sure if that's true, but that's what I tell people."

Toodles was solid and muscular, and she liked to talk. "I came from the village, up by Point Hope. We didn't have indoor plumbing, used a honey bucket and it was no big deal. I saw my first toilet when I was six. I was terrified; I thought it was going to swallow me whole." She threw back her head and laughed. Her voice was musical and lilting, and it still carried a hint of a village accent. "Now when I go back I bitch about having to pee into a bucket. That's what they call progress." She set two steeping mugs of tea on the table and waved for us to sit down. "I almost lost it when I moved down here for college. You know the story: Native girl from the village goes wild in the big city and loses part of her soul." She stirred her tea, and I noticed a series of etchings over her right hand. "Willow branches, for serenity," she said. "Luckily, I didn't lose my soul. Know what saved me?" She leaned forward impishly. "I learned to make our Native foods: sage and mushroom sauce, fry bread, salmon cheeks marinated in dandelion greens and nettles. I enjoyed that so much that I learned the white man's cooking ways, too, went down to Seward and studied culinary arts and then advanced my learning at Le Cordon Bleu."

"That's where Barry went," I said. "That's my ex-husband. He's the chef down at the Hilton. And Captain Cook. And the Sheraton, too—he moves around a lot, contracts himself out and—"

"Barry George?" Toodles leaned forward. "Met him at a banquet. We exchanged chowder recipes: moose for elk. Your ex, eh?" She stared at me with her dark eyes. "That was before I got my private detective license." She patted her large but firm belly. "Enough of my story, what's yours?"

Sandee explained about Randall leaving her alone in a Vegas hotel room, she showed photographs, and handed over his Social Security number, birth date, and parents' names and address.

"You've called his old friends?" Toodles asked. "High school sweetheart? College roommates?"

Sandee shook her head no.

"People don't disappear. That's movie bullshit." Toodles straightened her large shoulders and suddenly looked imposing. "What they do is go someplace familiar and re-create their old lives, right down to how they arrange their living rooms. Kinda sad, isn't it? We're supposed to be the dominant species yet we have so little imagination." She held the postcards in her hands and closed her eyes for a minute, as if she were a psychic instead of a PI. Sandee fidgeted but I held out my hands for her to be still.

"Okay, here's the deal." Toodles opened her eyes and stared directly at Sandee. "Your husband probably dyed his hair one shade lighter or darker. If he wore contacts, he wears glasses now; if he wore glasses, he's switched to contacts. He's living with someone younger than he is, probably much younger, he's working... what was his profession before?"

"Accountant," Sandee said. "For a hospital chain."

"Now he's working as an accountant for a supermarket or warehouse club. He's driving the same make and color vehicle, has the same credit cards but different account numbers, follows the same daily routine, and goes to bed and gets up at the same time as before. The new girlfriend probably looks like you, or the way you looked when you were younger. He's re-created his life," she said more gently. "He just did it without you this time.

"It's a classic midlife crisis," she continued. "You wouldn't believe how often it happens. We are all so predictable." She sighed. "I took this job expecting excitement but instead found out how excruciatingly ordinary our lives are." She sipped tea and grimaced. "This one will be easy. I can have an address, phone number, and even photos in seventy-two hours."

"Sev-seventy-two hours?" Sandee stuttered. "I'm not sure if I'm ready."

"What's not to be ready? You're looking for the truth, and you'll get it." She excused herself, went into the kitchen, and came out with a plate of cold salmon and a peppery lemon basil sauce. "I made this last night, when I couldn't sleep. Dig in. The salmon's from the Yukon River—caught my share dipnetting last summer. Native rights." She folded her arms across the table and leaned toward me. "Now, you," she said to me in that lilted voice, "tell me more about that delicious ex-husband of yours."

Chapter 20

Wednesday, Jan. 25

"I STILL CAN'T GET OVER the fact that someone finds Barry delicious," I said to Sandee, as we cross-country skied along the Coastal Trail. Mexico in an Igloo was closed for the day due to a faulty hot-water heater, and we were using the time to get in our exercise so we could eat more later. "Do you think I overlooked too many of his good points? Everyone keeps saying what a great cook he is. I feel insecure, as if I missed something."

"You're not fat," she said, as we began to ski through the tunnel. "And you don't watch the Food Network or read gourmet magazines, so I'd say that cooking doesn't mean that much to you."

"I like to eat."

"We all like to eat," Sandee said, "and most of us eat too much."

"But I cook," I protested. "And bake. I'm always baking."

"It's not a passion, though. You're not a foodie, which Barry needs, and he's not into art, which you need. You loved each other but couldn't touch the other's soft shine."

"Soft shine?"

"You know, the place that's the deepest part of you, the thing that defines you, makes you the person that you are. My mother called it the soft shine, though she never found hers." Sandee laughed bitterly, as we skied up a small hill and around a curve. It was a cloudy day, the inlet on our right, huge chunks of ice moving slowly with the tide so it looked as if they were alive. We both breathed hard as we skied along the side of the trail classic style. A group of thin, athletic girls from the high school ski team zipped past us in their sleek tights and bright jackets.

"I hate them," Sandee muttered, as we plodded along. My back pricked with sweat, and the air felt cold and damp against my face. We skied in silence until we reached the downhill before Point Woronzof, where we stopped and looked out over the expanse of beach. The sun was setting, lighting the sky pink and orange, and off in the distance the few tall buildings that made up downtown reflected the light back so that it shined bright and fiery against the frozen water. We always paused before the hill, since it had a tricky curve at the bottom and neither of us skied well on turns, especially while moving fast.

"Here goes." Sandee dug in with her poles and pushed off. I waited until she was halfway down, then pushed off and flew down the hill, my skis picking up speed, my poles raised, my knees tucked down as I alternated weight from one leg to the other in an attempt to keep my balance. What is it about being out of control that is so enticing? Each time I skied a hill I didn't know if I would make it down without falling, and that made it special, something I both looked forward to and dreaded.

"Cross-country skiing is like love," Sandee said, as we trudged back up the hill, our ridiculous skis splayed out so that we took giant, lumbering steps. "Most of the time it's boring and mindless, just moving along and following the trail. Then you come to the hills, and going up can bring you to tears." She paused to take a breath. "Everyone thinks the downhills are the easiest parts, but that's when you're most likely to fall and get hurt. Do you get it?"

"Kind of." We crested the hill and skied past a woman walking a dog in a sweater.

"It's the effortless times that are the most dangerous, the times that you feel as if nothing could go wrong. That's when you need to beware."

"You sound like an ad for a horror movie," I joked, panning an announcer's voice. "She was happy and then...beware."

"Laugh, but think of it and it makes sense."

"This is about Toodles, isn't it?" I stopped so fast that a man skiing behind me crashed into the back of my skis. "Sorry," I yelled over my shoulder, and then I turned back to Sandee. "You're not afraid of what she's going to tell you. You're afraid of what she's not going to tell you."

Sandee's face was scrunched tight in the dim light.

"You never loved him, did you? At least not in the shiny-spot way. Oh my god—" My ski had hit a rough lump of snow, and I momentarily stumbled. "This is about guilt; that's why you hired Toodles. You're trying to pay for your guilt, the sin of your relief."

"Leave me alone," Sandee snarled, trying to ski ahead.

But I stayed by her side. "The Oprah Giant says that to love is the grandest thing we'll ever do in our lives," I panted. Now Sandee was picking up speed. "She says that—"

"Who in the hell is the Oprah Giant?"

I realized I had never told her, I hadn't told anyone. They knew about my dirty dolls but not about my messed-up and troublesome mind. So I explained about the diary and the blog and e-mail messages, and how each month offered a lesson to follow. I was sure she'd laugh or make a joke, but she surprised me.

"That's why you've changed." She squinted at me in the hazy purple twilight. "Don't get mad, but you're different, Carla. There's an air about you, a lightness. People notice, too. Look at Francisco. He's been coming in for over a year and suddenly he notices you. It's not a coincidence. There's this feeling about being around you lately, I can't explain it. It's sort of like eating a plum."

After I got back from skiing, I started mixing up biscuits. Right as I folded in the butter, the door slammed.

"That's that," Laurel sat down across from me and shrugged off her coat. "Now I can sleep in again."

I added milk and a handful of cheddar cheese. I was trying to replicate Gramma's cheesy biscuit recipe but couldn't get the spices balanced.

"So there I was sitting at my desk skimming through sales documents," Laurel continued. "I reached for the stapler but it was empty, so I pulled out a box of staples, and that was empty, too. Five thousand staples."

She looked at me expectantly. I looked back, waiting for more.

"Don't you *get* it? Five thousand staples! I had stapled five thousand times." She smacked the table. "I knew it was an omen. So I quit."

"Y-you quit?"

"No more documents, no more smiling and showing houses to couples happier than I am. I'm done."

"But what about money?"

"I'll stay here with you until I have the baby. Then I'll work something out with Junior. We can sell the house. The furniture alone is worth a small fortune."

I stared at her as if she were mad, but she was up rummaging through the cupboards. "The funny thing is, the minute I handed in my notice, my stomach rumbled and I felt hungry for real food for the first time in months. What's for supper? I've been craving deviled eggs all afternoon."

The phone rang while I mixed the dough up with my hands, butter and flour squishing through my fingers.

"Laurel?" I yelled, glancing behind me. She didn't even look up from her laptop. "Jay-Jay? Stephanie?" I yelled, but no one answered. Finally the machine picked up. I tensed, afraid it might be Francisco. I hadn't seen him since the night we ate with Barry. It made me shy, seeing the two of them together and knowing I had opened something I couldn't easily close.

"Clara Richards?" a clipped and unpleasant voice wavered through the answering machine. "This is Betty Blakeslee, over at Artistic Designs. We need to meet with you tomorrow morning. Would ten do?"

She paused as if waiting for an answer. "Our March client just canceled, and we're left with you or a man who makes collages from eggshells." Another pause. "Bring three or four of your strongest pieces, a short bio, and a recent photograph. Ten then?" The phone clicked, and I stood in the kitchen surrounded by spills of flour and milk.

"Oh my god," I said softly and then louder, "Oh my god!"

Stephanie and Jay-Jay rushed into the kitchen.

"Are you bleeding?" Stephanie screamed, looking around as if for weapons.

"Collages out of eggshells," I muttered, and then everything went dark and the dirty linoleum rushed up toward me.

I came to a few minutes later in Laurel's bed. She sat at the foot, tapping away on her laptop.

"You have butter in your hair," she said when she noticed I was awake. "I'm going to have to change the sheets."

"Did I faint?" I'd never fainted before, at least not when sober.

"Junior e-mailed," she replied. "He wants to talk. He said enough time has passed that we'll be able to be ourselves, not pure emotion. He actually said that—'pure emotion.' When did men start talking about feelings? It was easier when they were Neanderthals."

"Is it true?" I reached out and gripped her arm. "About the gallery? The call?"

"Betty Blakeslee is cheap. She tried to talk down the price of their house by a hundred thousand. I told her to stop being so conventional, and she requested a different agent." Laurel punched computer keys as she spoke. "Don't let her know I'm your sister, okay?"

"So it *is* true?"

Laurel nodded. "Tomorrow at ten. I confirmed, but don't worry. I disguised my voice with an English accent and said I was the nanny."

"I can't go tomorrow. I'm not ready." I looked wildly around the room. "I have nothing to wear." I jumped out of bed and was halfway to the closet before I remembered that Laurel had relocated my clothes to the hall coat closet.

"Don't worry about *her*," Laurel said. "She doesn't know how to spell, and her punctuation isn't that great, either."

I knew Laurel was trying to give me something. "Thanks," I said. "Really."

I rushed out to the living room and listened to the message over and over until Jay-Jay and Stephanie threw pillows and screamed for me to please, please, please get over myself.

LETTER #8

Dear Carlita Richards:

Wowee! We finally received a payment on your account.

While the amount doesn't come close to meeting your outstanding balance, we commend you for your efforts and look forward to continued payments.

Think of us each time you flush!

Pete and Paula Anderson
Big Pete's Plumbing and Pipes

Thursday, Jan. 26

My gallery interview was a fiasco. Betty Blakeslee sneered at my prospectus.

"Barbie doll figures in your art?" she said. "One of the *other* galleries does that. It's old news. The package you sent made it sound as if you were cutting edge." Her voice dropped flat, as if it exhausted her to have to talk with someone so obviously untalented. I took a deep breath and thought of the Oprah Giant's advice about managing conflict: *Stay centered. Breathe deep. Don't let anyone steal your focus.* I breathed deep, I tried not to let anyone steal my focus.

"These are different," I said. "They represent a story."

"Don't tell me," Betty Blakeslee sighed. "You were sexually abused and now have a drug problem. Believe me, I've heard it before."

"No," I said a little too sharply. "It's about running away from home, not *home* home but the home of societal expectations and women's roles." Sweat dripped inside my bra. "Once you open the door of change you can't go back. That's the loss part, and it hovers over everything. But here's the thing." I was on a roll suddenly, I felt great. "We don't understand our own subconscious so we're always creating what I call dirty doll obstacles and—"

"Oh, Timothy." She waved her hand and a swarthy man with mismatched socks trotted over. She introduced him as Timothy Tuppelo, the gallery director. I dutifully stuck out my hand but instead of shaking, he bowed stiffly and then stuck his finger in his mouth and busied himself with dislodging something from between his teeth.

"Timothy," she commanded, "that mediocre landscape would catch more light on the other wall." She examined her lavender nails and rubbed something from her index finger. "Angela's on bed rest and had to cancel her show." She sighed again. It was obvious she resented Angela for burdening her gallery plans with a difficult pregnancy. "The eggshell man sculpted a giant penis from rolled and pressed chicken shells. Just because *some* men are fascinated with their dicks doesn't mean the rest of us are." She turned and shouted at Timothy again. "No, not *that* way. Toward the light, hello! Yes, like *that.*"

She clapped her hands and glanced at her watch. "I have an eleven o'clock due any moment. Can you show yourself out, Clara?"

"Carla," I corrected. "It's Carla." But Betty Blakeslee was already striding down the hallway in her black pumps with their squat heels, her skirt hitting exactly midcalf. As soon as she turned the corner, I collapsed against the wall. Timothy Tuppelo hurried over with a cool washcloth, which he pressed to my forehead.

"I think I peed my pants a little," I sobbed.

"Happens all the time." His sleeve smelled of cumin and ginger.

"That woman sucks the blood out of everyone she touches." He gave the washcloth circular little pats. I sighed and slumped lower.

"You an artist?" I asked.

"Did a show last year with the Dockers in Seattle."

I was impressed. The Dockers was a well-known mother-daughter gallery team that sponsored one out-of-state show a year. The competition was fierce.

"I weld junk," he said. "Recycled art. This new one unfolds like a child's pop-up book."

After I pulled myself together, I thanked him and veered straight for Golden Donuts, even though it was miles out of the way. I ordered four jelly-filled, three cream-filled, and four chocolate éclairs.

"That's only eleven," said the skinny girl behind the counter.

"Eleven?"

"Twelve makes a dozen, that's what most people order."

"Do I have to?"

"I'll have to charge seventy-nine cents for each one otherwise. It's your choice." She shrugged as I stared into the glass case, unsure which donut to pick: The glazed? The maple-filled? The colored sparkles?

"I-I can't decide," I whispered, my chin wobbling the way it does before I cry. The girl looked startled. Then she pulled herself together and unfolded a box.

"Bavarian crème," she said in a matter-of-fact voice. "It's what my mom eats when she's depressed, and you're almost as old as she is." She arranged the donuts inside the box, tucked in the top. "Seven fifty," she said, and I handed her my credit card and she handed me back the donuts.

"Bye, now," she said. My hands were trembling by the time I got out to the car, and it took me two tries to open the box. The smell of sugar and fried dough filled my nose, and I breathed deeply. The first bite was so sweet, followed by the hit of cream against my tongue, that my eyes watered and soon I was crying, sobbing, rocking back and forth as I stuffed another donut into my mouth, and then another. I knew

I wouldn't get the show, that I would suffer the humiliation of being outshined by an oversized penis. I was devouring the fourth donut and feeling a bit queasy when the Oprah Giant's words popped into my head: "You don't have to believe in yourself, you just have to tell yourself that you do," she had said (and in my sugar-drenched daze I imagined her voice to be firm and slightly sardonic, like Alice, the housekeeper from *The Brady Bunch*).

"Our brains," the Oprah Giant had explained in this week's blog, "can't tell the difference between a truth and a lie. It believes everything we say, and every negative thought, from *I'm too fat* to *I'm not smart enough*, registers as absolute truth in our minds." Our task, she said, was to override the years of negative self-talk by saying two positive comments for every negative thought.

I put down the donut. "My work hangs in galleries around town," I said, my voice shaky and timid, as if I had no right to say such things. "My work is appreciated by many," I said, louder this time. I turned on the car and began driving home. Once I got started, I couldn't seem to stop. "I am a talented artist," I shouted out. "I am a successful mother. My sister and I have a perfect relationship."

The last one was harder, and my voice faltered a few times so that I almost skipped over it, but then I said it out loud, very low at first and then stronger and stronger: "I deserve the love of a good man. I deserve to have a show. I deserve to have money. I deserve—god damn it—I deserve to be happy."

Chapter 21

Sunday, Jan. 29

"Mrs. Richards, pssst, Mrs. Richards, are you, like, awake?"

I opened one eyeball to Stephanie's face peering down at me from where I lay on the living room floor in Barry's old sleeping bag. I immediately shut it again.

"Mrs. Richards?" Her hand shook my shoulder. "You've gotta wake up. I'm totally in trouble."

I didn't move. I had stayed up late after my Saturday night shift drinking wine and eating burned microwave popcorn, scared out of my mind to paint because how do you do something you love when it's suddenly been deemed lacking?

"I did an impulsive thing." Stephanie slid over until she was practically sitting on my head. "I don't, like, regret it, only the consequences, which are totally skewed out of proportion."

I sighed. The room was cold, so I pulled the sleeping bag over my shoulders and sat up. "Is someone dead? Did you wreck the car? What is so important that you had to wake me up at—what time is it?"

"Six thirty-three. And I totally have a reason because, Mrs. Richards, brace yourself. I won second place."

"That's nice." I leaned my head on my knees and closed my eyes. My neck ached and my mouth felt cottony and too large, the way it often does when I drink too much.

Stephanie snapped her fingers. "Hello, the creative writing contest? The one that's in the paper every year?"

It took me longer than it should have to comprehend. "Wow, Steph, that's great. That's incredible." I reached over and hugged her thin chest to mine. The local newspaper hosted an annual creative writing contest each year after Christmas, and it was all very hush-hush—no one knew if they had won until it was announced in the paper. It was like being a minor celebrity for a week or two, and because of this the competition was fierce. Two years ago a housewife won the nonfiction award with an essay "borrowed" from an obscure underground literary magazine. If the editor hadn't been up moose hunting at the time, no one would have figured it out. I worried that Stephanie might have cheated, though she didn't seem the type. Still, who knows what someone might do for a taste of success. Would I cheat if I were granted a show and guaranteed that no one would find out? I hope I wouldn't, I hope I'm more honorable than that, but probably I'm not. Stephanie snapped her fingers in front of my face again.

"Mrs. Richards, have you, like, heard anything I've said?"

I shook my head groggily and Stephanie rolled her eyes, started over. "My mother totally pounds at the door like an hour ago? I cannot believe you slept through it. So I open up and she's like, 'You've embarrassed me for the last time, missy,' and she throws the paper at me, can you believe it? The woman has been an embarrassment my *entire* life, and now *she's* playing the victim."

Stephanie's lip twitched the way Jay-Jay's does before he cries, so I made comforting little clicks with my tongue. "It was about her." Her voice was small and trembly. "About her drinking."

"The poem?" I asked. Stephanie nodded miserably. "Well, you have to admit, she does drink a lot."

"That's easy for *you* to say. She's not *your* mother."

"No, she's not," I agreed. I pulled my feet out of the sleeping bag and began putting on my socks; it was obvious I wasn't going to get any more sleep. "My mother drank, she still drinks," I admitted. "She doesn't get rip-roaring drunk, and no one knows but my sister, brother, and father, but she drinks and was never there for me or any of us, not really. She may have been impeccably groomed, but she was flat on her ass on the sofa by nine each night. So yeah, I know how you feel. You end up practically raising yourself, and it sucks.

"But Steph, you have to push that aside for now. You wrote a poem and it won an award—do you know how many people would kill to be in your shoes? If I could win a contest with my paintings, I'd go for it— I wouldn't care what my friends or sister thought. Okay, I'd care, but I'd do it anyway."

Stephanie pulled her oversized T-shirt over her knees and looked at me expectantly. *Don't look at me,* I wanted to scream. *I don't have the energy to hold anyone up.*

"I guess we should go now." She stood up and extended her hand to pull me up. "You'll totally understand when you check out the yard."

"Yard?" I followed her to the kitchen and slipped on my boots.

"You'll see." And maybe it was knowing the worst was over or having someone walk beside her, but she sounded cheerful again. I called for Killer and opened the front door. It was dark and cloudy, a light breath of snow across the porch steps. Below, scattered over the snow-covered lawn, were heaps of clothes and shoes, CDs and books, stuffed animals and candles stuck in old wine bottles. A dresser with only two drawers leaned against a spruce tree. A mattress sagged over a rock, sheets and pillows tossed around it.

"I think there's another load on the way so you'd better, like, keep down. My mother's got a mean aim when she's drunk."

I looked around. It was beyond sad—not only Stephanie's meager possessions splayed across our yard, but the fact that her own mother had kicked her out without even realizing she had already been living with us for over a month.

"I guess you're officially living with us now," I said. It was a stupid thing to say, a nothing thing, a comment meant to fill the silence, but it was also funny in a horrible-not-funny-at-all sort of way, and Stephanie snorted and covered her mouth.

"Officially," she gasped. "I'm officially living with you now." She sat on the porch and laughed until tears ran down her face. "Mrs. Richards, oh, Mrs. Richards, that was such a totally dumb thing to say."

After she pulled herself together, we hauled the stuff we wanted to save into the arctic entryway right inside the trailer, a little room designed to stop the flow of cold into the house. Then we carted the dresser and mattress to the curb; in our neighborhood, the quickest way to dispose of something was to leave it at the edge of your driveway.

"Mrs. Richards?" Stephanie said as we pulled off our boots. "Would you like to read my poem?"

"I'd be honored." She handed me the features section of the paper, which had been formatted like a small magazine. On the front was one of Stephanie's school photos, along with photos of a few other winners: a little boy holding up a copy of *Huckleberry Finn*, a guy in a fishing hat, a woman wearing an artsy muumuu.

"Someone must have clued in my mother," she said, sitting down at the table next to me. "She *never* reads the features, only the entertainment section to see who's at the clubs." She sat back and folded her hands in her lap, a humble yet proud expression around her mouth. I skimmed through the articles until I came to the high school poetry category. There was Stephanie's picture again, enlarged this time, with comments from a judge who called her "gutsy and bold, a refreshing new voice."

Mother

Stephanie Steeley
West High School

Hideous sweater, holes
in elbow, skin gray and wrinkled,

go ahead, raise another
beer to your ugly mouth,
who the hell am I to judge,
except to notice how your lips
tremble with the memory
of knitting needles, blood,
that pink blue dream
you couldn't wait to kill.

"This is good." I was stunned. I knew Stephanie wrote poetry, but I hadn't realized she was the real thing. "Honey," I said, reaching across the table and grabbing her hands. "Sweetie," I tried again. I wanted to tell her that her words were beautiful, that she was brave and kind and her heart, which would get her in trouble time and time again, would also be the thing that saved her. Instead I handed her the metal box where I kept Gramma's old recipes and asked if she wanted to help me bake.

"Mrs. Richards!" she cried. "I am totally ready to maneuver myself around a kitchen."

As we prepared *szarlotka*, one of Gramma's favorite breakfast treats, Stephanie told me about how she waited until the last minute to apply to the contest, how she revised her poem over and over, trying to get the rhythm right, how she agonized and worried and almost gave herself an ulcer over the title.

I worked the dough and painted in my head as Stephanie talked. Jay-Jay woke up when the pastry was almost finished, and he shoved a crumpled booklet toward me.

"Ask me some spelling words while we're waiting for breakfast but make sure you pronounce them right. I don't want my brain messed up so early." Jay-Jay was favored to place high in the upcoming Alaska State Spelling Bee and had been memorizing spelling words for weeks.

"*Anaglyph*," I said. "*Chinchilla. Brachylogy. Acropodium.*"

Jay-Jay spelled them all without a hitch.

"How long have you been practicing?" I worried he was studying too hard. "You don't have to win, you know? We love you no matter how you spell."

"I *know* that," he said. "Ask three more but don't go in order. *Cetology. Axunge. Blatherskite.*"

"Did you know," Jay-Jay said after he finished zipping through his words, "that a blatherskite is an incompetent person who talks too much?"

"You trying to tell me something, mister?" I leaned over and ruffled his head.

"Mom!" He jerked away. "Words are funny, aren't they?"

I told him that they most certainly were and to please run down the hall and wake his aunt for a special breakfast treat. When Laurel straggled in, we all sat down to a surprisingly pleasant meal. Stephanie read her poem and Laurel talked about the cute crib she had seen at Burlington Coat Factory, and the apple cakes filled our mouths and melted against our tongues, and each word we spoke tasted of burned sugar.

GRAMMA'S SZARLOTKA (POLISH APPLE CAKES)

- 6 peeled apples, chopped
- ½ cup sugar
- 2 big handfuls raisins
- 2 handfuls almonds
- 2 eggs
- 3 large handfuls flour
- 1 teaspoon baking soda
- 1 teaspoon baking powder
- Splash almond extract
- Splash cinnamon and nutmeg
- ½ cup brown sugar

Preheat oven to 400°. Throw everything into a big bowl, push up your sleeves, and knead like crazy. Pour into a pan, cover with brown sugar, and bake about 45 minutes. Tuck a napkin under your chin and eat with a large spoon. Need extra sugar? Plaster the top with whipped cream or Cool Whip. Share with good friends and family. Laugh. Always have seconds.

LESSON SIX

The Hard Task of Happiness

So you think you want to be happy? Sure you do! But looking for happiness is like shopping for a swimsuit in the middle of January. The stores are loaded with cashmere sweaters, and the few swimsuits to be found are the wrong size, the wrong color, or the wrong style for your figure. Here's what most people don't realize about happiness. That it's hard work. That the quest can leave you exhausted. That once you find it, there's no guarantee it will still fit the following year.

—*The Oprah Giant*

The Hard Task of
Happiness

Chapter 22

Friday, Feb. 3

I SAT IN THE KITCHEN in a Francisco-induced haze. Last night we had cuddled in his car and kissed until my mouth ached and my lips puffed up, until my head swooned and all I could see were colors swirling my eyelids: pinks and pale yellows, blues with their edges muted soft.

Then the phone rang, and I lunged for the receiver, sure it was Francisco. An unpleasant nasal voice filled my ear instead.

"Clara Richards? This is Betty Blakeslee over at Artistic Designs. My apologies for calling so early but the eggshelled dick collapsed last night and we had to call in a cleaning crew."

"It's, you know, um, Carla," I sputtered. Betty Blakeslee had the power to reduce me to a blabbering idiot.

"The artist wanted to change the show to a Humpty Dumpty mosaic, but I put my foot down and told him to get his dick out of my gallery."

"Well, of course," I blathered.

"We're out a show for March and have no time to look for anyone else. Our fliers have to go out by next Thursday. Timothy will contact you about the artist statement for your collection of..." She grappled to find the right word.

"Dirty doll paintings," I said. "The dolls are included as a subtext emphasizing the plight of—"

"Just make the deadline and we'll get along fine," she sighed. "I'll need ten to twelve quality pieces by the end of February."

After she hung up, I stood in the middle of the kitchen, unable to move.

"Mom?" Jay-Jay had come in from his bedroom and now tugged at my sleeve. "Your face is bloodless."

I sat down in a chair and smiled weakly. "I'm okay, honey."

He ran out to the living room, where I could hear him rousing Stephanie from the couch. "Wake up. Mom is totally vamping out."

Stephanie staggered into the kitchen, her hair matted, poetry stanzas smeared over her arms. "Yoo-hoo, Mrs. R, you in there?" She waved her hands in front of my face. I smiled a dumb, loopy smile.

"I got it," I said in a faraway voice. "The giant dick collapsed. I fucking got it."

"Do you think we should call my dad?" Jay-Jay said, worried.

Stephanie leaned closer until I could smell her stale, morning breath. "She'll be okay. I think it's something about her art."

"Betty Blakeslee," I murmured. "On the phone. Got. The. Show."

"Oh-my-god!" Stephanie squealed. "She got the show," she cried to Jay-Jay. "Do you know what that means, Mrs. R? We are both going to be totally famous." She paused to spread cream cheese over a bagel. "Everything comes true if you work hard enough," she told Jay-Jay. "My dream of meeting Tobias Wolff? It will totally happen. Like, it might not happen the way I imagine, but it will happen. Oh, wow, Mrs. R, this is so totally huge for you!"

I told Sandee about the show during our first cig dig. It was a brutal shift, and neither of us was in a good mood. She was happy for me, but I could tell she was distracted.

"Have you heard anything from Toodles yet?" I asked.

Sandee slumped against the wall. "I haven't called back. She'll probably charge in here looking for me. She seems the pushy type."

"Determined, not pushy. There's a difference."

"I suppose." She looked so miserable that I decided to cheer her up with my own insecurities.

"It's hard to be happy about the show when I know I got it by default." I tucked in my blouse and prepared to go back out to the dining room floor. "If the collage guy's penis hadn't collapsed, it wouldn't have happened."

"So?" Sandee grabbed a tray and wiped off the crumbs. "Life isn't fair. A lot of people get things by default."

"The other artists will sneer. 'Oh,' they'll say, 'she only got the show because the other guy's dick went limp.'"

"Stop." Sandee's hand covered my mouth. It smelled of tequila and salt. "You worked your ass off for this. Look at your hands." She grabbed my left hand and we both stared at the chapped skin, the swollen knuckles, the burns and scars from working on my doll art. "You deserve this, Carla. We'll go out tonight, we'll celebrate. Because you've friggin' earned it."

Later that night Sandee came by the trailer to pick me up for our night out. On the drive downtown, she veered off onto Thirteenth Avenue and headed down a curved side street. "I'm, ah, picking up Joe," she said. "I had told him before we'd go out to eat tonight, so you'll have to meet him." She sounded unhappy at the prospect.

"I thought he was mad about the Randall mess."

"He is, but he's working on it. That's what he said, 'I'm working on my anger,' as if he had just finished reading a self-help book. That was after I told him about Toodles. 'Oh, a private eye,' he giggled, and I almost smacked him. He thinks it's an old guy in a wrinkled suit, like Columbo. I didn't mention it was a woman. I didn't want to push the issue."

Joe was waiting outside a nondescript blue house. "Hey," he said to me as he climbed in the backseat, "you must be Carla. I've heard so much about you." He stuck his hand through the space between the two front seats and we shook as Sandee backed out of his driveway. "Sandee says you two are like sisters. That's cool—you can never have too many sisters. I have five myself."

"Five? I can barely handle one," I told him.

"Well, they're all back in Ohio." Joe was tall and solid, with a friendly, bearded face and dark brown eyes. He wore a black flannel jacket, jeans, and huge leather boots. "Heard you've got a show next month. Congrats. Betty Blakeslee is one tough lady. She hit a moose a couple of years ago, totaled her car, and stood out in the snow, forehead bleeding, shoulder hanging all crooked, and know what she says? 'I hope that moose had liability insurance.'" He and Sandee laughed as if this were the funniest thing in the world.

By the time we left the restaurant after our dinner, I staggered from too many glasses of wine. The sidewalk swayed deliciously as Sandee grabbed the keys from her purse and steered me toward the car. I slumped against the window while she drove to Joe's house and watched them walk to the doorstep, lingering for a kiss that made me suck in my breath, even in my sorry state. When she got back into the car she cleared her throat.

"Carla," she said as she pulled out onto Arctic Boulevard. "You aren't going to like what I have to say but I need to say it anyway." She braked for a light and looked over at me. Her lip trembled lightly. "I love him, okay?" She stepped on the gas and squealed across the intersection. "I hope you're happy now." She cut off a blue sedan and grazed the bumper of a brown SUV. "I hope you're fucking happy that I'm so miserably in love."

"Yeah," I said. "I am."

And I was, too.

LETTERS FORWARDED FROM JIMMIE DEAN
(LETTERS #9, #10, AND #11)

Dear Dirty Girl:

I love you nasty thing please send your wrinkled pants and shirts I have an ironing fetish and will make them smooth and crisp.

This will cost you nothing but my love.

Arnold J. Reynolds
Bliss, Idaho

Dear Really Real Doll creator:

I am a freshman at the University of Florida working on an alternative women artist project.

Please submit two photographs of the back of your head to the e-mail address below.

Sincerely,
Jessica Boogey

Dear You:

Did you get the dirty underpants I sent? Please send pictures of you in my underwear. I'll give you $20 for each one.

If you sit on the toilet I'll send $40.

Sincerely,
Bille Fosterhood Jr.
Highbee, Missouri

Sunday, Feb. 5

When good things happen, they don't necessarily leave you happy. That is a myth, a mistake in thinking, according to the Oprah Giant.

"Happiness can't be measured by how you look or how much money you make," she wrote in next week's blog (I snuck a peek ahead, hee-hee). "If you think that job promotion is going to make you happy, think again. You might be able to afford nicer outfits, but you'll be stuck in your same own self."

Maybe that's why I feel so ornery and unsatisfied, so anxious and irritable. I've finally been awarded an art show, something I've dreamed of for years. Yet I still have a leaky toilet, a dog that won't stop chewing my shoes, and a pregnant sister hogging my bedroom. My life is the same; the art show simply adds more worry to the mix.

"You're totally looking at it wrong," Stephanie said as she made coffee this morning before church. With her odd clothes, her eccentric stories, her badass background, she's the only one of us who sees fit to visit god on a bimonthly basis. "You don't *have* to totally worry about the show. It will be, whether you fret or not. Why waste the energy?"

She sounded suspiciously like the Oprah Giant. "Have you been peeking at my laptop?" I asked her.

She gathered up her purse and slipped on a pair of clunky-heeled boots. "Okay if I borrow the car?" I pointed toward the cupboard. She picked the keys up and then paused at the door. "I'll light a candle for you, Mrs. Richards, but I think it's going to take way more than that."

I was still feeling down when Francisco picked me up for a run on the Campbell Creek Trail. "You look like shit," he said. "You sick?"

I wiped my hand across my chin, where I was getting a pimple. "You'd think I'd be happy about the show, but I'm not. I mean I am, but I'm not. I wonder if I'm a chronic under-happier, like an underachiever."

"It's complicated." Francisco lifted the lid of the cookie jar. "Got any snacks? I forgot my Sport Beans."

I heard Laurel's feet padding down the hallway, so I pushed Francisco toward the arctic entryway. "Out, now!" I hissed. Laurel had woken me the night before to share her plans of eating her placenta after the birth, and I wasn't eager to hear her repeat the news. Francisco had Abraham and Mamie with him, so I brought Killer. They sat sizing each other up in the backseat. When we got to the trailhead, Francisco turned off the car and tucked the key in a clever pocket at the waistband of his expensive running tights. "Maybe you're overthinking it," he said. There was something in his voice that I didn't like. "A show doesn't have to be a big deal."

I watched as he pulled on a pair of lightweight gloves and wanted to kick him. "How far you want to go?" I asked. I wasn't much of a runner. I preferred Rollerblading, where the wheels did most of the hard work.

"A couple of miles." He unzipped his jacket and pulled on a bright yellow Windbreaker. "You wearing that?" He nodded at my fleece top. "You'll be too warm. A tech shirt and Windbreaker would be sufficient. The rule is: if you're not cold the first mile, you're overdressed."

"Thank you, Mr. Running Man." My voice was sarcastic, but as we headed down the hill at the beginning of the trail, I felt better. The snow crunched beneath our shoes and the cold air felt good on my face. Francisco kept the pace light and I ran slightly behind him, thinking of colors, not the whites and grays and tans of the winter woods we ran through but bold and vibrant purples and yellows, strung-out-on-a-mood shades, Picasso's crazy mind colors.

"To the left, to the left," Francisco yelled, pulling me out of my daydreams and over to the deeper snow on the side of the trail. Up ahead, a moose cow with a yearling calf lumbered toward us on their ridiculous legs, their awkward knobbed knees looking too insubstantial to hold their weight. "Grab the dogs and stay back," he warned, holding his arm out as if to shield me. The cow lurched closer, stopped, blinked, and turned back to the alder tree she had been munching on. There were faint white markings around her mouth, which looked bored and slightly laconic, like a teenager.

"Watch the calf," Francisco hissed. It was almost near enough to touch, and Killer, Lincoln, and Mamie strained so hard against my grip that my fingers ached. "Back," Francisco said. "Slowly." We inched our way backward on the trail, the cow lifting her head and watching us suspiciously.

"Shit, wish I would have brought my camera. My mom's got a thing about moose." Squatting there in ankle-deep snow, I realized that I knew very little about him. That's the way it is in the beginning, you think you know the person but there is something more to learn, and something else after that. It's like walking down a hallway with doors on either side. Sooner or later you have to decide to keep walking or open each door and find out what's inside. Francisco helped me up, and we brushed snow off our legs, turned around, and headed back where we had come from. "We'll take the Coyote Trail loop and head out behind the science center," he said. I released the dogs and we started running again. "Once, a few miles up from here, I was charged by a cow when I was on my bike," Francisco said, and I grunted. Such stories were commonplace in Alaska. Moose were touchy and temperamental, and most folks were more cautious around them than around bears. My favorite story was about a woman who had been bitten in the ass as she walked down the street. I opened my mouth to share this with Francisco, but he turned and told me that I shouldn't be afraid of success, that I needed to accept my potential.

"Potential? You sound like Dr. Phil. 'Go forth and accept thy potential,'" I mocked in a deep voice. "If it were that easy, do you think I'd be struggling?"

Francisco shrugged. "Maybe you like to struggle. Maybe you've gotten so used to it that it's a comfort."

Well, that was easy for *him* to say. He owned a nice house, drove a decent car, made a decent salary—what the fuck did he know about eating generic spaghetti sauce? A sly voice in my head said that if I hadn't spent so much on art supplies over the years I could probably afford better spaghetti sauce, but I ignored it and concentrated on resenting Francisco. "You wouldn't last a day in my life," I snapped.

"You're not so special," he said. "You aren't even that poor."

I didn't know what to say so I kicked him instead, a clever little kick that looked like a trip, but he knew better. "Ouch," he yelled. "You did that on purpose."

"I slipped," I protested.

"You did not. That was deliberate. I can't believe you kicked me." He sprinted away before I could defend myself.

"Go faster, see if I care." I was furious. I wish the moose had bitten him in the ass. "Killer," I yelled but she had taken off with the other dogs after Francisco, and I was alone. I could vaguely make out Francisco loping up the last hill, looking as smooth and relaxed as someone from a Nike commercial. I decided to hate him. What did he know about my life? What did he know about me? I fumed and stumbled down the trail, nodding at a couple on skis and moving over for three women walking abreast. When I got back to the car, Francisco sat inside reading an anthropology magazine. The passenger side was locked. I knocked on the window and he looked up in feigned surprise, but I knew he had locked it on purpose. We had both been through enough relationships that we were well practiced at such nonchalant battle maneuvers.

"I never want to see you again," I said as I slid in the seat and fastened my seat belt. Killer sat in the backseat and ignored me.

"So why are you here?"

"I need a ride home."

"Now I'm a taxi?" I didn't answer. "First you kick me and then you expect a ride home?"

"Spare the dramatics. I'd walk but I'm not dressed for it."

"Here." He threw me his jacket and I put it on and opened the door. "Killer, you coming?" I asked. She thumped her tail but didn't move. "Traitor!" I hissed. I had regressed to fifth grade.

Francisco let me walk almost a mile before finally pulling up beside me. I was cold and hungry, my feet numb, my gloves wet from chewing on the fingers. He leaned over and opened the door, and I got in. Killer pressed her nose against my neck as if in apology.

"I thought I'd give you time to cool off," he said. I didn't reply. I still didn't say anything. We drove in silence. We were both in the wrong; we both owed the other an apology, but we were both too stubborn to make the first move. Francisco cleared his throat right as we hit Northern Lights Boulevard. "I can burp the vowel song. Want to hear?"

I shrugged, and Killer and Mamie drooled over the seat back.

"A, E, I, O, and U," he burped in rapid succession. "And sometimes Y and W."

I glanced over at him. His hands were tight on the steering wheel, his eyes squinted as if unsure if they should look over.

"Cool," I said grudgingly. I touched his shoulder and burped out the letter U.

Tuesday, Feb. 7

"Well, duh, Mrs. Richards, of course you had a fight." Stephanie was French braiding my hair as practice for the show. I wanted to look artsy and thought braids might be the way to go. "It's because you mentioned you had problems."

"So? Francisco seems pretty secure."

"He's a man." She sprayed something evil over my head. "His life is totally based on ego. You mention problems and right away he thinks he has to fix them. So he lashes out."

"I don't think you're giving Francisco much credit. I kicked him first." She pulled a section of hair, hard. "Ouch," I cried. "Watch out, that's my head."

"Love is totally blind."

"I don't love Francisco, it's not that simple."

"It *is* simple. You love him, he loves you, and neither one of you totally thinks you're good enough for the other. Everyone thinks that."

"How old are you again, thirty-five?"

Right as she gave a last yank on my hair, someone banged on the door.

"Is Hammie coming over?"

"Nah, he's working."

"Laurel?" A familiar voice yelled from the porch. "I know you're there. I saw your car out front." Junior banged harder and Laurel ran into the living room, her laptop cradled in her arms.

"Get rid of him," she whispered loudly.

I started to get up but she pulled me down. "No, listen. Stay here and don't move, okay? He'll think no one's home and go away."

"Laurel!" More pounding. "I know you're in there, damn it." He kicked the door and Killer went crazy. Another kick and I jerked my arm out of Laurel's grasp and ran to the door.

"Stop it! You're going to ruin the hinges!" I yelled, as I opened the door. Junior stood inside the arctic entryway in a pair of wrinkled jeans and a misbuttoned flannel shirt. His hair was tousled and he needed a shave.

"I have to see Laurel," he said. "I know she's here. Tell her to get her ass out here. Now!"

"Chill out, dude," Stephanie yelled.

Junior pushed past me and into the living room. "Where are they?" he demanded. Laurel sat in the chair. She looked at him with such innocence that I knew she was about to lie. "Where are they?" he yelled again. I held tight to Killer's collar. If he leaned one foot closer to Laurel I would release Killer. She is a pathetically docile dog but faithful to a fault, and Laurel was now part of our family.

"I have no idea what you're talking about." Laurel folded her hands over her bulging belly and smiled up at him.

"My lucky socks, the ones I wear in court. They were in the laundry basket last week and now they're gone."

"That is *so* sad," Laurel said. "Maybe you could buy new ones."

"I *cannot* buy new lucky socks," he thundered. Killer whimpered and sat on my toes. "My mother dipped them in the holy water at Notre Dame. You can't buy that."

"I can't buy anything," Laurel said. "I have no money. My account has been frozen. Besides, you're not Catholic."

"You did this on purpose. You want me to fail."

"I worked a shitty receptionist job to put you through your last year of law school. Why would I want you to fail?"

"Because I didn't invite you back," Junior said.

"Invite me? It's my house, too. My name is on the mortgage, if you'd ever think to check."

"Please!" Stephanie waved a large orange comb like a weapon. "You guys are totally spreading negative vibes and it's screwing my psyche."

"I need the house," Junior said, and his voice was awful, awful. "I have nothing else."

He let out a little sob and fumbled for the door, his untucked shirt-tail bunched against his ass.

"Poor guy." Stephanie peered out the window and watched him slip down the driveway toward his car. "He's totally pathetic in this, like, endearing sort of way. It would make a good poem, but I'd have to use a lot of slumpy letters."

Laurel's face was pale, tiny drops of sweat lining her forehead. I turned the TV on low, went into the kitchen, and started mixing flour into sugar for Gramma's Polack Cinnamon Cake recipe, which she cut into squares and called Little Fat Sugars.

I added an egg, all the while thinking of Gramma baking, which made me think of Barry cooking, which made me wonder if what we all really want is to return home and feel special and loved, the way we feel when someone bakes us a pie or offers cookies fresh from the oven.

"I wonder why women don't kill men and chop them up in pieces." Laurel walked up beside me, stuck her finger in the mix, and licked it clean. "We kill them sometimes, but we don't chop them up and leave them all over the city. I wonder why that is." She reached in and grabbed another finger of batter. "Not that I want to kill Junior; he has his good points. But do you ever wonder why we keep doing it, trying to love men? Oh, I understand it from a procreation standpoint, but do we have to buy couches and curtains and set up house together?" She paused for a moment, a surprised look on her face. "Carly!" She grabbed my hand, sticky from the sugar, and placed it on her belly. "Feel."

Beneath my palm Laurel's belly was warm and hard. I waited a moment and there it was, a fluttering that rose and fell, followed by a larger wave, the small thump of an arm or a leg hitting the side of my sister's belly. My eyes filled with tears. I couldn't help it. I remembered that jolt, that mystery.

"It feels like being in outer space," Laurel whispered. "Like flying around the moon."

GRAMMA'S POLACK CINNAMON CAKES
(LITTLE FAT SUGARS)

- ½ cup sugar
- ½ cup brown sugar
- 2 bars of margarine
- 2 cups flour
- 1 egg
- 1 teaspoon vanilla extract
- 2 teaspoons cinnamon
- Small pinch nutmeg
- ½ teaspoon anise
- Pinch of salt
- 1½ teaspoon baking powder
- 2 cups heavy cream (or Betty Crocker icing, if you're lazy)

Preheat oven to 350°. Throw the sugar and margarine into a bowl and mix. Slowly fold in the flour. Add the egg, vanilla, salt, baking powder, and spices. Pour into three small cake pans and bake at 350° for 15–20 minutes. While cake cools, add sugar to cream until thickened and sweet, and whip into thickness. Swirl in streaks of cinnamon (about 1 teaspoon, depending on taste), frost layers with icing, and plop together. Serve with iced tea and a lot of hugs.

Chapter 23

Thursday, Feb. 9

I MET TIMOTHY TUPPELO at Organic Oasis after I got off work to talk about the art show flier. We each drank a shot of wheatgrass juice that turned our lips green and made small talk until our organic, whole-grain wraps arrived. Tiny squares of tofu leaked out.

"You're not going to like hearing this," Timothy said with his mouth full, "but Betty Blakeslee went ahead and wrote up the fliers. I have one on my laptop—I'll show you when I'm done."

"How bad is it?" I picked a mushroom out of my wrap.

"Here's the thing." He set down his wrap and wiped his mouth on a napkin. "Blakeslee basically owns the Anchorage art scene. She's the backbone. If she likes something, the community embraces it. If she doesn't, well, you're lucky to hang it in an after-hours bar."

"What did she say?" I picked out more mushrooms and arranged them over my plate in a flower shape.

"It's not what she said exactly." Timothy stalled as he chewed his last bite. "You have to remember that Blakeslee is sharp. She looks like an old society woman, but her mind never stops."

"Is this your idea of a warning?"

He pulled out his laptop, flipped the lid and punched up the gallery website. "Don't worry, it's not posted yet. It's still in administrative function." He punched a couple more keys and turned the computer toward me, the lid half closed so that I couldn't see.

"It might be best to not have food in your mouth," he said. "It's a little startling, but nevertheless powerful."

As he slowly opened the lid, I gasped so loudly that the waiter hurried over with a handful of napkins.

"Where's the spill?" he cried. "Is everything okay?"

Timothy waved him away as I stared at the screen. The flier was well-done—I had to admit that, even in my shocked state. The colors were vivid, and one of my *Woman Running* paintings had been imaged across the middle. Below that was a photograph of me followed by an artist statement I had never actually made. Pieces of it did sound familiar, so I guessed that Betty Blakeslee had taken bits of my submitted biography and interwoven it with things I said during the interview. (Had she been taping me? Was she that sly, that evil?) I read it out loud, Timothy leaning forward as if to shield my words from the surrounding restaurant patrons.

" 'Local artist Carla Richards balances the sphere of feminism with the burden of male dominance in her upcoming show, *Woman Running with a Box*,' " I read in a slow, sardonic tone. " 'An erotic artist who designs dolls for the upscale adult website thinkingbuttsandboobs.com, Richards captures the struggle of modern-day sexuality with a playful and uninhibited voice that challenges the barriers between the id and the ego.' "

I slammed the lid of the laptop down. "Jesus," I said. "You have to take it off the website; you can't print that. I have a son in school. I'm in the PTA." This wasn't true, but I could have been in the PTA, would have been if I only had more time. "You know what people will say? What they'll think?"

Timothy motioned for the waiter to clear our plates. "Feel like dessert?" he asked, but didn't wait for me to answer. "There's a carrot cake I can't resist—it's vegan, but don't let that fool you."

I placed my hand on top of his, hard, like the game we played as kids. "You're not listening. You can't print that."

"I told you, it's already done." He nodded at the waiter as he set down the cake and two forks. "I pick the fliers up from the printer tomorrow morning."

"That's cold." I picked up the fork but didn't eat. "That's nasty cold."

"It's art," he said, his mouth full. "It's brutal, but it's a *business*. Blakeslee is smart, and she knows what she's doing. I'll bet you sell at least one piece before the show even opens."

"She hates me. She can't remember my name. She calls me Clara."

"She's dyslexic."

I picked up the fork. The cake was rich and sweet, with chunks of carrots that broke up the softness. "Would you do it?"

Timothy paused, his fork in the air. "The show, you mean? With the flier?" He expertly cut the last hunk of cake into two even pieces, stabbing one with his fork and dangling it up in front of his face. "I don't have a kid but if I did, well, that would make it tough: my wants and needs against someone else's." He squinted at the cake and laughed. "Who am I fooling? I'd do it in a minute, and not because I'm selfish and self-centered, which I am, but because opportunities are few and far between." He motioned to the last piece of cake. "You want that?"

"Yeah, I do." I didn't, but I knew that he did and I was feeling spiteful.

"Nothing's what you expect," Timothy explained. "My first show was in a bowling alley in Tacoma. Christ, I almost pulled out but know what? Someone who knew someone who knew someone was there. Get my drift?"

"Yeah, your first show was lousy, too."

"Everyone's first show is lousy, except in made-for-TV specials." He waved at the waiter for the check. "Let me know tomorrow morning. But remember: if you piss off Betty Blakeslee, you're not going to get another show until she dies, and lord only knows how soon that will be." He threw two twenties and a five down on the table and got up to leave. Then he turned back and squeezed my shoulder. "Go home, talk to your kid. Let me know before noon tomorrow."

I peeked at the check: at least he tipped well, which was one point in his favor. On the short drive home I worried how people would react if they knew I made and sold dirty dolls. Would coworkers giggle at me behind my back? Would customers make rude comments and expect me to flash my tits? I couldn't stand the thought of kids teasing Jay-Jay or playdates being canceled because parents thought he came from a corrupt home. How do you choose between what's right for you and what's right for your child and the rest of your family, your life? How do you possibly make that decision?

Once home, I didn't mention the art show flier to Laurel or Stephanie. I sat at the supper table and ate the meatloaf I'd made (a little dry but spicy enough) and listened to Stephanie worry about her SATs. She was retaking the test next month to broaden her scholarship opportunities and was brushing up on advanced math skills.

"It's totally inconceivable that I'll ever use precalculus in real life." She shook salad dressing over her potatoes. "Even basic math is useless. Who balances checkbooks? It's like, hello! Why don't you teach us something we need to know?"

"School sucks," Jay-Jay agreed. "We have to write in longhand. Nobody *writes* longhand anymore. Pretty soon it will be an ancient language, like hieroglyphs."

Laurel ignored everyone and shoveled food into her mouth. When Jay-Jay reached for the last slice of garlic bread, she yelped and stabbed the back of his hand with her fork.

"Ouch!" Jay-Jay jumped up. "Did you see that, Mom? She *stabbed* me."

"The skin's not broken." I held his hand up to the light; it was almost as big as my own. "I think you'll live, honey." I scooted him back to his chair. "Laurel, apologize to Jay-Jay and then cut the garlic bread in half and give him the biggest piece."

"But I'm eating for two," she protested, tomato sauce smeared across her upper lip. "I *need* more food. My body is feeding a baby, a whole extra life." She bit into the garlic bread and chewed. "Jay-Jay's brain is already formed and really, Carly, if you had shared *your* food when you were pregnant, he wouldn't be as smart."

I put my plate in the sink, grabbed the leash, and called for Killer. My boots were still wet from earlier in the morning, and as I slid my feet into plastic bags to keep them dry, I lost my patience. "Why don't we live in Hawaii?" I screamed to no one in particular. "We could be sitting on the beach drinking foo-foo drinks. What in the hell are we doing in Alaska?"

Stephanie, Laurel, and Jay-Jay stared at me as if I were mad, as if it were obvious, as if living in a shabby trailer and eating meatloaf made with generic bread crumbs in the middle of the coldest part of winter was the best thing in the world.

I don't know why I headed up the street instead of down by the inlet. Spenard Road isn't a choice place to walk at night, even with a dog for protection. I was propositioned three times before I reached Barry's house.

I heard music as I walked up the front steps, country or maybe old jazz, a woman's voice, gritty and sad and rising up through them hard times. I knocked while Killer sniffed around the doorstep, excited because when Jay-Jay took Killer with him for weekend visits, Barry cooked her special meals—doggone it food, he called it. I was ready to knock a second time when the door opened. Barry was disheveled, his shirt untucked, his feet bare.

"Carla," he said, surprised. I realized that he had a woman with him.

"Listen, I didn't know. I'll come back another time or call you tomorrow." I tugged Killer's leash and turned to go, but she refused to budge. "Killer, move," I hissed.

"Ain't no big deal, we was just getting ready to eat." Barry fidgeted with his shirt hem as I pulled Killer across the steps, her toenails squeaking in the hard-packed snow. "Made up some meatballs and a nice salad. You hungry?"

"No, I just ate dinner."

"Bear?" a woman's voice called out. It was strangely lyrical, familiar; I loosened my hold on Killer's leash and leaned closer.

"Toodles?" I said, and then I called, "Toodles, that you?"

Toodles lumbered out to the living room and stood behind Barry. She had on one of his shirts and a pair of wool socks; her legs were dark and muscular. "Carla!" she cried, as if we were old friends. "Come on in." She opened her arms to welcome me and when I stepped forward, she hugged me. It was a hard, warm hug. She stood between Barry and me, smiling and holding each of our hands. "That must be Killer," she said. "She looks like a wolf from this side, see? The wolf makes a fierce brother or sister; she won't let you down."

I knew I should feel jealous. Here was a woman who was obviously going to be important in Barry's life, his first major relationship since our divorce. Yet I wasn't, or at least not yet. I squeezed Toodles's hand and smiled back. "I'd love to stay for dinner," I said, even though I had just eaten.

While they scurried around getting things ready, I sat at the table and told them about my show and the interview with Betty Blakeslee.

"She treats Native artists like crap," Toodles said. "My friend Susie Coyote had a show, and she made a huge stink that Susie was Navajo, not Alaska Native. As if it matters. Native is Native; we're all treated like shit. Susie mentioned that, and know what Blakeslee said? She said that Susie used too much orange in her work and could she tone it down, please? She's one cold woman."

I bit down on the appetizers Toodles set down in front of me, cucumber slices with a mini shrimp on top, covered in an orange sauce and topped with a curly slice of onion. The flavors tingled my mouth. "Wow, this is good." I ate two more before I decided to tell them the rest. "There's something else," I said. "Can I borrow your laptop?"

"Over by the couch." Barry motioned with his head.

I carried it out to the table and punched up the gallery site and then the administrative code Tim Tuppelo had given me. "This is the bad part. In fact, it might ruin me, or at least ruin whatever feeble standing I've managed to make in the community, which isn't much, mind you, but at least..."

"Can't be that bad," Barry said. "You ain't got a mean bone in your body."

"You'd better look at this first." I pointed to the laptop screen. "It's, well, it's just..." I laughed weakly and shoved another appetizer into my mouth.

Barry and Toodles walked over and stood behind me. I hesitated before opening the laptop lid. "Don't be mad," I said to Barry.

"Why would I be mad?" He leaned forward, his head right over my shoulder.

"No, it's...Okay, see for yourselves." I flipped opened the lid and waited.

Barry whistled. "Holy fuck. I know them dolls!"

"You— You do?"

"Gus got one from his wife, said it was a joke but he still talks about it." He squinted as if he had never seen me before. "How long you been doing this?"

I shrugged. "A couple of years, though they just took off last year."

"Thinking Butts and Boobs is the real deal," Toodles said. "It's like the *New York Times* of erotica. It's nothing to sniff at."

"But it's erotica," I said.

"So?" She walked back to the oven to check the meatballs. "It's not like you're starring in triple-X movies." She opened the oven door and poked the meat with a fork. "A couple more minutes," she said to Barry, and then she turned back to me. "Besides, whose business is it anyway?"

"Well, people will definitely talk. And there's Jay-Jay to think about."

"Jay-Jay's fine," Barry said.

"Fuck them." Toodles pulled vegetables from the refrigerator and started mixing a salad. "Not Jay-Jay, I mean the other assholes. Bear, hand me the sharper knife." Barry slid the knife across the counter as she continued talking, her words interspersed with the chopping of carrots and onion. "People can be cruel, believe me. Back in the village it was the white kids who had it tough, especially the half-breeds, which included me. We were worse than the whites because we didn't belong to either side. When I came here I thought I'd finally belong, but that didn't happen, either." She stopped to wipe her hands on her shirt. "So people talk." Toodles popped an appetizer into her mouth. "Big deal. Hold your head high and ignore them because, honey, you're about to have a show."

"Thanks," I said, surprised; I hadn't expected the woman sleeping with my ex-husband to be the one to come to my rescue. "I still think they should take the website off the flier, though."

"No way." Toodles shook her head. "Trust a private detective on this one. That mention is going to make you a shitload of money. It could be the thing that launches you."

"It's ready," Barry said, pulling the pan out of the oven. I sat down at the table with my ex-husband and his new lover and ate the moose meatballs Toodles made, the small red potatoes Barry made, and the cranberry-apple pie they baked together.

"I picked these cranberries up by Denali last year." Toodles helped herself to a second piece. "Ahhhhh," she said, and then she crinkled her nose and opened her eyes. "Something is missing. See if you can catch it, Bear." She forked a piece into his mouth and they closed their eyes, identical expressions on their faces.

Sitting there across from them, I thought of what the Oprah Giant had said about following one's true path and no matter how far you stray, sooner or later you'll be redirected toward your destiny. I wondered if the reason Barry and I had met was to have Jay-Jay, and if the reason we broke up was to direct Barry toward Toodles. Maybe that was even why Randall left, because if he hadn't, Sandee wouldn't have hired Toodles, who wouldn't have thought about Barry again. It sounded preposterous, but sitting there, I believed it with all of my heart, all of my being. I opened my mouth, took another bite of pie, closed my eyes, and savored.

Saturday, Feb. 11

I was happily smearing purple inside a dark shadow on my *Woman Running with a Box, No. 11* painting when something rustled against the sliding glass door that leads out to the porch. "Bullwinkle," I said, and Killer thumped her tail because we both knew that moose liked to cozy up to the trailer when the temperatures dipped. Last week a large male had slept on the porch, its bony head so close to the sliding door that its breath left moist spots over the glass. I hurried over to the door to take a peek, and two eyes peeked back at me. I yelped, and Killer Bee whimpered against my legs.

"It's me, damn it," a muffled voice yelled.

"Sandee?" I lifted the blinds again and there she was, her face mashed against the window, her nose flat and wrinkled pale.

"Open up, it's freezing out here," she yelled.

"Can't you go around to the front door?"

"No, I cannot *use* the front door. The squeak of the hinges might do me in."

I slid open the latch, which was lined with ice, and watched Sandee struggle through the snow that had drifted up against the door. Her hair was wet, her sweatshirt covered with food stains.

"Where's your coat?" I asked.

"My life is falling apart and you're worried about a coat?"

She pulled up a kitchen chair and started talking before she even sat down. "I got it. Not that I asked but Toodles came in to work tonight. I *told* you she was pushy." She lifted her head. "Did you make brownies? I swear I smell burnt chocolate."

I shook my head no. I had spent the night obsessing over why I wasn't painting as much as I should, and Stephanie had spent the night obsessing over the college applications she sent in months ago. Sandee sighed and continued: "I was in the middle of an eight-top of servers from the Sheraton, you know how well *they* tip, and suddenly Toodles scurries over to my table and waves a manila envelope in my face and I swear, all I could think of was that *Let's Make a Deal* show I watched as a kid. Remember how Monty Hall waved those envelopes in contestants' faces?

"So she places the envelope on my tray—she was very polite, I have to give her that—and she says, 'I was waiting for the right time, and then last night I dreamed of your body with a wolf head.' A wolf head, Carla, like it was predestined by something bigger than us."

She reached into her apron pocket and pulled out a folded tan envelope, salsa smeared across the top. "I can't open it. I tried, but my fingers won't work. Could you?" Her voice trembled and she swallowed a loud gulp. "But don't tell me, okay? I don't want to know where he lives or what he looks like or if he's with someone else. I just want to know that he agrees to the divorce."

I picked up the envelope. "You sure you want me to?" It was like opening my *Woman Running* box and how once those dirty dolls scampered out, I couldn't ignore them, couldn't pretend that they didn't mean as much as they did. "We could wait until later, give you time to consider your options—"

"Do it." Sandee's face was scrunched so tight I was afraid her forehead might crack. I slid the edge of my paintbrush beneath the envelope flap and tore it open. A picture of Randall fell out and I clapped my hand over it, but not fast enough. Sandee tugged it away. "He's fat," she gasped. "He's put on about fifty pounds." She shoved the photo over to me. Randall stood beside a heavyset woman with two heavyset blond boys, all of them holding fishing poles and smiling fat, silly grins. They looked ridiculously happy and sunburned. "Toodles was right," Sandee said. "The woman does look like me."

I held the picture closer to my face. The woman had Sandee's hair and facial features, though she was shorter with ungainly, splayed feet. "Well, that's that," Sandee said. "He's practically married himself."

"I thought that's what you wanted."

"I didn't want him to be *happy*. I wanted him to be miserable. I wanted him to suffer for his sins."

"Pictures don't tell everything."

"Maybe he'll die of a heart attack. Think he's fat enough?"

"No." I shook my head. "He's mostly chubby."

"Bastard." She smacked the photograph. "Look how fucking content he is."

I didn't remind Sandee that she never really loved Randall, not the way she needed to love someone, because she wouldn't have heard me, and besides, she already knew. I made her hot chocolate with the last of the Baileys, a nice, healthy shot, and then I bundled her up in the recliner with the extra quilt and a box of Kleenex. I curled up by her feet until she fell asleep and then crept back into the kitchen, turned on the lamp, and began painting again. The shadows I had been working on had dried to a rich magenta I found particularly appealing. I added small drips of yellow and white to lighten the shade and began spreading the shadow out toward the sky, adding more and more yellow so that it slowly faded into a pale, sultry gold. Then I called Francisco. It was the first time we had talked since our fight on Sunday. I didn't say that I was sorry or that I had missed him.

"Sandee found out where Randall is," I said instead.

"Carlita, it's nice to hear your voice." He sounded sleepy; it was 3:17 a.m. "Who's Randall?"

"Her husband, the one that left three years ago, no note or anything. You want to hear or you wanna sleep?"

"I want to hear." He laughed. "I think."

"He's living in Tonopah with a woman who looks like Sandee's high school picture."

"Makes sense." His voice picked up. "Everything repeats, it's the law of history. Everything has been done before, in one sense or another. It's kind of depressing but it takes the pressure off." He yawned. "Hey, I almost forgot. I Googled you. Your art. Your dirty-doll figurines."

"Oh. I'm painting," I told him, embarrassed. "For my show."

"That's the reason you did it, those paintings you left sliced up like a puzzle."

"A pie. They're shaped like a pie."

"Right. I saw those funny creatures frolicking around the bottom and thought, *Hmmm, those must be dirty dolls,* and so I Googled and there they were."

"Oh." Obviously it wasn't possible to separate my artistic life from my romantic life, at least not with Francisco.

"Come over," he said.

I sucked in my breath but didn't say anything.

"I just got back from a short trip to Bethel. They didn't feed us on the plane. All I had for dinner was a stale donut."

"I'm not cooking."

"I know."

"I'm supposed to be painting."

"I know."

"Maybe," I stalled, "when I finish shadowing."

"I'll leave the door unlocked. Don't mind the beasts. I usually throw socks to settle them down."

I hung up and stared at my canvas. The Woman Running stared back with my eyes, my grandmother's chin, my sister's wrist, Sandee's chest, and Stephanie's mouth. Francisco was right: nothing was original or even new. We painted what was familiar, and that was how we lived. You couldn't really blame Randall for picking a woman so much like Sandee; probably he couldn't help himself. He was a weak man, and like most weak men he had to leave one woman in order to feel strong for the next. Maybe I would tell this to Sandee in the morning. I rinsed out my brushes and moved my canvas to the closet so that it didn't accidentally fall over, and then I pulled on my coat and checked on Jay-Jay. He slept with the blanket kicked down to his knees, his hands curled slightly, as if waiting to receive something. I kissed each palm; then I slipped out the door and drove to Francisco's without bothering to even change my underwear.

"I didn't change my underwear," I said after I let myself in the front door.

"I didn't either." In the soft glow of the night-light, his sheets were pale green. "Come on in." He drew back the covers and I hesitated. He was wearing boxers with skulls printed across the front. "A gift from my brother, get it, because I'm an anthropologist."

"I get it." Lincoln pressed up behind me, his paw stepping on my foot. "Ouch," I said, and then I kicked off my pants and crawled in beside Francisco. We lay beside one another without touching.

"This is odd," he said. "Does it feel odd to you?"

"Yeah. Sex is always awkward at first."

"Who said anything about sex?" And then he laughed. "Come here, Carlita." His arms were around me, his legs twined around mine.

I suppose I should write about sleeping with Francisco for the first time and his skin, which is more golden than mine, and so warm. And his mouth, hungry and fierce and how it covered me, how it became mine, and what it took and what it gave and what it was like as I lay there with him, covered by him. I'd like to say that it was earth shattering, that lights blazed, that my head exploded, and while it was like that, it wasn't like that at all. It was simple and pure and deep and urgent, and afterward, my stomach felt full, as if I had eaten a good meal.

Chapter 24

Tuesday, Feb. 14

"MOM! KILLER CHEWED UP my Valentine's Day box," Jay-Jay yelled this morning as I scraped the burned edges from the toast. He ran out and threw a crumbled shoebox covered in tissue-papered hearts on the counter. "You've gotta fix it. The bus comes in eight minutes."

I pulled out the duct tape and got to work. Duct tape is the Alaskan staple. Every household has at least one roll, and since we live in a dilapidated trailer we have four: the standard gray plus green, yellow, and bright red, which I used to cut out hearts and paste them over the chew marks from Killer's teeth. I added glitter and glued on conversation hearts. I was impressed; it actually looked good, but what else can you expect from duct tape?

"Cool," he said, snatching it up and running out the door just as the bus zoomed by. Poor Jay-Jay; he's been late forty-two times so far this year and recently brought home a note chiding me on my shoddy scheduling skills. Jay-Jay nudged me. "Mom, I don't want to miss library exchange."

On Tuesdays Jay-Jay's gifted class is bussed to other schools' gifted classes to do geeky and stimulating things like play Scrabble and chess and practice for the Junior Science Bowl the district puts on each year. I sighed and leaned over to tie my hiking boots. When I glanced up Laurel was standing by the kitchen table looking pale and unsteady. "I'm coming," she said, tying the sash of her fuzzy green robe and heading for the door.

"A coat," I cried. It was minus eighteen, and the car hadn't had time to warm up properly.

"I'm always warm," she said. "Pregnancy is nine months of having the flu and instead of getting better, you give birth." She smiled bravely. "Come on Jay-Jay, let's get you to school."

Jay-Jay wasn't pleased, since bringing Laurel meant he had to sit in the backseat. "It's insulting to see everything a millisecond after you guys," he complained.

After we dropped him off two minutes before the bell ("Run, Jay-Jay, run," I shouted as I braked hard and left impressive skid marks across the parking lot), Laurel decided to have breakfast at Village Inn.

"I want a pancake. Just one. I need that doughy sponginess in my mouth." Then she sagged against the headrest and closed her eyes. "Turn left on Northern Lights and go toward Forest Park." Her voice was flat and cold. "Keep going through the stop sign. It's the big monstrosity on the right."

I knew immediately that she was directing me to Hank's. "Are you sure?" I asked. "I don't think you're ready to face him."

"Oh, I'm not *facing* him," she said. "I have no desire to *ever* face him again. I need to get something back."

"Clothes?" I couldn't think of anything else that Laurel would risk such a confrontation over.

"No, my verve."

"Y-your what?"

"My verve. You know, my courage. It's Valentine's Day, damn it, and I'm not going to let him win. I'm going to, well, I don't know what I'm going to do, but I'm going to do something, Carly. He owes me, don't you see? Until I take back a payment I'll never be able to live with myself. Don't worry," she said quickly, "I'm not going to do anything illegal, I'm just going to make myself known in sly and devious ways." She smirked and looked over at me. I knew I should have talked her out of it, but she looked like herself for the first time in weeks. Her color was back, her eyes flashed, and her mouth curled into a smug little grin that reminded me of the Cheshire cat. I parked down the street from Hank's house, which was large and imposing and painted a haughty burgundy, and we both got out. It was windy and the moon hung fat and low, even though the sky had already lightened. We were caught in that transitory stage of it no longer being night but not yet daylight either, a watery blue transition that's impossible to capture in paint.

"Remember," Laurel said. "If anyone stops us, we're from the church."

"Which one?"

"Huh?"

"Which church?"

"*The* church," she said. "If you say it like that they'll be too intimidated to ask which one."

"But you have your bathrobe on."

"Priests wear robes and I can, too."

I knew we were going to be caught, and I wondered if Hank would be mad enough to press charges. I imagined Barry bailing us out in his ridiculous checked chef pants. He would drink coffee and tell hunting stories with the policemen. We would be there forever. "Do you have your phone so I can make sure Stephanie's around when Jay-Jay gets home from school?"

Laurel looked at me as if I were crazy.

"When we end up in jail," I said. "Have you thought about that?"

"It won't happen." She calmly wiped snow off a flowerpot, reached beneath it, and pulled out a key. "Come on, it's Tuesday. No one should be home."

She slid the key in the lock, snapped her wrist, and opened the door. Three fat dachshunds waddled toward us. "Don't get them excited or they'll pee on the floor."

It was too late and three puddles spread out across the living room floor, which was covered with an oddly shaped green rug.

"Good boys!" Laurel reached down to pet them, her voice high and childlike. "You pee on Daddy's floor, okay, yes you do, you do." She tugged me down the hall and up the stairs to a child's room. "Wait here while I look."

"Look for what?"

"I *told* you. My verve."

I sat on a bunk bed with a Buzz Lightyear quilt and read *Curious George* until Laurel yelled for me. She had the dresser opened and Hank's underwear scattered around her feet. "Go find scissors in the kitchen," she ordered.

I knew we were going to cut holes in all of Hank's underwear. It was in a novel we had both read years ago written by Margaret Atwood or one of those other plucky Canadian writers. I found two scissors, and Laurel and I spent the next half hour cutting small holes in all of Hank's boxers, briefs, and socks; then we sliced the buttons from his shirts. We hesitated when we reached his pants. "Holes?" Laurel asked, holding up a pair of gray flannel slacks. "Or zipper?"

We settled on the zipper and pulled and yanked until we managed to get them all off track. Then we folded and hung the damaged clothes back up again.

"This doesn't feel like enough." Laurel tucked the last shirt back into the drawer. "Shouldn't I feel triumphant and victorious?" When I didn't answer, she continued, "Mostly I feel sad. Look at these ties! Geometric shapes, like dancing cough drops. This is the man who will be the father of my child, Carly." She sat down on the bed and looked around as if she had no idea how she had gotten there. "What if my daughter has no fashion sense and everyone laughs at her and no one asks her to the prom?"

I grabbed her elbow and maneuvered her down the stairs, through the hallway, and out the door, propping her up against the porch while I locked the front door. Halfway back home I realized I had forgotten to slip the key back beneath the flowerpot, but that didn't matter. As soon as Hank saw the holes in his clothes he'd know who had done it. I hoped he would feel sorry about the way he had treated Laurel, but I doubted that would happen. Probably he was the kind of man who was unable to feel sorry for anyone except himself.

I was late for work and caught Mr. Tims's wrath.

"It's fucking Valentine's Day, we've got a full house, and you show up whenever you goddamn feel like," he yelled as I busily jotted down the specials and headed out to my section, which was already full. I smiled at all of the surly faces. Very few smiled back.

Sandee was in an equally foul mood. "I'm afraid Joe's going to propose," she said as she slammed her tray on the kitchen counter.

"You said that at Christmas and nothing happened."

"But he's hokey enough to make a huge romantic gesture on Valentine's Day. He's spent time in the bush without running water. It kind of goes with the territory."

I had no idea how living without a flush toilet could cause someone to be romantic. "What did he say when you told him about Randall?" I used my apron to wipe green sauce from the side of a plate.

"I haven't told him yet."

"You can't keep it from him." I arranged plates across my tray. The enchilada sauce was a runny, sticky mess today. "You're a couple now, and besides, he asked about the divorce. He asked *you*."

"It has nothing to do with him. It's between Randall and me." Sandee hoisted the tray to her shoulder and rushed out the swinging pantry door, a sprig of parsley sticking to the side of her face. As soon as I served my table, the hostess rushed over with a stack of menus. "You got four at Table Twelve and a loner at the corner booth," she said.

I wanted Francisco to be at my single-top but knew he was out working by Scammon Bay for the day and wouldn't be home until late. Instead I found Barry dressed in his work uniform; his ridiculous chef's hat sat neatly on the seat next to him. "Sorry to hog the table. I'll be out in a couple minutes."

"You want anything?"

"Nah, gotta get to work. A banquet's coming in, a hundred twenty-five vegetarians, won't even eat fish." He shook his head sadly. "Here." He reached into his coat and slid a small box toward me. I knew, from the shape, that it held jewelry.

"I don't understand," I protested.

"It's your Grammy's hairpins. They was behind the dresser when I cleared out of the house after we split. Kept wanting to give 'em to you but didn't seem the right time."

I had carried Gramma's hairpins around with me for years. They were silver and had tiny rubies along the edges, so small they were almost unnoticeable until the light hit them; then they shined. I had lost them when I was pregnant with Jay-Jay and had looked for weeks, weeping and mourning in my hormone-induced state.

"Thanks," I said, shrugging nonchalantly.

"Ain't nothing," he murmured. "Jorge still make them green enchiladas with the minced onions?"

"Want some?"

"Nah, trying to lose the gut." He patted his already shrinking belly. "Tell Jay-Jay to come over. I got a Valentine for him."

"Okay."

I watched him walk out, his pant cuffs dragging on the floor, and as soon as he was out of sight, I slipped the box into my apron pocket and hurried to the bar to pick up my drink order. I felt a twinge of grief, not regarding Barry as much as for the silly and foolish love we had shared, and how easily we had believed in dreams. Neither of us would ever love like that again. It was like surviving childhood and how you long to return even though you know it was never as idyllic as you imagine. Barry loved someone and I was in the process of loving someone, and our new loves would be more mature and stronger and more resilient. We would love with the love of impending middle age, of the knowledge that our bodies are fragile, and so are our hearts and spirits. We would be more tender, and more compassionate and more honest. We would be able to be all these things to someone else because we had loved each other first.

Thursday, Feb. 16

"Florida," Laurel said, looking up from her *1,000 Baby Names* book. "That's a pretty name, isn't it, Florida? Except everyone would associate it with a hurricane."

I was curled up in the living room tucked under quilts and blankets, picking yellow paint from beneath my fingernails. The city was still gripped in a cold spell, with nighttime temperatures dipping down to minus thirty; it hadn't reached above minus eight in over a week. Yet within that brutal chill lay lavender-hued shadows that were like nothing else. Evenings when I walk the dog the inlet glows ghostly pale and lightens everything so that it almost feels as if we are walking through clouds. I am happy then, no one else around, the wind so sharp and cold my face aches beneath my scarf.

The Oprah Giant says knowing what we want is the key to happiness.

"It's not what you think," she said. "That's merely a hodgepodge of family expectations, cultural norms, and your own defense mechanisms."

Instead, what we want is usually what we fear, and we fear it because we simultaneously believe we will fail to achieve it and think that we don't deserve having it. I worried about my own happiness quest. Was I reaching too high? Not high enough? Did I want too much? Too little? Was I suffering from lack of ambition? Self-confidence?

Gramma believed that donuts were the perfect symbol of happiness, and not fancy donuts but the simple cake version she made each Sunday, frying them up on the stove and blotting the grease off with napkins. A donut was sweet, nourishing, and light. It didn't weigh you down or pretend to be anything it wasn't, and it filled the belly in a slow and easy manner. You could eat three or four and not feel stuffed, which Gramma believed was the true worth of the cake donut, not that you could eat more but that while you were eating them you weren't thinking of more.

"I'm not having the amniocentesis test," Laurel said when she noticed me looking at the ultrasound photos scattered over the coffee table. "The doctor recommended it, but what's the point? So I can abort her if she's not perfect? What kind of person would do that?"

"There's different levels of not perfect," I said. "Some are pretty horrible. It's a valid concern."

"No." She pulled the quilt up around her neck. "I couldn't do it." She looked over at me. "Would you?"

I thought of Jay-Jay and how I would love him no matter what he looked like or if he were in a wheelchair and hooked up to oxygen, his neck too weak to support his head, like one of the students at his school. I would still love him, still rejoice when he smiled, still pass his room late at night listening to the comforting sound of his breath. But everything would be different, and he would never have the chance to be the person he is now. Though who knows what qualities he would have been given to make up for it, what gifts he could still give. "I'd have the test," I said quietly.

"And if something were wrong?"

"I don't know. I suppose that depends on the odds of the baby surviving. Why are you asking me all this?"

"You were the one who brought up happiness." She reached for the popcorn bowl and balanced it on her rounded belly. "What happens if my baby dies?"

"I thought we were talking about happiness."

"You can't have one without the other." She munched on popcorn. "Or maybe I'll be the one who dies."

I shivered and moved closer to Laurel. "You're not going to die and neither is your baby."

"You promise to raise her if I do?"

"Why are you even thinking about this?" I reached in and grabbed a handful of popcorn.

She shrugged and licked the salt from her fingers. For someone who thought she might die, she didn't seem very upset. "It could happen, that's all, and I'd be happy knowing she was with you. You might not realize this, Carly, but you're doing okay."

"Sure, if you die, I'll raise your daughter. Any special requests?" I asked sarcastically.

"Don't cut her hair short in the summer, like Mother used to make us do, and be sure she learns to swim when she's young. And don't let her wear high heels until she's sixteen; I don't want her ruining her feet." She leaned over, picked up a glass of orange juice, and took a long drink. "Folic acid," she said, and then she wiped her mouth with the back of her hand. "You'd think it would bother me, wouldn't you, talking about my own death? But it doesn't. You think it has to do with Gramma?"

I looked at her carefully. "Have you seen her?"

"No, but last night I dreamed she was running up and down the beach. She was younger and not as fat and had on one of those swimsuits with the skirts and she looked good, Carly, healthy and happy, and when I woke up I thought, *Whew! When I die I can visit the buffet as often as I like because no one will give a damn what I look like in my swimsuit.*"

"Laurel asked me to raise her baby if she dies in childbirth," I said to Francisco. We were curled in his bed reading old copies of *National Geographic*.

"That must have been tough."

"I said I would of course, she's my sister. But then I started thinking of all the things that could go wrong. She's forty, you know."

"That's not that old. She's having it at a hospital, right?"

"She wanted to have it in my bedroom but the doctor talked her out of it. Women still die in childbirth. You don't hear about it, but they do."

"She'll be fine." He patted my thigh. "Before long that baby will take over your trailer, teething toys all over. Worse than having dogs, at least at first." He laughed and turned toward me. "Have you ever thought of having another?"

"Dog?"

"No, baby. Another child."

"Yeah, I've thought about it." My stomach lurched, as if remembering both the comfort and misery of pregnancy.

"I've always wanted children. It just hasn't happened." He laughed wryly. "I have to know I'm leaving something behind. It's the anthropologist in me."

"You could donate at a sperm bank," I offered.

"I'd rather do it the real way." He snuggled against my shoulder. "You know, with a woman, not a specimen cup."

I tried to imagine it: a house, two small children running around the living room while big brother Jay-Jay tried to teach them complicated mathematical formulas. Francisco and me both older, heavier, and more weathered, but still loving toward one another, tender. Part of me wanted it; oh, I wanted it so much! But I was thirty-eight; by the time these children that hadn't even been born yet went off to college I'd be almost sixty. I wasn't sure I was ready to devote so much time to motherhood. I wanted to devote time to myself. I wanted to know who I was. I tried to explain this to Francisco.

"It would be different with a man around," he said. "You wouldn't be in it alone."

"I know," I said, and I did know. "It's just that—"

"Wait!" He slapped his forehead in mock parody. "We forgot the Valentines." Since Francisco had been in Scammon Bay on Valentine's Day, we had arranged to celebrate tonight, except we still hadn't made it out of the bedroom.

"Stay here," he said, as if commanding the dogs. I watched his ass as he scurried out of the room, muscles flexing as he walked.

"You've got a nice ass," I yelled out to him.

"Think so?" His voice was muffled. "My last girlfriend thought I was too bulky." He reappeared with a huge and ungainly package wrapped in brown paper, which he placed gently on the bed. "Sorry it isn't fancier. It was a bitch to wrap."

"Oh, well." I started to get up to get my present, but Francisco motioned me back to the bed.

"You first," he said.

I leaned forward and pulled the paper loose. Something jabbed my palm and my fingers hit the cool feel of bone. My heart sank. "Oh, how nice," I started to say in a feigned voice but then I shut up because I saw what it was: a pelvic bone painted with a silver-lavender sky, the inlet in the background.

"It's beautiful." I ran my hands over the curves.

"Feel that right there?" He guided my fingers to small cracks that ran along in the inside of the bone. "Those indicate childbirth. This woman birthed at least one child, probably more. We know from the scratches. Childbirth scars you down to the bone."

When he said that, chills ran down my back.

"It's lovely," I said. And it was, oddly yet truly lovely. "Now your turn." I pulled a small box from my backpack and handed it over. "It's wrapped better but don't feel bad, okay?" He laughed and lifted the lid. Inside were the leftover slices of the painting I had been giving him, along with a bottle of glue and sealant. "Once you put it together, it will have seams," I explained. "It will look mosaic, like a tapestry or a quilt. The cool thing is that each segment tells its own story, and when you put it together, the story changes and—"

His lips were on mine, hot and insistent. We made love again, the pelvic bone pressing my shoulder so that it almost felt like a hand reaching out, not so much for Francisco or me but for the heat between us and, dare I say it? The love.

LETTER #12

Dear Carla Richards:

Holy stethoscope!

Excuse our excitement, but your February payment not only arrived on time but was made out over the amount due.

We have therefore credited your account $9.75, available at the time of your next appointment.

Thank you for choosing Far North Pediatrics, where your children are our children.

Dr. Jennison and Dr. Harrison
Far North Pediatrics

P.S. Tell Jay-Jay we are all rooting for him at the spelling bee. Break a vowel, Jay-Jay!

Chapter 25

Saturday, Feb. 18

"D-O-D-E-C-A-R-C-H-Y," JAY-JAY SPELLED at the breakfast table this morning. "C-y-n-o-d-o-n-t. G-u-e-n-o-n."

Next Friday was the Alaska State Spelling Bee, and Jay-Jay was representing his school, having beaten out the top two sixth graders last month at the school bee. He had looked so small standing up on the stage with the older kids; he had to stand on his tiptoes to reach the microphone.

"It's totally random." He looked up from his sample word booklet. "They'll have these easy words and then wham! They'll throw in a hard one. *Cruel* and *crayon*, those are easy, you don't even have to think, and then suddenly it's *cruciverbalist*."

"It seems kind of mean," Stephanie said. "No one, like, ever uses those words, at least not real people."

"It's not about the *words*," Jay-Jay said. "It's about the preparation. You get rewarded for your commitment."

I closed my eyes and thought of soothing colors: titan buff, cobalt teal, Quinicidrone red. I planned to spend the entire day painting and warned everyone that as soon as I put on my headphones I would be gone; I wouldn't really be there.

"Okay if I go over to Alan's? We're filming his rock collection."

"Call the minute you get over there, not like last time..."

The door slammed and soon after, the phone rang.

"I didn't die," he said sarcastically. "I'm staying for lunch, and Mom, Alan's mom saw a poster of you in City Market and said it looked like your nostrils were flaring in triumph."

"I'm fucked," I said as soon as I hung up. "The fliers are up. Soon everyone will know I make dirty dolls." I leaned against the kitchen counter. "I hope no one scrawls nasty messages over our front door."

"Chill," Stephanie said. "You're totally overreacting. It's just sex. No one cares."

"Just sex," I snorted. "The Bible thumpers will want my head." I walked over to where Stephanie was sitting. "Do my nostrils flare? Tell me the truth, okay?"

She studied me a moment. "Well, they, like, balloon out when you're excited, but don't worry, Mrs. R, I read on the Internet that it's a sign of sexual generosity."

"Who's generous?" Laurel walked into the kitchen dressed in a hideous red-and-blue blouse and yellow sweatpants. From the side, with her stomach blooming out, she resembled Gramma.

"My fliers are up. Alan's mother saw them at—"

Laurel held up her hand like a traffic cop. "Spare me the details. I need to surround myself in serenity before class. Steph, you ready?"

"Totally."

Laurel was prepping Stephanie as a birthing coach alternate, in case I was stuck at work when her labor hit. She gathered up crackers, juice, cough drops, and the picture of Jay-Jay she was using as her focal point, the one taken on a clamming trip down at Nikiski. Jay-Jay stood in the sand in his oversized rubber boots, muddy and grinning and holding up a clamshell almost as large as his head. As soon as Stephanie and Laurel left, I pulled on my coat, tied a scarf around my neck, called for Killer, and headed down toward City Market. I needed to see the flier for myself. Maybe it wasn't as bad as I thought, I said to Killer as we walked. Probably it was half-hidden by notices for babysitters and dog walkers.

It wasn't. The flier was large, like a theater poster, and displayed smack in the middle of the entranceway; it was impossible to miss. My photograph smiled in a dopey manner, while my dirty dolls danced around the corners. It was garish, loud, obscene. I froze. I couldn't move.

"Miss, your dog can't come in here," a young boy working by the vegetables said, and heads turned. Did they notice the resemblance between my face and the one on the flier? I began to sweat, and before I knew it, I was tearing the flier off the wall. I had one side pulled down when a hand grabbed my wrist.

"You don't want to do that," a voice said. I looked over expecting to see the vegetable stocker but it was an elderly man in a bright red cardigan sweater.

"I-I don't?"

"No, dear." He released my arm and squinted at the poster. "It needs to be up. It's art." I gave him a grateful smile because he was right. It was art, and there was nothing to be ashamed of. "You should have made the naked women bigger," he said, pointing toward the dirty dolls. "I can't see their tits."

I walked back home with Killer, only to discover the furnace had died. The house was already getting cold, so I fired up the oven, threw a blanket over my shoulders, and called several repair shops. Furnaces were down all over town, they all told me, and no one was available until next week.

When I mentioned that my pregnant sister lived with me, one man promised to fit us in. "The missus was always cold when it come her time," he said. "Slippers, bathrobes, sweaters. Now she's going through the change and sleeps with nothing but a sheet."

The repairman ("Call me Ed!") arrived later that afternoon. He was in a glum mood but cheered up when he saw the furnace.

"She's an old one," he said as he knelt in the hallway and opened the door that housed the furnace's innards. "I'll do my best but she ain't got but a breath or two left."

Ed didn't look as if he had many breaths left, either. His pants sagged around his hips and his beard looked dull and tired. After two hours of clanking and tinkering, he declared the furnace officially dead and handed me a bill for $273.92. "'Course that's without the new furnie installation." He wiped his face with a dirty rag that magically appeared from his pocket. "Not sure how the pipes look, might have to replace 'em as well."

A new "furnie" would cost around $750, with an extra $300 or so for installation, unless we bought it from his shop; then they'd halve the setup charges plus kick in an additional 10 percent discount, along with a free calendar and coffee mug. I made plans for everything to be delivered Monday and walked him out.

"Ain't it a bitch?" he said as I opened the door and the cold snapped us in the face. He stared at me a moment too long. "You look familiar but don't think I ever been to this address before." He scratched his neck. "Maybe I seen you around town." He shook my hand with his greasy paw and drove off in his dilapidated truck. I settled down at the kitchen table and tried to figure out how to come up with over a thousand dollars by Monday. I was still there when Laurel got up.

"What *was* all that noise? I woke up twice and could barely get back to sleep."

I told her about needing a new furnace and how much it was going to cost.

"We alone?" she interrupted

"Jay-Jay is at Alan's, and Steph is out sledding."

She pulled the blanket tighter around her. "I don't want to be pregnant anymore. I'm tired of doing all the work. It took two of us to get this way, so why isn't Hank lugging thirty extra pounds and craving Dinty Moore beef stew?"

"Safeway beef stew," I corrected.

"Huh?"

"Safeway brand; you won't eat Dinty Moore," I said, but Laurel only sighed and played with her bathrobe sash. "Hit him where it hurts." I rummaged around the cupboard for the small saucepan. "Sue his ass for child support—weren't you talking about that earlier? Take him for everything you can get." I opened the freezer, retrieved my frozen credit card, and plopped it into the pan. I planned to bring it to a slow boil in hopes of unthawing it without ruining the bar code.

"I will, believe me. It was his penis that got me into this mess. Promise you won't say anything, but it was larger than most—not that I cared, but he expected me to *swoon*, which doesn't make sense when you think about it. Penis size isn't a character attribute or something he worked to achieve. It's genetics, pure and simple, and aside from sex, a big penis isn't really that useful—it can't stop global warming or feed the hungry."

I scooped my credit card out with a pair of tongs and laid it gently over a paper towel. It looked okay to me, maybe a bit shinier than normal but seemingly undamaged. I flipped it over. My signature was blurred but still recognizable.

"It's not that I *didn't* appreciate it," Laurel kept on. "I just wasn't willing to worship it, which I'm thankful for now. Look at me, Carly! Look at the things my body can do!" She gave her massive belly a loving little thump. "I'm growing a baby, a whole separate life, isn't that the most amazing thing?" She reached for a package of crackers and crammed two in her mouth. "Why are you cooking your credit card?"

I sighed and told her again about how much the furnace was going to cost and how I had to thaw my credit card out in order to charge the repairs.

"There's no other way." I held the card in my palm. It felt slippery and warm, like holding someone's hand. "It's just that...remember how I told you I had had a little bit of trouble with my finances, right? Well, the credit counselor has really straightened me out. I'm down to just a few thousand on four cards, my interest rates are manageable, and by next year I should be totally debt free." I almost mentioned the

Oprah Giant's diary program but slammed my mouth shut at the last moment.

Laurel smeared jelly over the crackers and licked her fingers. "Do we have any Chunky Monkey left? And maybe a little bit of chocolate sauce to go over it, and whipped cream and oh, Carly, if I could have a cherry on top it would be perfect. I have a busy afternoon ahead of me."

I got out the ice cream, fixed Laurel a sundae, and decided to make one for myself, too. I sat down beside her and dug in. "Remember the time . . . ," I began, but she was already waddling her sundae back to the bedroom. "Knock if you need to come in," she said over her shoulder. "I'll be working through most of the afternoon and will probably take off after supper to do the rest in person. You seeing Francisco tonight?"

"He's giving a talk up in Healy."

She didn't answer, so I put the ice cream away and decided to make bread. Gramma used to say that baking bread was like giving birth, that it took a long time, was often painful, and you never knew what you'd end up with but knew you'd love it nevertheless. She baked bread every Wednesday, the middle of the week, six dark and dense loaves filled with herbs and nuts. My favorite was caraway seed and rosemary bread, which Gramma made with just enough buttermilk to give it a tang, but I was sticking to a basic white and whole wheat flour mix. My loaves were usually misshapen and soggy in the middle, but we ate them anyway, tearing off pieces and smearing them with margarine while they were still hot.

After the yeast bubbled ("It trying to talk," Gramma used to say. "Imagine the stories it know"), I added shortening, salt, sugar, and milk, then measured out the flour—the final and most important step, according to Gramma, who varied the amount according to the weather, precipitation, and time of day. Afternoon bread demanded more flour, so I added an extra handful. Then I began to knead. It was my favorite part, the whole reason I baked bread: the feel of the dough, sticky yet determined, and how it clung to my hands one minute, retreated the next. It was a dance: punch, fold, press, pat. Gramma never followed a recipe when she baked bread but it always came out perfect, at least to us, though she always found a flaw. I don't think she was ever completely happy with a loaf. I lightly patted my ball of dough with oil. Some people oiled the pans instead, but Gramma claimed that disrupted the natural *istota*, or the heart and soul, of the bread. I covered the dough with a dish towel, placed it on top of the warm oven, and checked the clock. As I waited for it to rise, I looked over my *Woman Running with a Box, No. 13* painting. It was one of the last in a series of fifteen, and the woman was racing in the Iditarod Sled Dog Race, her hair flowing behind her as she mushed across the Bering Sea. Scattered across the sled were a slew of dirty dolls: Suck Me Sammie hung from the front rails; Pearl Necklace Polly and Darcie Do-Me-from-Behind sat on the supply pack, arms raised like beauty queens waving from a float. On the floor Fisting Fred bent over, his overly large ass exposed for all the world to see, each gigantic cheek covered in newsprint: "due to the economic decline," it said on the left side, and "according to witness testimony" on the other.

"I'm fucked," I said to Killer. The Iditarod is regarded as sacred, the last great race in a state slowly modeling itself after every other state in America. Insulting the Iditarod is like insulting Jesus. As luck would have it, the ceremonial start took place in Anchorage the same weekend my show opened.

"I'm really, really fucked," I repeated to Killer. But the dough magically rose, and I stuck two misshapen loaves in the oven, the warm and yeasty smells filling the air so that all night I felt loved and protected.

WHAT WAS ON MY ANSWERING MACHINE

6:55 a.m. Mrs. Richards? It's Ed. I was over the other day about the furnace call and realized you're the gal from the art poster they was talking about after church. Never thought I'd meet a real-life celebrity. The missus wants to know if you'll autograph the repair bill, it would give her—*Click.*

12:56 p.m. Carla! This is Jenny Jeffers, remember? We worked together at the Captain Cook a couple of years ago. I just saw the advert for your art show. Wow. Sounds like you've been getting laid a lot. Let's get together and—*Click.*

4:23 p.m. Hey, Really Real Girl, if I pay you fifty bucks, will you spank me with a Ping-Pong paddle?

Monday, Feb. 20

"If there was music playing in the background of your life, like a Hollywood movie, what song would it be?" Laurel sat on the floor beside where I had been sleeping, her hands folded across her belly. "And choose carefully—that one song would have to stay with you your whole life."

"What time is it?" I pulled myself up. Stephanie was gone from the couch and I could hear murmurs from out in the kitchen. "Did I oversleep?"

"I think I'd pick something by Joni Mitchell," Laurel continued. "Or Carole King. It would have to be a woman—imagine having to listen to a man over and over again."

Out in the kitchen Jay-Jay and Stephanie ate pancakes. "But here's the thing"—Jay-Jay was talking about his fruit-fly project—"if I increase their food they eat more but less often, isn't that cool? If people could do that we wouldn't have to worry about getting fat."

"You should totally see the toilets in the gym," Stephanie said. "They're plugged from girls puking." She took a big bite of toast. "Most think I'm ano since I'm so skinny but it's just, like, my metabolism. My mom was totally thin before she started drugs. Now she fluctuates: fat, emaciated, fat, emaciated."

"What's *ano?*" Jay-Jay asked.

"*Anorexic,*" Laurel answered. She sat down and immediately began stuffing pancakes in her mouth. "I'll take leftovers if anyone's got them."

I huddled in the last chair. In less than two weeks my opening would be over and I could live my life as a normal person again, without the threat of shame and ruin hanging over my head each time I listened to my answering machine messages. To calm my nerves I decided to pay my bills ahead of time. The Oprah Giant says that procrastinating is a sign of fear. "How can you like yourself when you're afraid to face yourself?" she asked. The credit counselor was a bit more realistic. To her it was all about math: you have so much coming in and so much going out, and in between is what you live on. I got out my checkbook, credit card statements, and Jay-Jay's old calculator, and I jotted down numbers and signed checks as everyone talked around me. Laurel was still deciding on a baby name, Jay-Jay wondered if fruit flies ever committed suicide, and Stephanie worried about getting into Stanford.

"They send out the letters April first. Is that totally cruel or what?"

"Why would that be cruel?" Laurel asked.

"Hello! It's April Fools' Day."

I licked stamps and set the envelopes in the middle of the table; I would drop them off at the post office on the way to work. It felt good to get them out of the way. Now I could concentrate on my paintings. I was finished, except for touch-ups, sequencing, and titles. I had no idea if they were good or bad. Looking at them was like looking at Jay-Jay's or Laurel's face: familiar and dear, all faults visible yet muted by love. I was ready to ask if anyone needed anything at the store when I started to cry. I set my head down on the dirty tablecloth and sobbed so hard the salt and pepper shakers jostled up and down.

"Mrs. Richards?" Stephanie said, but Laurel shushed her.

"Let her be," she said. "She needs to get it out."

Chairs scraped against the floor as everyone got up. Water splashed; someone washed the dishes. Someone else took out Killer. And still I cried. I couldn't seem to stop. I momentarily worried about becoming dehydrated but then remembered I was close to the kitchen faucet.

Hours later I woke to the smell of grilled cheese sandwiches and lifted my head. Jay-Jay and Alan sat across from me eating an after-school snack while Stephanie told them a story of Hammie's pizza deliveries.

"And so then he totally tells the dude that they don't deliver to the Upper Hillside but the guy, like, insists that he ordered a pizza just last week and they totally delivered it. So finally Hammie drives all the way up these slippery roads out by like Prospect Heights and knocks on his door and guess who answers?"

"Wayne Newton," Jay-Jay and Alan shouted; they had heard him sing on a PBS special last night, and he was their new joke.

I fell back to sleep. Cupboards opened and closed, doors slammed, Stephanie's cell phone rang again and again. Alan's mother stopped by to walk him home, Killer threw up on the rug, and Laurel went over more baby names with Stephanie. When I woke for good it was dark, and Laurel sat across from me tapping away on her laptop.

"A Jimmie called about your dirty dolls and offered his good luck with your show."

"Jimmie?"

"He and his boy toy got kicked out of the nudist resort for wearing clothes." She snorted. "If my Realtor friends could see me now: living in a trailer, pregnant with a married man's child, and conversing with a gay man with a ten-inch dick."

"How do you know how big his dick is?" My neck hurt and I felt ornery.

"Jimmie 'Ten-inch' Dean? It doesn't take a rocket scientist to figure *that* one out."

I was eating my second egg sandwich when Sandee walked in the door. Her hair frizzed around her head, and she smelled of fajita grease. "Where were you?" She sat down in the chair next to me. "It was brutal. I was stiffed twice. Mr. Tims was furious you didn't show but I told him you were a waitress on the verge of a nervous breakdown and if he wasn't nice he could end up in your next show. That shut him up fast." She took a bite of my sandwich, and then another. "Nutmeg?" I shook my head yes, and she stared at me hard. "You okay? Your face looks blotchy and crinkled."

"I fell asleep on the kitchen table." I noticed that Sandee's fingernails were bitten and ragged. "You don't look so good yourself. What's up?"

"Laurel said you spent the day sleeping."

"So?"

"I don't want to overload you. It's just that Joe gave me an ultimatum. Either I file for a divorce or we cool it down until I *do* file."

"That sounds fair. Harsh, but fair."

"I didn't think you'd take *his* side."

I made another egg sandwich and waited for Sandee to cool down. "You need to do something." I placed half of the sandwich in front of her. "Call Randall or send him an e-mail. Just do something." I pulled my cell phone out from beneath a pile of painting supplies. "Call him. Or call Toodles and have her call him. Just call somebody." I pulled on my coat and motioned for Killer. "I'm walking the dog. You know how to work my cell, right?"

The cold hit me like a slap, and Killer whimpered as we walked across the road and down by the inlet. My teeth chattered, and I could feel the wind through my pant legs, but still there was something exhilarating about being outside in such cold. The darkness was deep purple, and the snow-covered mountains gleamed against the horizon. After I scooped Killer's poop up with an old plastic bag, we headed up the big hill toward home.

"It's done," Sandee said the minute I walked in the door. She had put on lipstick and combed her hair. "Randall wants a divorce, I want a divorce, I guess I'm getting a divorce." She laughed shakily. "I called Joe and he invited himself over to watch *American Idol*. I hope it's okay."

I nodded and pulled off my boots.

"It's not what you expect, is it?" she continued. "Love, I mean. It's nothing like movies or books. It's more like a Wednesday, a middle-of-the-week day, slow and ordinary."

I thought of what the Oprah Giant had said, that desire is based on unattainability. We seek what we can't have, and if we somehow manage to have it, we lose interest because we never really wanted it to begin with; what we wanted was the quest, the excitement of the chase, the validation of knowing someone wanted us so much they were willing to travel out of their comfort zone to try and catch us. It's dysfunctional and doomed to fail, which makes it even that much more intoxicating. I wanted to tell this to Sandee, but I yawned instead. The short walk had exhausted me.

"Go back to bed," she said. "I'll wake you when Joe gets here. And I'll call Mr. Tims and arrange for time off, as many days as he can spare."

"I can't afford it."

"You can't afford not to. You need to take care of yourself. Jesus, Carla, everyone here depends on you. What would happen if you got seriously sick? That's where you're heading if you keep going at this pace." She patted my butt. "Scoot. And not the sleeping bag on the floor either, but a real bed. Laurel can nap on the couch if she needs."

I trudged off to bed, crawled under the covers. It felt strange to sleep so high up, almost as if I were flying. I must have fallen asleep, because the next thing I knew Jay-Jay was shaking my arms and telling me that Joe was there. I stumbled out into the living room.

"Carly!" Laurel cried, as if she hadn't seen me in years. I sat down and was immediately handed a paper plate filled with a strange lump that appeared to be covered in gravy.

"That's my chickpea cutlet," Stephanie said proudly. "I'm totally thinking of going vegan."

"I'd be afraid to stop eating cheese and eggs," Laurel said. "I don't want my baby born without fingernails."

"This dude totally complained about a fingernail in one of Hammie's pizza deliveries last week," Stephanie said. "His girlfriend kept saying, 'Honey, I think it's mine,' but he bitched until Hammie comped the order. He peed on the dude's tires on the way out, to get even."

"Like that guy who lived with wolves," Jay-Jay said excitedly. "He drank *tons* of beer and peed around this huge square to mark his territory."

"The wolves peed right over it again," Joe said. He sat beside Sandee drinking generic root beer and sawing away at Stephanie's cutlet, which had the consistency of cooked rubber. He looked perfectly at home.

I fell asleep again as Sandee told a story about a customer at Mexico in an Igloo who tried to pay his bill with wolf pelts. When I woke hours later, the house was silent and Stephanie was curled up in my usual spot on the floor. I found Laurel in the kitchen eating raw chocolate chip cookie dough without the eggs.

"It's been bothering me," she said the minute I walked in. "I kept brushing my teeth because I couldn't figure it out. So I got out my camera and look, tell me what's wrong, okay?"

I lifted the camera and peered at the preview window and there we were, all of us—Stephanie, Sandee, Joe, Laurel, and Jay-Jay. We were all smiling (although I had drool on my face from napping), not the fake smiles people put on for the camera but real and imperfect smiles: our mouths opened too wide, our eyes crinkled, the sides of our faces wrinkled.

"Something's wrong. I can't put my finger on it and, Carly, it's driving me crazy."

I didn't say anything for a long minute. "We look happy, that's what's wrong. We all look happy."

Chapter 26

Wednesday, Feb. 22

ONCE, GRAMMA SET UP a scavenger hunt for me. I was in high school and much too old for children's games, but I went along with it anyway. The theme was food, and each clue spelled out the ingredients for a recipe I was instructed to cook. I can't remember what this was, only that it didn't turn out; maybe I burned it or added too much salt. Before long, Gramma grew impatient at my clumsiness and took over.

"What, now you cannot read the letters?" she said, shaking the map over the counter and explaining each clue to me. I didn't mind being scolded and I especially didn't mind my grandmother taking over cooking duties. I sat at the table and told Gramma the story of Frida Kahlo, who Gramma loved because she had the strongest "flue-flue," which meant that she had balls. Mostly, though, she adored Diego, who was fat and messy in most of his photographs.

"That Frida a lucky woman," she'd say. "She got the gift and the fat man."

Then she'd make *placki kartoflane*, potato pancakes. Talking about Diego got Gramma so riled up that she often kept right on cooking: pork chops, meatballs, *golabki*, cabbage and mushroom pierogi, and raisin and raspberry jam jelly rolls. Platters filled the counters, the tables, overflowed out into her messy living room.

Remembering this made me hungry for potato pancakes, so I rooted around the refrigerator, lined up all the ingredients, and started grating potatoes and carrots. I was mixing in flour and eggs when Laurel shuffled into the kitchen in her oversized slippers. The chair pulled out and slammed back in again, and as she rearranged herself to get comfortable, I prayed she wouldn't start in with her stupid questions. I had too much to worry about this morning: I still hadn't fixed the shading in my last painting, and Jay-Jay's spelling bee was Friday. I mixed harder, the spoon *tap-tap-tap*ping the edge of the metal bowl.

"Listen, Carly," she began happily. "If you could be any type of punctuation mark, which would you be?" She paused and, when I didn't answer, kept right on talking. "I'd be a semicolon. There's something about that squiggly line with the little dot that commands respect. You pause but don't quite stop, like a yield sign. I used to be a period—I had that authority, that stop-right-here presence—but I think it's better this way, don't you?"

"I-I guess so." I leaned down to retrieve the skillet from the bottom cupboard when something hit me in the ass. "Ouch!" I jumped back. Something else hit me in the back of the shoulders and then the back of my head. "Stop it!" I turned around, ready to smack Laurel with the dish towel, when I noticed small bundles of money scattered across the floor.

"For the furnace." Laurel stuck her fingers in the jelly jar and licked them clean. "So you don't have to worry about more credit card debt. You might want to buy a better house someday, and Carly, your credit score follows you around. It's like your blood type. It's that important."

There was over a thousand dollars spread out around me, mostly in twenties. "Where did this come from?"

"I sold my clothes. Thank god I'm a popular size. If I were skinnier they wouldn't have gone so fast."

"You sold your designer outfits?" Laurel's clothes were her identity, and she kept them arranged in the closet through a complicated system of favorability. A purple blouse might hang next to a yellow blazer not because they coordinated but because she believed that if they came to life they would wear the same lipstick shade.

"I didn't need them any longer. I'm about to be a mother—what am I going to do with a white Anne Klein suit, or shoes with three-inch heels?"

"You're giving this to me? All of it?"

She shrugged. "I've been living here for months, eating your food and using your washing machine—which, by the way, makes a funny noise during the spin cycle. You might want to get someone out to look at it."

Tears welled up in my eyes. "Well, Laurel, I mean you didn't have to do this."

"I know." She wiped her sleeve across her forehead. Now that the furnace was fixed she was warm all the time and gave off a yeasty, almondy smell. "I posted everything on Craigslist and said I was moving so people would act fast. The hardest part was taking pictures. I had to put a sheet over your bedspread. No offense, Carly, but that sure is an eyesore and would have brought the prices down. I sold my Coach purse in less than five minutes. After that it was like dominos falling over: blouses, suits, shoes, pants, one after another after another. I mailed or delivered them myself; I didn't want anyone to know I was selling from a trailer. Like I said, stuff like that can really kill the price."

I grabbed her hand and squeezed. "Thanks." My voice was thick with tears.

"I thought I'd miss them but I don't. Oh, I miss what they represent, me as a well-dressed, competent woman; I miss that more than I can say. But I bought them when I was someone else. They don't belong to the person I've become. Don't get me wrong, I have no intention of wearing discount maternity rags all my life. After the baby comes I'll find another job and buy a new wardrobe, though probably not as expensive. Paying three hundred fifty dollars for a blouse no longer makes sense."

She got up and pulled a new jar of jelly out of the cupboard, sat back down, and licked the lid. "I know you've always seen me as strident and overly materialist and maybe I was, though a lot of it was put on for my job. Once you adopt a persona, it's hard to shrug it off. But once it's gone you can't pull it back on again, not when you've moved so far from what you once were." She paused for a moment and looked down at her hands. "I'm not getting back with Junior, am I?"

I wanted to say, *Sure you will* in a hearty, fake voice, but I didn't. "I don't know," I started, and then I was more honest. "Probably not."

Laurel had jelly smeared across her upper lip. "You'd think it would bother me more, but it doesn't, or at least not yet." She slurped jelly in silence. "Next week you take your paintings down for your show."

"Ummmmm."

"I'm glad, Carly. I really am. Maybe we're both getting what we want, you with your show and me with my baby. I always expected my life would be a straight line but it's turned all curvy, and the oddest thing is that it's so much better this way, even living in this trailer and having almost no money. I wonder why that is?"

"It's happiness," I said again, blushing slightly, as if I was talking about sex or feminine hygiene products.

"Happiness?" Laurel leaned forward. There was jelly in the corner of her mouth. "Do you really think this is what happiness is?"

"Maybe." I ladled the potato pancakes over the griddle and watched them bubble up with the heat. I could feel Laurel waiting for a better answer but I couldn't give it to her. I shrugged and said it again: "maybe."

Friday, Feb. 24

"Don't sit too close to the front because that's dumb," Jay-Jay told us when he came out to breakfast. It was the day of the Alaska State Spelling Bee, and he wore freshly ironed pants (thanks to Laurel) and a neat oxford shirt (ditto), and his hair was freshly slicked back. "And don't yell or clap too hard when I get a word right."

We all nodded, though of course we were planning on sitting up front and we would all clap too hard.

"Do you have your lucky charm?" Laurel was on her third piece of toast. "Tuck it in your right pocket, this way the luck will come to you. The left is for releasing luck out to the universe."

"Yeah, yeah," Jay-Jay mumbled. "I just hope I don't miss an easy word." He wiped his mouth on his sleeve. "Last year this kid went down on *dolphin*; you could tell he knew it, too, but there was a disconnect between his brain and mouth."

"Nervous?" Stephanie asked.

He shrugged and went to put on his shoes. No one spoke much on the drive downtown, and after I left Jay-Jay and Laurel off at the curb, I pulled into the Fifth Avenue Mall parking garage. I wore dark glasses in case anyone recognized me from my art show poster, and Stephanie had on a vintage polka-dot dress that swirled out from her hips and army boots, with striped socks sticking out the top.

"Hammie's totally skipping economics to come." She sidestepped a discarded Coke can. "He hates spelling; you should see his e-mails. I wrote a poem about it but I think I totally hurt his feelings. Now he mostly texts. Men are so sensitive, Mrs. Richards. Their egos are, like, totally fragile."

Laurel saved seats for us down front, seven in a row—Barry was coming as soon as he filed next week's produce order, and Francisco promised to be there after his work meeting. Parents and family sat in the outside aisles and spelling bee contestants in the middle. I spotted Jay-Jay in the seventh row, sitting between a freckled girl and a chubby boy.

"Jay-Jay," I yelled, frantically waving my arms. "We're over here, honey."

He glared and pretended I didn't exist. The parents looked far more nervous than the kids. My hands were sweating, and I worried I hadn't worn enough deodorant. I asked Laurel if I smelled, but she had her shoes kicked off and wasn't listening.

"Even my feet are fat," she complained. "Even my toes—look!" She pulled off her socks and wiggled her chubby toes at me. "It's so hard being pregnant, I had no idea. The birthing instructor says that once we go through childbirth we'll forget everything bad about being pregnant. Do you think that's true?"

I thought of my own labor, which had lasted thirty-six hours. I still remember the pain, so hot and immense I was sure I was going to die, yet behind it something so strong and binding that the moment Jay-Jay lay on my stomach, his face all scrunched and mashed from the birthing canal, his hands curled into angry fists, I recognized him immediately, recognized his face, as if I had known him a long time ago. "Yes, I think it's true," I said, squeezing Laurel's arm. She smiled over at me, just as the spelling announcer walked up onstage. He had on two-toned loafers and was introducing the three judges in a laconic tone when Sandee slid into the seat next to Laurel.

"Mr. Tims sends his luck, along with everyone else from work," she whispered loudly.

After we heard the rules (no walking up and down the aisles or entering/exiting while a speller was spelling), the first speller bravely approached the stage and spelled her word correctly. So did the next, and the next. Francisco arrived after the first miss, and I clutched his hand, my mind slowly wandering. I didn't notice Barry come in, or Hammie. I swirled colors around and was busy re-creating Monet's *Water Lilies* (I was having problems with the petals, which looked like vaginas unfolding across the water) when Laurel elbowed me in the side.

"Wake up," she whispered. "It's almost time."

I blinked. Jay-Jay's row was filing down to the front of the auditorium, fifteen elementary and middle school students in their too-big spelling bee T-shirts. Jay-Jay was the smallest; he barely came to the shoulder of the kid behind him. He looked so defenseless! So vulnerable! Those big kids were going to eat him alive.

"Help," I gulped to Laurel, my fingers tightening around her wrist. "I can't bear it."

"He'll be fine," she said with such confidence that I immediately sat up straighter. "He's strong—he won't buckle under pressure."

We sat silently, barely breathing as Jay-Jay made his way across the stage and stood in front of the microphone. His left shoelace was untied, and his spelling bee T-shirt bagged around his knees.

"*Pugnacious*," the announcer said, and Jay-Jay drew himself up, leaned closer to the microphone, and spelled it perfectly.

"Fuck," Barry whispered loudly; heads turned. "Don't think I'll make it through another round."

It was heartbreaking watching kids go down and how they struggled, their faces scrunched, their hands pulling at their T-shirts. By the time the first round was over, we were all exhausted. We waited in line for the restroom, then sat in the lobby eating the butterscotch cookies Barry had made. Jay-Jay sat with us and chattered; he didn't seem the least bit concerned about the pressure.

"Were you scared?" Sandee asked. "It looked so lonely up there."

"You don't notice." Cookie crumbs flew from his mouth. "You zone out until nothing exists but you and the word. It becomes, like, this entity, and you've gotta fight to find the letters."

"It's totally Zen," Stephanie said. "It's like the ultimate battle of the subconscious with the leftover regime of the status quo."

We all nodded as if we knew what she was talking about; it seemed the polite thing to do. More kids went down in the second round, as the words became progressively tougher: *Klompen. Mutafacient. Parchment.*

By the time Jay-Jay reached the stage more than half of the participants had been eliminated. He squinted in the overhead lights.

"*Perpendicularly*," the announcer said.

"Should have brought my Dramamine," Barry moaned, his arms folded around his belly. The rest of us leaned forward as if to urge Jay-Jay on. He drew in a breath, closed his eyes, and stepped up to the microphone.

"*Perpendicularly*," he said in a clear voice. "P-e-r-p-e-n-d-i-c-u-l-a-r-l-y."

There was no break before the next round, which took down even more kids, but Jay-Jay spelled *rarefaction* without a hitch. At the noon lunch break we walked to the Snow City Cafe and Jay-Jay devoured the Fourth Avenue Special, carrot cake, and two mugs of hot chocolate. Sandee told a story about a woman Joe had arrested for poaching a lynx; Laurel revealed her latest baby name: Lavender Blue. And Stephanie told about the kid in her honors English class who was suspended for having the principal's name tattooed on his ass.

"It's totally hypocritical." She slurped a vegan soup with root vegetables floating across the top. "Just last week we had this assembly and they totally went on about free speech and it's like, hello! It's his ass—he can tattoo it with anything he pleases."

It felt colder walking back to the spelling bee, the air damp from the inlet, the wind in our faces. Barry, Francisco, and Hammie walked in front to block the worst of it, but still our teeth chattered. The afternoon session clipped along at a faster pace, with the auditorium slowly emptying. Soon only three rows of participants remained, and then two. Jay-Jay walked up to the microphone each round with a determined set to his shoulders. I wanted to weep. I wanted to run up onstage and pull him down, drive him back home where it was safe and everyone loved him and there were no failures. I sat between Laurel and Francisco, and each time Jay-Jay bounded up onstage in his scuffed Nikes, they grabbed my hands, held tight. Barry jiggled his foot, tore his program to shreds, moaned softly.

By three p.m. there were only twelve students left. Then nine. Then six. Jay-Jay spelled his words without a hitch, but I could tell the strain was getting to him. His face was pinched, the bottom of his T-shirt damp from the nervous motion of his hands. Soon it was down to four. A girl in a plaid jumper missed and her mother challenged the judges. Jay-Jay strolled over during the short recess. He was very pale. He leaned his head on Barry's shoulder, closed his eyes for a moment. "Dad?" he said. "Remember that fish you caught and threw back even though it was regulation size?"

"The one I called Tommie?" Barry said. "He put himself up a real good fight. Couldn't make myself kill him after that, like he earned my respect. Hated letting him go but damned if I didn't look at him and think, *This guy needs to live more than I need to eat.*"

Jay-Jay was called back onstage. The boy with the thick glasses lost, and Jay-Jay was left with an eighth-grade girl who had made it to the final four the last three years in a row and lost each time. This was her last year in the competition. Her hair was scattered, her lips chapped. Her mother and father sat behind us. They were from a village up by Barrow, and you could tell they didn't have much money, that they lived hard lives, worked hard jobs. Jay-Jay and the girl looked so small and alone up there in the spotlight, spelling back and forth. The girl stumbled on *altazimuth*, but regained her composure.

Jay-Jay's next word was *quinquagesimal*. I knew he knew it—it was one of the words he had a little song about. He paused for a moment, looked right in our direction, let out a small shudder, and began.

"Q-u-i-n-q-u-a-g-a-s-i-m-a-l."

"Sorry, that is incorrect," the announcer said.

"Shit," Laurel said. "Damn, damn, damn."

The girl spelled the next word, *uxoricide*. There was a small hush and her parents leaped up and screamed. Jay-Jay shook her hand, accepted his second-place trophy, and posed for newspaper photos.

"Honey, you did so well, we're so proud of you." Sandee hugged him hard. I glanced at Barry. We both knew Jay-Jay had thrown the competition, and we were both proud yet confused.

"That girl needed it more," Barry whispered to me. "We ain't got much but them, well..." I knew what he meant. Being relatively poor in Anchorage was one thing; in the bush, where there was often no running water, questionable schools, major alcohol problems, and few opportunities, it was quite another. The fact that this girl made it to the spelling bee finals year after year, beating out the rich big-city kids who had it so much easier, was a small miracle. We all shook her hand and made small talk with her parents, who knew Francisco from his trips up north. Stephanie and Hammie left early to stop at the store on the way home to buy supplies for our second-place party.

"You're going to be in the paper," Sandee said when we all gathered in the kitchen to eat cake. "That reporter talked with you longer than the winner."

"He smelled funny," Jay-Jay said. "And his teeth looked slippery."

"I'm totally showing everyone at school," Stephanie said. "I'm saying, 'This is my little brother and he's totally awesome.'"

When I went to tuck Jay-Jay into bed hours later, I knew he was about to confess. I could see it in his eyes, the need to tell the truth, to lay his burdens at my feet.

"Mom?" His voice sounded small and uncertain. "I did a bad thing. I, well..." I sat down on his bed and waited for more. "I knew the word but pretended I didn't." He burst into tears. "I didn't *want* to lose, Mom. I didn't plan on it. It just happened." I held him and rocked back and forth.

"Shhh," I whispered. "It's okay; you did a good thing, a brave thing. Shhh."

"It was her last year, Mom; she really wanted to win." He hiccupped. "I have five more years, plus I *know* I'm smart." He rubbed his nose. "Know what she said to me during the break? That she wants to go to college 'cause no one in her family has ever been. But she said it like she didn't really believe she would." His face crumbled and he started to cry again. "I wanted to win so much, Mom, I really did."

"I know, honey." I held him tight and kissed his hair. "I know."

WHAT THE CUSTOMERS SAID AT WORK

Woman at Table Nine: Did you wash your hands? No offense but the adult entertainment field is ripe with bacteria. Please tell me you don't use the customer bathrooms, do you?

Man at Table Eleven: If I give you forty dollars, will you autograph my ass?

Jose (the cook): Do your boobs really think or only your ass?

Chapter 27

Sunday, Feb. 26

"MOM? WAKE UP, Sandee's here."

"Sandee?" I rose up on my elbow. The living room was dark except for the glow of Stephanie's digital alarm clock. "What time is it?"

Jay-Jay's watch face lit up. "Four twenty-seven," he said. "She's in the kitchen, and Mom, she's all dressed up."

I stumbled out to the kitchen, wincing in the bright overhead light. Sandee sat at the table wearing a sleeveless blue dress and matching shoes. Her hands were folded, and she looked scared and determined.

"What happened?" I cried.

She looked up and tried to smile. "We did it."

"Oh my gosh, you're married?"

"Joe had information on a judge about an illegal caribou, so he agreed to shuffle the paperwork for a quickie divorce, as long as we hand everything in within a month." She stopped to breathe. "So we got married, though technically it won't be official until the divorce comes through. We just got in from Fairbanks on the red-eye."

She held out her hand, a silver wedding band flashing. "Joe had matching bands made, see? There's a moose, mountain goat, and bear running across the side. I thought it would look awful but it's quite elegant." It was, too. The figures were small and well-crafted. I was envious of the design. She leaned her head against my shoulder and wept.

"Hush, now, good for you," I murmured, patting small circles across her back. "Where's Joe?" I asked. She wiped her eyes and laughed.

"He went to the supermarket to buy food. I think he's bringing a cake."

"Well, for heaven's sake, of course you'll need a cake. This is your wedding day."

"Is this going to get mushy?" Jay-Jay complained.

"Probably."

A minute later Joe stumbled in carrying so many grocery bags he could hardly walk. "I got distracted," he said. He had on a camouflage suit jacket and pants.

"You match my dad's truck." Jay-Jay peered inside the bags. "Look, Mom, he bought the lazy-way rolls in the canister." He turned to Joe. "My mom always makes homemade, but I like these better." He tapped the can against the counter until it popped. "Did you see that? It's got an air pocket with compressed air."

While Jay-Jay arranged the rolls over a cookie sheet, Joe stood behind Sandee, grinning. "A quickie wedding," he said. "Imagine the story we'll tell our kids." He nudged Sandee's arm and laughed. "Everyone will think we're pregnant."

Sandee wiped her eyes, and he cupped her head in his hand. "We're having a regular ceremony this spring, in a church like normal folks; this one was just for us." He looked down at her and I almost melted from the expression in his eyes. "Tell her the story, San, about why we decided to do it."

"Wait, I have to wake up Stephanie. She'll kill us if she misses this." Jay-Jay raced out to the living room, and a minute later Stephanie straggled out and sat cross-legged on the floor against the cupboards, Killer's head across her knees.

"What about Aunt Laurel?" Jay-Jay asked.

"Let her sleep." I wasn't sure if Sandee and Joe's story would make her sad or give her hope. Sandee leaned her head back against Joe's chest and began.

"Joe and I had been talking about getting married since I heard from Toodles. I hadn't said yes, but I hadn't said no, either. Besides, I wasn't divorced yet. 'We could be engaged,' Joe said. But I didn't want to be engaged. I wanted to either be married or not married. I had been living in limbo for three years. I was tired of the in-betweens.

"I thought I was going to say no. I wasn't ready for another relationship. There was so much I needed to do: file for divorce, sell the house, buy decent shoes. But I must have known I was going to say yes, and that I was only waiting for a sign.

"Then I ran into Toodles at the craft fair last weekend and she told me the most beautiful thing. Hollow bones, it's a Native expression for emptying yourself out so that you can be filled with the spirit. I thought of how light it would feel to empty myself of my burdens, how freeing to feel nothing but air inside my bones. Later that night I turned to Joe and said yes. I didn't think he'd know what I was talking about but he said, 'Good, I already bought the rings.'"

Sandee and Joe looked at each other and laughed so hard that they leaned into one another. Their faces shone, their eyes were wet and bright. They held each other and laughed and we all laughed, and when Jay-Jay opened the oven, the smell of cinnamon hit us in the face.

"The rolls are done, Mom," he said. I got up and pulled the cookie sheet from the oven, and we ate store-bought rolls with milk and hot chocolate, and when Laurel stumbled out and joined us, we told her the story over again, and laughed again, and we stayed together like that until the sun rose and Joe and Sandee headed back to his house to start their marriage.

"Wonder how long it will last." Laurel ran her finger through the cake icing and licked it off.

"The marriage?" I asked.

"No, the food they brought over." She began unpacking the bags Joe left behind. "Olives and hummus and bread. Ever wonder why there's rye bread and rye crackers but not rye muffins?" She didn't wait for an answer. "And brownies." She happily opened the package and lifted one to her mouth. "They're probably doomed as a couple. Marriage is like a brownie: sweet, rich, and fattening, but not necessarily nourishing." She licked her fingers. "But then again, who knows? Statistically, someone's marriage has to work." She attacked the second brownie. "Yours didn't, mine didn't, and her first one didn't, either." She burped softly and dug out a third brownie. "They do look cute together, don't they? And marrying in camouflage? That takes guts, even in Alaska." She burped again. "I wonder who will be next."

"Next?" I lifted my hands out of the dishwater.

"Toodles and Barry? You and Francisco? Me and someone I haven't met yet?" She started on the fourth brownie. "It's hopeful in a pathetic sort of way, isn't it, how we refuse to stop believing in love?"

What was on my answering machine

"Carla Richards? This is James Hendersen, arts editor for the *Anchorage Daily News*. I'd like to set up an interview for your upcoming *Woman Running with a Box* show. It sounds as if you're ready to send a kick in the face of the Anchorage arts world. My number is 555-3436. Leave a message soon, I'm on deadline. Bye."

Tuesday, Feb. 28

The opening is in three days.

Three.

Fucking.

Days.

I am falling apart. The Oprah Giant says that chaos is an opportunity to realign the soul, but I'm not sure what she means or what to do about it, either. I can take my car to the mechanic to get an alignment, but I can't imagine asking my gynecologist or family physician for a soul adjustment. Probably they'd write me a prescription for antibiotics and send me on my way.

"What color do you think my soul is?" I asked Laurel. She looked up from her cereal, surprised: that was the kind of question she was supposed to ask me.

She slurped milk and squinted at me. "Yellow—or wait, maybe a silver blue, warm but not like a Hollywood movie fake. Why?"

"I have an interview I don't want to do tomorrow and an opening I don't want to attend Friday."

"That leaves today and Thursday free." She poured a second bowl of cereal. "That's more than a lot of people. If we lived in Iran, you wouldn't have the luxury of art world humiliation." She chewed for a moment. "And I wouldn't have the luxury of an unplanned pregnancy. I'd probably be stoned to death, like that woman in the news." She pointed her spoon at me. "They purposefully use small stones, to prolong the agony. I wonder how long I'd last."

"How long what?" Jay-Jay sat down in the chair next to me. He had on a T-shirt that said, "Charles Lindbergh had big feet and big dreams." When no one said anything, he started talking about his fruit-fly project, which he had decided to enter in the upcoming science fair. "The thing about fruit flies," he said, his mouth filled with cereal, "is that they multiply so fast that you think, *Oh, another one.* They all look the same, so you don't think it's a big deal. It's like seeing a guy with a beard and mustache and realizing that *all* guys with beards and mustaches look the same. We group things together, see, because our minds seek patterns."

After everyone left for school and Laurel snuck off for a nap, I armed myself with a roll of green duct tape and circled around my paintings. It was beginning to get light outside and the air was filmy and gray; everything looked dreary and depressing. Why hadn't I stuck to more conservative subjects, outdoor scenes or chubby-faced toddlers hugging kittens? My paintings were an embarrassment, a mistake. A woman running through the woods with naked Barbie dolls clutching the edge of her coat—what the hell did that mean anyway?

I imagined the snickers, the snorts, the superior comments: *you call this art?* It was suddenly perfectly clear—I was about to make a monumental fool out of myself. I slumped down in the corner and leaned my head against the cupboards as Killer Bee watched in alarm—the floor was her territory. It was comforting down there, and safe; crumbs and small pieces of vegetables (broccoli? spinach?) littered the linoleum around me. I was on the floor, at the basest level—I could sink no farther.

When the phone rang, I didn't move. I counted the rings: three, four, five. I was sure it was Betty Blakeslee calling to cancel the show. "April Fools' a month early!" she would squeal. "Did you think I was serious? Did you truly think someone of my standing would contaminate her gallery with your pathetic scribblings?"

"Carlita," Francisco's cheerful voice boomed. "Are you having doubts? Do you need a confidence-boosting lunch? I'm stuck here at the lab, but we could do a picnic if you don't mind packing. I'm thinking peanut butter sandwiches, applesauce, chocolate milk, and cookies. A thermos would be cool if you've got one, especially if it's a superhero. Meet me at the lab whenever you can and"—*Click.* The machine cut him off.

I momentarily hated him: how dare he be so cheerful in the face of my humiliation! The last thing I needed was to be around someone so together and balanced, I knew that. I was positive of that. Nevertheless I started spreading peanut butter over bread and packing lunch. I even found an old Power Rangers thermos of Jay-Jay's in the cupboard, not exactly a superhero but close enough. I added carrot sticks, pickles, and the few remaining brownies from Sandee's wedding party. Then I divided everything into two separate bags, wrote our names on each with Magic Marker, left a note for Laurel, and headed outside. It was still absurdly cold but slowly warming; a Chinook wind was forecasted for later in the evening, and already the air felt less tight, more flowing. I hadn't bothered changing out of my sweatpants and old black sweater, and my hair was pulled back in a messy ponytail. At the last minute I grabbed *Woman Running with a Box, No. 10* and ran out to the car with it. By the time I pulled up in front of the ugly building that housed the anthropology lab, my stomach was growling, even though I had just eaten breakfast a few hours before.

"Hey," Francisco said as he opened the door. He looked tired, and a thin line of stubble marked his chin and cheeks. "Come on in. We have to keep the doors locked at all times, not that many people would steal bones, but you can sell anything on eBay."

Inside it was dim and cool, with shelf after shelf of bones and partial skeletons and chipped rock artifacts. There was barely room to walk.

"Look at this." Francisco led me over to a makeshift room in the back where a strange hunk of metal lay submerged in a large tub of water. "It's the toilet from an old ship that sank around Homer." He leaned over to wipe the corner. "We keep it in solution to wash off the rust. It's a slow process—it's been here for months."

I followed Francisco back inside, and he showed me what he was working on, a series of flint points and tools excavated around Aialik Bay. "And here's my baby." He opened a dim drawer and brought out a padded box. "This is from the Smithsonian Institute, from a site up in Greenland. We're comparing cold climate growth patterns." His hands reached carefully inside the box and brought out a partially reconstructed skull and set it in my lap. The empty eye sockets stared outward, and part of the mandible was missing. "Of course this is all cast; the real set is too valuable to send across the world. Still, there's something here, can you feel it?" He picked up my hands and placed them on either side of the cranium, which was cool and hard beneath my touch. "Now close your eyes and imagine this woman's life. She was about twenty when she died. Stress fractures on her humerus indicate she carried heavy objects, I'd guess stone and wood. The lifespan back then was about thirty, so she died midway through, though still considerably young." He patted my hand. "I'll shut up now so you can concentrate."

I closed my eyes and waited. At first there was nothing but the sound of the air vents and muffled traffic from outside. Then I felt it, a flicker like a breath, followed by another, and another.

"Feel that?" Francisco whispered into my hair. I could smell the musty, stale smell of his sweat, slightly moist but not repugnant. I moved closer, laid my head against his chest, listened to the secret rhythm of his heart: *ta-da-dum, ta-da, dum.* I thought of Laurel's baby and then of Jay-Jay, the first time the midwife put a stethoscope to my ears and let me listen to the heartbeat, so familiar that it was as if I had been waiting to hear it my entire life.

"It's the sound of the past," Francisco said. "We can all hear it; most of us just don't know how to listen."

I turned and kissed him. We held each other for a while and then I asked if he'd like to see the painting that would help conclude my *Woman Running* series. "I'm not sure what it means," I told him with a shrug, as if it meant nothing, as if showing it to him was as easy as smiling. I pulled off the paper, set the painting against the smudged counter, and stared at it with alarm. My Woman Running stood on top of a mountain dressed in a puffy down jacket, the wind flying her hair out from her head. Her back was half-turned so only her profile could be seen. Her hands were raised, her feet perched at the edge of the drop-off, her muscles tense. She looked poised to jump but was throwing dirty dolls off the side of the mountain. They tumbled through the air, their skirts flung up, their genitals exposed. The woman, from what could be seen of her face, wore a look of terrified joy. Behind her, a bear approached from one direction, two men with rifles from another.

"Holy fucking Jesus." Francisco whistled. "It's not what I expected for an ending, yet in a way it's *exactly* what I expected. It's so visceral and primal." He squeezed my hand and we sat and stared at my strange painting. The woman's hair almost glowed, and there was a power in her jaw, a fierce determination, as if by hurling the dolls over the side of the mountain she was, what? Releasing her fears? Her past? All the things she wanted but knew she would never have?

"I'm not sure who the woman is," I told him as we unwrapped the sandwiches. "She looks a lot like me, doesn't she? At first I thought she was my grandmother, then I thought she was my grandmother's sister; remember I told you she was lost in the war? No one knows what happened to her, can you imagine?" Francisco set the bone into my lap, as if it were a baby. The slight weight was comforting, familiar. "I used to help Gramma write letters to relief organizations, but there was no record of Lizzie."

My sandwich lay next to the bone. It was an odd juxtaposition, something ancient and something modern. I could hear Francisco's breath, the slight wheeze when he exhaled; he must have been catching a cold. I clutched the bone tighter to my belly, hoping it would speak, tell me the secrets of life. I sat with it for a long time. When I looked up, everything appeared drearier and shabbier.

"I'm getting old," I said. "I'll be forty in two years."

"I'm forty-four," Francisco said. "You've never asked, by the way."

I shrugged. "It doesn't matter. It's just that I thought I'd know more by now."

"Sometimes," he said as he leaned forward, as he began to take me in his arms, "I carry around a piece of bone in my pocket or sock." His mouth was warm, warm. "It makes me feel less alone," he whispered against my breast, his lips tickling.

We are always alone. I understood that even as our bodies came together, even as they fit so naturally, even as we strained and cried out and our sweat dripped over each other and I sank so deep inside of him I swear I could trace the shape of his bones with my teeth. We are always alone. But still. Sometimes, we aren't.

LESSON SEVEN

Moving On

Endings aren't easy. You have to let go, and who ever teaches you how to do that? But you did it, girlfriend, you were brave enough to look deep inside and reclaim those parts you lost or left behind. From here on, you will walk backward and forward, and every step will be bathed in the beauty of your true self.

—*The Oprah Giant*

Chapter 28

Wednesday, March 1

I WOKE EARLY. The sky was clear, the moon curved low in the sky as I sat in the kitchen, just me and the dog and all that quiet. I was still sitting there when Jay-Jay, all scrubbed and ready for school, slid into the chair next to me.

"Meriwether Lewis killed himself," he said as he reached for the cereal box. "You know, Lewis and Clark? Three years after he got back, though some people think he was murdered." He munched thoughtfully. "He couldn't handle his job after being out in the wild. Mr. Short says he was ill-suited for bureaucracy."

"Like Thoreau," Stephanie yelled from the living room. "They say he totally died a virgin but everyone treats him like a god. Then there's poor Emily Dickinson and all those snide remarks about her editor."

Jay-Jay ignored her and kept talking. "He was staying at this inn and there was a guy that didn't like him..."

I nodded and stuck four pieces of bread into the toaster. Today was the day I had to drop my paintings off at the gallery, and I needed the comfort of toast.

"...but they didn't do a very thorough investigation," Jay-Jay was saying. "They didn't have CSI back in those days. They didn't even know about fingerprints."

"Or germs," I said.

"I think he was murdered," he continued, as if I had never spoken. "'Cause who is going to shoot themselves two or three times?"

With that he grabbed his books and went out to the living room to wait for Stephanie. After they left, I carried my paintings out to the car. Each one was lovingly covered with brown packaging paper, the edges folded and taped as if gift wrapped. I pulled down the backseat and stacked them carefully, remembering how I used to strap Jay-Jay in his car seat, how I checked the latch two and three times, worried that it might come undone, that I might lose him. I locked the car (in case someone was waiting to steal my work), then went back inside and pulled on my hat and scarf.

Before I could drop off my paintings, I had to suffer through my newspaper interview. I had fretted for hours over what to wear. Francisco, who has been interviewed by national magazines, said to wear whatever reflected the tone of the story. I had no idea what this meant, so I asked Joe, who often appears in the newspaper chiding people for careless behavior after a bear attack.

"Speak definitively," he said. "Reporters try to get you to say what they want you to say, so don't let them lead you on."

All of this terrified me, and when I showed up at the newspaper, my hands were clammy with sweat. The lobby was high ceilinged, with a security guard sitting behind the desk. I was given a visitor badge and directions to the newsroom. Inside was a madhouse of phones ringing, computers beeping, and people talking and shouting. James was younger than I expected, and had blaring red hair and freckles across his face.

"Carla!" He stood up and shook my hand. "Let's go somewhere quieter." I followed him down the hallway to a cafeteria area with large windows. "I apologize for not being able to meet at your house." He stopped at the far table. "I have short deadlines and need to turn this around."

"That's okay," I murmured, imagining this man in our trailer noticing the ripped linoleum, the sagging furniture, the mismatched dishes.
"The house was kind of a mess."

The interview began better than I expected. James's questions were
easy, and the more I talked about myself, the more relaxed I became.
I balked when he mentioned my dirty dolls. "I, ah, well..." I paused
and then thought, *The hell with it,* and so I told him the truth. I told
him that I lived in a trailer, worked as a waitress, and was a single parent, and one night while looking for ways to make extra money, I came
across Thinking Butts and Boobs's contest announcement and entered. I
told him how I kept this hidden for years, how I was afraid what people
would think, how it felt to work on the dolls late at night when everyone was asleep: how freeing it was, and how it opened up something
inside of me, as if by confronting taboos I was able to knock down the
spaces of my own fears and limitations.

"What about the sexual components?" he asked.

"Excuse me?"

"Are you making a statement behind the sex, or using the sex to
make a statement?"

"Ah, both," I said. "I mean, sex is everywhere, and it influences everything we do. Yet we have to pretend that it isn't there and that we're
using our heads and our logic, when we're actually reacting on primitive
urges we can't really control. It's kind of absurd, when you think about
it. In this day and age, when we're supposedly so liberated, a woman
still can't like sex too much or she's labeled a slut. Yet if she doesn't like
it enough, she's labeled frigid."

"So you consider yourself sexually liberated?"

"I don't even know what that means. Does any women really know
what it means to be sexually liberated, when we all model our behavior
around the desires of men?"

I had no idea where my ideas were coming from. It was as if all of the
time I had been working on my dirty dolls and painting I had secretly
been filing words away, hoarding them in my skull until it was time to

use them again. By the time the interview was over, I was exhausted. I drove like mad to the gallery, where Betty Blakeslee was waiting. She didn't look pleased.

"A man with large feet dropped off a bone," she said. "I hope it's not authentic. I don't have the paperwork for human remains."

"Francisco is an anthropologist," I said, as if that explained it. "Besides, it's not real, it's a cast of this woman who lived—"

"Spare the gruesome details." She nodded at my paintings. "Take those to the back, Timothy is waiting. Chop, chop." She clapped her hands as if to hurry me along.

"Good stuff." Timothy whistled as he tore off the wrappings. "Color scheme is justified, and these figures speak to the alter ego." He closed one eye and then the other. "There's this underlying sadness or grief... Whoa, what's that you're holding?"

"A bone."

He waited for more.

"A skull from a woman who lived in Iceland centuries ago. Her bones were discovered during road construction."

"Can I touch it?"

"It's only a cast," I said, almost apologetically.

He reached over, smoothed his hand across the edge. "Pow-er-ful." He smelled his hand, as if for verification. "Maybe I should work in bone, can you dig it? Animal bones reaching toward the mythical heavens." I pulled the bone protectively toward my chest and hurried off to the bathroom, which was one of those one-room multisex types with no stalls. I placed the bone on the toilet, where it stared at me with blank eye sockets as I washed my hands. When I turned around a young woman with my grandmother's eyes sat smoking on the toilet, the bone placed securely on her lap.

"So you're the artist," she said, and I knew right away this was Lizzie, my grandmother's sister, the one who was lost in the war. "I thought you would be taller. And bustier." She had a slight, musical accent, nothing like my grandmother's guttural English. She was thinner, too, with the athletic build of a dancer. She puffed on her cigarette, which emitted no smoke, and sighed.

"I used to draw, did Anka tell you?"

"Who's Anka?"

"She changed her name?" She barked out a laugh. "Anka was always the storyteller."

"Gramma? Her name was Bethany because the midwife—" I stopped suddenly; how was it that I had never realized Bethany wasn't a Polish name? "I suppose your name isn't Lizzie, either."

"It's Elka, but people call me Lizzie." She paused to rearrange her legs. How odd that both she and my grandmother had chosen to come back in a bathroom? How many ghosts sit on toilet seats?

"Anka thinks I left because I was worried about Mama's safety, but really it was because of a boy. Jerzy was older and in the *Żegota*, the Polish resistance. He had higher aims than love; he was trying to save lives. But I was barely sixteen. I had never been with a man before; I couldn't think straight.

"I followed him around the country, sleeping in fields and wading through the underground sewer tunnels; often I was the only girl. When he asked if I would carry papers to Warsaw, I brushed off the dangers. I was sure his love would keep me safe, I was that silly.

"The mind is a terrible thing, Carla. It can make you believe whatever you want." She sighed. "For months I travel back and forth to Warsaw on the trains smuggling papers in my coat lining. Things in the city are terrible, many are people dying, and many more are hungry. The ghetto is hellish but it's not so good for us Poles, either—we are being squeezed from both sides, the Russians and the Nazis; there is little left for us.

"A few weeks before Christmas I am stopped as I get off the train. Maybe someone turns me in, who knows? So many people are starving. The Germans make rules about food rations, maybe 250 calories for Jews, 650 for Poles, over 2,000 for Germans. Turning in Jews and the resistance is good money. You think, *Oh, I would never do that.* But your son or daughter is starving, think of what you might do, eh?

"They grab my coat, rip the lining, and it all falls out: fake birth certificates and German citizenship papers. I know I am dead and it is going to be bad; they are not going to do it quick. I push away and run, zigzagging the way Jerzy told me, so the bullets will have a harder time catching me. It is the strangest thing, running like that, it is like I run forever, and even though I am scared, I also feel the peace, as if everything in my life has led up to this moment of me running. The first bullet hits me in the side, it is a burning pain, and then two more in my leg and hip. I keep running, and then I am down in the snow; it is red—how did the snow get red? I am crawling and there is a light in front of me, and so much warmth down my sides, like angels heating my skin, and right before it goes dark I think, *Now Anka will live.*"

My aunt folded her hands around the bone. I waited for more but she appeared to be done. "Gramma waited all those years," I told her. "She kept the kitchen light on so you'd be able to fix yourself something to eat."

She looked over at me and sighed again. "I couldn't visit Anka. It would have destroyed her. Yes, this is true. We cannot always handle the things we think we want."

"So you had to tell me? The day before my opening?"

"You wanted to know. You asked in your paintings. A woman running with those funny little dolls." She stood up, set the bone back on the toilet seat, and peered at herself in the mirror again. "What do you think of my hair?"

"You're dead," I snapped. "Who's going to see you?"

"That is no reason not to look my best." She sounded so much like Laurel that I wanted to slap her.

"But you're, you're..." I stopped and took a breath. "You tell me this tragic story of dying young and then worry about your hair?"

"It happened a long time ago." She shrugged. "If I did not die by the Germans, probably I die by the Russians or starve. People ate grass and tree bark. We were so hungry for so long. That is why Anka kept herself so fat."

I stared at her in disbelief.

"How I die, that is just part of my history. It is not so very much, really." She turned her head slightly. "It is not my face you have painted," she said. "Many women are running."

Her hand reached for the doorknob.

"You can't just leave," I screamed. "You can't tell a story like that and just leave."

The next thing I knew Betty Blakeslee was shaking me, and I opened my eyes to her face, so close I could see the tiny hairs beneath her face powder. "If you're taking drugs please don't flush them down the toilet," she said. "The last girl caused a flood."

"I fell asleep." I pulled myself up off the cold bathroom floor. "I was talking to my aunt and fell asleep."

Betty Blakeslee glanced around the room and sighed. "Preshow jitters. November's artist collapsed in the middle of the street and was almost hit by a bus. Imagine the lawsuit." She marched toward the door. "He was a bleeder, and anemic, too. I was hoping you would be normal but I suppose that's too much to ask."

The door slammed and I was alone with the skull bone again. I watched it out of the corner of my eye as I washed my hands, willing it to bring back my aunt, but of course that didn't happen. It must have been a dream—the idea that my aunt had been part of the Polish resistance was preposterous. Things like that didn't happen in my family.

I carried the bone back to the gallery space, where Timothy Tuppelo was busily shuffling my paintings around the room. "The order isn't that important," he said, as if I had never left. "Most people have the attention span of a fish. What they need are small, isolated moments." He grabbed my shoulder and yanked me to the right. "That wall?" He pointed to a bare space in the corner. "You want to make sure that each turn reveals a strong piece. Art clientele are snobs and first impressions are everything."

I pondered that as we hung the rest of the paintings and then stood back to give the room a look. I gasped. My woman moved through the various stages of her life, growing up and then growing older, lines appearing in her face, along with the first few gray hairs.

I clutched his arm. "Do you think this is me? Tell me honestly, okay? Because that's what everyone sooner or later says."

"It's cool." He patted my arm and made cooing noises. "We always fear our subconscious."

I had no idea what he meant.

"You need to go get high, have a drink or two, bleep out for the afternoon." I didn't say anything. "Yeah, it's you," he finally said. "So what? We can't escape the self. It's the whole basis behind art. If we didn't feel conflicted, we wouldn't bother picking up a paintbrush."

I thanked him for his help, told him I'd see him at the opening, and slipped out the door. The sun glistened tiny sparks in the snow, so everything looked magical, like jewels shining. I was halfway to the anthropology lab before I realized where I was going. Francisco opened the door on the first knock. "I'm making oatmeal," he said, as if it were the most normal thing in the world to find me at his workplace cradling his bone against my chest. "It's microwaved, but I added nuts and dried fruit."

I followed him inside the dusty lab and sat at a table covered with massive, curved bones. "Whale ribs," he said. "Aren't they beautiful?" He placed two bowls of oatmeal between the ribs and sat down at his cluttered desk.

"I brought your bone back. Thanks." I set it down carefully on a pile of papers. "The craziest thing happened." I sat down on the arm of his chair. "I saw my aunt in the gallery bathroom, sitting on the toilet seat, perfectly alive." I stopped for a minute, unsure if I should go on. "She told me she was shot smuggling papers for the Polish resistance."

"The *Żegota*," he said.

"You know?"

"I researched it in college, for my junior project. I was looking for my grandfather's brother."

"You're not Polish."

"Norwegian Jew. An uncle on my mother's side was killed in the camps."

"Shit."

"That's probably why I do this, you know, reconstruct the past." He nodded in the direction of the whale bones. "I'm trying to make sense of why things happen. Why death happens, but also life. It's kind of amazing when you think about it."

"So you believe in ghosts?"

He reached over and pressed my hand between his palms. "No, not ghosts. I believe we carry the memory of our ancestors in our genes and sometimes, maybe when we are weak or our defenses are down, we pick up fragments of the past, you know, like a radio station late at night."

"So I imagined it all?"

"We see what we want to see."

"It's almost my opening," I whined. "I just wanted to be happy."

Francisco rubbed his thumb over the vein in the back of my hand because he knew me well enough to know that happiness is the last thing I want. Oh, it's so simple, love. It's not what they tell you, fireworks and ripping each other's clothes off. That might happen in the beginning, but it's not the whole story. Real love is quiet and simple. It's someone holding your hand and allowing you to be snotty when you're scared. It's someone not letting go.

COLLEGE ART SCHOOL REPLIES: LETTERS #13, #14, AND #15

Dear Carla Richards:

The admissions committee has reviewed your application and regrets that it is unable to offer you a place in the California College of the Fine Arts Fall program.

While your work is strong in design elements, it lacks basic compositional focus.

We wish you luck in your academic future.

Dear Carla Richards:

After reviewing your application we regret that we must decline admission to the Seattle School of Art program.

We found your work strong in compositional focus yet lacking in design elements.

We wish you success in your artistic endeavors.

Dear Carla Richards:

The selection committee has reviewed your application and regrets that it cannot offer you a position at the Idaho School of Art and Photography.

Your work showed strong design and compositional focus yet lacked basic line structure.

We wish you the best in all your artistic pursuits.

Thursday, March 2

Holy fucking shit, tomorrow is the opening.

Someone help me, okay. Please?

Please.

Chapter 29

Friday, March 3

"Mom, did you see this? Mom?" Jay-Jay shook me awake early in the morning, so early it was still dark. "Mom, you're in the paper. Your face is on the front page."

"Wh-what?" I sat up and Jay-Jay shoved the newspaper into my hands. My face smiled out from the middle. LOCAL ARTIST SHOWS A SASSIER WAY TO PLAY WITH DOLLS, the headline blared.

"Uh-oh, this is not going to be good," I muttered.

"They spelled your name wrong once and said we lived in a manufactured home, not a trailer," Jay-Jay said, "and they called the restaurant an upscale Mexican establishment, but other than that it's okay."

"Shit." I scratched my leg. "Why are you up so early?"

"I'm bidding on fruit-fly accessories on eBay." Like mother, like son. I skimmed the article. The reporter had gotten most of the quotes right, but the angle was wrong. It was as if he was writing about me the way he wanted me to be, not the way I really was. Still, the photograph of my painting was great, and it took up almost half the page. The downside was that he used the word *erotic* five times, *pornography* three times, and *dirty dolls* twice.

"I hope this doesn't negatively influence you at school."

"Are you kidding? Mrs. Clampsen will drool the next time you come in. She goes overboard when she's around hotshots. You know the coolest thing?"

"What's that, honey?" I decided to make French toast to celebrate my opening. I doubted I could eat a bite, but cooking would tame my nerves.

"This means I'm probably going to get into the Berkeley program. Stephanie won the poetry contest, you got your show, Aunt Laurel got pregnant, and Dad got a woman." He counted off on his fingers. "Next is my turn."

"You'll get in," I reassured him. "Your essay was brilliant."

"You're my mom, you have to say that."

"No, I don't." Jay-Jay had written about the sea otter at the Alaska SeaLife Center down in Seward that had gotten trapped in the drainage pipe and died two days after we had gone down to see it. The essay was funny, spirited, and sad enough to bring tears to my eyes. "You just may grow up to be a writer," I told him.

"Yeah, yeah, yeah," he droned, and sat down and ate his French toast without a peep.

"Honey?" I said, right before he headed out the door for the bus. "Be careful at school; I mean, the pieces in my show are kind of risqué, and some of the kids or parents might get ideas..."

"Mom! It's just sex, it's no big deal." The door slammed and I was alone with Killer.

"Boy, oh boy, they sure make you sound different than you really are." Laurel read the paper and ate Jay-Jay's leftover French toast while I obsessed over what to wear to the show. She lowered the newspaper and stared at me. "What is that around your neck?"

"A scarf."

"No, no," she clucked. "Your neck is too long for scarves, you look like a giraffe. Try a chunky necklace instead. And something lower cut. You're the artist of a sexy show; you need to look the part."

"How?" I had on a short skirt, low-cut shirt, and high-heeled boots. I thought I looked sexy.

"Sexiness is not what you're wearing, it's what you're not wearing, get it?"

I shook my head no.

"Oh, for heaven's sakes, must I have to do everything?" She pulled herself up from the table and waddled after me to the bedroom. Half of my closet lay across what was now her bed. She rummaged through the stack, discarding most of it on the floor. "Is this all you've got?"

"Except for your and Stephanie's clothes."

We finally decided on a soft, gauzy skirt of Stephanie's, Laurel's silk blouse, Francisco's belt, Sandee's boots (with toilet paper stuffed in the toes because they were too big), and Barry's old hunting cap cocked sideways on my head. "Something's missing," Laurel said, examining from either side as I paraded back and forth across the living room. "Wait, I know—don't move." She ran into Jay-Jay's room and came out with a handful of his friendship bracelets. "Hold out your wrist," she demanded, and as she slid them on I realized that it was as if I was getting married. Along with Gramma's hairpins I had something from everyone I loved. Knowing this made me feel better. It's not that I felt I couldn't fail, because I knew I could and that I very well might. It was that I knew that I could stand tall no matter what, clothed as I was in my friends' best intentions.

Five hours later found me crouched in the back closet at Artistic Designs, hiding from Betty Blakeslee and the hordes of well-dressed people intent on talking about me in the third person.

"*She* needs to work on her shading."

"*She* should have taken it one step further."

"*She* has the oddest mind."

Out in the gallery, my work filled the walls, all of my mistakes and failings in full view. It was agonizing.

My show was deemed a success, at least by the Powers That Be. I sold four pieces, and Betty Blakeslee predicted I would sell more by the end of the month. She still thinks of me as Clara, so that is how everyone addressed me. "Clara," they said, "such lovely work, so original, so fresh, so stunning."

I wasn't too worried about what people called me; it was the money I concentrated on, and all it would do for me, for us. Four paintings totaled almost three thousand dollars after the gallery's cut. I could pay off my Visa and part of my MasterCard, put some away for Jay-Jay's summer Berkeley camp, buy baby clothes for Laurel, lunch at Simon & Seafort's for Sandee, a nice bottle of wine for Barry, and of course more painting supplies for me and maybe even a—

The door slid open and I quickly slammed it shut with my foot.

"Carla, it's me," Francisco whispered loudly. "Everyone's looking for you."

"Shhhh," I hissed. "They'll discover my hiding place." I tried to close the door but he pushed it back open again.

"Come on, toughen up." He tugged at my arm and I smoothed my skirt and walked back out in the light. Betty Blakeslee made a grab for my arm but Francisco intercepted with a brilliant swerve. I was busy listening to a man explain what was wrong with my brushstrokes when I noticed a fat woman in an ugly flowered dress staring up at my *Woman Running with a Box, No. 5* painting. Her mouth was open and she breathed garlic fumes. I excused myself and ran over.

"What are you doing here?" My voice pitched too high; heads turned. "You aren't supposed to be here."

"I want to see dirty paintings." Gramma pointed to the bottom of the canvas. "Some of them dolls got my face." She said this matter-of-factly, as if she always expected her face to show up on a painted Barbie doll with its boobs hanging out.

"Please don't talk to yourself," Betty Blakeslee hissed in my ear. "It looks bad to the clientele."

I wanted to tell Gramma that I had seen her sister and she was okay, she had been found, but it didn't seem the right time. She followed me around as I mingled, shook hands, and made small talk with artists, wannabe artists, and people who referred to themselves as art connoisseurs. It wasn't that much different from waitressing, really. All I had to do was pretend to be the person everyone wanted me to be, except no one left me a tip.

By the end of the evening I was drained. My legs felt shaky and my left eyelid wouldn't stop fluttering. I stood at the door with Betty Blakeslee as if in a wedding receiving line, and shook hands and murmured remarks to people who acted as if they knew me. Gramma sat on the floor by the buffet table, stuffing olives into her mouth. I thanked Betty Blakeslee for a lovely opening, thanked Timothy for all of his help, and finally escaped out the door, where I smacked into a woman waving a picket sign with "Down with Dirty Dolls!" blared across the front. A handful of others waved similar signs and chanted, "We've had enough, burn the smut."

"Ah, shit, it's the born-agains." Laurel opened her coat to show off her round belly. "They wouldn't dare harass a pregnant woman."

A man in a plaid jacket jutted a sign in her face and yelled about decency and God's plan for the universe, which, obviously, didn't include women running with pornography.

I stood there, incredulous. "Weren't you supposed to be here at the beginning of the show?" I asked.

"We just read about it in the paper," said a familiar-looking woman in an expensive sable coat. I peered closer.

"Mrs. Hendricks?" I said. "Is that you?" I couldn't believe it! Jay-Jay and Sophie were friends. I often drove them to gifted activities together. "How's Sophie's science project?"

"She's almost done." Her sign sagged. "Congratulations on Jay-Jay's spelling bee place."

"Thanks," I said, and then she raised her sign and began chanting again: "We've had enough, burn the smut."

"We could totally take them," Stephanie said.

I looked at our group: Laurel and Jay-Jay, Sandee and Joe, Stephanie and Hammie, Barry and Toodles, and me and Francisco. We looked cold and invincible. We looked as if we could defeat an army.

"Leave them be," I said with a shrug. "If they want to freeze their asses off, it's their problem."

"This will totally bring more attention to your show," Stephanie said. "They're doing you a favor in a, like, pathetic sort of way."

We stopped at the light on Seventh Avenue and, as if on cue, we all threw back our heads and looked up at the sky, which was murky from the city lights, hazy, no stars to be seen, but still we knew they were up there. I could hear my heart beating against my chest: *thump-thump, dum, da, dum. I had a show,* I imagined it singing. *A show, a show, a show.*

Everyone slowly left, two by two, Laurel and Jay-Jay climbing in the back of the car while Francisco and I sat up front.

"I can't believe it's over," I said as we sped toward L Street. "All that work and the anticipation, the worrying and wham, four of my paintings are gone. I'll probably never see them again; I won't know if they'll end up in someone's living room or den or hallway, and then years from now they'll find themselves in someone's attic or basement or even donated to a thrift shop." I watched the lagoon fly past as we drove toward Hillcrest Drive.

"Maybe you'll be famous and we can move into a bigger trailer so you won't have to sleep on the floor," Jay-Jay said. "And, Mom? We could get another dog. Killer's lonely."

I leaned my head against the window as an odd warmth rose through my chest.

"If so many people hadn't felt the need to criticize my work, it would have been an almost perfect evening," I said.

"Uh-oh, wouldn't want that," Francisco teased. I stared over at him, the dashboard lights reflecting across his beautiful face, and I thought of what I always think of when I feel loved and nourished and safe.

I thought of Gramma. I thought of food.

LETTERS #16 AND #17

Dear Jay-Jay Richards:

Congratulations! You have been chosen as a scholarship recipient to the Berkeley Mathematically Gifted Youth Summer Camp July 15–July 29.

Based on the selection committee's analysis of your academic record, letters of recommendation, and outstanding essay effort, you qualify for a $3,500 award plus work study options up to $200 per week.

Please return the enclosed information by March 15.

We look forward to seeing you at Berkeley this summer.

Sincerely,
Jeffrey Foggerty
Admissions Coordinator
Berkeley Mathematically Gifted Youth Summer Camp

Dear Stephanie Steeley:

Congratulations!

On behalf of the Office of Undergraduate Admissions, it gives me great pleasure to welcome you to Stanford University's Creative Writing Program.

A financial aid package will be arriving soon.

We once again congratulate you on your outstanding academic achievements and look forward to meeting you soon.

Best,
Ian Schaffer
Dean of Admissions and Financial Aid

P.S. The Creative Writing Department was impressed by your poem, "If I Eat Lunch with Tobias Wolff Do I Tell Him He Has Spinach between His Teeth?"

Sunday, March 5

Of course I knew I would cook a meal to celebrate my last diary entry—what else is there to do when you reach the end but eat? I planned a lavish Polish dinner filled with Gramma's favorites: *golabki, zupa koperkowa, mizeria*, and for dessert, *chrusciki*. I lugged the wobbly kitchen table into the living room and covered it with an old sheet. That did little to subtract from its lopsided, shabby appearance, but no matter. This was my dinner, and this was how I lived: messily and impulsively, with little semblance of order.

We ate buffet-style from the pots and pans lining the kitchen counters, all of us crowded around the table, our elbows and legs bumping. When we were halfway through the *zupa* (soup), Barry jumped up, a jelly jar of cheap wine raised in the air.

"A toast," he yelled, and he stood there, unsure of what to say. Finally he sat back down, grabbed Toodles's hand on one side and Jay-Jay's on the other. "I meant a prayer," he said. "For the food."

We held hands and bowed our heads as Barry cleared his throat once, and then twice. "Bless this, ah, food," he stammered. "Ah, and all the hard work Carly done and, ah..."

Jay-Jay's voice suddenly rang out, clear and smooth. "Bless this food, and may it nourish our souls and hearts with praise," he sang.

I looked up, surprised.

"Gifted sessions at the Bible school." He shrugged.

We ate and talked, ate and argued, ate and told jokes and laughed. Laurel worried about her baby's feet, Sandee complained about work, Stephanie revealed plans to ambush Tobias Wolff at Stanford, and Jay-Jay offered an analysis of his fruit-fly research that none of us understood, but still we listened and we praised.

"That reminds me of a bear problem out by Tok," Joe began as Sandee rolled her eyes.

I thought of the Oprah Giant's last blog post. "Happiness is like trying to catch the fog," she wrote in purple and pink font. "You can walk and walk and never realize you've reached it until you look back."

Was happiness really that simple? I pushed back my plate and headed to the kitchen for dessert.

"Need help?" Toodles asked, but I motioned her down with my hand. I had a feeling that Gramma would be waiting in the kitchen and she was, standing by the sink, wearing the same awful dress she had on at my gallery opening.

"That man, he a looker." She pointed at Francisco. "Like the Galloping Gourmet if he got skinny."

I shrugged. "He's okay."

"This ain't so good." She pinched the *chrusciki* with her fingers. "Too heavy."

"It's fine." I shooed her hands away. It was one of my favorite desserts, a bow-shaped pastry Gramma called angel wings. After I sprinkled on powdered sugar, I laid my hand on her fat shoulder.

"I saw her," I said softly. "I saw Lizzie."

Gramma clutched her throat. "*Ach*," she groaned. "What she say?"

I wasn't sure how much to tell her. "She died a hero but don't worry, it was quick."

I expected Gramma to cry, but she wiped her finger over the pastries and licked off the sugar instead. "That why you make the *chrusciki*," she said. "You have a celebrity."

"Celebration," I corrected. When I turned back, she was gone.

"*Do widzenia*," I whispered. Good-bye.

I carried the plate out to the living room. *Chrusciki* is a dessert Gramma reserved for special occasions, meant to be eaten with the ones you love. She believed the pastry wings spread open and flew through the belly.

I told this story as I served the pastry. "If you place your hands on your stomach, you supposedly feel angels," I said.

"Wild." Stephanie put down her fork and placed her hand across her belly. Laurel and Jay-Jay did the same. We sat there, all of us, our hands against our bellies as we waited to feel the flutter of angel wings.

GRAMMA'S CHRUSCIKI (ANGEL WINGS)

- 6 egg yolks
- 1–2 whole eggs
- 3 cups flour
- Pinch of salt
- ½ teaspoon vanilla extract
- ½ cup sour cream
- Cooking oil
- 2 teaspoons sugar
- ⅛ teaspoon anise
- Pinch of cinnamon
- Powdered sugar (for topping)

Separate eggs, beat yolks, and slowly fold in the rest of the ingredients except for sugar, anise, and cinnamon. Knead until smooth and then roll out, cut into strips, and fold into bow-like shapes. Fry in hot oil until browned and sprinkle with cinnamon, powdered sugar, and anise.

Makes enough for one single mother and her beautiful son; one pregnant sister and her soon-to-be-born daughter; one best friend and her fish-and-game husband; one teenage surrogate daughter and her, like, totally awesome boyfriend; one ex-husband and his new girlfriend; one bone-loving anthropologist; and one fat, hungry Polish ghost.

Reading Group Guide

DISCUSSION QUESTIONS

1. When she first begins her diary, Carla hopes that it will bring her solace. Do you think keeping a diary is mostly therapeutic, or can diaries bring more than just comfort? Have you ever kept a diary?

2. Carla's grandmother used to say that "sins make you fat." What did she mean by this? What "sins" are weighing Carla down?

3. Carla and Sandee are both initially hesitant about falling in love again. How do their past experiences with men differ? How does each woman try to protect herself from future heartache?

4. When talking about her relationship with Barry, Carla says that divorce is "not simple...and the break is never clean." Is this always true of divorce, or is there something about their relationship in particular that prevents the two of them from moving on?

5. What finally convinces Carla to agree to a date with Francisco? Why do you think she gives him another chance after he stands her up?

6. Carla's Gramma visits her four times after her death—the night Jay-Jay was born, during Laurel's appointment at the clinic, at the gallery show, and at the final dinner. What do you think these occasions have in common? Does Carla believe she is really seeing her grandmother's ghost?

7. Throughout the novel, Carla is afraid of what people will think of her when they find out she makes dirty dolls. Why do you think she continues to do it, when there are other, less risqué ways to make extra money?

8. Why is Carla so quick to welcome Stephanie into the family when she has so many others to take care of? Do you think her attitude toward Stephanie would be different if Carla hadn't had an abortion?

9. According to the Oprah Giant, it is a common myth that people will be happy when good things happen to them. Do you agree with the Oprah Giant? Where does happiness come from, if not from positive experiences and good fortune?

10. Compare Carla and Laurel's relationship at the beginning of the novel with their relationship at the end of the novel. What has changed between them? How has Laurel's situation allowed her to better understand her sister?

11. Carla is never quite sure who the woman in her paintings is. Who do you think the woman running with a box represents? What is she running from?

AUTHOR Q&A

Carla starts keeping a diary as an emotional exercise, but it gets very juicy very quickly. How would your own diary compare to Carla's?

Oddly enough, I've never kept a diary, not even as a young girl. I've tried journaling, but it felt too self-conscious, as if I were talking to myself, though I suppose all writing is talking to oneself. Still, if I did keep a diary, I'm sure it would venture toward juiciness. When my son was younger and I needed extra money, I wrote erotica. Some of this I published under my own name, and during PTA meetings and school functions, I lived in fear of angry mothers with Pokémon notebooks banishing me from the room. There were also a few horrible months when, had anyone Googled my name (and since I was a news reporter at the time it's inevitable that people had Googled my name), an erotic poem of mine entitled "Ode to My..." Well, okay, needless to say the C-word appeared in the title, and this C-word also appeared as the top link to my name. I'd like to say that this prompted me to stop writing erotica, but alas, it didn't.

Food plays a very prominent role throughout the novel. Is cooking a passion of yours? Where did the recipes come from?

I'm a vegetarian who veers toward the vegan side, and I love to eat. I love my vegetables. I was the kid in elementary school who ate everyone's spinach at lunch, which made me extremely popular. When depressed, I walk through the supermarket produce aisles and it always perks me up: all those blushing peaches and fragrant oranges, those round and firm radishes, those phallic cucumbers. Food is so erotic. We slide it in through our lips. We caress it with our tongues. We close our eyes and swallow.

Ironically, for all my love of food, I am a lousy cook, a truly lousy cook. I actually messed up Jell-O once when my son was sick. Which is why I live on stir-fry. And if I overcook it (which I so often do), I simply douse it in hot sauce before chowing down.

The recipes in the book? I made them up, mostly based on what I remembered from childhood. While I might be a horrible cook, I am a fairly decent baker. However, the recipes aren't meant to be perfect, or even to turn out each time. Like love, recipes are fickle. Sometimes they bless you and other times they turn on you. I wanted this to be the case with Carla's recipes, and I wanted that very unpredictability to mirror the tone of the book.

In the book, you claim that women dress up their fantasies down to the "the shape of the barrettes and the shades of toenail polish." Out of curiosity, what do the barrettes and nail polish look like in your fantasies?

Well, since I'm a runner my fantasies usually involve a pair of Nike running shoes and a tattered hair tie, and my nail polish is always chipped. But my fantasies *are* very detailed. I spend a lot of time deciding on the outfits: A running skirt or shorts? Tank top or sports bra? A Garmin or a regular old running watch? As I mentioned in the book, how the man looks doesn't matter so much, as long as all of his parts are strong and healthy. That said, I wouldn't chase Steve Prefontaine out of my fantasies unless, of course, his outfit didn't coordinate with mine.

Carla appears to have a very strong sense of family, even though her relationship with her sister is a little trying. Are you very close with your own family? Are there any Laurels in the bunch?

I am close to my two sisters (my third, and middle, sister died ten years ago), and my youngest sister and I are very, very close. I don't really have a Laurel in my family, though I think that we all harbor bits of Laurel inside ourselves, you know, the way we try to keep our lives neat and controlled while simultaneously making choices that introduce chaos. I read somewhere that love burns brightest inside our mess, and I wanted to show that with Laurel. I wanted to drag her through the mud. I wanted to force her to peel off her armor and see the beauty of her own complexities.

I love the fact that Carla and Laurel have a "trying" relationship. Don't most of us, with the ones we love the most? Don't we reserve our worst behaviors for those with whom we feel the safest, those we know will accept us no matter what?

I suppose I wanted to create a world where everyone was flawed and issues didn't magically resolve themselves, a world that resembled one of Gramma's recipes. Because really, how many people's lives follow a narrative arc?

You have a son, though he's a bit older than Jay-Jay. How much of Jay-Jay was inspired by your own son? More importantly, can your son spell *quinquagesimal*?

Yes, I do have a son, who is in college now, and yes, I originally based parts of Jay-Jay on him, though the more I wrote, the more Jay-Jay became his own self. I was a single mother and we lived in a small and cluttered house, and everywhere there was mess and books and dog hair, and things were always breaking down and we never had enough money, yet my son remained stoically optimistic and cheerful. I remember once the toilet overflowed and sewage seeped into the house; the stink was awful and many of our things were ruined, yet my son sat on the kitchen counter happily taking apart the toaster, and the first thing he said to me was, "Mom, what's for lunch?"

This is what I wanted to capture with Jay-Jay, the sense of vulnerability coupled with an almost adult wisdom, that innocent sense of truly believing we are the shapers of our own fate. Yet I also wanted Jay-Jay to contrast Carla's faults because, face it, children recognize their parents' failings and weaknesses, and they forgive us in ways we are unable to forgive ourselves.

Can my son spell *quinquagesimal*? Unfortunately, he probably can.

Where did the idea for the dirty dolls come from? Are there any Barbie doll parts on your kitchen table?

Years ago one of the Anchorage art galleries put out a call for entries for a Barbie-doll-themed show. I decided to submit a piece, even though I'm even worse at art than I am at cooking. I bought a couple of Barbie dolls, some felt and glitter, and got to work. Before long the kitchen overflowed with Barbie and Ken parts, colored paper, doll clothes, and stray shoes, along with tubes of expensive paint, brushes, and my son's X-Acto knife. One night, as I was in the process of attaching multiple breasts to Ken's chest, my son walked in. It was about three a.m. and I huddled on the dirty kitchen floor, dog hair sticking to my bare legs, naked doll arms and legs scattered around me.

"Mom?" My son stepped forward, his foot flattening a bald Barbie head. I ignored him and pounded Ken's torso into submission. "Mom?" my son said again. "I don't think you're okay."

The truth is, I wasn't okay at all. I fell asleep on the floor that night and when I woke the next morning I saw it all for what it was: paint smears and doll parts jammed this way and that and behind it all, me pretending to be someone I wasn't. I threw everything away, though the episode stayed with me, not the actual making of the dolls but how quickly I had become possessed by it, almost as if part of my childhood forever lurked in my mind, waiting to mix with my adult self.

I don't have any Barbie doll parts on my kitchen table, though I do have a Barbie doll sitting on the mantel over the fireplace, and for years I kept a chewed-up Barbie doll arm on my bookshelf. The cat finally dragged it off. I haven't seen it since.

For the novel's setting, you chose your home state of Alaska. How do you think this setting influences the characters and the story in a way that another state wouldn't?

Well, Alaska is a peculiar and unique place filled with peculiar and unique characters. There's a saying up here about the men: the odds are good and the goods are odd. And maybe it's the freedom of so much vast and open land, so much wilderness at our back door, but people up here allow you to be yourself. It's one of the greatest gifts of Alaska. Nonconformity is welcomed. Oddness is celebrated, especially in smaller towns. (I recently moved back to Anchorage after living for almost two years in a small, coastal Alaska community at the end of the road system and it truly was like stepping inside a *Northern Exposure* episode.)

I set *Dolls Behaving Badly* in Alaska because I wanted my characters to move about less restrained than had they, say, lived in a lower forty-eight city. I also wanted to develop personalities that were quirky yet believable from an Alaskan sensibility. You could plunk Carla, Barry, or Francisco down anywhere in Alaska and they'd fit in.

Alaska also feels closer to the spirit world. There are so many contrasts and extremes, so many variations of light and dark, cold and colder, that it's easy to believe in ghosts, easy to expect the unexpected. Does Gramma's ghost really appear or does Carla simply imagine it all?

Does it even matter? In Alaska, people have spiritual epiphanies while climbing mountains and kayaking alongside whales. Why not while in the bathroom at an abortion clinic?

Mostly, I set the book in Alaska because it's the only place I've ever lived that's felt like home. I know it sounds corny but I wanted to give the same to my characters; I wanted to tuck them somewhere safe and wondrous, yet at the same time I wanted an environment that would offer struggle and challenge. It was inevitable that I chose Alaska.

Francisco and Carla have an unconventional courtship, which is made all the more apparent by his gift of human bones. What is the strangest gift you've ever received from a man?

Well, I'm a bit unconventional and I do live in Alaska, so my idea of a gift isn't flowers, chocolate, or jewelry but real things, things associated with the natural world: a stone from the top of a mountain and a jellyfish floating around an old ceramic bowl. I've also received strands of wolf hair, dried moose poop, pieces of bear scat, and an almost perfectly preserved baby moose skull. Are those strange? I dunno. Except for the jellyfish, which died, I still have all of them.

Three of the central female characters in the novel, Carla, Sandee, and Laurel, each have an unsuccessful first marriage, though at least one of them finds love again. Was this a conscious decision on your part? Is there a specific message you want your readers to take away about love and marriage?

I wanted to write a book that centered on women finding strength within themselves. I wanted them to lean on one another and argue with one another, to both fail and succeed, and do so regardless of, or maybe in spite of, men. Too many books end with the fairy tale, the woman meeting the "perfect" man, and when you look around, you realize how misguided that is. Most of us do find love, but we find it at the wrong time or with the wrong person, and it's never perfect. If anything, love is messy. It complicates life. It forces change. It spirals out of control.

I wanted my readers to know that it's okay to be alone, that having a man in your life is a gift but so are so many other things: sisters and sons, neighborhood babysitters and dead grandmothers bearing sugar-laced recipes.

Mostly, though, I wanted to celebrate life. I wanted to highlight small and ordinary moments because I think too many women spend too much time worrying and obsessing about how they look and if their hips are too fat or their teeth white enough that they forget to live their own lives. I wanted to create a world filled with ordinary women living ordinary lives and, in the midst of doing just that, finding small pieces of extraordinary joy and strength.

One of my favorite parts of the book is when Stephanie punches the protester at the abortion clinic. I love the solidarity of the act, and how blasé she is about it: she simply marches up and does what needs to be done. I suppose this is the message I want to get across: To behave badly. But to do so with love.

AUTHOR'S NOTE

The idea for *Dolls Behaving Badly* came to me in the bathroom. In the bathtub, to be exact. I was a single mother working double shifts at an Anchorage restaurant, and each night after I put my son to bed I filled the bathtub with hot water, lay back, and read novels. Sometimes I stayed there for hours.

One night—it was winter, I remember, and storming—I suddenly heard a voice, a woman's voice, heavy with a Polish accent. "*Ach*, my feet hurt." And did I imagine this or did a Polish grandmother close the toilet seat, sit down, take off her shoes, and massage her gnarled and veined feet?

Well, I was tired at the time, and probably slightly dehydrated. I closed my eyes and when I opened them, she was gone.

But she came back. She followed me up mountains, as I swam laps at the YMCA pool, and while I drove my son to school. She pushed her way into my life, and no amount of pushing could convince her to leave. Soon I looked forward to her visits, and I began jotting down the things she said.

Before long other voices appeared: Carla's sardonic tone, Sandee's wisdom, Laurel's slight whining. I wrote everything down; I wrote on envelopes and the backs of grocery bags, and slowly it came to me, not the book so much as the idea for the book. I saw it so acutely it was as if remembering images from a movie: a woman with scattered hair living in a trailer and raising a child by herself. I saw the mess and disorder, the stacks of unpaid bills, the overflowing laundry basket, and behind it all, strands of love and obligation so thick they threatened to strangle her.

It took me seven years to finish *Dolls Behaving Badly*. During that time I quit waitressing and began working as a journalist. I graduated from my MFA program. My son entered middle and then high school. I fell in love and later, out of love. I got a dog and two cats, and then a couple fish. My life, like Carla's, was messy and hectic and filled with unexpected love and turmoil.

Sometimes even now I think: I wrote a book. I really and truly wrote a book!

Other times I think: What if I hadn't taken a bath that night? What if I had showered instead?

But mostly, I find myself cocking my head as if listening for their voices: Gramma and Carla, Stephanie and Jay-Jay, Laurel and Sandee. They're gone now; I had to let them go. I hope that they're happy, wherever they are now, and that they found what they were looking for, these imaginary characters that became more real than the actual living, breathing people in my life.

Maybe one day it will happen again. I'll walk in the bathroom and Gramma will be sitting on the toilet seat. "*Ach*," she'll say, "my feet hurt." And we'll eat Polish pastries and talk, and maybe we'll write another book together, who knows?

I've been waiting. I've been taking a lot of baths.

About the Author

CINTHIA RITCHIE is a former news editor at Alaska Newspapers. She spent eight years as features writer and columnist at the *Anchorage Daily News* and received her MFA from the University of Alaska Anchorage. *Dolls Behaving Badly* is Ritchie's first novel. She lives in Anchorage with her partner and pets.